Hope's Path

Hope's Path

Carrie Carr

YellowRoseBooks
a Division of
RENAISSANCE ALLIANCE PUBLISHING, INC.
Nederland, Texas

ISBN 1-930928-18-1

First Printing 2001

9 8 7 6 5 4 3 2 1

Cover design by Mary Draganis

Published by:

Renaissance Alliance Publishing, Inc.
PMB 238, 8691 9th Avenue
Port Arthur, TX 77642

Find us on the World Wide Web at
http://www.rapbooks.com

Printed in the United States of America

To my family—

Mom and Dad, who show me each and every day what real love is all about.

Kenneth and Judy, whose unwavering love and support kept me going, and who gave me Kailee and Kennedy—the best niece and nephew I could ever ask for.

Janna, the sister of my heart, who not only laughs at my jokes, but always lends me an ear to bend or a shoulder to cry on.

Karen, who's given me her love and friendship, and has become the daughter of my heart.

And last, but most definitely not least, my wonderful partner AJ—who gives me the courage to dream, and who makes those dreams come true. Always and forever, my love.

Chapter
1

The brooding figure on the porch swing peered tiredly into the evening gloom. Anxious blue eyes scanned the darkened road. *She should have been home hours ago, Lex worried. Maybe I should jump into the jeep and make sure she didn't break down on the road somewhere.* The dark-haired woman groaned softly as she climbed to her feet. *I should never have sat down,* she thought disgustedly, feeling the ache of overused muscles.

"Lexie! What are you doing out here without a coat on? You're gonna make yourself sick." Framed in the doorway stood a short sturdy looking woman who fussed good-naturedly at the rancher. Hands on her hips, the middle-aged housekeeper cocked her graying head at the tall form that had suddenly appeared in front of her. "Now get yourself into this house and go upstairs and clean up for dinner." Her nose wrinkled in disgust. "Maybe you should soak in the tub for a bit. I don't think a shower will get all of the dirt off."

Lexington Walters crossed her arms across her chest and glared down at the older woman. "Are you saying that I smell?"

Martha swatted the imposing figure with a dishtowel and grinned. "No...if you could smell, I wouldn't have to

tell you to take a bath," she tsked. "Is there any particular
reason why you're sitting out here in the dark in just your
jeans and tee shirt?"

Lex bit her lower lip and released a heavy sigh. "My
coat and boots are in the mudroom, and I was
just…umm…sitting out here thinking for a bit." She tried
to look innocent, but failed miserably.

"Honey, Amanda will be home any time now. She
called about twenty minutes ago." Martha reached out and
grasped a muscular forearm. "Good lord, child. You're like
a block of ice." She pulled the tall woman into the foyer
and closed the door behind them. "Now get upstairs before
you catch your death." Martha continued to lead her charge
through the house until they were at the foot of the stairs.

Lex pulled out of the housekeeper's grasp. "I'm fine,
Martha. I'm just worried about the problems we seem to be
having with the fence." She had spent the entire day in the
sleeting rain repairing yet another section of fence. *Three
sections in two weeks. There's got to be something, or
someone, causing this.* What compounded the problem was
the slow, near-freezing rain that had been falling off and
on for the past week. *No way of tracking whoever is
responsible for it since the rain just washes the evidence
away,* she thought angrily. *I'm just glad it hasn't begun to
completely freeze. That would make this damned uncomfortable to work in.* Lex felt a warm hand on her chilled
cheek absently wipe at a spot of mud. "What?"

Sympathetic brown eyes gazed into her own. "Go on
and get into the tub, Lexie. I'll send her up as soon as she
gets home, okay?" Martha pulled the soaked, black cowboy
hat off the dark head.

"Am I that transparent?" the rancher asked as she
wiped the damp hair away from her eyes. "She's only been
gone for one night." When Lex saw the knowing look on
Martha's face, she gave the older woman a wry smile and
shook her head. "Never mind. I don't want to know the
answer to that." She gave the small shoulder nearest to her
a gentle squeeze and turned to trudge wearily up the stairs.

As she walked through the master bedroom, Lex glanced around and smiled at the subtle changes in the once spartan room. *One month.* She noticed the small knickknacks that now adorned the dresser and several bookshelves by the fireplace. *And it already feels more like a home.* A quilt that had been made by Amanda's great-grandmother was spread out across the foot of the massive oak bed. The bright covering gave the otherwise dark room a sorely needed splash of color. When Amanda came to stay, the two women had a long and thoughtful discussion and decided to just share the master bedroom. Amanda had been afraid of crowding Lex, and the dark-haired woman had thought that having separate rooms was a complete waste. The older woman was only able to sway her partner by pointing out that it would be less work for Martha if they shared. Lex also had argued that the master closet had more room than the guestroom closet, even with her clothes already inside. *Damn, I miss her.* With a heavy sigh, she started running her bath water.

* * * * * * * * * *

Amanda Cauble shook her head as she walked up the stairs. She had just been thoroughly chastised by the feisty housekeeper for working too many late hours. *Martha certainly has no trouble expressing her opinion,* she marveled as she stepped into the master bedroom. Amanda ran her hand through her shoulder length blonde hair. *I can't help it if it's taken me over three weeks to reorganize the office. But I think that the worst is over for now.*

The young woman sighed deeply, sat down on the bed, and removed her high top sneakers. "Ooh...that feels great." She stretched her legs out and wriggled her toes. Amanda looked around the darkened room. *Martha said Lex was upstairs, but I don't see her anywhere.* The only light was the flickering fire in the fireplace, and... "Ah-ha!" Green eyes sparkled mischievously when she noticed the light that peeked out from under the bathroom door.

She rose from the bed and stepped quietly to the closed door. Amanda opened it slowly. She slipped in and smiled tenderly at the sight in front of her.

The rancher was slumped so low in the bathtub that her dark head was barely visible above the water. Amanda could see the dark rings that were prominent under Lex's closed eyes. Her friend looked so peaceful that the young blonde almost hated to disturb her. *She hasn't been getting much sleep or at least that's what Martha told me.* The housekeeper had confided to her downstairs that Lex had been up early every morning for almost two weeks.

"I'm so glad that you're home," Martha greeted the realtor warmly as Amanda stepped into the kitchen. She happily accepted the strong embrace from the young woman. "Maybe you can help me get Lexie to slow down a little and take it easy."

"What are you talking about, Martha?" Amanda perched on the small stepstool that sat next to the counter where the older woman was preparing dinner. "Is Lex all right?" She quickly grabbed a carrot from the cutting board on the countertop.

Martha slapped the hand away half-heartedly. Strange having someone here now that actually enjoys vegetables. The little imp has even gotten Lexie to try them. *"She's fine, so far. But I'm afraid that she's been working herself almost to death around here lately." She continued to chop vegetables for the stew she was working on.*

Amanda dropped the hand that had been on its way to grabbing an enticing stalk of celery. "Are you sure about that? She's been back at the house before me every night, and she doesn't leave in the mornings until I do." She frowned slightly. Martha can sometimes be a little overprotective, I know. But...

"Oh, honey. You really don't know, do you?" The older woman patted Amanda's hand. "Roy told me that she's up hours before daybreak, repairing fence by the headlights of the jeep. Then she comes back to the house before break-

fast and gets cleaned up. "

"*I wonder why she hasn't said anything to me about it?*" *Amanda mused aloud.*

Martha rubbed Amanda's arm comfortingly. "She probably just didn't want to worry you, honey. We both know how busy you've been getting your office in shape." She scraped a pile of chopped vegetables into the large pot. "And you know how Lexie is, dear."

The blonde nodded. "I sure do, Martha." She stood up and brushed her hands down her black jeans. "And I plan on taking better care of her, starting right now." She hugged the older woman gently. "Thanks for telling me." Amanda stepped back and walked to the door. "Is she...?"

"*Upstairs. I sent her up almost half an hour ago." Martha smiled and turned her attention back to her stew.*

Amanda felt badly. She knew that Lex was always up before her but never thought about how much earlier. More than once, she had found herself being awakened tenderly by the attentions of the already dressed rancher. *Which had its own perks,* she remembered with a fond smile. *I enjoyed helping her get undressed. But I should have realized something was going on with her before now.*

"Hey," Amanda murmured softly as she stepped closer to the tub. "Lex?"

Blue eyes blinked open slowly and a slightly dazed look appeared on Lex's face. "Amanda?" she croaked, then cleared her throat. She sat up slightly and rubbed her eyes. "You're home." *Brilliant, Sherlock. What are you gonna do for an encore? Tell her you're taking a bath?*

"I sure am." Amanda knelt beside the tub. She reached over and placed her hand on a tanned cheek. "You look totally worn out, honey."

Lex leaned into the touch. "Been a long day." She turned her head and kissed the delicate hand. "God, I missed you." Her voice broke slightly on the last word as Amanda met her halfway. Small hands tangled themselves into her damp hair as the younger woman pulled her close.

Lex accepted the kiss eagerly, needing the contact with her partner to affirm that Amanda wasn't a dream.

Amanda could feel the almost electrical surge course through her as the older woman desperately deepened the kiss. She pulled back and inhaled deeply. "Why don't you get out of the tub so we can continue this conversation in the other room?" She gasped as Lex raised her slender form out of the water. Six feet of combined softness and muscle stood in front of Amanda as water sluiced from the rancher's well-toned body. *God, every time I see her like this my knees go weak,* her mind sputtered. Amanda found herself being lifted and then carried into the bedroom as insistent lips captured hers once more.

* * * * * * * * *

The ringing of the telephone beside the bed woke Amanda. She reached quickly to answer it as her eyes fuzzily tried to see what time it was. *One-thirty in the morning? Who on earth?* "Hello?" she whispered quietly, trying not to disturb the still sleeping figure wrapped tightly around her body. Lex's soft cheek nuzzled her belly gently.

"Who the hell is this?" an annoyingly nasal voice demanded. "Put my damn sister on the phone."

Hubert. That figures. Amanda rolled her eyes. She really didn't want to wake Lex up since the older woman seemed to finally be resting for the first time in almost two weeks. "She can't come to the phone right now." Amanda winced slightly as her lover mumbled and snuggled even closer. "Can I take a message and have her call you back?"

The voice on the other end of the phone exploded. "You're her little...piece...aren't you?" Hubert practically screamed. "Put Lex on the goddamn phone, you worthless whore."

Amanda held the phone to her chest for a moment. She didn't want Hubert's raving to wake her friend. As she forced her emotions under control, Amanda whispered into the handset, "You can either leave a message, or I can just hang up on you now. I'll tell Lex in the morning that you called. It's your choice, Hubert." She jumped slightly when the phone at the other end was slammed down. *Jerk.* She carefully turned off the ringer and replaced the handset. Amanda smiled as she felt Lex worm her way up her body until her dark head was nestled snugly under the younger woman's chin.

She felt a surge of emotion and hugged her partner to her tightly as she tried to hold back tears. *I won't stand by and let anyone hurt you, Lex,* she swore silently. *Even your own brother.* The young woman took a deep shuddering breath and buried her face in the thick dark hair.

Lex woke up and lifted her head slightly. "Hey." She shifted her body until she was lying next to Amanda. The rancher raised a hand to turn on the lamp next to the bed. Seeing the tears on the blonde's face, she pulled Amanda into a strong hug. "What's wrong, sweetheart?"

"Nothing, really," Amanda sniffled, as she snuggled deeper into the embrace. A gentle kiss on her head caused her to lose her composure again. *Damn.*

"Amanda," Lex gently forced her lover's face upward, "look at me, please." The dark-haired woman felt her heart ache as she wiped the tears away with her fingertips. "Don't tell me it's nothing, love." She took a deep breath and tried to get her own emotions under control. "I can't stand seeing you like this."

Amanda sucked in a huge gulp of air then pulled one of Lex's hands to her face and kissed the palm. "Sshh. It's just after I hung up the phone, I got to thinking." She smiled ruefully. "And I guess it's getting close to that time of the month for me because my emotions went completely off the scale." She leaned up a little and gave the older woman a tender kiss.

"Mmm." Lex returned the offering, then pulled back suddenly. "Wait a minute. What do you mean, you hung up? Did the phone ring?" Not giving Amanda time to answer she continued, "Who in the hell would be calling at..." she glanced at the alarm clock, "almost two o'clock in the damn morning?"

Oops. Should I? "Umm. It was your brother. He thought that he had to talk to you right then, but I got him to think otherwise." Amanda braced herself for the impending explosion, which oddly enough didn't come.

Lex chuckled. "Oh, really?" She reached over to turn off the light, then scooted into a more comfortable position on the bed. "Good for you." She pulled Amanda into her arms and placed a soft kiss on the younger woman's head. "Thank you, sweetheart."

Amanda tucked the covers up around them to ward off the chill of the room. "You're welcome. But aren't you curious as to why your brother would be calling in the middle of the night?" She wrapped her arms tightly around Lex and snuggled closer.

"Not particularly." The older woman sighed as she felt sleep pull at her once again. "He used to do it all the time, because late at night was the only time I'd ever be in the house." She struggled to hold back a yawn. "It had gotten to the point that he was calling at least two or three times a week. So I turned off the phone up here and let him rant at the machine." The last few words quietly faded away as Lex dropped off to sleep.

"Goodnight, honey," Amanda whispered as she gently lay her head back on the rancher's chest and joined her in slumber.

* * * * * * * * *

"I'm glad to see that you two are still alive," Martha teased as Lex followed Amanda into the kitchen the next morning. "I was about to send up a search party." She smirked as Lex stuck out her tongue.

The rancher pushed her companion into a nearby chair and grabbed two coffee mugs from the cabinet. "Good morning to you too, Martha." Lex kissed the housekeeper's graying head and then swatted her on the rear.

"Aaaack!" The older woman spun around and waved a

spatula. "You're not too big for a whipping, young lady."

Lex backed away and lifted her hands up to ward off any blows. "Now hold on, Martha. You wouldn't want to break a perfectly good...umm...thingy-whattzit, would you?" She turned to Amanda, who had a hand over her mouth trying to stifle her laughter. "You're not helping, you know."

"Don't blame me. You're the one who can't keep her hands to herself," Amanda snickered. She quickly wrapped her own hands around the steaming mug that Lex had placed in front of her. "Mmm, thanks." The young woman leaned over the cup and inhaled deeply of the rich aroma.

"I've never seen anyone enjoy their coffee quite as much as you do, sweetheart." The tall woman sat down next to Amanda and leaned back in her seat. The front legs of Lex's chair rose a few inches off of the ground.

Martha walked by and tapped Lex lightly on the back of the head. "How many times do I have to tell you not to lean back in your chair?" She placed a full plate in front of each woman. "I swear, you haven't changed a bit in fifteen years." Before the housekeeper could turn away from the table, she found herself sitting on the grinning rancher's lap. "What?"

"I don't think I could do this fifteen years ago, could I?" Lex stood up and lifted the older woman with her.

"Put me down, you little rat." Martha quickly clasped her hands behind Lex's neck. "You're gonna hurt yourself. Lexie!" she squawked as she was tossed gently in the air and caught again.

Lex sat back down, but kept her hold on Martha. "That any better?" she asked, as the older woman climbed off of her lap.

"You!" Martha swatted her on the shoulder and then walked across the room. Neither woman at the table noticed when she reached into the sink.

The rancher gave Amanda a saucy grin. She completely missed the diabolical smile on the housekeeper's face.

Splat!

There was total silence in the kitchen. The quiet was finally broken when Amanda laughed so hard that she fell out of her chair with a solid thump.

The dark-haired woman stood up. A wet dishtowel hung off of her head and soapy water dripped down her face. "Martha," Lex growled as she pulled the sodden clump from her head. She stalked slowly to the older woman who had her hand to her mouth with a shocked look on her face.

"Oh, Lexie. I didn't realize that my aim would be that good." Martha's eyes widened when she noticed the look on the tall woman's face. She slowly backed away. "Now, honey, don't do something that you might regret later."

Halfway to her quarry, Lex stopped. As a slow smile spread across her face, she gently tossed the wet cloth back into the sink. "Paybacks, Martha." She glared at the house-keeper and wiped her face off with a sleeve.

Martha laughed. "Whatever you say, dear." She tossed a dry towel to Lex, then turned her attention to the stove. "Just remember who cooks your meals and cleans your clothes."

"Yeah, yeah. I've been telling you for years that I could do all that myself, you know." Lex sat back down at the table. She looked down at the young woman still on the floor next to her. "Are you going to sit down there all day?" Smiling, she offered a hand to Amanda.

"Thanks." The blonde allowed herself to be pulled up off the floor. Amanda sat down in her chair and shook a warning finger at Lex. "You two are hazardous to my health."

The dark-haired woman smirked over the rim of her coffee cup. "Not my fault you can't control yourself," she chuckled. "But I'm not complaining."

Amanda blushed and directed her attention to the plate of food that the housekeeper had placed in front of her. "Thanks, Martha," she murmured as a small hand patted her shoulder gently.

"Don't worry, honey. She's always been sassy like that. I'm used to it by now." The older woman sat down at the table with a heavy sigh. She looked over at Lex, who still had a devious grin on her face. "Stop looking at me like that, or I'll have to break a spoon on your backside for sure."

"Like what?" Lex was the picture of wide-eyed innocence. "I'm just eating breakfast." She took another large bite of food and winked at Amanda.

The blonde rolled her eyes. "Oh, please. Save it for someone that doesn't know you like we do. Now behave yourself, or I won't tell you who I saw at the office yesterday." Amanda attacked her own plate with gusto as she ignored the blue-eyed glare from across the table.

"Well?" Lex asked patiently. She leaned forward until she could look into Amanda's eyes. With a teasing note in her voice, she whispered, "You gonna tell me, or will I have to force you to talk?"

Amanda leaned forward and placed a quick kiss on her friend's nose. "I'm sooo scared." She sat back in her chair with a sweet smile. "But, I guess I might as well tell you. Do you remember the dinner party at my parent's house?"

Lex rolled her eyes. "How could I forget? It was the most fun I've had in years."

"Smart aleck." Amanda slapped Lex lightly on the arm. "Now hush, or I won't finish my story."

"Fine." Lex zipped her mouth shut, locked it and threw away the imaginary key. She raised her eyebrows at Amanda who shook her head and sighed.

"Thank you, I think. Do you remember the man sitting next to you at the table? Mark Garrett?"

Lex nodded, but didn't say anything. She smiled at Amanda who gave her an exasperated look.

"Oooh, you!" Amanda threw her napkin and hit the smirking woman in the face.

"What is it that makes you two throw things at me this morning?" Lex asked as she tossed the napkin back to Amanda. She gathered more food onto her fork and continued to eat.

Amanda sighed. "You really don't want an answer to that question, do you?" She took another bite of food. Swallowing hastily, she continued. "Anyway, Mark came into the office yesterday and said that he had quit his job."

"Really? Well, that doesn't surprise me much. He seemed pretty tired of it all." The rancher stood up and started to carry her plate to the sink. Lex noticed that Martha had finished, so she quickly grabbed the housekeeper's plate as well.

Martha sputtered and stood up. "I can do that, you know." She was about to continue when she noticed the serious look on the blonde woman's face. "But, if you two will excuse me for a minute, I have a load of laundry that needs to be checked." She quickly slipped from the room, allowing Lex and Amanda some privacy.

Amanda smiled at the retreating figure, then sighed. "Where was I? Oh, yeah. Mark said that he'd quit about two weeks ago, but kept getting threatening phone calls and nasty letters, and he was becoming afraid for his family's safety." Amanda put her fork down on her plate. She looked up at Lex, who stood with her back against the sink. "And he thinks that my father is behind all the threats."

Lex crossed the room quickly, and knelt down beside Amanda's chair. She placed a hand on the younger woman's thigh and squeezed gently. "What makes him think that, sweetheart?"

Amanda looked down into concerned blue eyes. "Because Mark has a lot of inside information on my father's company. Information that could do serious damage to him if it ever got out."

"I don't think Mark is the type to resort to that sort of thing, do you?" Lex murmured, raising a hand to caress Amanda's cheek. She smiled as the green eyes closed, and Amanda leaned into her touch with a soft sigh.

"Mmmm." Amanda turned her head slightly and kissed the callused palm. "No, I don't think so either." She opened her eyes again and gave her partner a sad smile.

"But you know my father. He doesn't trust anyone." She watched as her hand dropped to Lex's head and her fingers slowly combed through the dark hair.

The rancher smiled again. *God, I love the feel of her hands in my hair. One touch turns me into a quivering mass of jelly.* "Umm, Amanda?" Lex blinked, trying to fight the lethargic feeling stealing over her. "You were going to tell me why Mark was in your office yesterday, right?"

Amanda took a deep breath, then released it slowly. "Sorry." She smiled down at the older woman. She captured the hand that still caressed her face and stood up. "C'mon. Let's go sit in the den. You can't be too comfortable kneeling on the floor."

"Oof," Lex grunted, as she allowed Amanda to pull her to her feet. "You're right about that." She stretched, and sighed with relief when several audible pops came from her back. "God, that feels better." The dark-haired woman grinned at the look she was getting from Amanda. "What?"

"That sounds so painful. One of these days you're going to do that, and part of you is going to fall off," Amanda teased, pulling Lex out of the room by her hand. She led her friend down the hallway. "I swear, you pop and creak more than my old car."

Lex laughed. "Yeah, I guess I do. And it's a hell of a lot older than I am." She glanced through the large window in the den. "Damn, it's nasty looking out there this morning." Lex guided the smaller woman to the window, where they both could look out. "This is the coldest it's been around here in years. It might even stay cold enough today or tomorrow to snow and have it stick." She looked down at Amanda, who was firmly attached to her side. "I'm glad you made it home last night before it started getting bad, sweetheart."

As she snuggled even closer, the blonde woman nodded. "Me too. I'd much rather be stuck out here with you than sitting at my grandparents' house worrying about what kind of trouble you were getting into."

"Me? Trouble?" Lex turned them away from the window and to the sofa. "I don't seem to get into any trouble unless you're involved." She flinched as an elbow jabbed her in the ribs. "Ouch!" She sat down and suddenly found her lap full of a green eyed blonde. "Oh, so now I'm furniture?"

Amanda chuckled and wrapped her arms around the taller woman's neck. "Yep." She leaned forward and kissed the tip of Lex's nose. "Pretty comfortable too, I might add."

Lex slid her arms around the smaller woman's back and pulled her closer. "Oh, yeah?" She captured Amanda's lips in a gentle embrace. As she felt small hands tangle themselves in her hair, Lex moaned. She tried to pull back slightly. "I thought we were going to talk?" she whispered, just before those same hands pulled her closer to Amanda's face.

"Later," Amanda breathed, as she gently wrestled the older woman onto her back and continued her attack.

* * * * * * * * *

"Mmm," Amanda sighed from her sprawled position on top of Lex. "Sorry about that." She idly played with a button on the older woman's shirt. "I can't believe I fell asleep like that."

Lex continued her gentle stroking down the smaller woman's back. "Don't worry about it, sweetheart. We didn't get much sleep last night. A short nap didn't hurt either one of us." She chuckled ruefully. "Besides, if we had continued what we started, Martha would have gotten an eyeful. I didn't close the door when we came in."

"Oh, God. That could have been embarrassing." Amanda raised up and peered over the sofa. "Although with the way the sofa is facing, she couldn't see anything anyway." She was about to pick up where they left off when there was a frantic knocking at the front door.

"Who in the hell could that be?" Lex grumbled, as she worked her way out from under Amanda and started to the door. She almost ran into Martha in the hallway. "I'll get it," Lex assured the housekeeper who stopped and stared at her. "What?"

Martha stepped forward and buttoned the dark-haired woman's shirt. "You open the door dressed like that, and you'll catch a chill," she teased.

"Oops," Amanda laughed from the doorway. "My fault. I was trying to find a place to warm my hands." She smiled sweetly at the rancher.

Lex glared at her, then turned to answer the door. "I'll warm your..." she mumbled. Opening the door, she stepped back in surprise. "Ronnie? What are you doing out in this weather? Get in here before you freeze to death." She opened the door further to allow the young man to step into the house.

"Sorry, Ms. Walters but Roy asked me to come and get you." The teenager pulled a damp baseball cap from his head. Ronnie Sterling had been working for the Rocking W Ranch for only a few weeks—ever since Lex had signed the papers to be his legal guardian. His older brother Matt was sitting in the county jail awaiting trial for the theft of several thousand dollars worth of cattle, breaking and entering and attempting to murder Lex.

Amanda stepped forward and grabbed the young man by his arm. "Come inside by the fire and get warm. You can talk to Lex in the den." She led Ronnie into the den and made him strip off his coat. "Sit down here," she directed him to the chair closest to the fire, "and Lex will bring you some hot chocolate." The young blonde gave her lover an engaging smile.

"Hot chocolate. Right." Lex turned around and almost knocked over the housekeeper. "Sorry about that, Martha."

Martha laughed. "Honey, you go on in there and find out what that young man has to say. I'll bring enough hot chocolate for all of you." She patted the tall woman's side and turned to the kitchen.

Lex started into the den then stuck her head back out of the doorway. "Don't forget the marshmallows!" she shouted out after the retreating figure. She turned back around and smiled at the two sitting in front of the fireplace. "Well? What good is hot chocolate without marshmallows?" The rancher stepped over to where Amanda was sitting across from Ronnie. She sat down on the arm of the smaller woman's chair. "Okay, Ronnie, what is it that Roy wanted you to tell me?"

"Another section of fence was cut last night, Ms. Walters." The young man blushed when he saw Amanda place her hand on the rancher's thigh. He had heard from the men in the bunkhouse about the relationship between the two, but found it hard to believe that these two beautiful women could be "that way." *I thought that all gay women wore leather and chains, and had lots of tattoos.* When Lester had explained to him about Ms. Walters and her friend, he told the cook that his brother said that those kind of people were sick and perverted. *Boy, did I get yelled at that night. But, they don't look like perverts. Just like two people who care about each other. Hmmm. Maybe Matt was wrong.*

"Damn! This is getting ridiculous." Lex jumped up and paced the room. Turning her attention back to the young man, she sighed. "Okay. Which section?" She noticed the look on Amanda's face and saw the young woman raise a hand to beckon her. Lex walked back over to the chair and grasped Amanda's hand and allowed herself to be pulled back down.

Ronnie looked at their joined hands then quickly turned his eyes toward the fire. "Umm. He said it was the northwest corner. He's moved all of the cattle out of that section, because he was having trouble getting to the fence to repair it."

Martha bustled into the room with a large tray. "Hot chocolate, with marshmallows, as requested." She carried it over to a nearby table and set it down. "Well? Get yourselves over here before it gets cold. I've got a pot of chili cooking, so if you'll excuse me." The small round woman scurried out of the room before anyone could say anything.

Lex laughed. "You heard the lady, Ronnie. C'mon." She stood up and grabbed a mug which she handed to the young man. She picked up another steaming cup and turned to Amanda, who had stepped up beside her.

"Thanks, honey." Amanda accepted the warm drink gratefully. "Why is it so hard to reach the fence in that section, Lex?" She followed the tall woman over to the nearby loveseat and sat down. "Is it because of the weather?"

"No, not completely. Although with the weather being the way it is, it's gonna be even more difficult." Lex watched with a smile as Ronnie sat back down in front of the fire, his attention directed towards the flames. "The fence blocks off a small canyon, which has a nasty little drop off to the adjacent property. About the only way to actually reach it is by horseback, because of the rough terrain and all the rain we've had. The jeep would just get stuck."

Amanda turned slightly, so that she could study the older woman's eyes. "You're going, aren't you?" she said, as more of a statement than a question. "Isn't that what you pay all those men to do?"

Lex set her mug down on a side table. "Yes, I am." She reached over and grasped the small hand nearest her. "And yes, it is what I pay them for. But everyone except Lester, Roy, and Ronnie went into town yesterday for the weekend. They've been working themselves extra hard these past couple of weeks, so I thought they deserved a break." Lex looked into Amanda's eyes with determination. "And I won't ask them to do anything that I won't do, sweetheart. You know that."

"I know, Lex. It's just that you've been working harder than any of them. When do you get a break?" Amanda pulled the large hand up to her lips and kissed the knuckles gently. "And don't bother denying it, either. Martha filled me in last night." She saw the slight grin on the rancher's face.

"Martha has a big mouth." Lex opened up her hand and ran her fingertips along the younger woman's jaw. "But I had already decided that since you'll be home a few days next week helping Martha get ready for Thanksgiving, I'd take that time off, too."

Amanda smiled and leaned into the rancher's touch. "I think I'll like that. This past month has been so busy for us both; it will be nice to spend some quiet time with you." She allowed her eyes to leave Lex's face for a moment and focus on the young man near the fire. "I think we're embarrassing our guest, love."

Lex glanced over at Ronnie. "Yeah, I think you're right. Why don't I go upstairs and get changed, and you spend a little time with our young friend? Maybe find out what his plans are for the holiday?"

"Good idea, honey." Amanda smiled as her lover stood up. She regretfully released Lex's hand. "Please wear a warm shirt. I hate when you go out with just a tee shirt under your coat." Before Lex could open her mouth to argue, Amanda continued, "Hush. I heard about what you wore yesterday."

The tall woman lifted an eyebrow at that remark. "Damn that woman. Do I have no secrets left?" Lex shook her head. "I'll take care of her later." She'd started for the door when Amanda's voice stopped her.

"You'll do no such thing, Lexington Marie Walters." Amanda waggled a warning finger at the older woman. "All she did was answer my questions, so you leave that poor woman alone."

Lex stood in the doorway and grinned. "Yes, dear." She gave the blonde a mocking salute and started for the stairway.

Chapter 2

Amanda stood at the back door fussing with Lex's coat. "You have the radio, right?" she asked as she straightened the collar for the third time. "And the thermos of coffee that Martha poured up for you? And..."

Lex leaned over and captured the younger woman's lips in a soft kiss, effectively silencing Amanda. She pulled away after a moment and smiled tenderly. "Yes, sweetheart. I have so much damned stuff that Cannonball is never going to speak to me again. Stop worrying. I've done this dozens of times." Cannonball was the horse that Lex had purchased the previous week at an auction. He was a couple of years older than her horse Thunder, but the black stallion had thrown a shoe the previous afternoon. Lex knew that she could replace the shoe, but then would never hear the end of it from Dan, the farrier that she had hired specifically for that job.

"Maybe. But I've never been stuck at home waiting for you when you were out those dozens of times." Amanda lifted her hand and tilted the black hat away from Lex's eyes. "You'll be back by this afternoon, right?" She searched the tan face above hers, memorizing every inch. "Something just doesn't feel right to me, Lex. Please be really careful?"

"I promise, love. I'll be very careful," Lex assured her.
She placed a gentle kiss on the blonde's forehead. "I've
got too much here to stick around for to take unnecessary
risks." She stepped back a pace and grinned. "And, I promised to take you Christmas shopping next weekend. There's
no way in hell you're gonna let me get out of doing that, is
there?"

Amanda laughed. "You're darned right about that,
Slim. Who else can I wrangle into carrying all my packages for me?" She sobered when Lex reached for the doorknob. "Could you do me a big favor?"

Lex stopped, and gave the young woman a questioning
look. "Sure, baby, name it."

"Well, since I was going to work in the office this
morning, checking some stuff on the computer," Amanda
bit her lower lip, "do you think that you could radio in
every once in a while and let me know you're okay?"

Lex smiled. *She's just so damned cute when she looks
at me that way. No way I could tell her no. God, I've
turned into a complete wad of mush.* "Umm, okay. How
about on the hour? That way I won't be disturbing your
work too much."

The younger woman gave Lex a bone-jarring hug.
"How about every half hour, so I'll be able to concentrate
on my work and not worry about you so much?" She felt
strong arms wrap around her and return the squeeze. Soft
lips captured hers once more, and for an instant, the world
around them melted away.

Lex finally broke off the kiss and took a deep breath.
"Yeah. Okay. Thirty minutes. No problem." She let her
forehead rest on Amanda's. "You're really good at that,
you know." Lex took a deep breath and reluctantly released
the smaller woman. "God, Amanda, I love you. But I really
gotta go now."

"I know, sweetheart. I love you too. Every thirty min-
utes, right?" Amanda opened the door and shivered. "God!
That north wind is horrible." She pulled on Lex's sleeve.
"Come back sooner if the weather gets any nastier, okay?"

The rancher turned slightly. "Yes, dear." She winked and then stepped off the porch to where Cannonball was patiently waiting. Lex swung up into the saddle and adjusted the saddlebags that held the thermos of coffee. "Thanks for getting a bag of stuff together for me, Amanda. Now get into the house before you freeze." She waved and turned her prancing mount towards the north trail.

Amanda closed the door and then peered out the window until she could no longer see the horse or rider. "Be careful, love," she whispered as her hand touched the slightly cold glass.

"I take it she's gone?" Martha stood in the kitchen doorway, drying her hands on a dishtowel.

The blonde woman sighed and turned away from the door. "Yeah. I don't know why she doesn't just leave it for the guys to take care of tomorrow or even Monday." Amanda looked at her watch then followed the housekeeper into the kitchen.

Martha guided her over to a seat at the table and sat down in the chair next to her. "Honey, I asked her that very question before she went upstairs to change." She poured coffee from the nearby carafe into a waiting mug. "Here. You look chilled."

"Thanks, Martha." Amanda held the mug close to her body and took a cautious sip. "You did? What did she say?" She reached over and grabbed a cookie from the platter.

"Lex was afraid that even though Roy moved the herd from that pasture, some of the cattle or horses would get back in that area and fall off that drop off." The housekeeper shook her head. "We've never had this kind of trouble before. I sure would like to know why someone is doing this. It just doesn't make any sense."

"I know. It's so strange. Right now it's only vandalism. Lex told me that there were no cattle hurt or missing, that she's aware of." Amanda looked at Martha with a worried expression as a thought occurred to her. "Oh, God!

What if this is my father's way of getting back at Lex and me?"

Martha reached over and patted the young woman's hand comfortingly. "Let's not jump to any conclusions, dear. There could be all sorts of reasons why this is happening." She leaned back in her chair with a smile. "I talked to Charlie yesterday. He's going to have some Deputies help patrol the fence line with the hands. We'll get this figured out."

Amanda returned the older woman's smile. "Did you invite Charlie to dinner on Thursday?" She knew that Lex had already invited the Sheriff, but Amanda enjoyed making the housekeeper blush for a change.

"Well, as a matter of fact, I did. He said that the Wades were going out of town to her sister's for the holiday, so he was just going to have a microwave dinner and watch football. I straightened him right out," the older woman chuckled. Sheriff Charlie Bristol was Martha's long-time boyfriend, and had been trying for years to get the sweet woman to marry him. At the moment, he lived in a boarding house in town. But, if Lex and Amanda had their way, he'd be taking up residence in Martha's comfortable home in the near future. The modest home, built near the main house when Lex remodeled the ranch several years previously, had been a gift from the rancher when the housekeeper had refused a room in the main house. The woman had been like a mother to her, and Lex refused to let her go on living like a common servant in a small room behind the kitchen.

"Good. My grandparents will be here, and I hope to hear from my sister in the next day or so." Amanda had even extended an invitation to her parents, but her mother had called Anna Leigh and asked that she pass along their regrets. *She wouldn't even talk to me. I had to get the message from my grandmother. Which is just as well, I suppose. I have no idea where we'll seat everyone as it is.* "Umm, Martha? I hate to ask a silly question, but so far we have at least eight people confirmed for Thanksgiving dinner. Where on earth are we going to seat them all?"

The housekeeper laughed. "Oh, honey, don't you worry. We have a huge table that we set up every year in the sitting room. Lexie always moves everything out of there for the day." She gestured around the kitchen. "Since the mud room opens up to both rooms, we always haul all the food and goodies through there. It also keeps traffic in the cooking area down, so I don't have quite so many feet to trip over."

"Good idea." Amanda glanced down at her watch. "Oh. I've got to get to the office—Lex should be radioing in any time now." She refilled her coffee mug and stood up. "I've got some work to do on the computer, Martha. Just holler if you need me for anything." The young woman left the room before the housekeeper could say a word.

"I can't believe that young woman actually got Lexie to agree to check in with her." Martha shook her graying head as she cleaned up the table. "That's absolutely amazing."

****

The cold wind cut through Lex like a knife, which caused her to pull her hat down a little further over her eyes. *Damn. I must be getting soft—this never used to bother me before,* she sighed to herself. *But at least the rain has stopped for now.* Lex glanced at her watch, smiled, and pulled the hand-held radio from her coat pocket. "Amanda? This is Lex."

A slight crackle from the radio, then a rushed voice returned, "Hi, Lex. Is everything okay?" Amanda sounded slightly breathless.

"Everything is just fine. I'm almost there." Lex nearly dropped the radio when Cannonball stumbled on the path. "Easy there, fella." She patted the dun-colored gelding gently on the neck. A garbled message from the radio caught her attention. "What was that, Amanda? This gully I'm in seems to be blocking your signal."

"Oh. Well, I just asked if you're warm enough. The wind seems to have picked up here at the house. And...the weather...a little later in the day." Amanda's voice continued to break up.

Even though it was close to noon, the heavy cloud cover made visibility poor. Lex strained through the gloom to see her destination. The fence stood barely a hundred yards away from where she was. Another blast of cold, damp air almost took her breath away. "Sweetheart, you keep breaking up. Can you read me okay?" She had to pull back on the reins as Cannonball pranced sideways, obviously agitated. "Whoa, boy. Easy there."

Another burst of static came through the radio. "...ex? I can't...you. Are you...yet?" Amanda was sounding frustrated. "Can you...me? Lex?"

"Amanda? I'm in a bad spot, love. I'll radio you when I get onto higher ground, okay?" Lex pocketed the radio and dropped effortlessly from the saddle. She led the nervous horse to a large tree near the broken fence and tied his reins loosely to a branch. "Stay here, buddy. These trees should block off the worst of the wind." The tall woman gave him another gentle pat, then grabbed her bag of tools and moved to the break in the fence.

Lex pulled the collar of her coat tighter, trying to ward off the icy wind. "Damn! I think it's getting colder. And those clouds look like they could break loose any minute now." She dropped to one knee and studied the strands of wiring lying on the ground. *Not broken. Definitely cut.* A far off bawling sound from in front of her caught the rancher's attention. *What the...*She regained her feet and stepped forward cautiously to investigate.

Up ahead, near the edge of the drop off, stood a small calf. It appeared to be tangled up in some small brush as it stood in one place and continued to cry. Rust colored with a white face, the young animal cried more plaintively when it spotted the tall figure walking in its direction.

She held out her arms in a non-threatening manner as she tried to keep the animal calm with her voice. "Hold on, little guy," Lex tried to soothe. "I'll get you out of that mess in no time." Glancing to her right, she noted the drop off. "Now you try to stay calm, or we'll both end up down there." She squatted down beside the calf and cleared the brush away with one hand. Leaning down to get a better look, Lex cursed. "How in the hell did you get a rope tied around..." A heavy weight slammed into the back of her head, and Lex felt a moment of weightlessness before everything went black.

* * * * * * * * * *

The blonde woman paced frantically around the office mumbling under her breath. "I don't like this at all. Something just doesn't feel right." Amanda came to a halt next to where the radio was stationed. She reached for the microphone, then stopped. "She said she would radio me back as soon as she got to a better spot. It's only been about ten minutes," she muttered.

"Everything okay, sweetie?" Martha walked into the office carrying the carafe of coffee. "I thought you could use some more coffee." As she watched the young woman pace the floor in front of her, she amended, "Maybe not. Amanda?"

"Oh! God, Martha. You startled me." Amanda spun around. "Did you say something?"

The housekeeper set the carafe down and walked over to stand by Amanda. "I asked you if everything was okay." Martha placed a small pudgy hand on the younger woman's shoulder. "You look a little frazzled, honey."

Amanda patted the hand gently. "I don't know, Martha. Something just doesn't feel right. Lex told me that she would radio me right back, and that was almost fifteen minutes ago." She took a deep breath and shook her head. "I know. I'm probably just imagining things, but I can't help it."

"Maybe not, child. Sometimes our hearts tell us more than we realize." The older woman steered Amanda to the chair behind the desk. "Sit down for a minute and try to relax." The blonde followed her instructions. "Now tell me all about it, dear."

"It's hard to describe, Martha. Like an ache in my stomach, and a heaviness in my chest." Amanda had a faraway look in her eyes. "And the longer I sit here, the worse this feeling gets." She jumped up and grabbed the microphone from the radio. "Lex? Honey, can you hear me?" Releasing the catch, all she heard was static. "Come in, Lex. Please?"

Martha stood next to her, a worried look creasing her face. "She should be there by now. And the reception from that part of the property has never been a problem in the past." She walked over and picked up the telephone. "I'm going to call Roy and get him over here." The housekeeper dialed a number on the phone and waited patiently for an answer. "Lester? This is Martha. Is Roy over there?"

"Yeah, he just finished up at the barn and is on his way to get cleaned up. What do you need?" the old cook grumbled.

"I need him over at the main house, pronto. And tell him to dress warmly. We've got an important job for him to do," Martha snapped, not in the mood for their usual good-natured bickering.

Lester stopped immediately when he realized that something was wrong. "Right. He'll be over in a couple of minutes." He paused, then added, "If you need anything, Martha, you just let me know, okay?"

The housekeeper allowed a tiny smile to escape. "I will, Lester. Thank you." She hung up the phone and saw Amanda heading to the doorway. "Where are you going?"

"Upstairs to change. I'm going with Roy when he gets here." Amanda left the room before Martha could stop her.

****

A throbbing ache in her head caused Lex to slowly open her eyes and try to look around. *Ahh. Bad idea, Lex-*

ington, she berated herself, closing her eyes as she took a shallow breath. *Damn, that hurts.* Lex tried to move but found herself partially buried underneath several large tree branches. *If I fell, how did I end up under this stuff?* The dark-haired woman searched her fuzzy brain for an answer. *Wait a minute. I didn't fall. Something or someone hit me from behind. Probably tossed this crap down on top of me afterwards.* She tried to turn her body upwards, but the weight of the branches and several sharp pains stopped her. "Aaah, damn!" Lex groaned. Sounds of static coming from her right coat pocket caught the rancher's attention.

"Lex? Honey, can you...me?" Amanda's worried voice broke through the static.

"Amanda?" Lex tried to reach the radio in her pocket, but her right arm was pinned under her chest. "Shit!" Another sharp pain made her stop moving immediately. She closed her eyes and concentrated until the pain eased to a more manageable level. *Okay. Let's just try to figure out what hurts so damned bad.* She decided the best place to start was her toes, so Lex tried to wiggle them inside her boots. The movement caused more pain along her back. "Ow. Wrong idea."

The radio crackled again. "Come in, Lex. Please?"

The injured woman tried to reach the radio again, this time with her left hand. But her left arm was twisted up around her head, and the debris covering her had Lex completely pinned down. "Dammit!" she growled, then winced as the movement caused more discomfort. Her pounding head was lulling the rancher into a dreamy haze. She tried to fight her heavy eyelids, but to no avail. *Maybe if I just rest for a minute, I'll have enough energy to get out of this mess before Amanda worries too much.* The darkness pulled her under once again.

* * * * * * * * * *

"Are you sure about this, Miss Amanda?" Roy questioned as he saddled the two horses in the barn. The young blonde woman stood just outside the stall, bundled up against the cold. "She probably just had some radio trouble because of the weather and stayed to finish repairing the fence." The ranch foreman glanced over at Amanda's steadfast form. "We'll probably meet her along the trail."

Amanda uncrossed her arms and sighed. "I'm sure, Roy. I've got to do this, okay?" She walked over to where a sturdily built brown and white mare was saddled and ready to go. "Hey there, Stormy." The paint pony had been a recent gift from Lex, who constantly teased her about the gentle animal's size. Amanda rubbed the horse's nose and whispered, "You're going to help me find her, aren't you, girl?" A light nuzzle to her chest was the pony's only answer.

Roy led his horse out of the stall. "Okay. But don't look to me for protection when she catches us, okay?" he teased, trying to lighten the mood. Truth be told, the foreman was concerned as well. It wasn't like his boss to be out of contact when she promised differently. *But I'm not about to tell this young lady that. Martha would have my hide for sure.*

"Don't worry, Roy. I'll protect you." Amanda smiled slightly as she pulled Stormy from her stall. "I'll take full responsibility for this little trip, okay?" The small blonde and her horse followed Roy outside. Amanda mounted up and waited to see which direction the foreman would take. "Well? Let's get this party started before the weather gets too nasty."

The older man sighed. "Yes, ma'am." He directed them towards the north trail without another word.

Half an hour later, they came upon Cannonball. He looked uncomfortable and wet, leaning under a large tree. Roy pulled his horse up near the jittery animal and dismounted. He stepped over to the horse that stomped and then glared at him.

"Hey, there." The foreman ran his hand along the animal's neck to check for anything out of the ordinary. Amanda climbed down from her mount and stood behind

him. Roy turned her. "He's tied to the branch, and everything looks okay." They both looked around the clearing
for a glimpse of the missing rancher.

"Right. So that means she's got to be around here
somewhere." Amanda shivered as a strong gust of cold,
wet air blew her slightly backwards. *Great. Just what we
needed. More rain.* She followed Roy's lead and tied her
horse to a nearby tree. "Where do we go from here?"

The foreman pointed to the north. "If I have my bearings right, the fence line should be just over there." He
pulled a rifle that had been sheathed in a scabbard on his
saddle. "C'mon. It's less than a hundred yards this way."
Roy led Amanda through the trees until they came to the
fence. The broken strands of wire were still lying on the
ground, and a large canvas bag was sitting nearby. "She
made it to the fence okay." He knelt down and checked the
ground near the fence. "Nothing unusual here."

Amanda stood next to him while she tried to see
through the now misting rain. "Did you hear something?"
she asked the kneeling man.

Roy looked up at the young woman. "Hear what?" He
cocked his head to one side and listened intently. "All I
hear is the damn wind and rain."

"Shh! There it is again." She held up a warning finger.
"It sounded like a cry."

He closed his eyes and concentrated. "I don't...Wait!
Yeah. I think it's coming from over there." The foreman
pointed past the fence to a pile of shrubbery. "Do you see
that, Miss Amanda?"

The young woman nodded. "I think so. It looks like a
small animal." She started towards the sound.

Roy reached up and grabbed her arm and held her
back. "Wait. That's near the drop off. Let me go first,
okay?"

Amanda stopped and shrugged. "Sure." She helped
him to his feet and gave a small smile. "Well?"

Roy shook his head. "Yes, ma'am." He picked up the
rifle and started towards the brush. "Stay right behind me

though, okay? That's a really nasty drop off over there."

"No problem." Amanda placed her hand on his back and followed in his footsteps. "Lead on."

The small calf stood in the chest-high brush crying. As the two people worked their way closer, it tried to step to them, but seemed to be stuck.

"Looks like it's tangled up in something." Roy turned to Amanda. "I'm going to check it out. Why don't you stay here, away from the edge?" He waited until the younger woman nodded. "Could you hold this for me, please?" The foreman handed her the rifle.

Amanda held the gun and looked around nervously. "Is this thing really necessary?" she asked as he slowly crept to the bawling animal.

Roy glanced at her over his shoulder. "Probably not. But I'd rather be safe than sorry." He turned his attention back to the calf. "Take it easy, little guy."

"Okay, I can see that," Amanda agreed, looking down at the ground under her feet. There were several pairs of footprints in the mud, and she noticed that one set looked to be made by sneakers. She looked at Roy's feet, then her own. They were both wearing boots. *And Lex ALWAYS wears boots. Where did these tennis shoe prints come from?* She was bending down to look a little closer when she heard Roy curse.

"Damn. This little fella has been tied to the brush with rope. Who in the hell would do something like that?" He worked carefully to free the calf from its snare. "This was no accident." A few more flicks of his wrist, and the calf scrambled away, running to the opening in the fence. "You're welcome," Roy yelled, looking up at Amanda with a smile. He could see the intense concentration on her face as she studied the ground around them. "What's up?"

The young woman pointed to the churned up ground beneath their feet. "What does this look like to you?"

Roy peered down at the ground, touching the earth with his gloved hand. "Sneakers? And pretty recent, too." He watched as Amanda slowly stepped to the edge of the drop off, leaning forward to look below. "Careful, now."

Amanda dropped to her knees weakly. "Oh, no," she cried as she leaned her body near the edge. "Roy, look."

The foreman rushed to her side to peer down the side of the overhang. "Jesus. How in the hell..." Due to the quantity of branches and limbs that covered it, he could barely make out the sprawled figure below.

"Lex!" Amanda yelled, searching frantically for some way to reach the bottom. "Can you hear me?" She turned sideways to grab Roy's arm. "She must be seriously hurt. We've got to get down there."

"Hang on just a minute, Miss Amanda. Let me go get some rope, all right?" Roy jumped to his feet and raced back toward the horses.

The blonde woman continued to look for a way to reach her lover. "Lex! C'mon, honey. Let me know you're okay, please?"

A familiar voice called to Lex and nudged her from unconsciousness. *Amanda?* The dark-haired woman slowly opened her eyes. *God, I must be hallucinating.* She struggled to take a deep breath, then gasped as the movement caused her extreme pain. *Ah, jeez. Not good, Lexington.* Lex listened carefully, as she hoped to hear the voice again.

"Lex? God, please, answer me, or move, or something!" Amanda half-shouted, half-cried. "Dammit! Listen to me!" she pleaded as she wiped tears from her face.

"Amanda?" Lex murmured quietly. *It really is her.* "Can you hear me?" she choked out as the pain became more intense. *Gotta do something so she'll know I'm okay.* Lex took a quick inventory of what her physical condition was. *Not much I can do, but maybe...*

The small blonde lay practically on the edge of the overhang, looking for any sign that her partner was alive. Roy returned carrying a long coil of rope. "Okay. If I can find something to tie this off to, I can drop over the edge and check her out. We're gonna have to get back to the house and get the jeep, though." He looked frantically around for something to anchor the rope to.

"The jeep? But I thought we couldn't get it up here?" Amanda kept an eye on the unmoving rancher below.

Roy tied one end of the rope to a small tree stump. "We can't. But if we take the east road from the bunkhouse, we'll end up on that path down there." He pointed to what looked like an indention in the grass below, not far from where Lex was lying. "It'll take about an hour and a half to get to the ranch house and then drive back here. But we really need to check her out, first." He pulled on the rope to check its sturdiness. "I sure hope this damned thing will hold me."

Amanda grasped his hand with a fierce strength. "It probably won't hold you, but I know it will hold me." Her green eyes blazed with determination. "You can hold it until I get down there, and then hurry back to the house for the jeep." When she saw him about to argue, Amanda held up a hand. "Wait. Listen to me, please." She nodded to the still figure below them. "I'm lighter, younger, and would be able to keep her calmer than you would. Besides," she flashed him a tired smile, "you know the way back up here. I don't." They both looked down at Lex.

"Hey! Did you see that?" Roy pointed with excitement. "I think I saw her hand move."

Amanda bit her lip and stared at the unmoving form. "Are you sure? I don't..." Then she saw it. The fingers on Lex's left hand wiggled slowly. "Yes!" She wrapped her arms around the startled man and laughed. "She moved."

Roy blushed and pulled away slightly. "Umm. Okay. Let's get you down there so I can get back to the house." He tied the rope around Amanda quickly, making a harness. "Once you get down there, I'll lower the supplies to you, okay?" He unloaded the rifle and handed her the cartridges.

"What are these for?" Amanda gave him a funny look.

"However the boss got down there, it wasn't an accident. I want you to have the rifle with you, just in case." He handed over the weapon and helped Amanda drape it over her shoulder using the attached leather strap.

Amanda took a deep breath and nodded. "Okay. I don't like it, but you're right." She shifted the gun around until it was somewhat comfortable on her back. "Be sure you get in touch with Sheriff Bristol before you leave, okay? He needs to know about this."

Roy nodded. "Right. C'mon. Let's get you down there, Miss Amanda." He stood up and coiled the rope behind him, using his right arm and back to brace the strands.

"Okay." Amanda slowly worked her way over the edge, sliding down until only her head was visible to the foreman. "See you in a bit, right?" She gave Roy a half-hearted smile.

"You sure will, miss. Just sit tight, and I'll be back in no time." Roy winked at Amanda as he lowered her from sight.

A few minutes later, Amanda was at the bottom of what appeared to be a ravine. She quickly untied the rope and allowed Roy to pull it back up. The small woman stumbled over to where Lex lay unmoving. "Lex?" She removed some of the debris from her lover. "Honey? Can you hear me?"

"Amanda?" Lex gasped, as she felt small hands lightly touch her hair. "Are you really here?" Her voice was barely a whisper.

"I'm here, love. Let me try to get some of this stuff off of you." Amanda carefully cleared away the smaller limbs and brush. "What happened to you?" She leaned down to hear what Lex tried to say.

The rancher almost cried in relief when she realized that Amanda was actually with her. "God. I thought you were a dream." She felt a gentle hand on her face. "I...I don't remember much." She felt another large limb being removed from her body, and groaned in appreciation.

Amanda heard the groan and stopped. "Oh, God. Did I hurt you?" She had removed enough to get a close look at Lex's face. The rancher's eyes were closed, and there were several still-bleeding scratches on her cheek and forehead.

She was afraid to move Lex since she knew that the rancher had fallen almost thirty feet.

"No...didn't hurt." Lex mumbled, fighting off another bout of unconsciousness. "Relief..."

A shout from above got Amanda's attention. "Miss Amanda! I'm sending down all the supplies now. How is she?" Roy had tied the saddlebags to the rope and was cautiously lowering them to the ground.

Amanda looked up at the foreman. "She's out again, but she seemed pretty coherent when she was awake." She untied the bags and carried them over to where the rancher lay. "Please hurry, Roy. I don't know what kind of injuries she has."

The foreman waved at her. "On my way. I left the radio in one of the bags, in case hers is broken." He disappeared from sight.

" 'manda?" Lex's voice was a hoarse croak.

The younger woman dropped to her knees beside the still-pinned rancher. "I'm right here, sweetheart." She brushed dark bangs away from Lex's scratched and muddy face. "Roy's gone for help. He'll be back really soon." She felt tears burn her eyes.

"Cold." Lex could feel the pain take over again. "Can't feel..." Her eyes closed slowly before she could say anything more.

Chapter
3

Amanda spent the next half-hour trying to make her partner more comfortable. She had the majority of the debris cleared away from Lex's body, but there were still several limbs that were just too heavy for her to move without risking more injury to the rancher. Inside one of the bags that Roy had left was an emergency kit that contained several shiny thermal blankets. Although Amanda was more than a little concerned about how well they actually worked since they were so thin, she covered Lex with the flimsy material the best she could.

"Lex? Can you hear me?" The young woman cleaned off Lex's face with a damp cloth. "C'mon, honey. Wake up for me, okay?" The rain had stopped for the moment, and it looked as if the afternoon sun was trying to make an appearance. "I wish I knew what happened. And if you fell, how did all this stuff end up on top of you? It doesn't make any sense." She ran her fingers through Lex's hair.

One blue eye blinked partially open. "I'm not real sure myself. I remember a calf..." Lex's voice was hoarse, but stronger than before. She was able to look at Amanda without having to move, since the blonde was kneeling on Lex's right. "How long have I been out?" When she saw the tears falling from the younger woman's eyes, Lex almost cried herself. "God, baby. Please, don't cry. Everything's gonna be okay."

"Sorry." Amanda sniffed and wiped her face with the back of one hand. "It's just that you were unconscious, and I didn't know how badly you were hurt, and I can't get all of this stuff off of you, and..." She knew she was babbling, but couldn't stop.

"Amanda." Lex stopped her in midstream. "I'm fine. Just pinned down and sore. It doesn't feel like anything is broken." *Although I can't feel my legs—but that may be due more to the cold than anything else. No sense in scaring her.* "And even though I'm really glad you're here, how did you find me?"

Amanda took a deep breath. "Are you sure you're okay? You keep fading out on me." She strroked the tangled dark hair.

Lex closed her eyes tightly, then reopened them. "Yeah. Just got one hell of a headache. Now tell me how you got here, sweetheart."

"Well, when you didn't radio back like you said you would, Martha and I got concerned." *Try scared to death, but she doesn't really need to hear that right now,* Amanda thought to herself. "So she called Roy, and he saddled up a couple of horses. We found a calf tied to some bushes up there." She pointed with her free hand, the other still unconsciously stroking her lover's dark hair. "And then I saw a lot of footprints near the edge. When I looked down, I could see you lying here." Amanda stopped as her throat closed with tears. "I couldn't tell if you were..." She couldn't even say the word.

"Sshhh." Lex struggled to pull her right arm out from under her body. She wanted to try and calm the younger woman somehow. The weight of the branch still lying across her back stopped her. "Damn."

Amanda stopped her quiet stroking and placed a gentle hand on her lover's shoulder. "Please stay still, Lex. Roy should be back soon with help."

The rancher stopped her struggle. Lex allowed her head to fall forward slightly until her forehead was resting against a sturdy limb. She had landed on top of a small patch of cedar, and the overwhelming fragrance of the tree was getting to her. *Dammit. I hate feeling helpless like this. God.* She could feel the fuzzy feeling returning, but was determined to fight it. *I keep going out like that, and Amanda's gonna be scared to death.* "Amanda?" Lex whispered as she turned her head slightly sideways. "How long has Roy been gone?"

"A little over an hour, I think." Amanda glanced at her watch. She studied the glassy-eyed look on her companion. "You're not looking too good, love. How are you feeling?" She played with the rancher's hair again. When her hand grazed the base of Lex's skull, the older woman gasped and flinched.

"Ow. Think you found a sore spot, sweetheart," Lex tried to joke, but she could feel the sharp pain radiate all over her head.

The younger woman knelt down until she could look closely into Lex's eyes. "Oh, Lex. I'm so sorry." She leaned forward and studied the older woman's scalp. "God, you're bleeding."

Lex closed her eyes as Amanda gently probed the back of her skull. "It's not that bad. Just a little tender."

"Yeah, right." Amanda pulled a square of gauze from the medical kit and placed it over the wound. "This certainly explains the reason you keep nodding off. You've probably got a concussion, honey." She emptied one of the bags, then placed it under the rancher's face. "Here. This should make you a little more comfortable." Amanda wiped Lex's face with the damp cloth.

"Thanks." Lex tried to swallow back the pain that was coursing through her body. She opened her eyes and gave the young blonde a grateful look. "I'm really glad you're here."

Amanda stopped what she was doing and gave Lex what she hoped was a smile. "I'm really glad I'm here, too.

Just wish I could do more." The honking of a horn cut off
what she was about to say. Turning around slightly,
Amanda could make out the form of Lex's truck heading
towards them. "Thank God. Roy's here."

The dark green Ram pick-up pulled to a stop just a few
yards away from where the rancher was lying. Amanda
almost cried with relief when the ranch foreman jumped
from the vehicle. An older, bearded man stepped from the
passenger side and followed him. "Lester?" She turned
back around and leaned down closer to Lex. "You're not
going to believe this, honey. Roy actually got Lester to
leave the bunkhouse."

Lex chuckled, then winced. "You're kidding me. The
only time that old man ever gets out is to go to town and
buy groceries. Martha can't even get him up to the main
house very often." Her headache was worsening, and Lex
knew she didn't have much time. "Amanda," she whispered, "I'm going to have to rest for a bit, okay?" The
rancher closed her eyes and allowed sleep to claim her
once again.

"Lex?" Amanda leaned down and whispered into the
rancher's ear, "Hang in there, sweetheart. We'll get you
out of here in no time." She left a trembling kiss on Lex's
scratched brow.

"How's she doing, Miss Amanda?" Roy asked as
Lester helped him carry a six-foot long plank of compressed wood. They put the door-sized piece down close to
where Amanda was kneeling, and Lester went back to the
truck to gather some more supplies. The foreman dropped
to one knee next to the small blonde and placed a gentle
hand on her shoulder. "Martha said that she was conscious
for a bit?"

The housekeeper had been waiting for Roy when he
pulled the horses up to the back of the ranch house.
Amanda had radioed ahead so that Martha was prepared,
and she had everything organized so that he could return
immediately. She had also contacted Lester and had him
load up Lex's truck with the supplies—the two of them

were pacing the kitchen floor when the foreman finally arrived.

Amanda covered his hand with her own. "Yeah. She's been in and out for the last half-hour. I think she has a concussion, Roy. There's a nasty gash on the back of her head, and her eyes look really out of focus." She looked back down at the unconscious woman. "Aren't we going to wait for an ambulance?"

Lester stepped over to the other side and looked down at the remaining limbs that pinned the rancher. "Only have the one in town, and it's in the shop. Besides, I don't think it could make the trip over that so-called road." He rubbed his thin gray beard with one hand. "But Martha sweet-talked Doc Anderson into making a house call. I think she promised him pork chops for dinner." He gave Amanda a sly wink. "He should be there by the time we get back to the house."

"Great. Then let's get the rest of this stuff off of her and get out of here." Amanda was about to stand up when Roy stopped her. "What?"

"Miss Amanda, I think Lester and I can handle the heavy stuff. But we're gonna need you to keep her as still as possible, just in case her back or neck is hurt."

Amanda nodded. "Okay." She moved around until she was sitting in front of Lex, then placed a hand on each shoulder of the still woman. "How's this?"

Roy smiled. "Perfect." He got a strong grip on one end of the branch that was lying across Lex's back. "Let's get this one first, Lester. It looks to be the biggest." The older man nodded and the two of them slowly lifted the large limb. "Damn," Roy groaned. "This thing weighs a ton." When he saw the upset look on Amanda's face, the foreman could have slapped himself. "I'm sure she's okay. The brush she landed on helped a lot."

The young woman looked up fearfully as Lex moaned and stirred a bit. "Sshh. Stay still." Amanda leaned forward and whispered softly into the rancher's ear, "Lester and Roy are here to help, but you have to stop moving."

Lex tried to wriggle free from Amanda's grasp. "Hurts," she mumbled as she attempted to turn her head.

"Honey, please." Amanda released the rancher's shoulders and gently held Lex's head immobile. She bent down until she could look into Lex's face. "Listen to me, Lex. We're going to get you out of here, but you have got to keep still."

"God," Lex muttered as she slowly opened her eyes. With the large limb removed, she was able to slowly raise her left hand and lay it on Amanda's arm. "I'm okay, sweetheart. Just really sore." She started to turn her head, but Amanda's firm grip held her immobile.

"Dammit, Lex. I said to stay still," the blonde snapped, her nerves raw and on edge.

The one blue eye that was visible opened wider at the sharp tone. "Sorry." Lex stopped trying to move her head and sighed.

Amanda's eyes widened also. "No, Lex. I'm the one who's sorry." She leaned forward and dropped a light kiss on the rancher's face. "Guess I'm still a little rattled. I didn't mean to jump down your throat like that, love."

Lex smiled. "Well, I can't say that I blame you, sweetheart. I should have listened to you the first time. I'm sorry you've had such a...Aahhh!" The last piece of wood was removed from her lower legs and caused a sharp pain to shoot across Lex's back.

"What is it, Lex?" Amanda felt a surge of panic rise in her chest. She looked up at Roy fearfully. "What did you do?"

The foreman gave her a reassuring smile. "Just got the last of this mess removed, Miss Amanda." He approached until he could kneel down and meet the rancher's gaze. "Boss, do you have any feeling in your legs?" He hated to ask that question in front of Amanda, but Roy wanted to know just how careful they needed to be. He had seen enough serious injuries over the years to know when to be cautious.

"Oh yeah. Hurts like hell." Lex flashed him a pained

smile. "Never felt anything hurt so good, though." She moved both feet slightly with a grimace. "Don't think anything's broken, but I bet I'll be a solid bruise for a week or so."

"How about your neck?" Amanda asked in a shaky voice. She had released her hold on the older woman's shoulders, and one hand stroked Lex's cheek gently.

Lex turned her head slightly and kissed the small palm. "My neck is fine, sweetheart. I just have a headache—everything else seems to be intact." She looked at Roy. "But I could sure use a little help getting off this damned brush. Never did care for the smell of cedar."

Roy grinned. *Oh, yeah. She's just fine.* "Sure thing, boss. Just let us know if we start to hurt you any." He motioned to the still quiet Lester, who reached over and got a gentle grasp on Lex's right leg. "Miss Amanda, if you'll support her head, we'll try to do this as easy as possible."

Amanda smiled down at Lex. "Let us do all the work, okay?" Her partner looked as if she were about to argue. "Please?"

Lex looked into the worried green eyes of her lover and sighed. "Yes, dear." She winked.

"Thank you." Amanda kissed the dark head. "Now, just relax." She braced Lex's head with her hands and nodded to Roy.

The foreman looked at Lester as they slowly rotated the rancher's body. When they had gotten Lex turned onto her left side, the injured woman bit off a pained groan. All movement stopped as Lex fought the urge to scream.

"Stop," Amanda yelled to the men. "Oh, God. Lex." She held the rancher's head perfectly still as terrible visions played in her mind. *We've paralyzed her. I knew we shouldn't have moved her. What if she has internal injuries? Moving her may have punctured a lung, or worse.*

"Amanda," Lex's quiet voice broke through her mental chastising, "it's okay." Her jaw was clenched in an effort to control the agony she was in.

"No...you..." Amanda stuttered as she watched the dark-haired woman fight the pain. "We hurt you, didn't we?"

Lex opened her eyes slowly. "No, baby. It's just my arm. I must have landed on it wrong. I'm fine, really."

Lester grabbed one of the emergency blankets and cut a long strip from it with his knife. "No problem there, Miz Lex. We'll just tie it down until the doc can take a look at it." He gently and efficiently tied Lex's right arm across her chest. "That ought to help."

"Thanks, Lester." Lex took a cautious breath. *Doesn't seem like anything is broken inside, thank God.* She offered Amanda a gentle smile. "Sorry about that, love. Didn't mean to scare you like that."

Amanda returned the smile gratefully. "It's okay, honey. Guess my nerves are shot." She looked at the two men sheepishly. "C'mon, guys. Let's get Lex into the truck before she turns into a Popsicle." A damp mist was falling, and the blonde thought she might have seen a snowflake come down as well.

Fifteen minutes later, a very grumpy Lex was lying in the bed of her truck. Over her objections, they had tied her down to the plank of compressed wood. After the earlier scare, Amanda had demanded that they not continue until the rancher was completely stabilized by the board.

"Are you sure you don't want to ride up front with the heater?" Roy asked the young woman for the third time. "Lester can ride in the back and help keep her still."

Amanda walked wearily up to the truck with Lex's old hat in her hands. She had searched for several minutes to find it because she knew how much the battered Stetson meant to her lover. "No, thank you, Roy." She climbed into the back and sat next to the injured woman. "I'll be more comfortable back here."

Lex smirked at the foreman, who was peeking over the edge of the truck. "Give it up, Roy. I haven't won an argu- ment with her yet." She gave the blonde a loving smile when her hat was placed near her head. "Thanks, sweetheart."

"No problem." Amanda twined her fingers with her friend's, even though Lex's uninjured arm was pinned in place by the restraints. "We about ready to go?"

Roy saluted. "Yes, ma'am." He climbed into the front of the truck and started it up. "I swear, Lester. It's never a dull moment around this place."

The old cook shook his head. "You got that right. We need to get the boys back to the ranch, pronto. I don't like the smell of this."

* * * * * * * * *

Amanda paced back and forth in the hallway next to the master bedroom. She stopped every so often and listened at the closed door, then sighed and continued her circuit. "What could be taking so damned long?" she grumbled, angry that she had been asked to leave the room almost an hour before by the kindly doctor. She was about to knock on the door when Martha appeared behind her.

"How's it going, honey?" The housekeeper had a large covered tray in her hands. "What are you doing out here in the hallway?"

"He kicked me out, Martha," Amanda huffed incredulously. "He said that I was getting in his way and aggravating his patient." She looked down at the tray. *There's more than one way to skin a cat. I think I just found my way back into the bedroom.* "Do you want me to take that in for you?" she asked sweetly.

Martha shook her head. "Oh, no. You're not getting me into trouble too, young lady. Dr. Anderson wanted you out here for a reason, and I'm not about to cross him." She felt pity for the young blonde. "But you can open the door for me, and I'll put in a good word for you, okay?"

Amanda took a deep breath and nodded. "Okay. But can you at least find out what's taking so long? I'm really getting worried." She reached for the doorknob and almost screamed out loud when the door opened instead. "Oh."

Dr. Anderson pushed the door the rest of the way and smiled. "You can both come in now, ladies." He smiled apologetically at Amanda. "I'm sorry I ran you out like that, honey, but I really needed to get her calmed down before I could check her out. She was more concerned about you than her own injuries, so I had to remove the distraction."

Distraction? I'm a distraction? Good grief. If she hears that, I'll never live it down. "That's okay, I understand." Amanda started to move around him and stopped. "Is she okay?"

"She's going to be fine, dear. As a matter of fact, I gave her a sedative earlier and she's resting comfortably right now. Just try to keep her in bed for a couple of days, if you can." Dr. Anderson opened the door wider for Martha so that she could carry the tray into the room. "I'm afraid she won't know you're here, Amanda, but you're more than welcome to sit with her for a while."

Amanda stepped quietly up to the bed where Lex was peacefully sleeping. The rancher's face had been cleaned, and the scratches that looked so bad earlier now appeared minor in the soft glow of the bedside lamp. Her right arm had been splinted and heavily wrapped with an elastic bandage, and was draped casually across her stomach. The young woman turned to face the doctor who had moved to stand beside her. "How is she, really?"

Dr. Anderson shook his head and chuckled. "Very lucky, actually. She has a concussion, and I had to put six stitches in the back of her head." Before Amanda could ask, he continued, "I know. But Lexington was so agitated, that knocking her out for a while was the lesser of the two evils." *And the language that young woman knows even made me blush a time or two.*

"I certainly don't blame you there," Amanda murmured. "She can be pretty bull-headed at times." She turned and brushed the dark bangs from the resting woman's eyes. "What about her arm?"

"I think it's just severely sprained. But I need you to

get her in to the office first thing Monday morning so that I can take a complete set of x-rays of her arm and her back." The elderly doctor patted Amanda on the shoulder. "I swear, the girl must be part feline to fall that far and not break any bones."

She sat gingerly on the edge of the bed as her legs gave out in relief. "She's really okay," Amanda mumbled, more to herself than anyone else in the room.

Martha put the tray down on a nearby table. "That's really great news, Doc. Why don't you come downstairs, and I'll fix you up a plate of that dinner I lured you out here with?" She took one last relieved look at the still form on the bed before ushering the older man from the room.

Amanda watched the door close, then turned her attention back to the woman lying in the bed. "So much for our quiet Saturday, huh?" She closed her eyes and took a deep breath.

"Not my fault," Lex mumbled as she opened her eyes. "At least not this time." She blinked several times as she tried to focus on Amanda's face. "Umm, sweetheart?"

"What is it, honey? Do you need anything?" Amanda looked worriedly down at her lover. "Are you warm enough? How about some water? Maybe..."

Lex lifted her left hand and covered the babbling mouth. "Sshh. I was just going to suggest that maybe you would like to get cleaned up and changed." She removed her hand and caressed the younger woman's jaw.

Amanda closed her eyes and leaned into the touch. "Mmm, that's a good idea. I've got to put some fresh sheets on the bed in the guest room anyway." She kissed Lex's palm.

Did I miss something here? "Why? Is Dr. A. hanging around for the night? I told him before he gave me that damned shot that I was okay." The rancher struggled to sit up. "Maybe I should just go down there and..."

"Stay still, honey." Amanda put her hand on Lex's shoulder. "No, he's probably going to be leaving right after Martha feeds him. I just thought that it would be better for you if I wasn't bouncing around on the bed all night. You really do need to get your rest."

"You're kidding, right?" The dark-haired woman dropped back against the pillows with a heavy sigh. "There's no way in hell I can get any rest if you're sleeping across the hall." She looked down at the quilt that covered her. "I didn't get any sleep the night you were gone."

The quiet admission tore at Amanda's heart. "Oh, Lex. I'm so sorry." She saw the light blush that covered the rancher's face. "Can I tell you a secret?"

Lex looked up and saw the green eyes filled with unshed tears. "Sure, sweetheart."

"I didn't get any sleep either. My grandmother teased me unmercifully yesterday morning."

"Mandy, dear, are you feeling all right?" Anna Leigh stepped into the kitchen, concerned that her granddaughter was up so early. The young woman usually had to rush to get ready for work, because she would normally sleep as long as possible in the mornings. "It's barely five o'clock in the morning." She sat down at the table with a slight yawn.

Amanda carried two mugs of coffee from the counter and sat down next to her grandmother. "I'm fine, Gramma. I just couldn't sleep."

The older woman smiled knowingly. "Uh-huh. Was there something wrong with your room? I've been telling Jacob that we need to replace that mattress for quite some time now."

"No. It was perfectly comfortable." Amanda peered over the rim of her mug as she took a sip. Just too big, and very lonely. I can't believe I miss her after only one night. *"Guess I'm just not used to it anymore."*

"Missing something, or someone, dear?"

The young woman sighed heavily. "God, yes." She blushed when she realized what she had said. "Lord, I can't believe I said that." Amanda covered her face with her hands.

Anna Leigh patted her on the arm. "Oh, honey, you're absolutely priceless." She watched as her granddaughter ran her hands through her shoulder-length hair. "Don't feel too bad, Mandy. I haven't been able to sleep away from your grandfather since we've been married."

"Really? That's a relief." Amanda wrapped her hands back around her coffee mug and stared into it. "But please don't tell Lex. She'll probably think I'm crazy."

"Your secret's safe with me, dear." Anna Leigh took a sip of her coffee. "But you'd better put on a little extra makeup this morning, or everyone at the office will figure it out." She enjoyed the shocked look on the young woman's face. "Or else they'll think you had a REALLY good night."

Amanda leaned down and kissed Lex tenderly on the lips. "Now," she inhaled deeply to control her emotions, "if you'll give me a few minutes, I'll get cleaned up and we'll see what Martha has brought up for dinner." She stood up, wiped her eyes with her hand, and walked into the bathroom. "I'll be right out."

The rancher closed her eyes with a weary smile. *Damn, she's cute. How did I ever get so lucky? Must have done something right, sometime.*

* * * * * * * * *

THUD!

"Dammit!"

Amanda woke up with a start and rolled over, only to find Lex's side of the bed empty. "Whatzit?" she mumbled as she looked around frantically. *Where is she? God, what time is it?* She blinked a couple of times and peered through the darkness to focus on the alarm clock. *Twelve-thirty in the morning?*

THUNK! THUNK!

There it is again. Where is that noise coming from? Amanda climbed out of bed and noticed the light seeping from under the bathroom door. She slowly opened the door and peered inside. "Lex? Is everything okay?"

"Umm." Her lover's sheepish voice came from the vicinity of the bathtub. "Everything's okay...sorta."

"What do you mean, sorta okay?" The blonde stepped further into the room. "Oh, Lex." *Don't you dare laugh, Amanda Cauble,* she sternly warned herself. She quickly covered her mouth with her hand and asked, "Are you okay?"

The tall woman was lying sideways, butt down in the empty tub, wearing only the boxer shorts that she normally slept in. Lex looked at her friend with a sheepish grin. "Yeah. I'm fine. But since I can't use this arm," she waved her bandaged right arm around, "I seem to find myself stuck."

Amanda chuckled. "Looks like it." She stood directly in front of Lex and crossed her arms over her chest. "And just what were you planning on doing at this time of night?"

"I thought I'd take a bath. Dr. A. told me not to get the bandage on my head wet, but I felt so damned dirty that a nice soak sounded good." She raised an eyebrow at Amanda. "Well? You gonna help me get out of here, or do I need to just wait until Martha comes in to clean?"

"Hmm." Amanda appeared thoughtful. "I dunno. I ought to make you sit there for a while and suffer, since you didn't have the sense to wake me up and ask for help."

Lex sighed. "Okay. What's this gonna cost me?" She tried her best pitiful look. "You shouldn't pick on me, you know. I'm injured."

Green eyes sparkled with glee. "Uh-huh. Are you saying that your bad judgement was brought on by the head injury?" Amanda could barely contain her laughter. *Does she have any idea just how adorable she looks right now? Probably not.*

"Would it get me out of this mess with my dignity intact?" Lex bargained.

"Nope."

"How about if I throw myself on your mercy? Do any penance that you see fit?"

Amanda brightened at that offer. "Really? You'd do whatever I asked?"

The rancher looked at her friend with suspicion. "Yeah, okay."

"Cool." The younger woman offered her hand to Lex. "Here. Be careful now." She slowly pulled the tall form from the tub, but didn't release her grip until Lex was steady on her feet. "You got dizzy and lost your balance, didn't you?" Amanda accused as she wrapped an arm around the naked torso. "Good grief, Lex. You feel like a block of ice."

Lex leaned into Amanda gratefully. "Well it's the dead of winter, what did you expect?" She looked down at the blonde. "I really would feel better after a bath."

"Oh, really?" Amanda steered Lex back into the bedroom and guided her onto the bed. She leaned down and nibbled on the rancher's ear. "How about a nice warm sponge bath? That way you won't get too chilled, and I get to have a little fun too?" She raised her head as she felt a strong hand glide up her back under her nightshirt.

"That sounds like a pretty good idea to me." Lex continued to explore the younger woman's back with her left hand. "Although I can think of something else that we could do for fun." She tried to lean up for a kiss, but was stopped. "What?"

Amanda dropped down and kissed the strong chin below her. "Not tonight, dear, you have a headache." She laughed. "I've always wanted to say that."

A pitiful groan was her only answer.

* * * * * * * * *

"Good morning, honey," the housekeeper cheerfully greeted Amanda as she walked into the kitchen the next morning. "How is Lexie doing?"

Amanda reached into the cabinet for a coffee mug.

"She's really hurting this morning. I didn't even have to force her to stay in bed." She peeked over the older woman's shoulder. "You want me to take that tray up for you?"

Martha covered the tray and smiled. "That would be really sweet of you, Amanda. I was just about to bring it upstairs."

"I don't mind. You have enough to do around here without waiting on us hand and foot." Amanda gathered up the tray and started for the door. "Is there anything I can do to help you around here today? I'm going to make sure Lex takes her pain medication, so I'll be free pretty much all afternoon."

"Well, I..." A knock on the front door interrupted Martha's answer. "That must be Charlie. He told me on the phone yesterday that he wanted to have a talk with Lexie." She hurried to the door and opened it. "Charlie Bristol. Get in this house." Martha grabbed the Sheriff's arm and pulled him inside. "What have we told you about knocking around here? You're family."

The tall, thin man took off his hat and grinned. "Hello, honey. Nice to see you, too." Charlie winked at Amanda, who was standing at the foot of the stairs with the tray still in her hands. "Good to see you, Amanda. How's Lex doing?" The housekeeper had briefed him on the rancher's condition yesterday. Since the lawman thought of Lex as the daughter he never had, he had personally driven over to Dr. Anderson's home earlier that morning to get a complete medical report. *If I find the son of a bitch that did this to her, I'll wring his neck myself, and save the taxpayers a load of money.*

"She's okay. Just really sore." The young woman began her trek up the stairs. "And probably hungry." Halfway up, Amanda called over her shoulder, "Give me a minute to get this stuff settled, then come on up. I know she'd love to see you."

"Well? Are you gonna stand there in your coat all morning, or will you be joining me in the kitchen for some coffee?" Martha winked at Charlie before she made her way back to the rear of the house.

The lawman stood silently for a moment with a silly grin plastered on his face. *I think I fall deeper in love with that woman every time I see her. Maybe Amanda has an idea on how I can get her to say yes.* Charlie had proposed to the housekeeper at least once a month for the past ten years. Even though Martha returned his love, she gently continued to turn him down time after time. *I'll just keep asking her until she says yes just to shut me up,* he vowed as he followed her slightly rounded form into the kitchen.

****

"Please, Lex. Just take the darn pill." Amanda had cleared the dishes away and was now trying to convince her stubborn friend to take something for the intense pain she was experiencing.

Lex took a deep breath and closed her eyes. "It's not that bad." She leaned back against the headboard of the bed, sweating from the exertion of putting on a nightshirt.

Amanda sat down gingerly to the left of her. "What's the big deal? You're supposed to rest for a few days anyway."

"I just don't want to spend our only day together sleeping when I'd rather be spending the time with you," Lex admitted. "I've...uh...really missed you lately." She opened her eyes and searched the younger woman's face.

"Oh, honey," Amanda framed Lex's face with her hands, "do you really think that I could leave you when you're feeling like this? I've already called my grandmother, and she's agreed to take care of things at the office for a few days." Amanda's grandmother, Anna Leigh Cauble, was the retired owner of Sunflower Realty. She had recently turned the management over to her granddaughter after she had to fire the previous manager for misconduct.

Lex smiled. "Really? You're going to stay home for a day or two?" Her blue eyes lit up like a small child's at

Christmas.

Amanda returned her smile. "Try for longer than that. Gramma told me to take the entire week off. She says someone has to keep their eye on you, and poor Martha needs all the help she can get." She leaned forward and captured the rancher's lips gently with her own. She felt Lex tangle her left hand in her hair as she deepened the kiss.

"Ahem." Martha stood at the doorway with a blushing Charlie right behind her. Since her head only came up to his chest, the sheriff had a very good view of the activity on the bed. "I don't think that's what the doctor had in mind when he said for you to stay in bed, Lexie," the housekeeper teased as she stepped into the room.

"Oh, God," Amanda laughed as she buried her head in the dark-haired woman's chest.

Lex smirked at the older woman as she ran her fingers through Amanda's hair. "You got a better way to keep me in bed?" She felt her lover laugh again.

Charlie choked as he tried to stifle a chuckle of his own. "She's got a point, sweetheart." He closed the distance between himself and Martha and wrapped his arms around her.

"Don't encourage her." Martha playfully slapped the arm that was settled around her ample waist. "She's hard enough to live with as it is."

"I can imagine she is." Charlie kissed the top of the older woman's head, then walked over to the bed and kneeled next to it. "How are you doing, sweetheart?" He placed his hand lightly on Lex's leg. "Doc tells me you were pretty damned lucky out there." *Scared me to death when I heard, poor kid.*

Lex grimaced at the older man. "To tell the truth, Uncle Charlie, I hurt like hell." She looked down at her right arm, which was still heavily wrapped. "And I feel like a total idiot, letting someone get behind me like that."

Amanda sat back and ran a hand through her hair. She then turned around and snuggled up on her lover's good side. "Why don't you two pull up a seat and get comfortable?" She grabbed a medicine bottle and a glass of water from the nearby table, and handed Lex a pill. "And you. Take one of these before I have to get tough with you."

"Yes, dear." The injured woman took the offering meekly as her eyes twinkled. Lex swallowed the pill with a frown. "Yuck!" She continued to drink from the glass until all the water was gone. "Nasty stuff."

Charlie stood up and brought two chairs closer to the bed. "This is a semi-official visit, honey." He waited until Martha sat down before he continued. "I sent a couple of men to check out the area. Is there anything you can tell me that might help?"

Lex felt Amanda grasp her uninjured hand. "It was definitely a set up; that much I know for sure." She squeezed the smaller hand and sighed. "The fence was cut, and a small calf had been tied to some brush near the edge of the drop off. When I went over to cut him free, I felt something slam into my head, and then everything went black." She pulled the younger woman's hand up and kissed the knuckles. "Next thing I knew, I was lying at the bottom of the ravine covered by a bunch of limbs and branches."

"Have you gotten any threats lately, Lex? Something that might explain why someone would do this to you?" Charlie had pulled a small notepad from his shirt pocket, and was busily taking notes.

"No. Not that I can think of." Lex was already feeling the effects of the medication that she had taken. "And if someone wanted me dead, why didn't they just shoot me?" She heard a sharp intake of breath as Amanda realized where these questions were leading.

Amanda looked up at her friend with a serious expression. "That's not completely true now, is it? You've had two separate threats in the last month." She saw understanding in the blue gaze. Turning her attention to Charlie, Amanda bit her lip. "Rick Thompson threatened her at my grandmother's office last month in front of several witnesses."

The lawman nodded. "That's right. I'd forgotten all about that." He added Rick's name to his notes. The ex-manager of Sunflower Realty had been fired when it had become known that he had sent Amanda on a wild goose chase to the Rocking W ranch. She was supposed to talk to Lex about selling the large piece of property. On the way to the meeting, her car was washed off the old bridge that led up to the ranch, and the dark-haired woman jumped into the raging creek to pull her from the water. Rick had thought Lex was involved in his dismissal, and had made several threats to get even when he was arrested at the office later on that week.

"That little turd," Martha muttered. She had never liked the man, and made a mental note to ask Roy to have some of the boys keep a closer eye on the ranch house until Lex was back on her feet.

"And then there's my father," Amanda uttered quietly, looking down at their linked hands. "He made some nasty threats when we were in California."

Lex struggled to keep her eyes open. "Sweetheart, I honestly don't think that your father would resort to something like this. Besides, how did they know I'd be the one checking the fence? I think it's more likely vandals that were afraid I'd catch them, so they did what they could to give themselves time to escape." She felt her eyelids grow too heavy to keep open.

Amanda released Lex's hand and kissed her cheek. "Rest well, love." She looked at Charlie and Martha with a quiet smile. "Why don't we go downstairs and discuss this a little more? She'll be out for hours." She rose carefully from the bed.

Martha nodded and stood up. "Good idea, honey." She stepped over to the bed and placed a light kiss on the sleeping woman's forehead. "Foolish child. She's gonna drive me crazy before this year is out, that's for sure." She grabbed the discarded food tray and headed for the door. "You two coming downstairs with me, or do I have to drink that whole pot of fresh coffee all by myself?"

Charlie looked at Amanda and grinned. "Gotta love a woman like that." He offered her his arm with a bow. "Shall we?"

"Yes, I do believe we shall." Amanda accepted his arm with a curtsy. "Thank you."

Chapter
4

"You idiot. I'm paying you to keep an eye on her, not kill her." He had to pull the phone away from his ear to protect his hearing. "Good God. Have you no sense? What if they figured out that you did it?" the voice continued to rant.

The victim of the tirade sighed. "Look. I *was* keeping an eye on her. And I really had intended to just cut the fence and then leave. But when I saw that *she* was the one there, I couldn't resist," he chuckled. "When I saw her lying at the bottom of that ravine, I honestly thought I'd killed her. So I threw some stuff over the edge to try and hide the body."

There was a short silence from the other end of the line. "It's somewhat of a shame that you didn't succeed—it would have certainly made things a lot easier for me." Papers shuffled in the background. "Okay, here is what you're going to do. I want you to keep a high profile— make a nuisance of yourself. That should come easily for you."

"What? Are you out of your mind? They'll lock me up for sure." The underling's voice was incredulous. "You don't pay me enough to go to jail for you."

"Listen to me, you fool. If you go into hiding, you'll be the first person that they will suspect. You're probably already on top of their list. Trust me, the best place to hide from these backwater bumpkins is right under their noses," the intelligent voice commented. "You might even try threatening her in front of some of them. They'll never figure you to be that stupid." *Although I could vouch for your lack of intelligence. Where did I go wrong? I should have hired a professional when I had the chance.*

The man looked around his cluttered living room. He noticed, not for the first time, the empty food cartons lying around. *I really should get someone in here to clean this place up sometime.* He took another deep swallow from his beer. "Okay. But if they bust me, I'm taking you down with me."

"Don't even try to threaten me, you worthless little pissant. I can make you disappear in a heartbeat...permanently."

"Umm, yeah. Sorry about that. I wasn't really threatening you, honest. I'm just a little nervous about getting caught, you know?" He ran a trembling hand across his forehead. "I didn't mean nothing by it."

"Just remember who's in charge, and you'll be fine. I want you to make yourself *very* visible for the next few days, got it?"

"Yeah, I got it." Once his boss had hung up the phone, the man threw his can of beer across the room. He proceeded to throw things around the living area until he wore himself out. "Damn you, Lex Walters!" He stood in the middle of the destruction, panting heavily. "I can't wait until you get what's coming to you.

* * * * * * * * *

The rest of the morning and afternoon went by peacefully at the ranch. Amanda would go upstairs every so often to check on her friend, but spent most of the day sharing stories with Martha and Charlie. The sheriff left in the late afternoon because he wanted to get back into town. He needed to organize the reports his men would be turning in after their investigations. Martha allowed him to leave only after getting his promise to be back at the ranch early on Thursday for Thanksgiving dinner.

The young blonde looked at the computer screen and sighed. She had decided to work on the ranch finances for Lex since the older woman tended to get overly stressed whenever she tried to handle the paperwork. Amanda had always enjoyed working with numbers, and Lex had happily handed over the bookkeeping duties to her after one especially trying night of attempting to balance the ledger.

Amanda rolled over in her sleep only to find herself alone in bed. She glanced over at the alarm clock and saw that it was almost one o'clock in the morning. The sleepy blonde slipped on the colorful robe that had been a gift from Lex and padded quietly down the stairs in search of her lover.

The young woman spotted a light coming from the den and moved toward it. Amanda stepped into the den and found that the light was actually leaking out from the attached office. She stood in the doorway for a moment and watched the dark-haired woman. "Lex?"

The rancher looked up from the computer screen and rubbed her eyes. "Amanda. What are you doing out of bed?" She pushed her chair back from the desk with a sigh.

"I got cold." Amanda smiled as she stepped into the room.

"I'm sorry, sweetheart. I should have checked the fire before I came downstairs." Lex didn't notice the glint in the green eyes when she apologized.

Amanda approached the desk slowly. "It wouldn't have helped," she stated as she stepped in front of Lex and stopped. "I missed you." The blonde climbed into the older woman's lap, facing her, and straddled her legs. She put her arms around the rancher's neck with a sultry smile.

"You can't honestly tell me that you'd rather play on the computer than come upstairs and play with me." Amanda bent down and gave the startled woman a passionate kiss.

Lex wrapped her arms around the smaller woman. *"Mrrumph."* She pulled away regretfully. *"God, baby, you sure make it hard to say no."* She trembled slightly when Amanda placed gentle kisses on her neck. *"But I've been...ah..."* Lex put her hands on the voracious woman's shoulders and gently pushed her back. *"Please, Amanda. I've got to get these damn ledgers to balance. I have a phone conference with Mr. Collins first thing in the morning to discuss the next quarter."*

"Okay." Amanda sighed, somewhat heartened by the genuine regret in the blue eyes across from her. *"What seems to be the problem?"* She chuckled as Lex spun the chair around to allow them both to see the computer screen without unseating her.

"See right here?" Lex used a long finger to point out a number on the screen. *"This figure should match that one."* She touched another part on the display.

Amanda twisted around until she had a clear view of the computer. *"May I?"*

Lex lifted Amanda until she was facing the screen completely, but still situated on her lap. *"Be my guest."* She rested her chin on her friend's shoulder and wrapped her arms around the small waist. Lex closed her eyes as she listened to Amanda type.

"There you go."

"How did you...?" The rancher opened her eyes and looked at the screen. *"Damn."* The figures matched. *"I've been working on that for well over an hour. How did you figure it out so quickly?"*

Amanda leaned back into the warm body she was cradled against. *"Guess my college years weren't a complete waste of time."* She tilted her head as Lex kissed her neck. *"Mmm. I've always loved playing with numbers."* The young woman smiled as she felt insistent fingers loosen the tie on her robe.

Lex placed her lips near her lover's ear. "What would it cost me to have you help with the bookkeeping around here?" she whispered as she gently bit Amanda's earlobe.

"Oh, God." Amanda almost melted onto the floor. "For this kind of payment, I'll do just about anything you ask." She felt herself being lifted as Lex carried her into the den and placed her carefully on the sofa. "Oooh, yeah. You've just hired yourself a bookkeeper," she growled and welcomed the tall woman into her arms.

"Are you okay, sweetie?" Martha asked from the office doorway. "You look a little flushed."

Amanda looked up guiltily. "Umm, yeah. I'm great. Just going over the books for Lex." She ran a hand over her face to try and dispel the blush. "Do you need my help in the kitchen?" She had told Martha earlier to come get her whenever she needed help starting dinner. When she had first moved in they had made a pact as far as the household chores. Martha would let Amanda help with the laundry and the cooking, and the younger woman wouldn't get in her way when she did the rest of the housework.

Martha shook her head. "No, nothing like that, dear. I just came in to tell you that your grandmother called a few minutes ago."

"She did? I didn't hear the phone ring." Amanda looked at the offending item. "Is everything okay?"

"That's because Lexie keeps the ringer turned off in here so it won't disturb her. Mrs. Cauble was just checking in to see how our patient was doing." The housekeeper moved into the room and sat down. "Are you real busy?"

"No, not at all. What's wrong, Martha?" Amanda could see that something was on the older woman's mind.

"That business yesterday scared the living daylights out of me," she admitted. "Do you really think that some-one is out to get my Lexie? Who would do such a thing?" Martha looked down at her lap, then lifted her head and met Amanda's gaze. "I've alerted the boys down at the bunkhouse, and they're going to keep a close eye on the house until she's feeling better." She leaned forward with an intense look on her face. "My little girl has finally found happiness, and I'll be damned if I'm gonna let some low life ruin that. They'll have to go through me to get to her."

Amanda stood up and stepped around the desk, then knelt at the older woman's feet. "I know, Martha. I feel the same way." She gripped both of the housekeeper's hands tightly. "When I look at you, I can see where Lex got her beautiful heart from. I wish that I would have had half as good a mom growing up as she did."

Martha pulled Amanda to her and enveloped the smaller woman in a fierce embrace. "Honey, I thank the good Lord for you each and every day." She stood and helped the young woman to her feet. "Now let's stop all the serious talk, and go check on the cookies that I left baking in the oven. They should almost be ready."

"Oooh, cookies." Amanda followed her dutifully out of the room and down the hallway. "What kind?" she asked as she took a deep sniff of the air.

"Brown sugar." Martha stepped into the kitchen and made her way to the oven. "Be about another minute, dear. Why don't you go ahead and get yourself a glass of milk?"

Amanda smiled. "Mmm, my favorite. But I think I'll run upstairs real quick and check on Sleeping Beauty. Maybe she'll be awake, and I can take her some cookies, too." She stepped out into the hallway and screamed. "Aaaah!"

Martha rushed out of the kitchen in a panic. She found Amanda back against the wall with one hand over her heart. Lex stood a few feet away dressed in gray boxer shorts and an unbuttoned black nightshirt. "What are you doing out of bed?" the housekeeper demanded.

"You scared me half to death," Amanda chastised as she willed her heart to stop pounding. "Martha's right. What *are* you doing out of bed?"

Lex was propped against the banister with her injured arm held closely against her body. "I was bored and tired of lying in bed." She inhaled deeply. "Cookies? Smells like brown sugar." She pushed away from where she had reclined against the stair post and slowly limped into the kitchen.

The blonde looked over at Martha and shrugged. "You raised her."

"Good lord. Just had to toss that one in my face, didn't you?" the housekeeper joked as they followed Lex into the kitchen.

"I hate to break up your little gabfest, but could one of you come over here and help me with the milk?" Lex stood at the cabinet holding a clear container of milk. "I can't get the damned lid off."

Amanda shook her head and smiled. "Poor baby." She walked over and grabbed another glass. "You want one too, Martha?"

The housekeeper laughed. "No, thank you, dear." She pulled the tray of cookies out of the oven. "I bake them. I don't usually eat them."

"Really?" Amanda was intrigued. "Are they safe?" she teased as she poured two glasses of milk. After she returned the bottle to the refrigerator, she gently buttoned the rancher's shirt. "Looks like I get to pamper you a lot for the next few days, huh?" The blonde looked up into Lex's eyes with a tender smile.

Lex returned the smile. "I guess so. Thanks," she whispered and kissed the shorter woman on the forehead.

Amanda grabbed both glasses and ushered the rancher to the table. "Sit down, tough stuff." She watched with concern as her friend moved stiffly to a chair and sat. "You look like you're completely miserable."

"It's not that bad, sweetheart. I'm just really stiff from lying around for so long." Lex shifted around uncomfortably in her chair as she picked up her glass with her left hand. "I think I'm more sore today than I was yesterday."

Martha stepped up beside her and touched the top of her dark head. "Honey, there was a good reason the doctor told you to stay in bed for a few days. You have to give your body time to heal." She waited until Lex looked up into her eyes. "After you eat I want you to go back to bed, okay?"

Lex wanted to argue, but she relented when she saw the concern reflected on the older woman's face. *Besides,* she thought, *I really do feel like hell.* "Yes, ma'am." *Maybe I can talk Amanda into joining me. This might not be so bad after all.*

"Thank you, Lexie." Martha leaned down and kissed her charge on the cheek, and then moved away from the table with purpose. "Don't fill up on cookies. I'll heat you up some stew."

Amanda chuckled. "She's got you pegged, sweet-heart." She reached for another cookie. "But don't worry, the stew is really good."

The housekeeper cleared her throat from across the room. "That goes for you too, young lady. You barely touched your lunch today."

"Ha!" Lex grinned triumphantly. Then she realized what Martha had said. "Are you feeling all right?" She covered Amanda's hand with her own. "You're not coming down with something, are you?"

"I'm fine, love. Guess I'm just a little tired." Amanda squeezed her lover's hand. *Of course, I spent the entire night watching her sleep. No wonder I'm a little tired.* The younger woman didn't even lie down for most of the night, for fear that she would try to snuggle up against the injured woman in her sleep.

Lex sighed. "Amanda. What am I gonna do with you?" She looked down at the bowl of stew that Martha had set in front of her. "Mmm. You're right. This smells fantastic." She began to eat, then paused to yawn. *Damn. Hope I don't fall asleep in my bowl.*

"That settles it then. After you finish your dinner, it's off to bed for you both." Martha settled into another chair. "You girls will need your rest since you have to be up early in the morning."

Amanda looked at her quizzically. "We do? What's

going on, Martha?" She ate her stew hungrily.

Martha gave Lex a no nonsense look. "You're going into town first thing tomorrow so that Lexie can get a complete checkup." She raised a hand when the rancher opened her mouth to speak. "No arguments. You can barely walk, and you're hurting so badly that you're not even trying to hide it."

Lex decided to concentrate on not spilling her stew. She was still shaky and her vision had not completely cleared up. *Probably a good idea.* Then she grinned to herself. *Oooh. Martha won't expect me to agree with her. This will be good for the shock value alone.* "I think you may be right, Martha," she murmured quietly while she kept her attention on her bowl.

"What?" The housekeeper dropped her spoon in shock. "Lexie? Oh, honey. If you're feeling that badly, maybe we should go this evening." She started to get up and clear the table. "I knew we should have taken you to the hospital yesterday."

Lex looked up with a sneaky grin and then tried to look innocent. "Maybe I'd feel better if you would bake me more cookies."

Amanda almost choked on a mouthful of stew. "Oh, God. That's funny." She coughed a couple of times and took a large drink of milk. "She got you that time, Martha."

Martha sat back down with a sigh. "I swear you're gonna be the death of me one of these days, Lexie." She shook her head and continued her meal.

"Sorry, Mada," using her childhood nickname for Martha. "I just wanted you to relax a bit. You worry too much." Lex smiled again. "But if it would make you feel better, you can tuck me in tonight and read me a story."

"Just wait until you get better, young lady. I'll take a spoon to your backside," the older woman threatened, but she couldn't keep the smile from her face.

Lex was stopped from making another sarcastic remark by the ringing of the phone.

"I'll get it." Amanda practically leapt from the table and raced across the kitchen. *Thank God. I think Lex was about to get herself into more trouble.* "Walter's residence, Amanda speaking." She saw the rancher's scowl out of the corner of her eye. Lex had asked her several times not to answer the phone that way. She had stressed that it was just as much Amanda's home as it was hers, but the blonde stubbornly refused. *We're going to have to come up with a compromise before Martha ends up being a referee.* The voice on the other end of the line caused her face to scrunch into a frown. "Hold on just a minute, I'll see if she's available." She held the receiver to her chest.

"Who is it, Amanda?" Lex tried to turn around in her chair, but a sharp pain in her back stopped her. "Dammit."

"It's your brother. Do you want me to just take a message?" Amanda whispered. She didn't want to see Lex get upset, which was always a good possibility whenever her brother was involved.

The rancher slowly climbed to her feet, barely able to hold back a pained groan. "No. He'll just keep calling until I talk to him." She held her hand out for the phone. "Let's see what he wants now." Lex allowed Amanda to drag a chair from the table and help her sit down. "Thanks," she whispered. "Hello, Hubert. What can I do for you this time?"

"For one thing, you can tell your little...girlfriend...to drop the damn attitude. I'm not amused," Hubert's nasal tone whined. "She thinks she's better than me, and I'm tired of it."

Lex sighed. "Hubert, you're imagining things. And, for the record," she looked over at her lover with a smile, "she *is* better than you. Now what do you want?"

Hubert was livid. "Now you listen to me, you perverted bitch. Don't you dare talk to me that way. I'll..."

"Shut up!" Lex barked, then instantly regretted it. She fought back a wave of dizziness as her head pounded. "You've got exactly one minute to tell me what you want before I hang up." She closed her eyes and leaned back in the chair.

"Fine. I got some papers in the mail Friday that require your signature. I left a message on your damned machine yesterday, but you didn't bother to return my call." The older man sounded like a petulant child. "Do you want me to bring them out to the ranch, or will you be in town sometime this next week? I need to send them back as soon as possible."

The rancher opened her eyes and caught Amanda's worried look. "I'll be in town tomorrow, Hubert. We'll drop by the office then, okay?" Lex winked at her friend.

Hubert laughed humorlessly. "My, oh my. Miss High and Mighty is actually going to sully herself and grace the little people with her presence. Why I ought to..."

"Goodbye, Hubert." Lex hung up the phone in the middle of his sarcastic speech. "Asshole," she muttered, then glanced over at Martha. "At least he won't be bothering you any more tonight."

The housekeeper stood up and walked over to where Lex was sitting. "Sweetheart, let's get you back upstairs and into bed. You're looking a bit pale."

"She's right, Lex." Amanda reached down and helped Martha pull the dark-haired woman to her feet. "C'mon. If you're a good girl, *I'll* tuck you in and read you a story."

Lex released a tired chuckle. "That's the best offer I've had all day." She draped her left arm over the blonde's shoulders, and felt Martha wrap an arm around her from the right. "I must be doing something right," she joked.

"What makes you say that, dear?" Martha asked as they helped her slowly up the stairs.

"I've got the two prettiest ladies in the state of Texas hanging all over me." Amanda tickled her ribs while the housekeeper lightly slapped her rear end. To which she indignantly responded, "What?"

Chapter 5

"Oh, stop pouting. You're not going to win this one, so don't even try." Amanda glanced at her friend out of the corner of her eye. She was straining to see over the dash of Lex's truck and was afraid to take her eyes off the road for more than a moment. During the night, the temperature had dropped to around twenty degrees, and the blonde woman was worried about hitting patches of ice on the road to town.

Lex continued to stare out of the passenger window. The early morning sun glinted off of the frost in the passing fields, and she had to squint in deference to her headache. "I'm not pouting." Her heavy sigh caused condensation to form on the inside of the window. The rancher used her good hand to idly draw a small circle on the glass. Her right arm was still heavily wrapped with the elastic bandage, and Martha had made her wear an old sling to keep it close to her body. *Stupid doctor. I've been banged up worse than this before. Why do I have to go all the way into town for a couple of bruises and a damned headache?*

As the truck reached the outskirts of town, Amanda

tried again. "Honey, you can't really blame him for wanting you to go to the hospital instead of his office. Especially when you told him about the headache and the pain in your back." She knew that Lex did not like being fussed over, and she thought that her friend was probably a little frightened about what the tests might show. "He said it was just a precaution."

"If it's just a precaution, why did you make me pack an overnight bag?" Lex turned away from the window to study the younger woman's profile. "What did he say to you?'

"Doctor Anderson asked me to have you pack a bag in case the tests took longer than he thought. I guess he was afraid to ask you." Amanda reached over and patted the nervous woman's leg. "Now just relax. I promise that I'll be there with you the whole time, okay?"

Lex moved her hand away from the window and placed it on top of Amanda's. "You must think I'm acting like a child. I'm sorry, sweetheart." She raised their hands and kissed the young woman's knuckles. "Forgive me?"

Amanda smiled. "Oh, I don't know. How do you plan to make it up to me?" She felt a small thrill chase down her back as the rancher nibbled on her fingers. "Okay. You win."

"Yeah?" Lex murmured as she continued her gentle assault. "So, I'm forgiven then?" she persisted. She looked up as the truck pulled to a stop. "We're here?"

They were in the parking lot of Somerville Community Hospital. The older brick structure was only four floors, since a majority of the townspeople went into the larger cities for most of their medical needs.

Amanda parked the truck near the side entrance as Doctor Anderson had requested. He had told her that he didn't want Lex walking any further than necessary, and that they'd be able to check her in at the nurses' station just inside the door. "Yep. We're here." She switched off the truck and turned sideways in her seat to look at the dark-haired woman. "You want to stay here while I go inside and get someone to help you?" She knew it was probably pointless, but she had to try.

"Nah. I'm fine." Lex smiled at her and unbuckled her seat belt. "Let's just get this over with, all right?" She watched as her friend climbed out of the truck and hurried around to open her door. "Thanks."

"Any time." Amanda smiled as she helped her partner from the vehicle. "Lean on me, okay?"

Lex wrapped her good arm around the shorter woman's shoulders. "I always do, love." She smiled to herself when Amanda walked very slowly toward the hospital entrance. "Sweetheart, I won't break, you know.

"I'm sorry...I just..." Amanda stammered, embarrassed at being caught coddling her lover.

"Don't be. I just don't want you to worry. I'm fine, really," Lex assured her.

Amanda chuckled. "Don't worry? Why not ask me to do something easier? Like eat your cooking?" she teased as she tried to steer the conversation away from serious matters.

They'd almost reached the side entrance when Dr. Anderson met them outside with a wheelchair. "Good morning, ladies." He exchanged amused glances with the small blonde. "Hello again, Amanda." He focused his attention on Lex. "Lexington, have a seat. I'm not going to let the hospital gossips say that I don't treat my patients right."

Lex eyed the contraption warily. "I really don't think I need that, Dr. A."

The smaller woman had already maneuvered the rancher near the chair. "Consider this another one you're not going to win." She met Lex's stubborn glare. "Don't try that look with me, Slim. I'm not intimidated."

She released an aggrieved sigh, but Lex allowed Amanda and the doctor to assist her into the chair. "This is ridiculous. I'm just a little sore."

"Uh-huh. Tell me another one." Amanda patted her on the shoulder, then wheeled her to the hospital. She leaned

down until her mouth was right next to the rancher's ear.
"Behave yourself and I'll give you a nice hot oil massage
when we get home." Amanda kissed the ear before moving
away.

Dr. Anderson laughed at the blush that colored the
injured woman's face. "Well now, Lexington, I was going
to get onto you for being so pale, but it looks like you've
developed quite a bit of color in your cheeks." To escape
the possible wrath of the dark-haired woman, he quickly
led them through the automatic doors and to the nurses'
station.

"Good morning, Dr. Anderson," a middle-aged nurse
greeted them. "I see you found your patient." She smiled at
the woman in the wheelchair. "Good morning, Lexington."

Dr. Anderson nodded. "That's right, Gina. Didn't even
have to send out a search party."

Lex waved at the petite woman with her good hand.
"Nice to see you again, Mrs. Fowler. Have you heard from
William lately?" The gray-haired nurse's son had worked
at the ranch the summer before he graduated from high
school three years before. After graduation, the lure of
adventure called him into the Army. The last postcard that
Lex had received from him had been postmarked Germany.
Much to her amusement, the young corporal had hastily
scrawled her a teasing note about the beautiful *Fräuleins*
he had found.

Nurse Fowler laughed. "Just last week, as a matter of
fact. He has leave next month and will be coming home for
Christmas."

"That's great. Tell him I said hello." Lex gestured over
her shoulder. "Mrs. Fowler, have you met Amanda Cauble?
She's living at the ranch now."

"It's nice to meet you, dear." Understanding dawned in
the older woman's gray eyes. "You're Anna Leigh and
Jacob's granddaughter, aren't you?"

Amanda smiled. "Yes, ma'am. It's nice to meet you
too." She unconsciously placed her hands on Lex's shoulders. "Do you know my grandparents?"

The nurse nodded her head. "Oh yes, I certainly do. I'm on the historical committee with Anna Leigh." She smiled at the closeness between the two younger women. *Anna Leigh was right. Looks like Lexington finally found what she's been missing all this time. And such a nice girl, too.*

"I hate to break up this little chat, but I'd really like to get started on those tests." Dr. Anderson gently took control of the wheelchair. "C'mon, young lady. Let's get you settled and changed into one of our fancy gowns."

"Can I...?" Amanda started, but was stopped by a raised hand.

The nurse sat a clipboard down on the counter. "Why don't you and I take care of the paperwork first, then I'll show you where the cafeteria is and you can grab a cup of coffee?"

Amanda watched as Lex was wheeled down the hallway. *I'll be right there, love. Hang in there.* She looked at the kindly nurse and smiled. "I promised Lex I would stay with her while the tests are being run."

"Honey, she's a big girl. I'm sure she'll be just fine." Nurse Fowler patted her arm. "All we really need is her signature on the bottom of this form—everything else we already have on file." She glanced up as Amanda signed the paper.

"It's okay. She gave me power of attorney a couple of weeks ago," Amanda assured her. *And what a surprise that was, too,* Amanda remembered fondly.

Lex worked late with the ranch hands that day, not coming back to the house until almost midnight. Amanda was beside herself with worry because she had heard that they were searching for lost cattle in remote areas of the property. The rancher hadn't been seen or heard from in over five hours, and all the hired help had returned to the bunkhouse hours earlier.

Amanda had fallen asleep on the sofa in the den while waiting up for any word of Lex. She was startled out of a deep sleep by the sound of the back door closing and heavy boots treading slowly down the hall. The worried young woman jumped off of the couch and peered around the doorway. "Lex? Is that you?"

The dark figure moved towards her slowly in the darkness. "Amanda? Sweetheart, what are you doing up this time of night?" Lex kept her distance, however, allowing only the barest glimpse of her profile in the dim light.

"I was worried about you. Are you all right?" Amanda took a step closer, only to have the rancher step back. "What's the matter?"

Lex held her hands up to ward off any contact. "I'm a mess. No sense in you getting all nasty because of me." She took another step back, moving nearer the staircase. "Why don't we go upstairs? I can get cleaned up, and you can get to bed. I'm sorry for keeping you up, but I lost the radio I was carrying."

The younger woman closed the distance between them. "You haven't answered my question. Are you all right?" The closer she got the more she could see and smell. Lex was covered from head to toe in dark and reeking mud.

"I'm fine. Just tired and really stinky." Her white teeth shone from a gunk-covered face. "I'm really sorry you were so worried. I was kinda stuck for a bit." Lex turned and motioned for Amanda to precede her.

After the rancher got out of the shower, she told Amanda about her day. The first part of the afternoon was spent tracking. She finally caught up with the missing cattle after dark. They had somehow fallen into a pit of mud, and Lex had worked for the next several hours to dig them out. She figured that the radio was lying somewhere at the bottom of the pit, since she couldn't find it in any of her pockets.

"I'm sorry that I worried you." Lex was lying on her left side with her hand propping up her head.

Amanda mirrored her friend's posture. "I think it was more the uncertainty than anything else. Not knowing if you were okay." She looked deeply into Lex's eyes and whispered softly, "I wouldn't be able to survive without you, Lex. You've become such a part of me."

They settled down to sleep after a long talk. Lex tried everything she could to assure the younger woman that she wasn't going anywhere, and that Amanda would always have a home on the ranch.

Two days later, Amanda woke up alone. She rolled over to Lex's side of the bed and saw a large manila envelope with her name on it lying on the rancher's pillow. She opened it and cried softly. Inside were signed and notarized papers giving Amanda Lorraine Cauble complete power of attorney for the Rocking W Ranch and Lexington Marie Walters. The note on top of the papers said it all: 'This just makes it legal. Forever yours, Lex.'

****

"See? I told you I was fine." Lex grumbled as they drove to Amanda's grandparent's house. Dr. Anderson had put a sturdy splint on her right arm and instructed Lex to keep it immobile for at least a week. The test results showed considerable bruising and swelling along her back and shoulders, but no permanent damage was detected. Lex took great enjoyment in her condition and continued to harass the younger woman. "Spent half the damn day proving my point, but I think it was worth it." Her last words were slightly slurred since she was fighting the effects of the sedative she had been given earlier.

Amanda cut her eyes over at her jubilant friend. "God. You can be such a poor winner sometimes." She stuck her tongue out at Lex. "Be nice, or I'll tell Martha that the specialist said for you to stay in bed for the rest of the week."

Lex glared at her. "You wouldn't." She registered the smirk on the younger woman's face. "You would."

"Yep. My silence is not cheap." Amanda continued to watch the road in front of her. She could almost hear the wheels turning in Lex's mind. *I can't wait to see what she comes up with next.*

"Not cheap, huh? Are you saying that you can be bought? Just at an inflated price?" Lex was enjoying this conversation. Her mind was fuzzy, and seemed to be getting worse. *Damned medication. Feels like I'm about half drunk.*

Amanda turned the truck onto her grandparent's street. "Well." She pulled up in the driveway and shut off the engine. "I'm just saying," she unbuckled her seat belt and leaned towards her friend, "that for the right price, I'll keep your secret."

The rancher raised her left hand and tangled it in the blonde hair to guide Amanda closer. "You will, huh?" she whispered, their lips only a breath apart.

"Yeah," Amanda growled as she covered the older woman's lips with her own. "Wanna hear my price?" she asked after they broke apart breathlessly.

"Uh," Lex had to clear her throat. "Uh-huh. I sure do."

Amanda kissed her again. "You have to promise me," she dropped a quick peck on Lex's lips, "to stay," another one, "in bed until Thursday. I promise to make it worth your while."

TAP TAP TAP!

The knocking on the passenger window caused both women to break apart quickly. An older man stood outside the truck with a big smile on his face. "You two gonna play kissy-face all day, or are you coming inside to visit?" Jacob Cauble teased.

"Hi, Grandpa." Amanda wiggled her fingers at him as she blushed. She regretfully pulled herself away from Lex and climbed out of the truck. The small woman circled the vehicle and almost knocked her grandfather to the ground with the force of her embrace. "I've really missed you."

"Hello there yourself, Peanut." The tall man wrapped his arms around Amanda, lifted her and spun her around. "I've missed you too." He deposited her gently on the ground and studied the young woman carefully. "How are you doing, sweetheart?"

Amanda gave him a relieved smile. "Much better

now." She stepped around him and opened the passenger door on the truck. "You ready to be sociable, Lex?"

Lex grudgingly accepted Amanda's help in climbing out of the truck. "Thanks." She leaned a little shakily against the truck. "Hey, Jacob. How's everything going?" She was really feeling the tranquilizer Dr. Anderson gave her before they left. *Sneaky old goat. He slipped an extra one in, I'll bet.*

Jacob tried to hide the grin that threatened to break out over his face. "Never been better, honey. Would you like some help getting into the house?" He winked at Amanda, who pulled a duffel bag from the back seat of the truck.

"That would be great." Lex took a wobbly step towards the older man. "I seem to have a little problem with my legs right now." *Not to mention how blurry everything is.*

"Watch out, Lexington. I think my husband is putting the moves on you," Anna Leigh's voice warned from behind him.

Amanda closed the truck door and turned around. "Gramma." She stepped over to the petite woman and enveloped her in a hug. "Long time, no see," she teased.

Lex and Jacob stepped around them as the older man supported most of her weight. "I think Jacob needs to be the one who watches out," Lex chuckled. "I may just run off with him myself." He was the grandfather that Lex never had, and she adored him. She allowed him to lead her into the house as Amanda and her grandmother stared in surprise after them.

"Sorry, Gramma. The doctor gave her another sedative before we left so she'd get some rest this afternoon." Amanda linked her arm with the older woman's as they followed the pair into the large, comfortable home.

Anna Leigh laughed. "Oh, honey, she's something else." She sobered and slowed their walk momentarily. "How is she really, Mandy? She looks so pale."

"Her arm is severely sprained, and she has a couple of nasty bruises on her back, but Dr. Anderson said that all of the tests came back negative." Amanda followed her grandmother into the house. "He was pretty concerned about the head injury and wanted to keep her overnight, but I promised to get her to rest here instead. That's why she's acting so goofy. He gave her a shot of something before we left the hospital."

The two Cauble women watched in amusement as Jacob escorted the tall woman up the stairs. "Almost there, honey," he encouraged her. "Just a few more steps."

"Did y'all add a few extra steps since the last time I was here?" Lex questioned. "It sure seems like it."

Amanda exchanged grins with her grandmother and jogged up the stairs. She stepped up behind Lex and put her hands on the unsteady woman's hips. "How about an extra set of hands?"

"Good idea, Peanut. I think we're running out of steam." Jacob stood on Lex's left side with her good arm wrapped securely around his waist. "Think you can make it now, Lexington?"

Lex kissed him on the cheek. "Piece of cake, Jake." She turned her head slightly to wink at Amanda who was supporting her from the other side. "And you'd better watch those hands, Blondie. I could get the wrong idea." She giggled as they guided her to Amanda's old bedroom. "Damn, that's a hell of a walk. I'm pooped."

After she sat down, Jacob gently lifted Lex's legs and swung them up onto the bed. He patted her knee gently. "You get some rest, sweetheart. I'll see you later." He walked over and met his wife at the door. They watched for a moment as their granddaughter fussed over the extremely groggy rancher. "C'mon, love. Let's go downstairs and give these girls a little privacy. The coffee should be ready by now." He kissed Anna Leigh on top of the head before they turned and made their way back down the stairs.

"C'mon, honey. Stay awake for a few more minutes and help me get you comfortable." Amanda gently eased the sling off of Lex's injured arm as the older woman fought to keep her eyes open.

"Mmm. You tryin' to take advantage of me, cutie?" Lex murmured with a sly grin. "I gotta warn you. My girlfriend is the jealous type." She opened one eye as small fingers unbuttoned her shirt. "You're pretty good at that."

Amanda helped ease Lex into a sitting position so that she could remove her shirt. "Honey, this is going to hurt when I try to pull your sleeve over that splint." Dr. Anderson had wanted to keep Lex's arm immobile, so he put an extensive splint on her. The metal and foam brace covered her arm from her elbow to her knuckles. He told them both not to remove it for a week, when he expected Lex back for her follow up exam.

Lex sighed. "No problem." She reached up with her good hand and took a firm grip on the right shoulder of her blue cotton shirt. Pulling hard, she ripped downwards until the sleeve was lying down by her wrist. "There. No more sleeve." She grinned and closed her eye.

"Oh, boy." Amanda shook her head and removed the rest of the shirt. *She's gonna be upset about that later.* "Okay, sweetheart. Let's get this tee shirt on you now."

Chapter
6

Ten minutes later, Amanda stepped into the kitchen with a tired but relieved smile on her face. She ran her hands through her strawberry blonde hair to give it some semblance of order.

"You look worn out, Mandy. Why don't you come over here and sit down before you fall down?" Anna Leigh pulled out the chair nearest her. She watched with concern as the young woman dropped gracelessly into the seat. "Are you okay, sweetheart?"

Amanda smiled at her grandmother. "I'm fine. It's just been a really long weekend." She gratefully accepted the cup of coffee offered by Jacob. "Thanks, Grandpa."

"Anytime, Peanut." He sat down on the other side of her and laid his hand on her arm. "Anything we can do to help? You look like you haven't slept in days."

"I haven't." Amanda concentrated on the mug in front of her. "Every time I close my eyes, I keep seeing Lex lying at the bottom of that ravine." Tears spilled down her cheeks as she closed her eyes. "I thought she was dead. My entire world was gone."

Anna Leigh leaned over and wrapped her arms around the young woman. "Honey." She pulled Amanda close to her. "You can't think like that. She's okay."

The small blonde spun and wrapped her arms around the older woman as she cried harder. "Oh, Gramma." She buried her face in Anna Leigh's neck, unable to stop the tears. "I was so scared."

Jacob looked at his wife with understanding shining in his eyes. "I'm going to work in the office for a bit and give you ladies a chance to have a little chat." He stood, placing a soft kiss on Amanda's head before leaving.

After crying fitfully for several minutes, the young woman finally wound down. "I'm sorry I fell apart like that," she sniffled, and wiped her eyes with the napkin that Anna Leigh had given her. "I guess all of it finally caught up with me."

"Mandy, you have nothing to apologize for. I did the same thing once we got Jacob home from the hospital after his wreck," Anna Leigh assured her. Earlier in the year, Jacob had almost been killed when a drunk driver hit the car he was driving. Amanda had moved from California to help her grandmother temporarily, but never went back even after her grandfather's injuries had fully healed.

"You did? I never knew." Amanda looked at the older woman with a new respect. "You always seemed so strong, so in control." She saw the remembered pain reflected in the green eyes so much like her own. Her grandmother had been a source of strength for them all and spent every available moment with Jacob at the hospital. She had even held Amanda as the young woman cried in fear of losing the man who was more like a father to her than a grandfather.

Anna Leigh took a deep breath and smiled. "Poor Jacob. I think I scared him to death the night we brought him home from the hospital."

After sending Amanda out for Chinese food at Jacob's request, Anna Leigh bowed to his good-natured complaints and helped him get comfortable on the sofa in the den. He had argued that she could not get him upstairs without their granddaughter's help, and he was tired of lying around in a bed.

"My love. I can rest as well here as I can upstairs. I promise to take it easy." Jacob took Anna Leigh's hand in his and kissed her knuckles. His left leg was encased in a cast from hip to toe, and lying down flat proved to be quite painful. "It feels really good to just sit up normally for a change," he joked.

Anna Leigh knelt next to him and covered Jacob with a soft quilt. "I'm sure it does, Jacob. But the doctor said for you to not overdo it, or you'd be right back in the hospital." She felt a tightening in her throat. "And I don't think I could handle that right now." The weight of the past month came crashing down on the petite woman and crushed her spirit with remembered pain. "You almost..."A strangled sob escaped from her as Anna Leigh fell forward onto her husband's chest.

Jacob wrapped his strong arms around his wife and pulled her close. "Shhh. Everything's okay now." He felt her bury her head deeper and cry harder. Without thinking, he pulled Anna Leigh up into his lap and rocked gently. "That's it, sweetheart. Let it out. It's all going to be okay now."

"I'm sorry for falling apart like that, love. I don't know what came over me," Anna Leigh sniffled some time later. She pulled her head away from his chest and looked down. "How did I end up in your lap?"

Her husband looked at her sheepishly. "I'm not real sure myself, sweetheart," Jacob scooted back to make more room on the sofa, "but I kinda like where you are." He winked at her. "Wanna make out?"

She felt a gentle hand run down her back. "You're supposed to be resting, Jacob," Anna Leigh chastised, but she found herself not wanting to break the contact. "Well, I suppose a little snuggling couldn't hurt." She cuddled up next to her husband and kissed him gently. "I love you, dearest."

"And I love you, my beautiful wife." Jacob returned

her kiss as he pulled her closer.

Amanda reached over and wiped a tear from the older woman's face. She saw the strong determination and love that got her grandmother through the rough months of Jacob's recuperation. "I don't know how you did it, Gramma. I don't think I could ever be that strong." She inhaled a shaky breath.

"Honey, you're a lot stronger than you realize. I don't know of many who could have gotten through what you have in the past couple of months. Don't sell yourself short." Anna Leigh reached up and riffled the younger woman's hair. "Besides, you're *my* granddaughter."

"Well, you do have a point there," Amanda agreed. She had always considered Jacob and Anna Leigh more than just her grandparents. The older couple had welcomed her into their home every summer of her life, giving her more love and support than her parents ever had. "Thanks, Gramma."

Anna Leigh smiled. "Anytime, sweetheart. Now, why don't we go find out what kind of trouble your grandfather is into?" She stood up and stepped away from the table. "I swear, that man of mine can get into trouble walking through the house." Once the two of them reached the doorway, the older woman put her arm around Amanda. "Nice to see you got something from him."

"Gramma," Amanda chuckled as they walked out the door. "You sound just like Lex."

* * * * * * * * *

A gentle touch on her head brought Lex out of a wonderful dream. "Mmm." She opened her eyes slowly and saw the same face that she had been dreaming about. "Hey, there," Lex murmured, her voice rough with sleep.

"Hey there yourself, blue eyes. Nice nap?" Amanda continued her gentle ministrations with the dark locks. *I just love playing with her hair. It feels like silk on my fingertips.* "How are you feeling, honey?"

"Okay. Still a little woozy, I guess." Lex tried to sit up and dropped back to the pillow. "I guess I'm a bit more than a little woozy," she admitted to her friend.

Amanda studied her carefully. "I can tell. Your eyes still look a little glazed. But Dr. Anderson called and told me that I needed to get you awake for a bit so that you can eat and take your medication."

Lex blinked a couple of times and lifted her left hand to the younger woman's face. "Are you okay? You look like you've been crying." She struggled to sit up. "What's the matter, sweetheart?"

"Nothing." Amanda leaned into the touch and covered the hand with her own. "Had a good talk with my Gramma earlier." She searched the older woman's face with concern. "You doing okay?" she asked as she shifted her hand from hair to skin and checked her lover's forehead for fever.

"Fine." Lex gently batted the small hand away. "What kind of talk did you have with your grandmother that would make you cry?" She sat up a little more until she turned her arm the wrong way. "Damn."

The blonde helped Lex until she was in a more comfortable sitting position. "You can ask me for help, you know. You don't have to try to do everything yourself." She reached behind Lex and fluffed the pillows.

"I know."

"It wouldn't be admitting any weakness to actually let me help you every now and then," Amanda continued, as she fussed with the blanket covering Lex.

"Well, I..." Lex stammered as she tried to sneak a word in.

"You can just be so darned stubborn sometimes." Amanda stood up and walked into the bathroom mumbling, "I love you, and that means that I don't mind taking care of you when you need me to." She stepped back into the bedroom carrying a glass of water.

"Amanda?"

The young woman stopped next to the bed and sat

down beside Lex. "So if I want to pamper you every now and then, you should just...what?" Belatedly realizing that her patient had spoken, Amanda stopped in the middle of her tirade and looked at Lex.

The rancher smiled at her. "I don't mind you fussing. I just don't want you to wear yourself out, love." Lex smirked and held out her good hand. "You got something for me?"

Amanda sighed as she handed over the glass of water and a couple of pills. "You do that on purpose, don't you?" She waited until Lex was finished with the water, then took the glass back. "Just when I get a good rant started, you nip it in the bud by being agreeable."

"Well, there's no sense in being too predictable, is there? You'd get bored, otherwise," Lex teased. "And since you so kindly offered. Think I could get an escort downstairs?" She reached up with her good hand and waited until Amanda grasped it.

"I should bring your dinner upstairs, but I know how you are." She pulled the dark-haired woman into a sitting position. "Promise me that you'll come back to bed after we eat?"

Lex grinned. "You gonna keep me company? I get awfully lonesome up here all my myself, you know."

The blonde chuckled as she helped Lex slip on a pair of sweat pants. "Yeah, I could tell when I came up here that you were pining away for me." She snapped the waistband gently.

"Do I get extra points since I was dreaming of you?" the rancher queried as Amanda adjusted the sling around her neck. She looked down into the green eyes that were a few inches from her own. "It was a really good dream. I could give you...Mrrumph." A small hand covered her mouth.

"Hush. If you starting telling me about this dream, we'll both be late for dinner." Amanda stood on her tiptoes and replaced her hand with her lips for a quick kiss. She felt Lex's good arm snake around her back and pull her closer. "Lex." she broke off slowly as she tried to catch her breath. "You're not helping matters much, you know." She snuggled her face into the older woman's chest, being careful to avoid the injured arm. "And I think we'd better get you downstairs before those pills start to take effect. I don't think that I can carry you back up here like you can me."

Lex allowed the younger woman to wrap an arm around her left side. "Heh. It would be fun to watch you try." She walked cautiously through the bedroom and down the hall. "At least I can walk now. Guess whatever that old quack injected me with has worn off," she mumbled as they worked their way down the stairs.

The doorbell cut off any reply that Amanda was about to make. The two women stood on the stairway and watched as Anna Leigh went to answer the door. She waved at them as she passed by the stairs. "Hi girls. Let me get this, and then I'll give you a hand." When she reached the door, Anna Leigh opened it partially and then stopped. "What are you doing here?"

"I came to talk to you, Mrs. Cauble," a man's voice called from the front porch. "If you'll give me just a minute, I'll be gone before you know it."

Amanda and Lex stood at the foot of the stairs a few feet away. "Who is it, Gramma?" the younger woman asked as she took a step forward. Lex followed her cautiously.

The door swung open wider and Rick Thompson stepped inside. "What are you two doing here?" He pushed by Anna Leigh and moved to confront the younger women.

"Mr. Thompson. Do not barge into my home and yell at members of my family." Anna Leigh put a restraining hand on his arm. "I will be forced to call the sheriff and have you removed."

The large man looked down at the hand that was wrapped around his arm. His face softened slightly. "I didn't come here to cause any trouble, Mrs. Cauble. I really did want to talk to you, though." He glanced back

over at Lex, who had casually placed herself between him
and Amanda. "Damn, Kentucky. You look like hell."

"Thanks, Rick. Looks like that bruise on your chin
faded nicely." The rancher smirked. The last time she had
seen him was during a confrontation at the real estate
office where he used to be the manager. When Anna Leigh
had found out that Rick had sent her granddaughter on a
wild goose chase to Lex's ranch, she immediately fired
him and gave his job to Amanda. He had struck out at Lex
in anger, and Amanda used her kickboxing skills to knock
him to the floor.

Amanda stepped up until she was in front of the dark-
haired woman. "Why don't we all go into the den where
it's more comfortable?" She felt Lex's hand rest gently on
her shoulder and squeeze lightly.

"I came here to talk to Mrs. Cauble, not you." Rick
pointed an accusing finger at the small blonde. He turned
back to Anna Leigh. "I can't get a job anywhere in this
damned town, thanks to you."

"Now wait a minute. Are you accusing my grandmother of blacklisting you? That's ridiculous. She would
never do such a thing, even if you did deserve it, which
you do." Amanda stepped away from Lex and moved closer
to the seething man. "Have you ever considered that everyone in this town knows you?"

"Yeah? So what?" Rick crossed his arms over his chest
and glared down at Amanda. *What did I ever see in this little bitch?* "It's a small town."

Lex walked forward slowly until she was behind
Amanda again. "What she's trying to say, Ricky, is that
everyone else in town knows what an ass you are." She
smiled as Anna Leigh fought to keep the grin off her face.
"Why would anyone want to hire someone with a track
record like yours?"

Rick stepped forward and jabbed Lex in the chest with
a finger. "You'd better watch your mouth, Kentucky or I'll
break your other arm."

Anna Leigh grabbed his arm and pulled him away. "I

think you've had your say, Mr. Thompson. It's time that you left."

"I don't need this shit from you. Any of you." He spun away from the older woman and stomped to the door. "I'll finish with you later, Kentucky." Rick stormed out of the house and slammed the door behind him.

"Jackass," Lex mumbled. "Are you okay, Anna Leigh?" she asked, as the small gray-haired woman locked the front door.

Amanda wrapped her arm around Lex and hugged her gently. "I could ask you the same thing, honey. He didn't hurt you, did he?" She closed her eyes in relief at her partner's negative shake of the head.

"I'm just fine, Lexington. Why don't we all go into the den and sit down? You're looking a bit pale." Anna Leigh quickly stepped to Lex's other side and helped her granddaughter escort the injured woman into the next room. "I don't know what that man thought he could accomplish by barging in like that. Did he actually think I would give him his job back?"

Lex chuckled as they helped her sit on the loveseat close to the fireplace. "He's not the sharpest knife in the drawer." She groaned softly as she leaned back. "I'm guessing that he just felt like harassing someone, and you happened to be convenient."

"Maybe we should call Charlie. He did threaten you, Lex." Amanda snuggled down next to her friend. "For all we know, he could be the person behind what happened to you on Saturday."

Anna Leigh sat on the sofa across from them and curled her feet up under her. "I thought you said it was just thieves that you had stumbled across. What makes you think that Rick might be involved?"

"Did I hear you mention Rick's name?" Jacob walked into the room and took the place next to his wife. "Hello, sweetheart." His kissed her on the cheek. "What has that fool done this time?" He looked over at the two women snuggled together on the loveseat. "Hi, girls. Are you feeling any better, Lex?"

"Much better, Jacob. Thanks for asking." Lex smiled. "We had a visit from Rick a little while ago, but your beautiful wife ran him off." She winked at Anna Leigh who blushed slightly. "The poor idiot thought that Anna Leigh had blacklisted him because he hasn't been able to find a job around here anywhere."

Amanda poked Lex. "Be nice." She turned her attention toward her grandfather who was pulling his wife closer to him. "Charlie thinks that whoever has been cutting the fences at the ranch was after Lex personally." She saw the shock on her grandparent's faces and continued quietly, "Especially since several different people have threatened her over the past month or so." Amanda felt the arm that was wrapped around her stomach pull her closer.

Lex kissed the top of the blonde head under her chin. "We don't know that for sure, sweetheart." She gave the older Caubles a wink. "Besides, Rick isn't smart enough to pull off something like that without being caught. He can barely tie his shoes without help."

"I agree with you about the sense that boy has," Jacob nodded, "but he could just be the brawn behind the operation. Maybe someone else is calling the shots."

Anna Leigh gave both young women a glare. "Why didn't you tell us that you had gotten threats, Lexington? Maybe we could have done something."

"We didn't want to worry you unnecessarily, Gramma. There isn't much that anyone can do until Charlie gets more evidence," Amanda answered for them both.

"She's right. And, personally, I think that he's just been reading too many mysteries lately and is trying to play detective," Lex joked, trying to lighten the mood in the room. "Although, picturing him decked out like Sherlock Holmes is always good for a laugh." The tall thin sheriff was never without his silver cowboy hat and pressed brown uniform shirt. The thought of him dressed in a London gentleman's clothes and a deerstalker hat made Lex almost laugh out loud.

Amanda didn't have the same self-restraint. She giggled at the mental picture. "Oh, God. Charlie as Sherlock Holmes. Would that make Martha his Watson?"

The rancher lost her composure after that comment. The image of her housekeeper wearing a bowler and dressed as the famous detective's sidekick was too much for her. "Oh God, Amanda," she chortled, "that's a picture I really didn't need in my head." She leaned back against the sofa and closed her eyes.

"That would be a sight," Jacob agreed with a chuckle. He watched as Lex fell back tiredly. "I almost forgot the reason I came in here to begin with." He stood and pulled his wife up next to him. "I brought dinner home."

Anna Leigh found herself wrapped in her husband's strong arms. "And what great feast have you prepared for us this evening, darling?" She laughed as Jacob spun her around the room to imaginary music.

Jacob continued to twirl his wife from the room. "Only the best for our family, my dear. Take out from the Peking Palace."

Amanda laughed as her grandparents waltzed into the kitchen. She glanced at Lex, whose eyes were still closed. "Honey?"

Lex opened her eyes slowly. "Hmm?" She struggled to sit up. "What's up?"

"Grandpa picked up some Chinese takeout for dinner." Amanda ran a hand lovingly down the older woman's face. "You want me to just bring you some in here?"

"No. I'm fine." Lex raised herself upward. "I may need a bit of help getting off the couch, though." She smiled tenderly at Amanda. "Especially since I seem to have a lap full of cute realtor on top of me."

The young woman blushed and stood up. "Oops. Now how do you suppose that happened?" She reached down and carefully pulled Lex to her feet. "C'mon. Let's get in there before all the good stuff is gone." Amanda wrapped her arm around the taller woman and led her from the room.

****

The lone figure sat in the darkened room, the only light coming from a small lamp in the center of the desk. Impatient hands rifled through several stacks of papers as they searched for something. Photos were also strewn haphazardly across the desk, showing a dark-haired woman in many of the shots. Pictures on horseback, outside a large stucco house, or with a small blonde woman all had the same tall figure in each shot. It was one of the latter photos that the figure picked up and gazed at for a long moment. Angry eyes flashed as the hands ripped the photograph in half. "You will not get away with this," the impassioned voice growled. "I will see you burn in hell before I allow this to continue."

One hand reached to the side of the desk where the phone sat and dialed a number from memory. The other hand angrily discarded the torn photo into a nearby trash bin already filled with similar victims.

"Yeah?" a man's voice sleepily answered on the fourth ring.

"Have you done what I asked?" the brooding figure at the desk questioned without preamble.

The man on the other end of the phone became instantly alert. "Well," he stammered, "it's not as easy as you might think. I have to be really careful, you know."

A fisted hand slammed down on the desk. "Now you listen to me, you pathetic moron. I'm not paying you to think. Just do as you are told." There was silence for a moment as they both thought. "All right. Did you at least get the hospital reports?"

He sat on the edge of his bed and ran a trembling hand through his hair. "Yeah. She must be a goddamned cat. Not one broken bone—just a sprained arm, some bruises, and a concussion. Why?"

"Because, you idiot, if she's not seriously injured, then she'll quickly get back to business as usual. Which means..."

"Oh. I get it. Which means I can try again?" he interrupted, as he tried to get back into his boss's good graces.

The voice on the other end of the line almost screamed
in frustration. "No!" followed by a heavy sigh. "It means
that we'll be able to tell if she suspects anything by how
she goes about her daily business. I don't want anything to
happen to her. Not yet, anyway."

He stood and paced the cluttered room. "What the hell
do you want me to do, then? Follow her around and take
more damned pictures?"

Dead silence from the other end of the phone stretched
for a long moment. "Don't," the voice whispered menacingly, "ever take that tone with me."

"Okay. Okay. Sorry," he whined as he kicked an empty
beer can across the room. "But I hate to just sit around and
do nothing."

"Stop whining. I promised you that you'll get your
chance, just be patient. We must wait for the perfect opportunity."

He sat back down on the bed, then brightened. "I can
always mess with her truck. The weather is kind of bad
right now. No one would think anything of it."

"No! I don't want to take the chance of hurting..." The
mysterious voice caught itself before revealing too much.
"No. I don't want any more accidents right now. I'm looking into ruining her professionally and then personally. If
that doesn't work, then we'll try something more...perma-
nent."

****

"Jacob, that had to be the best Chinese food I've eaten
in months." Lex sighed as she leaned back away from the
table. Of course, the fact that almost every other bite was
fed to her by the small blonde next to her had nothing to do
with her enjoyment of the meal. Amanda had taken pity on
the rancher as she tried to eat with her left hand, and gave
her tidbits off of her own plate in fun. *Oh yeah. Definitely*

the best Chinese food I've had. Period.

The older man looked up from where he was putting the leftovers in the refrigerator. "I'm glad you liked it, honey. I've been having a hankering for Chinese for over a week, and I know it's one of your favorites."

Lex smiled at him in appreciation. "Thanks. Don't tell Martha, though. The last time she tried to fix stir fry she almost burned the house down." As proficient as the housekeeper was in the kitchen, she never mastered using the wok that Lex had given her one Christmas.

"That's okay, sweetheart. Your secret is safe with us," Anna Leigh assured her. She watched as the injured woman tried to hide a yawn. "Mandy, why don't you get Lexington upstairs before she falls asleep at the table? I'm sure she'd be more comfortable in bed than in that chair."

Amanda looked at Lex who shrugged sheepishly. "Guess that medication is really starting to get a hold on you, isn't it?" She studied the slightly glazed eyes. "Yep. It sure is." The younger woman stood up and smiled at her grandparents. "If you'll excuse us, I'll escort Her Majesty to our room." She held her hand out to Lex. "C'mon, tough stuff. Nap time."

"Yes, mother." Lex allowed herself to be pulled up out of her chair. "You gonna read me a story, too?" she teased as the blonde wrapped an arm around her waist.

"If you're good, I will. I may even bake you some cookies later, if you behave," Amanda teased as she helped her friend out of the kitchen. "I'll be back to help with the dishes in a little bit," she called over her shoulder.

Anna Leigh waved her off. "No need, honey. Why don't you get some rest too? We're going to make an early night of it ourselves." She winked at her husband, who grinned happily.

Lex chuckled as they walked back up the stairs. "Have they always been like that?" she asked the smaller woman.

"Oh, yeah. For as long as I can remember. I used to wonder what was wrong with my own parents. I rarely saw them in the same room, much less acting as if they actually cared for one another." Amanda felt her companion lean a little more heavily on her. "Are you going to be able to make it up the stairs? Maybe I should get Grandpa." The weight immediately eased off of her.

"Nope. I'm fine." The taller woman looked down at her lover. "Guess I just got a little carried away with my leaning. Sorry about that." She stood up a little straighter and took in a deep breath. "Let's go."

They walked the rest of the way in silence, as Amanda was lost in the memories of a childhood spent with indifferent parents and loving grandparents. She wordlessly sat Lex on the edge of the bed and pulled her sweatpants off, leaving the rancher in her flannel boxer shorts and tee shirt. A gentle touch on Amanda's face brought her back from her musings.

"Amanda? What's the matter, sweetheart?" Lex was somewhat unnerved by her usually chatty friend's reticence. She looked up into the soft green eyes and saw her partner come back to her.

The blonde shook her head and smiled. "Nothing. Just thinking." She helped Lex swing her legs onto the bed and covered her.

Lex wasn't giving up easily. "About what? You looked a little lost there for a bit." She blinked and struggled to keep her eyes open.

"Nothing important, really. I just remembered a time when I was younger. I asked Gramma why my parents weren't like her and Grandpa." Amanda sat down on the other side of the bed and clasped the rancher's hand. "She told me that different people show their love in different ways. And that Mother did love Daddy, but she just had a different way of showing it." She felt her hand pulled to Lex as the older woman kissed her knuckles. "I guess Gramma just didn't want to tell me that my parents had more of a merger than a marriage." Tears of past hurt fell from her eyes.

"Oh, sweetheart." Lex pulled the young woman close. She felt Amanda curl up next to her and tuck her face against her neck. "Shhh. It's okay." The rancher felt help-less as her lover continued to cry. She whispered quiet words of reassurance to the younger woman as she stroked the blonde head.

Amanda stopped crying after a few minutes and raised her head. "I don't know what's gotten into me today." She sniffled, smiling as Lex wiped her face with a corner of the sheet. "That's the second time today. I'm sorry, Lex."

Lex smiled and stroked the soft cheek with her thumb. "You have nothing to apologize for, love. I think the past few days just caught up with you." She looked down at their tangled bodies. "Not that I'm complaining, but don't you think you'd be more comfortable out of those clothes?"

"Probably," Amanda agreed, blushing. "But I want to go downstairs and tell my grandparents goodnight, first." She regretfully pulled away from the long form stretched out on the bed. "I'll be back in a few minutes, okay?"

"Sure," Lex yawned. "Give them my love." She closed her eyes and quickly fell asleep.

Amanda stood at the doorway for a long moment and studied her sleeping lover. The scratches on her face were almost healed, and the bruises were already fading as well. *Looks like she's going to be just fine. I don't know how Martha has survived this all these years.* The housekeeper had confided to her one afternoon that Lex was always get-ting into some type of trouble. She shook her head and went back down the stairs.

She saw a light coming from the den and altered her direction. Poking her blonde head cautiously around the corner, Amanda saw her grandparents speaking to another person. She could only see the back of a man's head where he was sitting on the sofa.

Anna Leigh saw her granddaughter standing at the doorway and beckoned to her. "Mandy. Come on in, we have a visitor."

The young woman stepped into the room and the guest stood up. He turned to face her and smiled. "Hello, Miss

Cauble." Mark Garrett held out his hand. "I hope you don't mind me dropping in unannounced like this."

Amanda took his hand and returned his smile. "Please, call me Amanda. I thought we had settled that in the office last week." She sat down and waited for him to do the same. "You're always welcome, Mark. But what brings you here this evening?"

Anna Leigh answered her question. "He brought some flowers for Lexington. Wasn't that thoughtful?" She pointed to a large arrangement of mixed blooms on a nearby table.

"Very." Amanda eyed the flowers appreciatively. "But that really wasn't necessary, Mark."

"Well, I dropped by your office to leave some paperwork, and one of the ladies there told me that your friend was hurt in an accident." He looked over at Jacob and Anna Leigh. "Lex and I got acquainted when we sat next to each other at the fall dinner party." Mark turned his attention back to Amanda. "I really enjoyed her company then, and I just wanted her to know that I wished her well."

Jacob decided to steer the conversation into a different direction. "That's great, Mark. You were telling us that you used to work for our son?" He saw his granddaughter visibly relax. "Why did you quit?"

Mark nodded at the older man. "Yes sir, I did. But I was ready for a change of scenery. I wanted to move my family somewhere that my children could grow up safe, yet educated. Lex had told me about Somerville, and it sounded like a really good place to settle." He smiled at Amanda. "Especially since I know I can trust the local realtor."

"That's true, you certainly can," Jacob agreed heartily. He gave his granddaughter a wink. "This town's always had real good luck with the women from that office." His wife gave him a playful slap on the arm. "Hey," he protested in response.

Amanda laughed at her grandparent's antics. *They never stop. Just like newlyweds.* She smiled inwardly. *Or like Lex and me. Cool.* "Lex is going to be sorry that she missed you, Mark. She's upstairs resting right now."

"Oh, that's fine. I'm certain I'll see her around sometime. It is a pretty small town." The young man stood. "I didn't mean to stay so long, anyway. I'm sure you folks have things to do."

"And I'm sure you want to get back to your family." Amanda stood with him. "Where are you staying?"

He shook his head. "They're still in New Mexico. I decided to come on ahead and find us a house first." Mark allowed Amanda to escort him to the front door. "Hopefully I can have them here for Christmas."

"That means you'll be all alone at Thanksgiving." Amanda made a quick decision. *Lex did say the more the merrier, right?* "Why don't you join us at the ranch this Thursday for Thanksgiving dinner? We'd love to have you."

"Oh, I couldn't impose on you like that." Mark stopped just outside the door.

Jacob and Anna Leigh stepped up behind Amanda. "If I know my granddaughter and Martha, there'll be more than enough food to go around," the older man laughed. "Besides, it would help even things out some. I think Charlie and I will be the only men there. We could use your help."

"You love being surrounded by women, you nut." Anna Leigh poked her husband in the ribs. "But Jacob's right. There will be plenty of food, and you'll be more than welcome."

Amanda reached out to shake Mark's hand again. "Then it's settled. I need to go into the office in the morning for a little while, so if you'll give me a call there I can give you directions to the ranch." She stepped out onto the front porch with him. "Thank you so much for bringing the flowers by, it really was very thoughtful of you. I know Lex will appreciate them."

Mark ducked his head and smiled. "It wasn't much. Just tell her I hope she's feeling better soon, and I'll see you all Thursday." He released Amanda's hand and walked to his car.

The Caubles stepped out onto the porch with Amanda and watched Mark drive away. "Such a nice young man," Anna Leigh commented. "Bringing flowers over for Lexington like that." She wrapped an arm around the younger woman's waist and pulled her close. "How is she feeling, dear?"

"She was falling asleep when I left her a bit ago," Amanda answered, as she returned her grandmother's hug. "I just came downstairs to tell you and Grandpa goodnight."

Jacob moved to Amanda's other side so that she was sandwiched between the two of them. "I'm glad you did, Peanut. We love seeing you both, but I hate for it to have been under these circumstances." He kissed the blonde head. "Are you going back to the ranch tomorrow? We'd love for you both to stay an extra day or so."

Amanda sighed happily as she soaked up the love from her grandparents. "Thanks. I think I'm going to try and talk her into staying an extra day. I'm afraid that if we go back to the ranch, she'll try to work. There's always something out there that needs her attention."

"That's a good idea, sweetheart. You can go into the office in the morning, and we'll keep an eye on Lexington for you." Anna Leigh looked her granddaughter in the eye and added sternly, "But right now I want you to go upstairs and go to bed. You look completely worn out." Her tone brooked no argument.

"Yes, Gramma." Amanda kissed her grandmother's cheek with a smile. "I'll see you in the morning." She hugged Jacob and kissed his cheek as well. "Goodnight."

Anna Leigh linked her arm with her husband's as they watched the young woman go back inside. "It's getting pretty cold, love. What do you say to hot chocolate in front of the fire before bed?"

"That sounds like a great idea, sweetheart. I'll take care of the fire if you want to bring in the chocolate."

Jacob followed his wife into the house and closed the door behind them.

* * * * * * * * *

Amanda stepped quietly into the bedroom and quickly changed into an oversized sleep shirt. It was actually one of Lex's tee shirts that she had stolen, but the rancher didn't have the heart to take it back. When she had offered to buy Amanda a nightshirt that fit, the younger woman had just laughed and declined the replacement. *I keep trying to tell her it isn't the size, or the style. It's because it's hers.* Lex had given her a look like she thought she was crazy, but didn't say anything else. *Probably the same reason I find her snuggling my pillow when I'm not there.* She looked at the bed and saw Lex lying flat on her back with a pillow hugged to her chest. *Not like she'll ever admit to it, though.* Amanda smiled as she crawled onto the bed next to Lex.

"Mmm. Amanda," Lex murmured in her sleep with a smile. She squeezed the pillow to her tighter, then frowned. "Amanda?" Her eyes opened slowly to see the blonde woman leaning over her with a huge smile on her face. "What?"

"Miss me?" Amanda leaned down and kissed her gently.

Lex blinked a couple of times. "Sure. How'd you guess?" She lifted her head and returned Amanda's kiss. "Have I been asleep long?"

The younger woman raised up and looked first at Lex, then at the pillow she was still hugging. "Comfy?" She chuckled at the look the rancher gave her. "No, honey, you haven't been asleep long. But you had a visitor earlier."

"Yeah? Who?" Lex watched with a fond smile as Amanda removed the pillow and took its place next to her.

"Mark Garrett dropped by with some flowers. He heard that you got hurt and wanted to pay his respects." Amanda snuggled close with a happy sigh.

The older woman began rubbing Amanda's back gently. "Really? That's kinda strange, isn't it? I don't even know him that well." She felt her eyes slowly closing against her will.

Amanda lifted her head up just enough so she could place a soft kiss on Lex's jaw. "I think he appreciated you being so nice to him at the dinner party." She burrowed back down on the rancher's chest. "I invited him to Thanksgiving dinner since he'll be away from his family. I hope that's okay with you."

"You can invite whomever you want to, sweetheart. It's your home too, you know," Lex yawned. "How did he know where to bring the flowers, though?" she asked as her eyes closed. "Goodnight, sweetheart. I love you." She pulled Amanda close and kissed the top of her head.

"I love you too, Lex. Sleep well," Amanda whispered as she heard the even breathing of her lover. *That's a good question. I know that the people in the office don't make a habit of telling strangers any personal information. I'll have to ask around in the morning.* She mentally shook her head. *Lord, I'm getting paranoid. They probably remembered seeing me talk to Mark and thought it would be okay, which it was. I've got to stop thinking that everyone is out to get us. Definitely need to quit watching those government cover up television shows.* She allowed Lex's steady breathing to coax her into sleep.

Chapter
7

"Good morning, Amanda." Wanda Skimmerly's cheerful voice greeted the young woman as she stepped into the office at Sunflower Realty. "We certainly weren't expecting you in this week." The older woman stood up and embraced Amanda in a heartfelt hug. "How's Lexington? Mrs. Cauble told us she had an accident."

Amanda returned the hug and stepped back. "She's doing just fine, Wanda. Thank you for asking." She linked arms with the curly-haired woman and led her into the office. "I just wanted to check in, since I was already in town," she explained. Amanda sat down behind the desk and waited until Wanda sat as well. "We'll be leaving for the ranch in the morning. If anything comes up, you can reach me at my grandparents until then."

Wanda smiled. "Don't you worry, honey. I'm sure we'll be fine. You just take care of Lexington." She stood up and straightened her maroon wool dress. "Do you think she'd be up for visitors this afternoon? I baked some brownies last night for her, and want to drop them by sometime today."

"I'm sure she'd love that, Wanda. Oh. That reminds me." Amanda stood and walked around the desk to sit on the edge. "Did anyone talk to Mark Garrett yesterday?"

"Isn't he that nice young man who came in last week?" Wanda asked. She thought for a moment and then shook her head. "I don't remember seeing him in here since last week. It was pretty quiet, and I suppose he could have come in when I went to the bank at lunchtime. But I didn't talk to him." She saw the confused look on the younger woman's face. "Is there something wrong?"

Amanda smiled and shook her head. "No, not really. Mark said that he stopped by yesterday and was told of Lex's accident." She stood and walked the other woman to the door. "He even brought flowers over to the house for Lex."

The older woman stopped and turned around. "How did he know where to find you?"

"That's what I would like to know." When Wanda opened her mouth to speak, Amanda raised her hand. "Not that it's a problem, I'm just curious. I guess with everything that's happened, I've become a little paranoid."

"Why don't I ask around? I really don't think anyone here would give out that kind of information, but it never hurts to be sure." Wanda patted Amanda on the arm. "If it's okay with you, I'll bring those brownies by for Lexington when I get off work this afternoon." The rancher had quickly become a favorite of the women in the office, since she would drop by unexpectedly with flowers or candy for Amanda. Her dark good looks and charming smile made many of them threaten to dump their husbands for her, much to Lex's embarrassment.

"That would be sweet, Wanda. I know she'd really appreciate the company." Amanda had left her lover propped up on the living room sofa, armed with a television remote control and a scowl. Lex had argued that she was ready to go back to the ranch today, but Anna Leigh had vetoed that notion immediately. The older woman had told Lex that she was going to lie there and relax, or she would call Dr. Anderson and have him give her another shot. Amanda left after the rancher made her promise to return as early as she could.

The older woman chuckled as she walked away. "I imagine she's probably driving Mrs. Cauble half crazy by now. She doesn't seem like the type who likes to sit around and do nothing."

Amanda crossed her arms across her chest and leaned against the doorway. *I probably should call Gramma and see if she's killed Lex yet.*

"Amanda? You have a call on line two," Lisa Pratt called from her desk nearby. The young woman had just graduated from high school the previous year, and was working part-time in the office while she went to the local community college. She idolized Amanda and harbored a secret crush on Lex.

"Thanks, Lisa. I'll grab it in my office," she told the young redhead as she made her way back around her desk. She sat down and picked up the phone. "This is Amanda Cauble."

"And my sister's latest conquest?" the man's nasal voice questioned through the phone.

The blonde rolled her eyes and shook her head. "Hubert? Why are you calling my office? Lex isn't here."

He released a heavy sigh as if talking to a child. "No shit. And she's not at the ranch, either. She was supposed to drop by my office yesterday to sign some damned papers, but never showed up." He softened his tone a little. "You wouldn't happen to know where she's hiding, would you?"

Amanda closed her eyes and pinched the bridge of her nose with her forefinger and thumb to ward off the impending headache that his voice always caused. *I can't believe this man is related to Lex.* "She's not hiding, Hubert. Lex had an accident Saturday and is recuperating." *Well, he is her brother. I'm sure he would want to know if she had been hurt.*

"That's her excuse for standing me up yesterday? I'm a busy man, you know." He paused for a moment. "She sounded fine Sunday. I think the bitch is just playing games with me." Papers shuffled loudly in the background. "These papers are important and they have to have her damned signature on them, since she's the owner of that stinking ranch. You tell her to get her ass over to my office immediately, or she could lose her part of the inheritance." His voice continued to rise until he was almost yelling.

"Inheritance? Does Lex know what these papers are for?" Amanda questioned him with concern. "Has someone passed away?"

Hubert laughed humorlessly. "It figures that the sound of money would catch your attention. Yeah. Somebody died, and we get something out of it. The problem is, there are some papers that require both our signatures." He took a deep breath and spoke a little more calmly. "So if you'll just get my high and mighty sister to take time out of her busy schedule, we can get this matter cleared up. Think you can handle that, honey?" he ended sarcastically.

The young woman bit her tongue to keep her comment to herself. *Jerk.* "What if I drop by and pick up the papers, have her sign them, and then drop them back off to you today? Will that satisfy you?"

"I'm not letting these damned papers out of my sight, sweetheart. Especially to a little floozy like you," Hubert snapped. "Now either get her over here, or tell me where to find her. Your choice."

Amanda winced. *No good options here. Well, better on our terms than his, I suppose. And he'll have to behave if my grandparents are there.* "She's at my grandparent's house, Hubert. Why don't you meet me there at..." The sound of the phone slamming down caused her to pull the receiver away from her ear. *Crap. Now I've got to race him to the house.* She grabbed her purse and briefcase and stood up. "Wanda!" she shouted as she left the office, "Call my grandmother and tell her I'm on the way home, and to not answer the door for anyone until I get there."

"Will do, dear. Is there anything I can do?" the older woman asked.

"Nope. That's it. Thanks." Amanda jogged out of the

office in a hurry, leaving behind several questioning glances.

****

The small gray-haired woman was curled up in the overstuffed chair, deeply engrossed in a murder-mystery novel. The only sounds in the room were the crackling of the fire and the deep, even breathing of the sleeping woman stretched out on the nearby sofa. *Poor Lexington. She tried so hard to stay awake until Mandy came home.*

As they spent a large part of the morning talking, the older woman learned more about this person with whom her granddaughter had decided to share her life. Anna Leigh had known the rancher for years, but had found, to her chagrin, that she didn't really know her at all. *I had no idea that she played the piano.* Lex had offered quite a bit of personal information about herself, as well as her thoughts on the future. She had confided to Anna Leigh that she had considered selling the ranch and buying a house in town so that Amanda would not have the long commute to work.

"It scares me, Anna Leigh," the younger woman admitted. "I'm afraid that she'll get tired of being so iso-lated from her family and friends and decide to leave." Lex *wiped a stray tear from her cheek. The medication that the doctor had prescribed brought her emotions closer to the surface, and she could also feel sleep pulling at her.*

"Have you talked to Mandy about all of this, honey?" Anna Leigh sat down next to the injured woman and clasped her left hand. Lex *shook her head. "I didn't think so. Because if you had, you would have found out that she loves that ranch. Probably more than you do." The older woman ruffled* Lex's *dark hair gently. "She was so thrilled when you asked her to handle the bookwork. She called me up the next day and said it made her feel like she was actu-ally contributing to the running of the ranch."*

Lex looked at her in surprise. "I had no idea," she whispered.

Anna Leigh smiled softly. "She loves the life she's living, Lexington. I've never seen my granddaughter happier than she is now." She watched as the rancher fought to keep her eyes open. "Why don't you take a little nap? Mandy probably won't be home until after lunchtime." She pulled the quilt up over Lex and patted the younger woman on her uninjured arm. "Go on. I've got some reading to catch up on."

"Okay. That sounds like a pretty good idea." Lex yawned and closed her eyes.

Anna Leigh shut the book she was holding and sighed. *Rawson Walters should be shot for deserting such a sweet girl.* She studied the still form fondly. *Although I can't fault the way that Martha raised her. She turned out better than anyone ever expected.* The shrill ringing of the telephone from another part of the house interrupted her musing.

"Sweetheart? Wanda from the office is asking for you," Jacob announced quietly from the doorway. He looked at the sleeping woman on the sofa and smiled.

"Thank you, love." Anna Leigh stood up and walked to her husband. She kissed Jacob on the cheek and took his hand. "Why don't you come with me? We can use the phone in the kitchen so Lexington won't be disturbed."

Jacob allowed his wife to lead him into the kitchen and settle him on the chair closest to the phone. Anna Leigh picked up the handset and then climbed onto his lap. "This is Anna Leigh. What's the matter, dear?" She knew that the realtor would only call her if there was a problem, and Amanda could not be found.

"I'm really sorry to bother you, Mrs. Cauble," the younger woman apologized, "but Amanda asked me to call you." Wanda had worked at Sunflower Realty for over eight years, but could never bring herself to call the older woman by her first name. "She said for you not to answer the door for anyone until she got home."

Good lord. What kind of trouble has that girl gotten into now? Anna Leigh tensed and felt her husband wrap his arms around her and squeeze comfortingly. "Did she say why?"

"No, ma'am. She sure didn't. But she got a phone call from a rather rude man right before she left. Or at least that's what Lisa told me." Wanda sounded slightly breathless, excited by the bit of intrigue.

"Okay. Well, thank you, dear. I appreciate you giving us a call." Anna Leigh sighed and leaned back into her husband's strong embrace.

"No problem, Mrs. Cauble. I'm glad I was able to help." Wanda hung up the phone quickly. She was anxious to call her husband and tell him the latest news.

Jacob nuzzled his wife's ear. "What was that all about, love? Is everything all right?"

The older woman hung up the phone and turned in his arms to link her hands behind his head. "Mandy asked her to call us. We're not supposed to answer the door until she gets home."

"What has that child done this time?" he wondered aloud. "I swear, it's always something with her."

"I'm not sure, but she should be home pretty soon, and then we'll find out." Anna Leigh leaned in and kissed Jacob tenderly. "But we have a few minutes to kill until she gets here."

He returned the kiss happily. "No sense in wasting a perfectly good opportunity, I always say," Jacob murmured.

The back door suddenly crashed open, and Amanda burst into the kitchen, breathing heavily. "Did I beat him?" She was about to close the door when Charlie Bristol jogged in behind her.

"What in the hell is going on? Is Lexington okay?" he panted, then stopped dead in his tracks. "Oh. Sorry folks." He took off his hat and nodded at the couple in the chair. "Nice to see you, Jacob. Anna Leigh."

Anna Leigh slowly climbed off of Jacob's lap and stood to shake the sheriff's hand. "Hello, Charlie. What are you doing here?"

The lawman glared at the young blonde woman, who had the decency to blush. "Actually, I was trying to catch up to little Miss Indy 500 over there. She broke nearly every traffic law on the way over here."

"Amanda Lorraine Cauble. What do you mean by driving like that?" Anna Leigh put her hands on her hips and scolded.

"I'm sorry, Gramma. Charlie. But I had to get here before he did." Amanda rushed out of the kitchen without any further explanation.

Charlie looked after the retreating figure. "Where on earth is she off to now?" He followed Amanda, curious. *Never a dull moment around these girls, that's for sure.*

"Shall we, my dear?" Jacob gestured with his arm in the direction of the departed sheriff. "I'm getting a little interested myself." He allowed his wife to precede him out of the room.

Amanda stood in the living room peeking nervously through the front curtains. She would intermittently turn and glance at the still form on the sofa then return to her vigil.

"Would you please tell me..." Charlie stepped into the room, but silenced when he saw Lex sleeping.

"Sssh!" Amanda spun around and warned. She waved the lawman over to the window. "Come over here and we can talk," she whispered.

He joined her at the window and looked outside. "What are we looking for?" he rumbled quietly. Charlie couldn't see anything out of the ordinary in the front yard—especially not something that would cause the normally cautious Amanda to drive like a maniac all the way across town.

Anna Leigh and Jacob walked over and stood close to their granddaughter. "What's the matter, Peanut?" Jacob asked in a low voice.

Amanda spared another glance at her sleeping lover, then turned her attention back to her grandfather. "Hubert is on his way over here."

"You've got to be kidding. What could he possibly want?" Charlie shook his head. He knew that there was no love lost between the siblings. The six-year difference in the ages didn't help, but the sheriff felt that the animosity that Hubert had towards his younger sister would never change. *That boy has hated her since she was born. When their daddy signed over the ranch to her instead of him, I thought for sure Hubert was gonna kill her.*

"I'm the rightful heir to this ranch!" Hubert yelled at his father. "She's just a damned kid." He jumped out of the chair he was sitting in and stood tall over the older man.

Rawson leaned against the rock fireplace in the den. He refused to back down, even to his volatile son. "Sit down, Hubert Wallace Walters. I'm not finished talking, boy."

Hubert pointed an accusing finger at Lex, who was seated next to Charlie on the sofa. "This is all your fault. Always kissing up to the old man, you little brat." He spun back around and glared at his father. "I went to college and majored in business so that I could run this hell hole. I've put up with the dirt, the flies, and the stupid animals all my life because I thought that when you retired, it would be mine. And now you're saying that she *is going to be in charge? That's ridiculous. What about me?"*

Lex stood up. "I'm just going to be the foreman, Hubert. Dad's still in charge." She looked over at Rawson questioningly. "Right?"

"That's right." For now, anyway. Rawson smiled at his daughter. Let's just see how she handles her brother. It'll be a good test of her character.

"That's bullshit." Hubert crossed the room until he was face to face with his younger, and still smaller, sister. He tried to use his size to intimidate her. "You ain't got the sense to run a business."

*"And you do?" Lex crossed her arms and gave him an
amused look. "Who did your homework during your final
semester?" She held out one hand. "You still owe me two
hundred dollars for that."*

*He grabbed Lex by the shoulders and shook her hard.
"You little smart ass. Always thought that you were better
than me, didn't ya?"*

*Charlie jumped up to intervene. As a favor to Rawson,
the sheriff had driven out to the ranch to be a witness when
he told his son about the ownership of the ranch. The
rancher didn't trust his eldest son, and thought that having
the lawman present would prevent any violence on
Hubert's part.*

*Lex raised her hands and grabbed Hubert's wrists. She
twisted his arms until the angry young man screamed in
pain. "There's no thinking necessary, Hube." She released
her hold and stepped back when Charlie put his hand on
her shoulder. "Back off, big brother. Before I have to hurt
you." She had been given self-defense lessons by the sheriff years earlier—and had only used them when absolutely
necessary.*

*"Calm down, honey," the lawman whispered in the
young woman's ear. "Everything's going to be okay."*

*Rawson laughed. "That's enough, kids. Hubert, I
expect you to still help out around here." He patted the
younger man on the arm and left the room, still chuckling
to himself.*

*Hubert glared at the rancher's back as he left, then his
eyes cut to his sister. "This isn't over, Lex. I'm not going to
let you take what's rightfully mine." He shoved Lex out of
his way and stomped out of the den.*

The thought sent a chill down the lawman's spine. *Oh,
lord. He wouldn't, would he? After all these years? Not
even Hubert could be that cold-blooded, right?*

Anna Leigh reached over and touched the sheriff's arm
with concern. "Charlie? Are you all right? You look like
you've seen a ghost."

He blinked and then shook his head to clear it. "Uh, yeah. I'm just fine. Thanks, Anna Leigh." Charlie gave her what he hoped was a convincing smile.

"Hubert called me at the office to say he had some papers that required Lex's signature," Amanda explained quietly. "He said that it had to do with an inheritance, and he had to get the papers back right away." She looked over at Lex's peaceful profile. "If you'll just give me a couple of minutes, I'll wake her up and fill her in."

Jacob gave his granddaughter a hug. "No problem, Peanut. We'll go make a fresh pot of coffee." He released her, put his arm around his wife and led her away from the window. He turned to the sheriff and smiled. "C'mon, Charlie. I think we still have some coffee cake left."

"Sounds good to me." The lawman nodded, as he followed the couple from the room.

Amanda barely noticed when they left, as her attention went to the still form on the sofa. She walked slowly over to where Lex was lying and sat down near the sleeping woman's hip. Still loath to wake her lover, she knew that she didn't have much time. "Lex?"

"Mmm?" The rancher turned her head and rubbed her cheek against the soft hand that was stroking it. "Amanda," she murmured, a slight smile playing on her lips.

"Honey, c'mon. You need to wake up." Amanda leaned down and kissed the sleeping woman's forehead. She continued to gently rub Lex's face with her hand.

The dark-haired woman leaned into the kiss and slowly opened her eyes. "Amanda? What time is it? Did I sleep the whole day away?" She looked around the room and tried to get her bearings.

The younger woman smiled down into Lex's face. "No, love. It's just a little after twelve. I came home early." Amanda helped the rancher up into a sitting position. "We're about to have an unwanted guest, I'm afraid."

"Yeah?" Lex rubbed her eyes with her left hand. "Damn, I gotta quit taking those pills. They really knock me on my butt." She blinked a few times and smiled at

Amanda. "So, who's this mystery guest, and how long do we have?"

Amanda found herself pulled up against the older woman's chest as she looked into Lex's sparkling blue eyes at close range. "Umm...well..." She stopped as insistent lips caught hers. A loud pounding intruded on Amanda's thoughts as she melted into Lex's arms. *God, I can hear my heart beating...no...pounding. Wait.* She pulled away regretfully. "I think he's here."

Lex gazed at her lover with a confused look. "Who's here?" Then she heard the loud thumping that came from the front door. "What the...?"

"Sshh. It's Hubert," the blonde informed her regretfully. "He has some papers that he insists you have to sign immediately. I thought it would be better to just meet him here and get it over with."

"Damn. I forgot all about that. Good thinking, sweetheart." Lex struggled with the quilt that covered her. "Help me look a little more presentable, would you?"

Amanda stood and removed the quilt. "You always look presentable to me, honey." She brushed Lex's hair out of her eyes. "Although right now, you still look a little out of it."

The pounding continued, and Lex smiled ruefully at Amanda. "You might as well let him in before he beats down your grandparents' door." She closed her eyes and shook her head. "Or, better yet, maybe I should answer the door." Lex attempted to stand, but was stopped by a firm hand on her shoulder.

"No. Please, Lex, just sit there and I'll go get him." Amanda removed her hand and backed away from the sofa. "If you really want to throw Hubert off balance, make him come to you." She stepped into the hallway and almost ran into Jacob.

The older man caught her and chuckled. "Whoa, there. You want me to answer the door, sweetheart?"

Amanda took the opportunity to wrap her arms around her grandfather and give him a hug. "No, that's okay. But I wouldn't mind if you decided to keep Lex company in the living room." She smiled at Charlie and Anna Leigh who both slipped quietly into the room.

"All right, Peanut. But I'm standing right there in the doorway, just in case." Jacob stepped back and leaned against the doorframe to the living room, crossing his arms nonchalantly.

"Thanks, Grandpa." Amanda gave him a sweet smile then turned to open the door.

Hubert Walters was standing on the porch, his hand poised to pound on the door again. "It's about damn time you opened the door. I almost froze my ass off out here." He pushed by Amanda and stormed into the house.

"Gee, wouldn't have been much left of you then, huh? Won't you come in?" Amanda mumbled sarcastically.

"Where the hell is she?" Hubert stood in the hallway looking around impatiently.

Jacob moved forward and raised a warning hand. "Son, if you don't calm down and watch your language, I'm going to have to ask you to leave."

Hubert stood and glared at the older man who was several inches taller than he was. *Obnoxious old goat. He's just as bad as his little tease of a grandkid.* "Okay, fine. I just came to see my sister, and then I'll get out of your hair."

"All right. She's in here." Jacob led Hubert into the living room. Charlie and Anna Leigh were already seated in opposite corners of the room, looking on with undisguised curiosity. Jacob walked over to the loveseat and sat down next to his wife. "Have a seat, young man." He pointed to a chair across from the sofa.

"No, thanks. This will only take a minute." Hubert stood in front of the sofa and looked down at his sister. She was unusually pale, with a bruise covering her right cheekbone and several nasty looking scratches on her face. He glanced at the arm that was immobilized by the sling and smirked. "Damn, Lex. You look like hell. One of your stupid horses finally throw you?"

Lex refused to be baited. "Thanks for your concern, Hube." She leaned back and indicated the briefcase in his hand. "You've got something that you want me to sign?"

He laid the leather case on the desk behind him and pulled out several papers. "Yeah. Just sign on the dotted line on pages four, eight, and the last page." He handed her the papers and a pen.

The rancher took the papers and began reading the top page slowly. *God, I hate all this legal mumbo-jumbo. Why can't they just print this stuff in plain English?*

"Just sign the damned things. You don't have to read them, I've already checked over everything," Hubert blustered.

"Either sit down and shut up, or leave and come back later. I *am* going to read every word before I sign anything," Lex informed her brother coldly.

Hubert slammed his briefcase closed. "For God's sake, woman. I told you I already read it. Haven't you listened to a word I said?"

Blue eyes blazed at him. "Just how much could you have read? I don't see any pictures here." Lex's headache was back full force, and she was tired of her brother's antics.

"You bitch!" Hubert stepped to the sofa angrily. When he reached his sister, he leaned down and grasped her shirt with both hands and yanked her to her feet. "Just sign the goddamned papers."

Charlie jumped up and grabbed the larger man by the shoulder. "Let her go, Hubert." He pulled Hubert away from Lex, while Amanda wrapped her arm around the injured woman. "I think you should leave, son."

"Get your damned hands off of me, old man." Hubert jerked out of the sheriff's grasp. "And I'm not your son." He grabbed his briefcase and stomped to the door. "I want those papers at my office before five o'clock today, Lex." Hubert left the room and then the front door slammed shut. Jacob followed silently behind him.

Anna Leigh hurried over to where Amanda was helping Lex sit back down. "Goodness, dear, are you all right?" She knelt at the younger woman's feet and placed her hand on Lex's leg.

Lex smiled tiredly. "Yes, ma'am. I'm just fine." She looked around the room at the others. "I'm really sorry for that, folks," she apologized quietly.

Jacob returned from locking the front door. "Why should you apologize for him? He's a grown man, although I'm afraid he doesn't much act like one." He stepped behind the sofa and patted Lex gently on the shoulder.

"Are you sure you're okay, Lex?" Charlie studied the rancher carefully. He wanted to chase after her brother and knock some sense into the man's head. *I need to find out where Hubert was on Saturday. Although the thought of him tossing his own sister off that ledge makes my blood run cold.*

"Relax, Uncle Charlie. He just caught me off guard, that's all. And I really didn't want to start a brawl in the Caubles' living room." Lex turned her head and winked at Amanda, who was looking at her with concern. "I'm fine, Amanda. Don't look at me like that."

Amanda smiled weakly and stared down at her lap. "Sorry." She didn't notice when everyone else left the room, leaving her alone with Lex. Her hand was gently grasped and then kissed. She looked up and saw the rancher smile at her tenderly. "What?"

The older woman studied Amanda's face for a moment. "You are so beautiful," Lex murmured as she gazed into the blonde's eyes. She released her grip and raised her hand to caress the younger woman's cheek. "Thanks for looking out for me, sweetheart. I didn't mean to sound unappreciative." Lex watched as Amanda leaned into the touch and closed her eyes. "I just hate to see you worry for no reason."

"Everything I do concerning you has a reason, Lex." Amanda opened her eyes and looked at her lover seriously. "Don't ask me to try and change that, because I can't. I told my grandmother that you are my entire world, but that doesn't even come close to describing what you mean to me."

Lex used her thumb to wipe away the single tear that dropped from her partner's green eyes. "Oh, sweetheart, I feel the same way about you." She leaned forward and kissed Amanda tenderly, then pulled back slightly so that she could make eye contact. "I know I don't talk about my feelings very often, but you are the most precious gift that I have ever been given." Lex kissed her lover again. "I swear by everything that I am that I will love and cherish you for the rest of my life." The rancher searched the younger woman's face. "I love you, Amanda Lorraine Cauble and I always will."

Amanda sat for a moment in silence. The older woman's words echoed in her mind as she wrapped her arms around Lex's neck. "I love you too, Lex," she murmured into the rancher's chest, as she closed her eyes and basked in the love that they shared.

Chapter
8

They sat tangled together for several minutes as Lex comfortingly rubbed the blonde's back with one hand. "Why don't we go see what your grandparents and Charlie are up to?" she whispered into the smaller woman's ear. "They're probably wondering what's taking us so long." Lex kissed her head and leaned back slightly.

"That's a good idea. But, aren't you curious about those papers? Hubert said it was an inheritance." Amanda gestured to the stack of papers that Lex had dropped. She bent down and picked them up off the floor.

"Nah. He was probably just saying that so I would hurry up and sign them. For all I know, it could be another one of his get-rich-quick schemes." Lex scarcely spared a passing glance for the items in question.

Amanda stood and offered the rancher her hand. "I don't know. He seemed pretty adamant about getting them back in a hurry. Knowing Hubert, I figured that meant it must involve money." She pulled Lex to her feet and wrapped an arm around her.

Lex chuckled. "I think I can make it to the kitchen under my own power, sweetheart. It's really not necessary for you to be my crutch."

"I know," Amanda smiled, "but I enjoy it." She tight-

ened her grip on the taller woman's waist. "So just relax
and let me have my fun."

"Seems like I've heard that line before," Lex teased.
She enjoyed watching the blush creep across the younger
woman's face.

"Ooh. I can't believe you said that." Amanda laughed
as they stepped into the kitchen. She fanned her face with
her free hand. *Jeez. The things that she can do to me with
just a few words.*

Anna Leigh looked up at the smiling women when they
entered the room. "Goodness, Mandy. You look flushed. Is
everything okay?" She could tell by the smirk on the taller
woman's face that everything was just fine. *I'd love to
know what Lexington said or did that caused that one. My,
she's red.* She winked at the sheriff, who sat across from
her at the table.

"Looks like someone could use a little cooling off,"
Charlie quipped. He raised his coffee mug at the rancher in
salute. "You're looking a lot better today, Lex."

Lex allowed Amanda to seat her at the remaining chair
at the table. "Thanks, Uncle Charlie. I'm feeling pretty
good." Which was true, she supposed. *Although this
damned headache is beginning to get on my nerves, and my
arm is still killing me. But it could have been a lot worse,*
Lex thought tiredly. *And damned if I'm not sleepy again.*

"Why don't you stay for lunch, Charlie? I just cooked
up a big batch of stew, and there's more than enough."
Jacob could see the indecision playing on the sheriff's
face. "It's the least we could do, since you haven't arrested
our granddaughter for her traffic indiscretions today." He
got up and walked over to the stove to stir the simmering
pot with a wooden spoon.

"Traffic indiscretions?" Lex glanced over at Amanda
who had taken Jacob's place at the table. "Exactly what
kind of indiscretions are we talking about here?" she questioned her friend.

Charlie ignored the pleading look that the blonde
woman gave him. "Seems like Amanda wanted to see how

many laws she could break between her office and here."

Amanda rolled her eyes. "You're exaggerating, Sheriff." She stressed his title. "I may have gone over the speed limit a bit, but I don't think..."

"Sixty-four in a thirty is more than a little bit, honey. When I saw that little Mustang fly by me, I thought I was seeing things." Charlie shook his head. "You scared me to death, young lady." *I thought something serious had happened to Lex. God, the thoughts that went through my mind at that.*

"I'm really sorry." Amanda looked properly chastised. "I didn't even see you behind me until I pulled up into the driveway."

Lex sighed heavily and braced her head with the hand she had propped on the table. "What am I going to do with you?" She closed her eyes and shook her head.

"We've been asking ourselves that same question for years," Jacob chuckled. "Hope you have better luck figuring it out." He winked at his wife and returned his attention to the simmering pot on the stovetop.

"Grandpa," the blonde woman huffed, although she couldn't hide the smile that was sneaking onto her face. "You talk as if I was a lot of trouble growing up." She shook a warning finger at Lex, who had a silly grin on her face.

Anna Leigh laughed at her granddaughter's antics. "Oh, honey. It's not that you were trouble, it just seemed to find you." She saw the glint in Lex's eyes.

"I knew it," Lex chortled, raising her head and slapping her hand down on the table. "My life has certainly gotten more exciting since you dropped into it, sweetheart."

Amanda gave the rancher an incredulous look. "That's not what Martha told me. Seems like you were always coming back to the house with something either scraped or broken."

Lex tried to look innocent. "I don't know what you're talking about." She gave Charlie an intimidating glare. *Not one word, Charlie.*

"Well, let's see..." Amanda closed her eyes and counted off on her fingers. "You rolled your truck and broke your leg."

"Not my fault—the weather was bad," Lex defended.

"Uh-huh. Okay." Amanda refused to let up, especially when she saw the daring glint in her partner's eyes. "Broken ribs, which you unsuccessfully tried to hide from Martha?"

Charlie exchanged amused glances with the Caubles. *These two are something else, that's for sure. I'm sure glad that Lex found someone who won't take any bull from her.*

Lex bit her lip in deep thought. "Umm." Her face brightened. "Oh, yeah. The cinch strap ripped while I was breaking a new horse. Again, not my fault." She gave the group around the table a triumphant smile.

Amanda shook her head. "How about the broken arm you had when you met my grandmother?"

The rancher was quiet for a long moment. "I honestly don't remember how that happened," she admitted ruefully. "But I'm sure it wasn't my fault either." Lex grinned when Amanda stuck her tongue out at her.

"That's enough, girls," Anna Leigh admonished, then decided to change the subject. "Lexington, dear, if you don't mind me asking, what exactly were those papers about that was so important?"

"To tell you the truth, I kinda forgot all about them." Lex looked at Amanda. "Did you bring them with you, sweetheart?"

The blonde smiled and handed the stack of papers to Lex. "Of course. I'm beginning to get a little curious about them, myself."

Lex took the papers and gave the younger woman a gentle grin. "Thanks, love." She began to study the papers carefully. "Hmm."

Amanda stood up and went to the cabinet that held the dinnerware. "I'll just get the table set for lunch." She grabbed a handful of bowls and spoons and brought them over to the table. When she placed a setting in front of Lex, she noticed that the dark-haired woman had placed the papers on the table and closed her eyes. "Lex? What's the matter? Does it tell you what this is all about?"

The rancher felt a soft touch on her shoulder and opened her eyes. "Yeah. Says that someone died last week, and left Hubert and me a rather large inheritance." She looked down at her hands and released a heavy sigh.

Anna Leigh reached across the table and patted the tall woman's hand. "Honey, who passed away? Someone close to you?"

Lex looked up at the older woman with a slightly puzzled expression. "My grandmother."

"Victoria's mother? But I thought you told me that she passed away when you were a child." Anna Leigh could read the hurt and confusion on the rancher's face. She knew that both of Rawson's parents were long dead, since they had left the ranch to their only son before Lexington was even born. When Anna Leigh first met the young woman, she felt sorry for her lack of grandparents, since the rancher had told her that they were all dead.

"That's what my father told me." Lex struggled to her feet. "If you'll excuse me, I'm really not very hungry right now." She stepped away from the table and departed the kitchen, leaving the papers behind.

Amanda looked at the shocked faces around the kitchen. "Umm. I'm going to go see..." She hurried out of the room behind her apparently distraught friend. After a quick search of the downstairs, she found Lex on the front porch. The blue eyes were staring off into the distance, not focused on anything in particular. "Mind some company?"

The dark-haired woman glanced back over her shoulder. "I'm afraid I'm not very good company right now." She turned her attention back to the passing traffic.

"Okay. Then I'll just stand here with you for a bit, if you don't mind." Amanda stepped over and rubbed Lex's back. "And I always think you're good company." She felt the tense shoulders relax slightly.

Lex turned around with a small smile on her face. "Thanks, sweetheart." She reached over and brushed the hair out of the smaller woman's eyes. "Sorry I left like that. It just felt like the room was closing in on me." She leaned up tiredly against one of the support beams.

Amanda stepped closer and ran her hand up Lex's unencumbered arm. "Do you want to talk about it?"

"There's really not much to say." When Lex saw the determined look on her partner's face, she relented. "When I was about eight or nine, I asked my dad about my grandparents. Seemed like all the other kids at school were always talking about theirs, and I was curious. He told me that they were all dead and not to bother him about it anymore." She remembered the conversation like it was yesterday.

Young Lexington came home from school excited about something she had heard in class. Her science teacher had explained that everyone received different characteristics from the people in their family, and that if they looked closely at their parent's parents, they'd see their own features on their grandparents' faces. She was curious about which family members she most looked like, and searched for her father to find the answers. "Daddy!" she went from building to building, yelling for the rancher.

Rawson Walters was in the hay barn repairing several rotted planks in the loft. He heard his young daughter cry his name and peeked over the edge. "Up here, Lex. You want to bring me that can of nails?"

"Sure, Dad." She dropped her backpack full of schoolwork and rushed to do his bidding. Lex would faithfully follow her father all over the ranch to help out as much as a nine-year-old possibly could. She hurried up the ladder to the loft, almost dropping the nails in the process.

"Careful, there! It'd take all day to get those picked up," the tired man admonished, as he took the can from his daughter. "What are you running around hollerin' about, Lex?"

Lex impatiently brushed her dark hair out of her eyes. "We learned some really neat stuff in school today, and I wanted to tell you about it." She held one end of the board that he was working on. "Well, I mean I wanted to ask you something about it."

The ex-rodeo rider looked up from where he was nailing the board. "Okay, so ask." He hated having these kinds of talks with the youngster. She was too bright for her own good, and was always asking him questions he was uncomfortable answering.

"Well, we were talking about heredity today in science, and how we're all made up of different parts of folks in our family." Lex's eyes were bright with excitement. "Then Mr. Ramsey said that if we looked at our grandparents, we could figure out where our different features came from."

Rawson felt a cold chill start in his gut. Don't ask me about them, please, he silently begged his daughter. "Yeah? So what's your question, hon?"

The young girl didn't notice the sudden loss of color in her father's face. "Where are my grandparents, Daddy? All the other kids talked about theirs, and I didn't know what to say." She saw an unusual look cross the rancher's face, but continued. "I don't remember ever hearing anything about them, and I was wondering why."

"Your grandparents are all dead, Lex. Not much to talk about." Rawson grabbed another board and started to hammer. "And I don't talk about them because there's nothing to say, so just drop the subject." He picked up a few more nails and looked his daughter in the eye. "Why don't you get back to the house and do your homework, and we'll go ride the south section of fence before it gets dark?" The rancher knew the best way to distract the young girl was by doing work on the ranch itself.

"Okay, Daddy. I'll be back in no time." Lex impulsively hugged her father before she took off back down the ladder, anxious to finish her homework. It wasn't until much later that Lex realized what her father had told her.

God, that hurt when I finally figured out what he had meant. Lex inhaled, then released, a deep breath. "Why would he lie to me about that? What purpose could it possibly serve?"

"I don't know, honey." Amanda looked up into anguished blue eyes. "I'm sure he thought he was doing the right thing." A cold blast of air caused her to shiver violently. "Why don't we go back into the house before you add pneumonia to your list of ills?"

The rancher nodded and allowed Amanda to lead her back inside the house and into the living room. "You're probably right, as usual." Lex grinned at the young woman as she was guided to the loveseat near the fire. "Umm, sweetheart?" She watched as Amanda covered her legs with the quilt. "Amanda?"

Amanda looked up from where she was tucking the edges of the quilt around her lover's legs. "Yes?" She was kneeling on the floor next to Lex's feet. "Maybe I should stir up the fire." She stood up and started to walk away, when the back of her belt was grabbed from behind. "Urk!" Amanda found herself sitting in the rancher's lap.

"Stop fussing, love. You're gonna completely wear yourself out." Lex pulled the younger woman closer. "Besides, I have a better way to warm up." She leaned forward and covered Amanda's lips with her own for a long moment. Lex felt her partner's hands tangle themselves in her thick hair as she continued her loving ministrations. She pulled back regretfully to catch her breath. "God, Amanda," she murmured, leaning her forehead against the blonde's.

"Yeah," Amanda gasped huskily, "me too." She heard voices coming closer, as her grandparents tried to join them without causing any embarrassment. "I think we're about to have company, sweetheart." She slowly slipped from Lex's lap to sit beside her. In a louder voice, Amanda asked, "What are you going to do about the forms, Lex? Do you want to sign them so I can take them back to Hubert?"

Jacob and Anna Leigh stepped into the room with

large smiles on their faces. "Hello, girls," the older man chuckled, "Are you okay, Lex?" He and his wife sat down together on the nearby sofa. "Charlie sends his regrets, but he wanted to go and check into something. He said he would call you later."

Lex smiled at Amanda's grandfather. "I'm fine, Jacob. Just needed to get a little air." She felt Amanda take her hand and squeeze it reassuringly. "Sorry about running out like that."

Anna Leigh waved her hand and scoffed. "Don't you dare apologize, Lexington. We were just concerned about you." She saw her granddaughter nod slightly and smiled. "You just let us know if there's anything we can do."

"Thank you, Anna Leigh," Lex acknowledged quietly. "I may just take you up on that." She looked sideways at her partner. "I need to find out more about my grand-mother. Would you...?"

Amanda pulled their linked hands up to her lips and kissed Lex's knuckles gently. "Why don't I do a little investigating and see what I can come up with?" She looked over at her grandparents. "Would you mind if I bor-rowed your computer?"

"Not a bit, Peanut. Why don't I see if I can give you a hand?" Jacob stood up and followed the young woman out of the room.

Lex watched them as they left. She took a deep breath and looked down at her lap. *My grandmother. I wonder why she never tried to get in touch with me?* She felt tears burn her eyes as she thought about what she had missed. *She had to know that I existed, didn't she? Maybe she was ashamed of me. I'm no great prize.*

"Lexington?" Anna Leigh's gentle voice broke into the rancher's musings. "Would it help to talk about it, dear?" She crossed the room to perch on the arm of the loveseat. "I've been told I'm a very good listener." She placed a comforting hand on the younger woman's shoulder.

"I don't...maybe..." Lex shook her head and blinked a couple of times to clear her vision. "I guess I'm just trying to understand why." She closed her eyes when she felt the older woman's hand make soothing motions on her head. "Why would my father lie to me about my family? And why did they never make an effort to get in touch with me when I got older?"

Anna Leigh sighed. "I'm not certain, of course, but from what I had heard at the time, your mother's father almost disowned her when she married Rawson. I didn't know either of them terribly well, since both Victoria and Rawson were a bit older than our son Michael." She got up and sat down next to Lex on the loveseat. "I do remember the write up in the newspaper, though. They said it was quite...interesting."

Lex looked at the older woman quizzically. "Interesting? It was just a wedding."

"Well, it seems that there was a slight altercation at the reception." *More like a brawl. The paper had mentioned it took hours to clean up. Several people, including the groom, ended up in jail.* Anna Leigh smiled gently at the younger woman. "I don't think your father got along very well with Victoria's parents."

"Just exactly what kind of altercation are we talking about?" Lex shifted slightly so that she could look directly at Anna Leigh. "And why was there a newspaper article on a simple wedding?"

The older woman shook her head. "It was so many years ago, and I may not remember the details very well."

"Please, Anna Leigh. I would really appreciate anything that you could tell me. I'm at such a loss here," Lex pleaded quietly. "Until today, I thought my grandparents had died before I was born. Maybe you can help me figure out why my father never told me about them." *And why they never bothered to get in touch with me.*

Anna Leigh took a deep breath. "Okay." She reached over to grasp Lex's hand. "But bear with me, dear. It was quite some time ago, and I didn't pay that close of attention to the gossip at the time." After the younger woman nodded, she began. "I know for a fact that the Edwards were not too fond of their daughter's choice for a husband. Victoria was such a sweet and quiet girl, and I think that Rawson brought her out of her shell, so to speak. Travis, her father and your grandfather, was going to cut her off from the family completely, or so the gossips said." The older woman shook her head sadly. "Melanie, your grandmother, talked him into allowing the wedding to take place. At least that was the buzz around town at the time. Since they were not from around here, it was pretty big news for a girl of her social standing to marry a working man." When she read the pain in Lex's eyes, Anna Leigh apologized. "Honey, like I said before, all of this is just hearsay. We don't know what really happened."

Lex took a deep breath and tried to smile. "It's okay. I guess it just sounded a little too familiar, that's all." She saw the look of realization cross the older woman's face. "I went through something similar with Amanda's father just a month ago. This hits a little too close to home."

"Oh, dear. I never thought of that." Anna Leigh gazed at the young woman sadly. "You know that Jacob and I love you as if you were our own granddaughter, don't you?"

"Yes, and believe me, you two are the best grandparents I could have ever asked for," Lex answered with a watery smile. "But I really would like to know about my family. Maybe I have a great aunt or uncle out there, or even cousins." She suddenly smiled. "Or maybe my grandfather is still alive. Think he'd mind meeting me?"

Green eyes twinkled. "Mind? Good lord, child. If he is alive, he'd probably be ecstatic. You are the spitting image of your dear mother." She reached up and wiped an errant tear from the rancher's face. "Let me finish my little story, and then we'll check on Mandy and Jacob's progress in the office, all right?" She waited until Lex composed herself, then continued. "Where was I? Oh, yes. The wedding went off beautifully, they said but things got a little...uncomfortable at the reception. Travis had a little too much to drink, and accused Rawson of marrying his daughter for

her money. Your father took that as an insult to Victoria
and punched his father-in-law, which caused a large brawl
to break out."

"Oh, boy. No wonder I never saw any pictures of my
grandparents." Lex shook her head. "But I swear that I can
remember a tall, dark-haired man at our house before my
mother died."

"You probably did. I think they used to visit when
your father would go out of town to the rodeos—although
after Victoria's funeral, I don't believe we ever saw either
of them again. But we really didn't travel in the same
social circles as the Edwards." Anna Leigh could see the
exhaustion on the rancher's face. "Why don't you let me
help you upstairs, Lexington? You look completely worn
out."

Lex fought off a yawn. "That bad, huh?" She blinked
several times and frowned. "I swear I'm gonna quit taking
those damn...uh, sorry...darn pills that old quack prescribed. They knock me on my rear."

"Let's go." Anna Leigh pulled Lex to her feet. "He
prescribed those because he knew that there wasn't any
other way to make you rest so you could get better. I'll
explain to Amanda where you are when I check on them."
She wrapped a steadying arm around the trim waist.
"Honey, you need to eat more. You're nothing but skin and
bones."

The rancher sighed as they made their way up the
stairs. "You sound like Martha." She chuckled at the
answering pat on her side. "Or Amanda, for that matter.
She's always on me about not eating right."

Anna Leigh tickled the taller woman's ribs. "Hush. Or
I'll sic Jacob on you to fatten you up." Her husband took
great delight in cooking, and was forever treating her to
rich meals. "Thank goodness I still do my walking every
day, or I'd be the size of a house by now."

"Now that's a threat," Lex murmured as she sat
heavily on the bed. "You'd never get rid of me then." She
yawned again as the older woman covered her with a blan-

ket. "Thanks, Gramma." Lex didn't even realize what she had said as she closed her eyes tiredly.

"Any time, honey," Anna Leigh whispered, kissing the already sleeping woman's forehead. "Pleasant dreams."

* * * * * * * * *

Amanda sat at the computer searching through county records, as Jacob continued to peruse the legal papers left behind by Hubert. "Can you find anything that tells where Lex's grandmother was buried?" she asked him as she surfed from site to site.

"I'm afraid not, Peanut." Jacob sat in the chair he had pulled around next to his granddaughter. "Although I do remember hearing that they came from Dallas at one time. Maybe you could try there."

"Good idea, Grandpa. Do you know what her maiden name was?" Amanda found yet another dead end and leaned back in her chair with an exasperated breath. "Is there anyone in this town we could call that might have known them? I really want to find something for Lex."

Jacob rubbed his chin thoughtfully. "I don't...let me think..."

"How about Reverend Nelson? Isn't he the one who performed the ceremony?" Anna Leigh answered from the doorway. "Perhaps he would know a little bit more about the Edwards than we do." She stepped into the room and leaned up against her husband, who promptly pulled her into his lap. "Jacob! Behave yourself."

"Not a chance, my love." The chuckling man pulled his wife close and nibbled gently on her neck. "Now what were you saying about Reverend Nelson?" Jacob tickled her ribs.

Anna Leigh slapped ineffectually at his hands. "Stop that." she giggled. "Mandy, tell your grandfather if he doesn't stop that this instant, he'll be sleeping in the guest room." She squirmed a bit more until her husband stopped his teasing.

Amanda laughed at her grandparent's antics. *That's what Lex and I am going to look like in forty years or so, I bet. They're so darned cute.* "Oh, I dunno. I think I'm on his side this time."

"Traitor," her grandmother huffed with a smile. "Anyway, I was saying that Reverend Nelson usually keeps really good records, and if anyone knows anything about Travis or Melanie Edwards, it would probably be him."

"Great. I'll just get Lex and we'll..." Amanda had jumped up and was halfway to the doorway when she realized something. "Where is Lex, Gramma? Is she in the living room?"

The older woman escaped her husband's loving grip and stood up. "I took her upstairs to bed, sweetheart. Her medication had about gotten the best of her." Anna Leigh crossed the room to stand next to her granddaughter. "She was in shock, I think. Finding out she had a grandmother that had been alive all these years really shook her up."

Amanda looked stricken. "Oh, no. Poor Lex. I should have been there for her." She started to leave the room when her grandmother stopped her.

"She's already asleep, Mandy. Lexington was fine, really." Seeing the look on the younger woman's face, she continued, "She was just the sweetest thing before she fell asleep, calling me Gramma just like you."

Jacob sauntered up behind his wife, wrapped his arms around her, and propped his chin on the top of her head. "That's great, sweetheart. Hopefully we can keep her in the habit when she's conscious." He winked at his granddaughter. "Why don't you go upstairs to check on her, and we'll see if we can't hunt down Reverend Nelson."

Anna Leigh nodded. "You look like you could use a little nap yourself, honey. Get some rest, and we'll call you down for an early dinner, all right?"

"That sounds like a wonderful idea. I'm beat, even though it's only," she looked at her watch in amazement, "two o'clock? Good grief." Amanda embraced both of her grandparents and planted kisses on their cheeks. "I'll see you both in a little bit, okay?" She turned and practically raced out of the room.

"She reminds me so much of you at that age, my love," Jacob chuckled in his wife's ear. "Never walking anywhere, always in a hurry." He ran his hands along her sides in a teasing manner. "It has been a busy day. Maybe we should take our own advice and get a little nap in ourselves?"

"Hmm." Anna Leigh took her husband's hand and led him from the office. "That's the best offer I've had all day, handsome." She pulled him up the stairs and into their bedroom, quietly closing the door behind them.

Amanda shut the bedroom door and tiptoed silently across the room. She studied the still form on the bed as she pulled on a tee shirt and a pair of shorts. Lex had rolled over on her left side, draping her injured arm across Amanda's pillow. Quietly, so as not to disturb the sleeping woman, Amanda slipped under the covers and gently raised Lex's arm, slowly rolling her over to her back.

"Amanda," Lex sighed. "Love you," she murmured in her sleep.

"I love you too, sweetheart." Amanda snuggled up next to the rancher and kissed her softly on the jaw. "Sleep well, my love. We'll get all of this mess figured out soon, I promise." She closed her eyes and joined her lover in slumber.

Chapter 9

Sheriff Bristol leaned back in his chair and rubbed his eyes. Several file folders were strewn across the desk in disarray. *Okay. So now we know that Rick Thompson has no alibi for last Saturday, and Hubert was "missing" for about four hours that day.* "Great. Two suspects, two motives." He was about to search through the folders again when his phone buzzed.

"Sheriff? I have Mrs. Cauble on line two for you, as you requested," his secretary informed him.

"Thanks, Lydia." Charlie picked up the receiver and pushed line two. "This is Sheriff Bristol in Somerville, Texas. May I please speak with Michael Cauble?"

The woman's voice on the other end of the line released a heavy sigh. "As I told the woman who called, my husband has been out of town on business since last Thursday. I do not expect him back until Wednesday evening, at the earliest. What is this all about?"

"I'm sorry to disturb you, Mrs. Cauble, but I'm investigating a crime." He pulled a notepad close and jotted down some notes. "Where can I reach Mr. Cauble? It's imperative that I speak with him on this matter as soon as possible."

"Are you insinuating that my husband is guilty of

something criminal?" Elizabeth Cauble's voice turned icy. "Perhaps you should just contact our lawyer."

The sheriff closed his eyes and rubbed his forehead, trying to postpone the incipient headache. "No, ma'am, I'm not insinuating anything. But a crime has been committed, and I'm pursuing each and every lead until I catch the person responsible."

Elizabeth's reply reflected her irritation. "If this crime happened there in Texas, what makes you think that Michael had anything to do with it?"

"Because your husband recently threatened the victim, ma'am. I'm following every lead, no matter how small or far fetched it may seem." Charlie felt like pounding his head on the desk. *Damned stubborn woman. I can't believe sweet little Amanda is even related to her.*

"Who is he supposed to have threatened? Were there witnesses? When was this alleged threat made?" Elizabeth's voice continued to rise until she was almost screaming. "How dare you!"

Charlie took a deep breath as he tried to think of how much he could safely say. "Your husband threatened Lexington Walters last month, Mrs. Cauble. It seems that he also attacked her in front of your youngest daughter."

The cultured woman's tone practically shook with rage. "That...pervert...said my husband threatened her? That's the most ridiculous thing that I have ever heard." She paused for a moment to get herself back under control. "She has my daughter brainwashed to think like her, too. You can't believe a word either of them say." Elizabeth laughed humorlessly. "Do you even know this...woman, Sheriff? She can't be trusted, you know."

"Mrs. Cauble," the lawman almost bit his tongue in two trying to control his temper, "I have known Lexington Walters since she was born. You won't find a more upstanding citizen, or kinder person." He waited a moment to let his words sink in. "And I promise you, I *will* get to the bottom of this. No one hurts my family and gets away with it. Good day, ma'am." Without allowing her an opportunity for further slander, he slammed the receiver back down on the phone and covered his eyes with a shaking hand. *God. What a hateful woman. Poor Amanda. And now her father doesn't seem to have an alibi either. This damned thing just keeps getting more and more complicated.*

The knock on his office door caused Sheriff Bristol to glance up expectantly. "Come in." Charlie smiled at the young woman who stepped into the room. "Amanda. Hello there. Come on in and have a seat." He stood and waved her into a nearby chair. "What can I do for you this morning, honey?"

Amanda sat down with a serious look on her face. "Lex and I were talking last night. We thought that we should tell you about someone else, even though he hasn't made any threats or anything." She had been awakened before dinner by gentle kisses from the rancher. The attentions led to them being late for the evening meal, much to her grandparents' delight. *I thought they'd never quit smirking,* Amanda thought with an inward grin.

"Okay. At this point, I'll take any help or ideas I can get." Charlie grabbed his notepad and turned to a clean sheet of paper. "Go ahead."

"Like I said, he hasn't threatened her or anything, and maybe it's just a coincidence, but..." Amanda raised her hands helplessly. "With the way things have been lately, we figured it would be better to be safe than sorry. Mark Garrett used to work for my father, but he quit a couple of weeks ago." The sheriff nodded. "Anyway, last week he showed up at my office saying that he wanted to relocate to Somerville. And, he showed up at my grandparents' on Monday with flowers for Lex."

Charlie scratched his head. "If he's new in town, how did he know where to find you?" Understanding dawned on his weathered features. "Damn. Do we know where this Mr. Garrett was on Saturday?" He wrote furiously on his notepad. "Do you happen to know where he's staying?"

The young woman shook her head. "No. He never told

me. Which is kind of strange, since I'm supposed to be finding a house for him. Mark didn't leave me any way to get in contact with him." Amanda stood up and walked over to the window to glance outside.

"How's Lex feeling today, sweetheart?" Charlie looked back at the door. "Is she still over at your grandparents'?"

"No. She's over at Dr. Anderson's getting a checkup." Amanda turned back from the window with a sheepish smile. "He ran me off and said that he didn't want to see me for at least two hours." She crossed back to the desk and leaned up against one corner. "Lex is hoping that he'll give her the okay to unwrap her arm, since it's not bothering her any more."

The sheriff chuckled. "She's always healed up quickly. I remember that it caused some interesting arguments between her and Martha." Charlie stood up and grabbed his hat. "Why don't you let me buy you a cup of coffee? The diner across the street also has a great cheese Danish."

Amanda smiled as she preceded him out of the office. "Sounds good, but only if you'll let me pay for it."

* * * * * * * * * *

"Ow!" Lex jerked away from prying hands. "Are you trying to kill me?"

The gray-haired doctor chuckled good-naturedly. "Calm down, Lexington. We're almost done." Dr. Anderson finished removing the wrap from her injured arm. "I thought that it wasn't hurting you any more?" He looked up into her wide blue eyes.

Busted. Okay, I can talk my way out of this. "Umm. It wasn't." Lex stopped to think. "But with all your twisting and jerking, it's a little sore now," she finished with a triumphant smile.

"Uh-huh." He turned the arm slowly and used his thumb and forefinger to test for swelling. "Can you make a fist?"

Lex closed her hand slowly. "Isn't that a dangerous thing to ask me?" She grinned down at the older man. "Especially with you in that position?" She flinched as he turned the still-bruised arm.

Dr. Anderson laughed at the mock threat as he slowly bent her arm at the elbow. "Easy now. The x-rays show that there was no permanent damage done, but it's going to be pretty sore for another week or so." He could feel her muscles tense as the young woman tried to keep from reacting to the pain. "It's looking a lot better, honey. You can leave it unwrapped, and I'll give you a list of exercises that will strengthen it properly." He handed Lex her shirt that lay on the table.

"Does this mean that I can go back to the ranch and not have to come back here any time soon?" Lex asked as she struggled to button up her shirt. "Damn." A knock on the door stopped her fumbling.

A tousled blonde head poked in the door. "Are you about through, or do I have to try and find something else to occupy my time out in the waiting room?" Amanda asked as she edged her way into the room. She noticed Lex standing by the examining table with her shirt unbuttoned. "Need some help?" she asked, as she made her way across to the rancher.

Lex smiled at her young friend. "Yeah. My hand still doesn't work too well."

"I'll just let you finish getting dressed, Lexington." Dr. Anderson stood in the doorway. "Stop by my office before you leave, and I'll have some papers for you to sign, okay?" He closed the door behind him.

Amanda finished buttoning the rancher's shirt and then wrapped her arms around Lex. "I missed you," she mumbled into Lex's chest. The blonde tilted her head back until she could look the older woman in the eye. "What did he say?"

"I'm fine. Gonna be sore for another week or so, but no permanent damage." Lex raised her right hand and slowly ran her fingers through Amanda's hair. "Dr. A. said he was going to give me some exercises to strengthen my arm, but I need to take it easy for a bit."

"That's great." Amanda found herself lost in the rancher's blue gaze. She slowly stretched up and met Lex halfway, their lips gently touching. "Mmm." Amanda reached up and clasped her hands behind the taller woman's neck as she deepened the kiss.

Lex wrapped her left arm around Amanda's back and pulled the smaller woman closer. She ignored the pain in her right arm as she continued to thread her fingers through the blonde hair. "Amanda." she felt the young woman turn slightly to run her hands down Lex's arms. "Ow!" Lex gasped, as Amanda inadvertently grabbed her sore arm.

Amanda jumped back as if she had been burned. "Oh God, Lex. I'm so sorry." She could see the pain in the blue eyes above her. "Are you okay?" The blonde took a tentative step forward and touched the clenched jaw. "Honey?"

"It's okay." Lex closed her eyes and took a deep breath through her nose. "Just a little tender, that's all." She blinked her eyes open and forced a smile onto her face. "See? No harm done, sweetheart." The sharp pain in her arm slowly receded. "C'mere, beautiful." Lex pulled the younger woman close and wrapped her arms back around Amanda. They stood quietly for several minutes, lost in each other.

"Is everything all right in here?" Laura, Dr. Anderson's nurse, poked her red head into the room. "The doctor said that he was ready for you in his office." She smiled at the rancher, who still had her left arm wrapped around Amanda.

Lex gave the nurse a wry grin. "Just great. We were just on our way out." She allowed Amanda to leave the office before her, winking at the young woman holding the door. "Thanks, Laura."

"Any time, Lex," Laura assured her. *Oh, how the mighty have fallen—and hard, too. She certainly deserves the happiness. Congratulations, my lucky friend.*

****

"Did you get everything on Martha's list?" Amanda questioned her friend. Lex was scowling at the road ahead of them and fighting the swirling wind to keep the truck on the road. They had just spent the last two hours fighting the crowds at the local supermarket, much to the rancher's discomfort. "Lex?"

"Hmm?" Lex turned her attention away from the road for a moment. "I'm sorry. Did you ask me something?" She looked down at the small hand that rested on her thigh.

Amanda lightly ran her hand up and down the denim-clad leg. "I was just wondering if you got everything at the store that Martha had asked for." She studied the sharp profile beside her. "What's wrong?"

Lex released a deep breath, then smiled at Amanda. "Nothing's wrong, sweetheart. I was just thinking." She gingerly grasped the younger woman's hand with her own. "I think that we got everything that Martha wanted." She smiled ruefully. "I hope." *Lord knows I don't want to make another trip to town tonight or in the morning.* She brought Amanda's hand up to her lips and kissed it tenderly.

"What's on your mind? You seem a million miles away." Amanda could tell that something was bothering her lover and was determined to get to the root of the matter. "I'd like to help, if I could."

"I know, love." Lex shook her head. "I was just wondering if Martha might know more about my grandparents. I've never really talked to her about them." She squinted as the afternoon sun came out from behind some clouds. "Guess it can't hurt to ask, right?"

Amanda nodded. "That's right. And I've got a few leads to follow up on the computer when we get back to the ranch." She smiled broadly as the truck traveled across the old bridge to the ranch. The hired hands had completely rebuilt it after a large tree had wrecked it recently. Proud of their accomplishment, they had asked Lex and Amanda to ride down to the structure a week ago. *It seems like a*

*lifetime ago that my car was washed into the creek from
here, not just a month. So much has happened. I nearly
drowned, was rescued by the most incredible woman in the
world, and fell in love. Sounds perfect to me.*

Lex watched her companion's face as Amanda's
thoughts drifted. She privately loved it when the younger
woman would get distracted like this. *The look in her eyes
when she's thinking turns me to mush. Jeez. Do I need to
get a grip, or what?* But she couldn't help but smile as she
watched Amanda gaze off far into the distance. "Now
you've gone off somewhere. Want to share?"

"Hmm?" The blonde turned her attention back to Lex,
who was smiling at her. *I love that grin. She looks like a
little kid that knows a secret.* "Sorry. Just reminiscing."
She scrutinized the way the light chased across the older
woman's face. "So much has happened in a month, hasn't
it?"

"Yep." Lex fought the truck as a gust of wind tried to
blow it from the road. "Best month of my life, if you ask
me." She maneuvered the vehicle down the recently renovated road. "Damn. I think it's gonna get nasty later on
tonight, sweetheart." The sudden jerk of the steering wheel
shot renewed pain to her healing arm. *I'm going to soak in
the tub for hours tonight.* Lex glanced over at her lover
with a devilish smile. *And I bet I can get some company, if
I ask nicely.*

Amanda watched as Lex grinned at her. "What?" She
glanced down at herself and then back up to meet the
rancher's smirk. "That's a sneaky look you have. What are
you up to?"

The rancher pulled the truck up to the house next to
the mudroom entrance. "I was thinking about how good a
long soak in the tub would feel tonight." She got out and
hurried around to open the door for Amanda. "And I was
wondering if you would care to join me." Lex reached into
the back seat of the truck to grab a bag of groceries, only
to have her hand gently slapped away by the younger
woman. "Hey," she objected.

"Dr. Anderson said for you to take it easy for the next few days. Martha and I can bring in the supplies," Amanda chastised. When she saw the older woman's face cloud, she added, "Why don't you go upstairs and get the bath water ready? I'm feeling a little dirty myself."

Lex laughed. "Ooh. That's a good one," she whispered into Amanda's ear. "I'll save you a spot, cutie." She swatted the blonde on the rear, then raced into the house.

"I'll get you back for that, Lexington!" Amanda shouted after the retreating figure, trying to keep a straight face. *Just when I think I have her figured out, she acts like a little kid. Big tough rancher...*not.

Martha stepped into the kitchen and was almost bowled over by a quick moving form. "Aaah!" She jumped back into the hallway holding one hand over her heart. "Lexie! I didn't even hear you drive up. Are you trying to give me a heart attack?"

"Sorry 'bout that, Martha." Lex grasped the older woman by her elbows. "Are you all right?" She led Martha into the kitchen and helped her to a chair. "Here. Sit down for a minute."

"Stop that." Martha swatted at the tall woman. "I'm not that old." She studied Lex carefully. The rancher had squatted next to her chair with her hands braced on the arms. "You certainly look a world better, honey."

Lex allowed the older woman to stroke her hair softly. She unconsciously leaned into the touch and closed her eyes. "I feel one hundred percent better, too. Guess a couple of days rest was just what I needed." A noise from the mudroom caused her to stand up and open the adjoining door. "Dammit, Amanda," Lex grabbed one of the three bags that the younger woman was struggling with, "I thought you were going to wait for help."

"I was, but there was no sense walking in empty-handed." Amanda carried her two bags over to the cabinet. Lex placed her bag beside the others and turned in the direction of the door. "Don't even think about it, Slim." The blonde grabbed the back of Lex's belt to curtail her progress. "You're going upstairs, remember?"

The dark-haired woman glared at Martha, who was snickering from her seat at the table. "Not one word out of you," she warned. Lex turned around and enclosed Amanda in her arms. "Why don't you let me help you with the groceries, then we can go upstairs together?"

Amanda kissed Lex on the chin, then ducked under her arms to get to the mudroom door. "Nope. I'll get the rest of the groceries and then bring the overnight bag upstairs with me." She slipped out of the room before the rancher had a chance to argue.

"Damn. I lost again, didn't I?" Lex asked the housekeeper, who was putting the groceries away. "I used to be a lot tougher than that."

Martha laughed. "Not really, honey. You just used to be a little bit better at hiding it, that's all." She stopped what she was doing to give the rancher her undivided attention. "I'm really glad that you're feeling better, Lexie. You scared me pretty good this time."

Lex stepped forward and pulled the older woman into a powerful hug. "I kinda scared myself, Mada." She found herself calling Martha by the long-relinquished childhood nickname more and more recently. She kissed the top of the graying head lovingly. "I'll try to do better in the future, okay?"

Tears burned the housekeeper's eyes. "See that you do, sweetie. I have too many years of hard work invested in you," Martha teased as the rancher released her. "Now get yourself upstairs before we both get into trouble." She gently patted Lex on her hip.

"Yes, ma'am." Lex playfully saluted the older woman and swiftly left the kitchen.

Martha wiped her eyes with one corner of her apron. *I'm glad your good luck is still holding, Lexie. I don't know what I'd do if anything ever happened to you.*

* * * * * * * * *

Later that evening the three women were enjoying coffee in the den when Lex decided that it was time to ask the housekeeper for her help. The rancher was comfortably seated in one corner of the sofa, with Amanda tucked securely between her legs. Lex rested her chin on the younger woman's shoulder as she looked questioningly at Martha. "Martha? Do you remember my mother's parents?" She felt Amanda's hands tighten on her own where they rested casually on the blonde's stomach.

"Well, yes, honey. I certainly do. Although I believe that the last time I saw them was at your dear momma's funeral." Martha shifted slightly in the oversized chair where she was sitting so that she could look Lex directly in the eye. "Why do you ask, Lexie?"

"Hubert received a letter and some legal papers this past Friday. Seems that we were named in the will of Melanie Edwards, our grandmother." Lex sighed. "Dad told me years ago that all of my grandparents were dead. Do you have any idea why he would lie to me like that?"

Martha's heart nearly broke at the anguished look on the young woman's face. "Oh, honey. I don't rightly know what your daddy was thinking. I hadn't been here that long when your poor momma passed away, but I do remember that Mr. Walters and his in-laws didn't get along very well. After the funeral, they took separate cars from the cemetery, and I never saw or heard from them again."

"But why would they not at least try to contact their grandchildren? What kind of people were they?" Amanda wondered aloud. She gently stroked Lex's left arm, careful to stay away from her injured one.

"Well, from what little contact I had with them, I can tell you that Mr. Edwards was a quiet, dignified man. Tall, dark hair, and very handsome." Martha smiled at the young couple on the sofa. "I do believe that's where your good looks came from, Lexie. Mrs. Edwards also had dark hair, but she was very small and had fair skin." She slapped her leg and jumped up suddenly. "I wonder..." She hurried to the doorway, then turned. "Well? Aren't you two coming?"

Amanda stood up and offered a hand to the still reclining rancher. "Where are we going, Martha?" She pulled Lex up and started for the door without releasing her hold.

Martha blushed slightly. "Oh. Just look at me. Must be getting old, or something. I thought that we'd check upstairs in the storage room, where Mr. Walters had most of Miss Victoria's belongings packed away. She probably kept photographs and letters from her family."

"I don't know." Lex balked at the door and pulled Amanda back with her. "It doesn't seem right—going through her things like that." *I remember packing a few things when I moved into the master bedroom, but it was only a box or two. I guess Dad kept a bit of her stuff out for sentimental reasons.*

"Honey," Martha walked back over to Lex and cradled the younger woman's face in her hands, "I truly believe that she'd want you to see anything she had. I'm just sorry we waited so darned long to do this."

Lex blinked back tears. *What is wrong with me? It's not like I ever really knew her. Martha has been more of a mother to me.* "It's not your fault, Martha. I should have asked about this long before now." *Get a grip, Lexington. You're worrying her for no reason,* the rancher chided herself. "C'mon. Let's go exploring." She kissed the older woman's cheek and left the den, pulling a somewhat startled Amanda behind her.

The storage room was actually an old bedroom, part of which had recently been converted into the guest bedroom. Lex opened the door and flipped a switch that activated a large fluorescent light in the center of the room. Martha stepped by the rancher and opened the dark curtains to allow the early evening light inside.

The housekeeper made her way over to the far corner of the room and opened a box. "I believe this is where Mr. Walters put everything. He boxed most of Miss Victoria's belongings up the day of the funeral and never stepped foot into this room again." She pulled a couple of silk scarves from the top of the box. "C'mere, Lexie. Amanda. This is the right box, all right."

Amanda gently led her lover over to where Martha stood. She leaned over and peered into the box curiously. "Oooh. Those are pretty." She watched as Martha reverently folded the items and continued her search.

"Wait. This looks like letters." Martha pulled the tied bundles from the box and handed them to a still-silent Lex. She dug a little deeper. "Ah ha! Bingo." The housekeeper pulled several large photo albums from the bottom of the box.

"All right. Good job, Martha." Amanda didn't notice when Lex quietly slipped from the room. "Hopefully these will shed some light on the mysterious Edwards family. Maybe I can check those notes and letters and find an address. Right, Lex?" she turned to ask her lover. "Honey?"

Martha looked to the open door. "I'll gather this stuff up and bring it downstairs. Why don't you go find Lexie? I think all of this shook her up more than she cares to admit."

The younger woman bit her lip and followed the housekeeper's gaze. "You're right. I'll meet you back downstairs in the den, okay?" She gave Martha's arm a reassuring squeeze and hurried from the room.

A search of the upstairs rooms came up empty, so Amanda continued her search downstairs. She finally found Lex in the sitting room, staring at a small photograph on the far wall. All of the regular furniture had been moved out the previous day and in its place were a long formal dining table and ten chairs. There had originally been twelve chairs until Amanda's parents had not-so-politely declined their invitation.

The rancher turned to the doorway and met Amanda's eyes. "Umm...hi." Lex dropped her gaze to the floor. "Sorry I left like that. I just needed to get some air."

Amanda crossed the room until she stood directly in front of the taller woman. She grasped the rancher's chin and gently forced Lex to look her in the eyes. "Hey. This is

me that you're talking to." She waited until blue eyes
sharpened and focused on her. "Please, honey, let me help.
Tell me what's bothering you."

"I'm not sure," Lex whispered as she put a long arm
around the smaller woman's shoulders and led her back to
the wall. She pulled the photograph down and handed it to
Amanda. "Even looking at this picture, I can't remember
anything about her."

"She's beautiful." Amanda took the framed portrait
from Lex and studied it carefully, then looked up at her
lover. "Sweetheart, you could be her twin."

The woman in the picture sat in a lush garden, wearing
a white beaded wedding gown. Her waist-length dark hair
practically shimmered in the sunlight. Blue eyes sparkled
into the camera with undisguised happiness. There was a
rugged looking young man standing behind her with his
hand gently placed on her shoulder. He seemed uncomfortable in the black tuxedo he was sporting. His hazel eyes
looked tired and weary, although he appeared to be barely
out of his teens.

"Yeah. I kinda think that's one of the reasons he left
home. I remind him too much of her." Lex peered over
Amanda's shoulder at the picture. "I feel bad, not being
able to remember my own mother. I wish I could have
known her."

The blonde turned and looked up into Lex's still face.
"But don't you see, love? You have a perfect chance to do
just that. I'm sure that's why she saved all of those
things—so that when you were older, she could share them
with you." Amanda reached up and touched the clenched
jaw. "She just had no way of knowing that she wouldn't be
here with you, that's all."

Lex wrapped her arms around the smaller woman and
buried her face in the soft blonde hair. "God," she gasped
as the walls that she had erected around her heart so long
ago began to fall.

Amanda felt the heavy sobs shake the normally strong
body in her arms. "It's okay, love. Let it go." She held on

tightly to her lover as Lex released emotions that she had held in control for so many years. "That's it, sweetheart." She continued to gently stroke the dark head until the convulsive tears slowed.

The older woman had practically crumbled to the floor, which forced Amanda to sit down in a nearby chair. Lex looked up from her kneeling position and drew in a large lung full of air. "I'm sorry, Amanda. I didn't mean to fall apart on you like that." She began to wipe her face with her shirtsleeve when a small hand halted her movement.

"Please don't apologize, honey." Amanda looked around, spotting a linen napkin on the table. She picked it up and gently dried the rancher's face. "How are you feeling?"

"A little foolish, to tell you the truth." Lex stood up stiffly and sat in the chair next to her friend. "I don't usually do that but it seems you bring out that part of me."

"Do you have any idea how good it makes me feel when you share yourself with me like that?" Amanda asked quietly. She grasped one of Lex's hands and pulled it into her lap. "It's like you're trusting me with something very special, honey. And I'll try to always be worthy of that trust."

Lex sniffled slightly and stared at their linked hands. "Worthy? Good lord, Amanda." The rancher lifted her free hand and brushed her knuckles against the blonde's cheek. "Of all the people in this world, you are the last one that should ever worry about being worthy of anything."

Martha struck her head in the room and looked around. "Is everything okay in here? I hate to bother you both, but there's a phone call for Amanda." She stepped the rest of the way into the room and noticed the picture now lying on the table. "I think it's your sister, honey."

Amanda smiled at Lex and stood up. "I love you." She kissed the rancher on the lips and started for the door, then hesitated. "Are you okay? I can call her back later, you know."

"Never been better, love." Lex returned the younger woman's smile. "Tell Jeannie hello for me, all right? Martha and I will be in the..." She looked up at the housekeeper with a questioning glance.

Martha laughed. "We'll be in the kitchen. You can keep me company while I get some things ready for tomorrow." She ruffled the rancher's hair. "Let's go, sweetie. I'll even give you some cookies."

"Sounds like fun. I'll see you both in a few minutes." Amanda waved as she left the room.

The dark-haired woman sighed as she climbed to her feet. Lex startled Martha by wrapping her arms around her and squeezing the housekeeper tight. "Thanks for putting up with me, Mada," she whispered quietly. "I love you." Lex kissed the older woman's forehead and then released her.

"C'mon, brat. I may even put you to work." Martha grabbed the front of Lex's khaki shirt and pulled the grinning rancher from the room.

Chapter
10

.

A muffled thump woke Amanda early the next morning. She raised her head from Lex's chest and looked around the dark room. "What was that?" she mumbled.

"Mmm." Lex moaned and wrapped her arms around the smaller woman. "Don't care. Go back to sleep." She placed a sleepy kiss on Amanda's head as she pulled her closer. "It's a holiday, and it's too damned early to get out of bed."

Amanda glanced up at the clock. *Six o'clock? And Lex is still in bed?* She casually reached up with one hand and touched the rancher's forehead. *No fever. Hmmm.*

Lex chuckled. "I'm not sick. I just don't feel like getting out of bed yet." She kissed Amanda's throat. "But suddenly I'm not sleepy any more."

"Oh, really? Do you have anything special in mind? Because I could...oooooh." Amanda felt a warm hand glide gently down her bare back. "That's nice." She ducked under the covers and blazed a trail down her lover's body with her lips.

THUMP, THUMP, THUMP! The pounding was louder this time.

A blonde head poked out from under the blanket. "Did you hear that?" Amanda cocked her head slightly, trying to pinpoint the location of the noise. She felt Lex shift slightly underneath her, so she rolled over to allow the rancher room to move.

"Dammit." Lex climbed out of bed and started for the door. "Sounds like someone is beating on the front door."

"Honey?" Amanda's amused tone stopped the tall woman before she opened the bedroom door.

With her hand on the knob, Lex turned around. "Yes?"

The younger woman got up and grabbed her robe from a nearby chair. She put it on, then picked up the shorts and tee shirt that were lying on the floor next to the bed. "Not that I mind the view, but don't you think it would be a good idea to put something on before answering the door?"

Lex shook her head in disgust and released the doorknob . "You're probably right." She accepted the clothing and dressed quickly. "No sense in scaring whoever it is before I strangle them." She kissed Amanda tenderly. "Why don't you climb back into bed, and I'll join you in a few minutes?"

"I don't think so." Amanda shook her head. "I'm going with you." She reached around Lex and opened the door. "I think I can hear someone yelling." She took a step, but was stopped when Lex grabbed a handful of her robe.

"Hold on there. Where do you think you're going?" Lex pulled the smaller woman back into the bedroom.

Amanda turned around and looked up into the rancher's eyes. "To answer the door, of course."

The tall woman ran a hand through her dark hair. "I'm not going to win this one, am I?" At the shake of the blonde's head, Lex rolled her eyes and sighed. "At least let me go first, all right?" She grasped Amanda's hand and stepped quietly into the hallway.

The loud thumping turned into pounding as they made their way down the darkened staircase. Amanda walked directly behind Lex, with one hand lightly touching the center of the taller woman's back. When they reached the foot of the stairs, Lex stopped.

"What?" Amanda whispered as her heart pounded.

"That son of a bitch," the rancher growled when she recognized the voice on the other side of the door. Lex turned around and placed a gentle hand on her lover's shoulder. "Stay right here, okay?" Before Amanda could argue she added, "It's Hubert. I don't know what's wrong, but he sounds really pissed."

The younger woman shook her head stubbornly. "All the more reason for me to be with you." When Lex opened her mouth to speak, Amanda covered it with her hand. "I know you're feeling better, but I have no intention of letting you face Hubert alone. So you'll just have to deal with it." She replaced her hand with her lips and left a quick kiss in its place.

"All right. But at least stay behind me. I don't trust him." Lex turned to the front door. The loud pounding was being punctuated by an occasional curse. She quickly opened the heavy oak door and stepped into her brother's flustered face. "What is your major problem this morning, Hubert?"

The angry man roughly pushed his sister aside and stormed into the house. "You never returned any of my calls, and you let me stand outside for over half an hour freezing my ass off." Hubert glared at Amanda, who had stepped up beside Lex and placed her arm around the rancher's waist. *At least my sister's taste has improved. This one's not bad on the eyes.*

Lex closed the door and gestured to the nearby den with her free hand. "Let's go in there to talk. If I have to listen to you whine, I should at least be comfortable."

"Fine by me. But I don't plan on being here very long." He brushed by the two women on his way to the den.

"Are you sure that you two are related?" Amanda whispered to her friend. "I mean, well, I know that you favor one another in the looks department, but he's such a...umm..."

"Whiney-ass?" Lex offered with a smile. "I think he crawled out of the shallow end of our gene pool." She

winked at Amanda. "C'mon. Let's go find out what we did
to deserve his ugly mug on our doorstep at six in the morning."

Amanda slapped her companion lightly on the stomach. "No more old gangster movies for you, honey."

Hubert stood by the fireplace, his arms crossed and an
aggrieved look on his face. " 'Bout time you two got in
here."

Lex led Amanda to the loveseat and then edged past
her brother. She knelt by the hearth to stir the still warm
coals, then added kindling and several small logs. "Shut
up, Hubert," she directed her uninvited guest. She continued to tinker until a cheerful fire blazed in the fireplace.
Satisfied with her results, Lex stood up and dusted off her
hands as she stepped back over to where Amanda was
seated.

"Lexie? What's going on in here?" Martha's voice
called from the doorway. The older woman entered the den
with a confused look on her face. "I thought I saw a light
on in here…" She was about to question Lex further when
she noticed Hubert stalking over to the sofa and sitting
down. "Is everything okay?"

Amanda patted the rancher on the leg and stood up.
"Everything's fine, Martha. Would you mind helping me
start a pot of coffee? I think we could all use a cup." She
linked her arm with the housekeeper's and escorted Martha
out of the room. The young woman could tell that Lex
wanted to talk to her brother alone. *But if he tries anything, I'll personally see to it that Lex becomes an only
child.*

"Okay, Hubert. Now tell me what's so damned important that I've got your lazy butt on my front porch this
early." Lex leaned back on the loveseat and stretched her
long legs out in front of her. She casually linked her hands
against her stomach and glared at her brother. "And make
it quick. I've got things to do."

"Yeah, I'll bet. More like you have a certain little
blonde to do," Hubert scoffed as he propped his muddy

feet on the coffee table in front of him. "I don't blame you, though. She's a hot little...UGH!" His remarks were cut off as Lex straddled his legs and pulled him up by his jacket.

"Shut your filthy mouth." Lex shook her brother as she held him a few inches off of the sofa. "I've tried to be nice because we're family, but I won't sit here and let you talk about Amanda like that." The pain in her still healing arm was excruciating, but she continued to shake the heavier man. "Now either tell me what's on your tiny little mind, or I'll gladly toss your ass back outside. And I won't..."

"Lex." Amanda stood in the doorway with a large tray. "What's going on here?" She hurried into the room and placed the tray on a nearby table. "Let him go, honey." Amanda stood behind her lover and gently tugged back on Lex's shoulders. "Please," she added quietly.

The tall woman slowly released her grip on Hubert's coat. "Watch your mouth," she growled lowly. "One wrong word, and I'll fix it so it'll be wired shut. Got me?" She gave him a rough shove.

Hubert sank back against the sofa. "I got you," he mumbled. "Don't have to get all bent out of shape." He rubbed his chest as Lex slowly eased away from him.

Amanda kneaded the rancher's shoulders as she pulled Lex back to the loveseat. "What happened in here? I was only gone for a minute." She looked over at Hubert, who gave her a nasty look.

"You'll have to ask her, I had nothing to do with it." He aimed his glare at Lex, who sat silently next to the blonde. "She's just a little touchy, that's all."

"Touchy?" Lex almost jumped off the loveseat. "You sorry son of a..."

Amanda grasped the rancher's left arm. "Stop it!" She ran her hand down the strong arm until she held Lex's hand. Giving it a squeeze, she softened her tone to a request. "Just stop it, please."

The dark-haired woman took a few deep breaths and leaned back. "Okay." Lex forced herself to relax and concentrated on the small hand holding her own. "Sorry." She looked over at Hubert, who gave her a smug grin. She returned the look with a serious one of her own. "You ever going to tell us what you're doing here, or are we supposed to guess?"

The smug look vanished from Hubert's face. "If you'd give me half a chance, I would." He made a show of dusting off the front of his jacket. "This damned thing cost me almost eight hundred dollars. You're lucky you didn't tear it." Before his sister could say anything, Hubert continued. "I want to know what you did with those papers. You were supposed to bring them back to my office."

Lex rolled her eyes and shook her head. "You came all the way out here for some stupid papers? Idiot." She squeezed Amanda's hand. "I wanted to check them out before I gave them back. I don't sign just anything, you know."

"What's there to check out? Just sign the damned things and give them to me." Hubert stood up and walked over to the fireplace to stare into the flames. "It's not that big of a deal." He glanced back over his shoulder at his sister, halfway afraid that she'd jump up and slam him into the hearth.

When she felt the body next to hers tense, Amanda decided to join the conversation. "Hubert, did you read those papers?"

Hubert looked at the young woman as if she had just sprouted horns on her head. "Of course I did. That's how I knew that they required both our signatures. Why?"

Lex sighed. "Why? You know that the papers have to do with an inheritance. Did you notice who passed away?" She was no longer angry, just disappointed that she was related to the man across the room. *He knows but I don't think he cares.*

"Yeah, so? It's not like we knew the old broad." Hubert turned away from the fireplace and stuck his hands in his coat pockets. "They didn't want to have anything to do with us, so why should I give a damn?" His voice was tinged with childhood hurt. *Always looking down their noses at Dad, like they were so much better than him...and me. We were better off without them.*

Lex stood up and walked over to him. "You knew she was still alive?" Her voice shook. "All these years you knew that our grandmother was alive, and you never bothered to tell me?" She ran her hands through her hair and stepped to the front window to look outside. The sun was slowly peeking out from behind the hills. *Looks like it's going to be a nice day for a change.*

"Doesn't it bother you at all that your grandmother is dead?" Amanda asked the big man quietly.

Hubert laughed humorlessly. "Bother me? Why should it bother me?" The look he directed at her was almost pity. "An old lady I haven't seen since I was a kid kicked the bucket and left me a large wad of money." He smiled. "Don't get me wrong, hon. I'm thankful but that's about it."

"Get out." Lex had turned around and was leaning up against the wall, her arms crossed over her chest. She pushed away from the wall and clenched her fists, and her voice vibrated with controlled emotion. "You cold-blooded bastard. I want you out of our house. Now."

Her brother walked over to her and looked her straight in the eye. "Oh, come on. You can't possibly have any feelings for someone who deserted us almost twenty five years ago." When he saw the menacing look on Lex's face, Hubert backed off a step. "Okay, I'll leave. But not until I get the signed papers back in my hands."

Lex shook her head and walked around the older man. "Fine. If that's what it takes to get rid of you, I'm all for it." She went into the adjoining office.

"So," Hubert looked over at Amanda, who was still sitting quietly on the loveseat, "you're still here, huh? Didn't think you'd like living out here in the boonies."

Amanda regarded him carefully. "As a matter of fact, I love living out here. It's beautiful, it's quiet, and there's not that many pests around," she smiled sweetly, "usually."

The rancher stepped back into the den and looked over

at her lover, who had a very satisfied smile on her face. *What is she up to? I guess I'll have to ask her later.* Lex had a large manila envelope, which she tossed at her brother. "Now get out. You're not welcome in our house."

OUR house? Sounds like the little gold digger has got her hooks sunk in good. I hope she takes my snotty sister for everything she has. "Gladly. This dusty old place has always given me a headache." Hubert shoved his sister out of his way and stalked out of the room.

Lex followed Hubert and watched as he fought with the front door. "Turn the handle, then pull," she offered sarcastically. "Usually works better that way."

Hubert yanked the door open and stomped outside. "Bitch," he mumbled under his breath. The big man cursed again as he slipped on the bottom step of the porch. "Damned run-down shack."

"He's rather cranky, isn't he?" Amanda observed wryly. She stepped behind Lex and wrapped her arms around the rancher's still body. "Are you okay?"

"Yeah." Lex closed the door and turned around in the younger woman's arms. "I'm just finding it hard to believe that my own brother would keep something like a living grandparent from me." She pulled Amanda close and buried her face in the soft blonde hair.

Amanda rubbed her back comfortingly. "C'mon. I hear a soft warm bed calling us." She turned and led the taller woman to the stairway. "Like you said, it's too early to be up, especially on a holiday."

Lex pulled her lover's hand up to her lips and kissed the knuckles. "I think you're right. We'll worry about all of this stuff later." She held on to Amanda's hand tightly as they walked slowly up the staircase. "Have I told you lately just how much I love you?"

"You may have mentioned it a few dozen times this morning." Amanda snuggled close to the taller woman. "I love you too, Lex." She steered the rancher into the bedroom and pulled the clothes from her body. "C'mon. We've got some serious snuggling to do."

* * * * * * * * *

Several hours later, Lex was seated at the kitchen table while Amanda and Martha worked at getting the dinner ready. "You sure there's nothing I can do to help?"

"We'd kind of like dinner to be edible, honey," Amanda teased, then turned around from where she was chopping vegetables. "What are you doing?"

In her boredom, Lex had balanced items from the table to construct a carefully built tower. The base of the tower was the wooden napkin holder that usually graced the center of the table, and sitting on top of that was a bottle of hot sauce that Lex used on most of her meals. Lying across the top of the hot sauce was a butter knife, and balanced precariously on each end of that were the salt and pepper shakers. Lex was studying the table as she tried to find something else to add to her creation.

"Nothing." Lex leaned back in her chair and grinned.

Martha glanced over her shoulder from her position at the stove. "Good gracious, Lexie. Now I know you're bored." She looked at the precarious structure and shook her head. "Isn't there something that you can find to do for the next hour or so? We should be finished by then, and you'll have someone to play with," she teased.

The rancher tried to appear offended, but the sparkle in her eyes gave her away. "Fine. I know when I'm not wanted." She rose and walked to the doorway. "I'll just go down to the bunkhouse and make sure that Ronnie and Lester don't forget where the house is." Since the rest of the ranch hands had families in town, Lex had given them the day off. She had invited the old cook and the teenager to the main house for dinner, since they were the only ones left behind.

Amanda washed her hands and walked over to where Lex stood. "Why? Can't you just sit back and relax for a while?" She placed her hands gently on the rancher's stomach. "Do you have to be busy all of the time?"

"It's not that." Lex smiled as Amanda unconsciously

played with the buttons on her faded blue flannel shirt. "I just need to get some air. I'm feeling kinda," she took a deep breath and sighed, "stir crazy." She caught the small hands and held them carefully. "But I'll take the jeep instead of riding, okay?"

"And a radio?" Amanda requested nervously. *Stop it. Give the poor woman a break, Mandy.* She looked down and watched as Lex's thumbs traced over her hands.

"Sweetheart." Lex waited until green eyes tracked to her own. "It's okay. I understand." One callused hand caressed Amanda's face. "If you want, I'll just hang around the house."

The blonde shook her head. "No." She leaned into Lex's hand and kissed the palm. "You go and enjoy yourself. I know how you hate to be cooped up for any amount of time."

Lex smiled. "I won't be gone very long, I promise." She leaned down and gave Amanda a kiss. "And I'll take a radio." The rancher hugged her lover and almost raced from the room.

"She's worse than a little kid," Amanda lamented to the housekeeper with a fond grin. "How ever have you stood it all these years?"

Martha moved from the stove over to where Amanda stood and enveloped the blonde in a heartfelt hug. "She's a handful, that's for sure. But I do believe she's met her match in you, sweetie."

Amanda returned the embrace happily. "You think so, huh?" She drew back and escorted the older woman to the window over the sink, where they both watched as the old jeep whizzed by the house. "I hope that shifting gears like that doesn't hurt her arm."

"Honey, if it did, we'd surely never hear about it." Martha patted her on the back and returned to the stove. "But at least she drove, instead of riding that huge horse of hers."

"I suppose." Amanda turned away from the window with a concerned sigh.

* * * * * * * * *

Another rut in the road caused Lex to grit her teeth together and bite back a groan. *Had to get out, didn't you, Lexington? Couldn't just watch a movie or something, could you?* She winced as the jeep hit another deep pothole in the dirt road. Thinking back to the earlier conversation with her brother, the rancher sighed. *All these years I had a grandmother. I wonder why she never acknowledged me?* Driving down the familiar road brought to mind when she was just a teenager.

Two days after turning sixteen, Lex had taken her test to get her driver's license. She hurried home to share her good news with her father. Not finding him at the main house, she jumped into the old truck that they used to distribute hay to the different fields and made the short drive up to the corral.

Rawson Walters was hard at work replacing a worn gate on the corral when he heard the old truck approach. He looked up to see his daughter braking to a stop nearby. When she practically jumped out of the beat up old vehicle, he shook his head. "Lexington. What are you doing? Slow down, girl."

"Hi, Dad!" The teenager raced over to where her father stood with an exasperated look on his weathered features. "You'll never believe it." Lex climbed up on the corral and straddled the top rail, one leg on each side.

"Won't I? What happened?" Rawson put both hands on the small of his back and stretched. "You didn't get into any trouble in school, did you?"

Lex laughed. "No. Not that I know of, anyway," she amended as she brushed her dark bangs from her eyes. "I got my driver's license today. Passed the test first try." The young woman was practically jumping up and down on the fence.

The rancher smiled at his daughter's exuberance. "That's great, honey. I guess I didn't realize you were old enough to take the test yet."

Lex felt part of her happiness fade. "I turned sixteen two days ago, Dad. Don't you remember? Martha made me that cake and everything." And she gave me that really nice shirt she made, but I don't want to tell him about that. He'll just get mad like he usually does when I talk about Martha.

"Oh, right. Well, that's good to hear. I was wondering why we had a cake for dessert that night. She usually makes a pie or cobbler." Rawson felt a twinge of guilt at forgetting his daughter's birthday. Guess it doesn't matter, though. She doesn't seem too upset. "So. Now that you're legal, you about ready to start taking on more responsibilities around here? I thought we'd start you off as foreman, and gradually work you into the rest of the duties."

The teenager bit her lower lip in thought. Her older brother had just gotten his business degree, and never failed to brag to her about what he was going to do when he took over the ranch. "Sure, Dad. If that's what you want. But what about Hubert?"

Rawson looked up into his daughter's face. "Your brother doesn't know a damned thing about ranching. He's more interested in making money than learning what to do around here." He patted her leg and then stepped away. "I'll talk to Hubert. Now since you're already here, why don't you jump down from your perch and help me finish up this gate?"

She smiled happily at the opportunity to work with her father. "Yes, sir." Lex jumped down and picked up one end of the gate. "Does this mean I get to go on the next buying trip?" She had always wanted to go to the auction in Oklahoma, which meant three days in a hotel—something that she'd never gotten to do.

"We'll see. But it also means that you'll be shadowing me for the next couple of weeks. There's a rodeo in Houston later next month that I want to try my hand at, and I want you to be able to handle things here while I'm gone. So get any homework assignments now, and tell your

teachers that you won't be in class for a bit."

"You want me to skip school? But..." Lex had worked hard all year at her perfect attendance. *"The Christmas break starts next month. Then I'll be home for almost three weeks."*

The rancher never understood what was so important about school to his daughter. *I've done okay without a lot of education. I just don't know why she's so all-fired hepped up about it.* Her father looked up with a serious expression on his face. *"I'll be gone by then. You need to learn all you can before I leave."* *What is wrong with this kid?* Rawson wondered. *I would have jumped at the opportunity to get out of school.*

Lex felt tears of anguish burn her eyes. *I won't cry. He'll think I'm still a kid.* She took a deep breath and cleared her throat. *"How about a compromise? I'll get up at four in the morning on Saturday and do whatever you ask. I'll stay up until whenever you say, and do it all again on Sunday."*

"Okay. But you'll also have to get up early every morning and work until time to leave for school. Then come home and work until eleven or twelve o'clock every night. Think you can do it?" Rawson was determined to make certain that his daughter had her priorities straight. *We'll just see how long she can do that before she begs to stay home from school. The ranch is more important than some stupid classes on history and literature.* *"Well, Lexington? Do we have a deal?"* He pulled off his leather work glove and held out his hand.

"Yes, sir!" Lex shook her father's hand firmly. *"When do I start?"*

Rawson laughed and patted her on the back. *"How about now? Let's get this gate finished up, and then we'll take a quick run down to the back pasture and check the fence there."*

Lex pulled the jeep up to the bunkhouse and slowly climbed out of it. She noticed that the building had been recently painted, and that the ground around it was freshly weeded. *Looks like Lester has been busy,* she mused as she reached the front door. Before she could knock, the door opened and Ronnie Sterling's smiling face appeared.

"Hi, Ms. Walters. I told Lester that I heard someone drive up." He had a towel around his shoulders that bore the remnants of recently cut hair. "Whatcha doing here?"

The old cook limped up to the door grumbling. "Hush your mouth, boy. Now get out of the way and let the boss in before she freezes to death." He grabbed the young man's arm and pulled him away from the door. "Sorry 'bout that, boss. He's kinda excitable."

"No problem, Lester." Lex stepped inside and closed the door behind her. She gestured to the chair in the middle of the room. "Setting up a barbershop?" The shining wood floor had a scattering of hair covering it, which Ronnie was already sweeping up.

"Something like that," Lester laughed and walked into the kitchen. "Care for a cup of coffee? Just made a fresh pot a little while ago." He waited until Lex sat down at the table before pouring her a mug. "You're looking a mite better than you were the last time I saw you."

Lex accepted the steaming mug and chuckled. "Thanks, Lester. I'm feeling a hell of a lot better, too. You guys about ready for some of Martha's cooking?" She watched with concern as the older man made his way slowly to the table and sat down. *Damn. I never really thought about it before, but Lester's gotta be pushing seventy by now. He's sure moving a lot slower than I ever remember. Guess I should be looking for an assistant for him, at least. Lord knows the old guy will never want to retire.*

Lester studied the rancher's face for a moment. "Sure thing, boss. Are you feeling okay? You're looking a mite pale."

"Huh?" Lex shook her head slightly. "Yeah, I'm fine. Just thinking." She picked up the mug of coffee and took a cautious sip. "Damn, Lester? Think you could make it any weaker?"

"Oh, sorry about that. Ronnie can't quite stomach the usual stuff yet. So since it was just me and him here, I made it a little lighter than normal." The old man blushed slightly. Lester's usually straggly beard had been neatly trimmed, and his hair had also been recently cut.

Looks like Lester is all cleaned up and ready to go this evening, Lex smiled to herself. "Can I ask you a question, Lester?" *Well, if anyone would remember, it would be him. The old guy's got a mind like a steel trap.*

The grizzled old cook looked up at the serious young woman. *She's sure come a long way in a really short time.* "Ask away, boss. I'll do my best to answer you." He considered the young rancher to be like a granddaughter. *She sure grew up great. Guess ol' Martha did right by her.*

"Do you remember my mother's parents? I know they just kinda disappeared from here after Louis was born." Lex couldn't face the old man any longer and looked down to study the coffee in her cup.

"Sure do. Right handsome couple, they was. But your granddaddy and old man never could get along. They had some mighty nasty arguments I seem to remember. Why are you asking about them now? I just always assumed you didn't want to have anything to do with them, since we never saw them after your daddy left." When he saw the lost look on the young woman's face, Lester unconsciously reached across the table and grasped her forearm. "What's the matter?"

Lex closed her eyes and took a deep breath. *I'm not going to fall apart in front of Lester. It'd freak him out for sure.* She opened her eyes again and patted his hand. "I just found out that my grandmother died, Lester. My father told me years ago that I had no living grandparents. And now I'm trying to figure out why he would lie to me about something as important as that." She stood up and walked over to the large window to peer out at the corral. "It just tears me up inside to think that I lost someone in my family I never had the opportunity to know. And that I lost the last living link to my mother."

Lester pulled himself up and started across the room to the tall woman. "What do you mean, the last living link? Didn't you talk to Travis?"

"Who's Travis?" Lex turned away from the window as the old man approached. "And why would I talk to him?"

"Why, he's your granddaddy, boss. I figured that he's the one who let you know about Mrs. Edwards' passing." Lester rushed forward as Lex, overwhelmed by the news, crumpled to the floor.

Chapter
11

Lex opened her eyes and saw Lester's concerned face hovering above her. "What happened?" she murmured. "Why am I on the floor?"

"Good lord, Miz Lex. Are you okay? You done scared ten years off of me." The old cook ran trembling hands down the reclining woman's arms. "You didn't have a relapse or something, did you?"

"No. I don't think so." Lex slowly rose to a sitting position to lean against the wall. She ran a shaky hand through her hair. "Did I hear you right? My grandfather is alive?"

Lester slowly climbed to his feet. "That's right. At least he was about a month ago when I got his last letter." The old man hobbled over to the radio that sat on the counter. "I'm getting too damned old for all this excitement," he grumbled. He picked up the freestanding microphone and hit the transmit key, signaling the radio at the ranch house. "Excuse me a minute, boss. I gotta buzz the main house before Ronnie gets there."

The rancher slowly rose from her position under the window and sat down at the kitchen table. "Why is Ronnie going up to the..." Understanding dawned in her blue eyes.

"Aw, hell." *Amanda and Martha will come unglued when he gets there.*

"He took off before I could stop him, boss. The little guy just happened to walk into the kitchen about the same time that you hit the floor." He put the microphone to his lips. "Main house, this is Lester. Do you read me?" He released the key and waited.

"Why the radio? Is there something wrong with the phone?" Lex asked, as they waited for a response from the house.

"I was going to tell you about it this evening. It was out yesterday morning when I got up." Lester gave the rancher a shrug of his shoulders.

A clear voice from the radio interrupted him. "I read you loud and clear, Lester. This is Amanda. Is something wrong?" She had been carrying the handheld radio around in her sweater pocket in case Lex called.

The old man glanced over at Lex with a worried look. The dark-haired woman had her arm propped up on the table and rested her forehead on her open hand. "Everything is okay, Miss. But Ronnie is going to show up there any minute now, all excited and upset. Just tell him that you talked to me, and that everything is all right."

"Why is Ronnie on his way up here? What's going on?" Amanda's voice had a slightly panicked tone to it.

"Lester, this is Martha." The housekeeper overheard the conversation and had gently taken the radio away from the distraught young woman. "Is Lexie there with you?"

Lex looked up and saw Lester growing frustrated. She stood up and smoothly took the radio microphone away from him. "Martha? Calm down. Everything is just fine." She leaned back against the kitchen counter and closed her eyes. "I had a little shock a bit ago, and kinda passed out for a minute. But I'm okay now, so just..."

"You passed out? Oh, Lexie. Maybe we should..." Martha was interrupted when Amanda seized the radio.

"Lex? My God, are you okay?" Amanda's voice trembled. "What happened?" She didn't wait for an answer.

"That does it. I knew you were going to overdo it. Just stay right there. I'll get the truck and pick you up in a couple of minutes."

"Wait!" Lex nodded thankfully at Lester when he brought her a chair to sit on. "Sweetheart, I'm fine, really. I just had more of a shock than I was able to handle, that's all."

Amanda took a deep breath and sat down at the kitchen table. "What kind of shock?" She heard a frantic beating on the front door. "I think Ronnie's here, honey." The young woman watched as Martha nodded and left the room. "Now, you were going to tell me what kind of shock would make you pass out."

The rancher chuckled. "Yeah, it does sound sorta strange, doesn't it?" She felt calmer since she could hear Amanda's voice. *Now isn't that pitiful?* "Lester just told me that my grandfather is alive, and I guess it kind of threw me for a loop." *Major understatement, Lexington old girl. More like knocked you senseless.*

Amanda felt a large weight lift off of her shoulders as she realized that Lex was okay. "Oh, honey, that's wonderful news. What else did he say?"

"I don't know. That's when I passed out," Lex admitted ruefully. "But we're about to make our way back to the house. Hopefully we can get Lester to tell us a little bit more about all of this."

Amanda smiled and waved at the teenage boy that Martha escorted into the kitchen. "Sounds great, love. I'll be looking for you." She rose and walked over to the window as if she could see where Lex was calling from. "I love you."

"I love you too, sweetheart. We'll be there in a few minutes, okay?" Lex looked at the old cook, daring him to say something about her use of endearments. She set the microphone down and laughed. "Ronnie made it there in record time. Maybe we should see if he wants to join the school track team."

Lester grabbed his coat from a nearby hook and pulled

it on. "Maybe so. Lord knows that boy has been a godsend for me. He never complains and is always looking for something to do." He went over to a nearby closet and grabbed a metal box and tucked it under his arm. *This should help her understand a little better where Travis and Melanie were coming from. Hopefully she won't hold their absence against them.*

Lex led the old man out of the bunkhouse and closed the door behind them. "Is that so? I'm really glad, Lester. He's had a rough life, that's for sure." She climbed into the jeep and waited for him to do the same. "What's in the box?"

"Something I think you'll be rather interested in, boss. I'm just sorry I didn't show you this before now." Lester looked at the young woman sadly. "I always assumed that you knew about your grandparents, but didn't want to have anything to do with them."

"Don't worry about it." Lex flinched as the jeep hit a particularly rough spot in the road. "Remind me to get some new shocks put on this old thing, would you? This damned road's going to beat me to death." They rode the rest of the way to the main house in silence; each caught up in their own thoughts.

****

Lex pulled the jeep up to the front of the house. She watched as Lester slowly pulled himself out of the vehicle and stretched. "You okay, Lester?" She walked around the rear of the jeep and joined the old man as they walked up the steps to the house.

"Just fine, boss. I reckon this cold weather is just messing around with my old bones. I betcha anything that we're in for a nasty storm soon." Lester limped up the steps next to the tall woman. "How 'bout you? You sure you're feeling okay?"

"Yeah, I'm fine. Just a little sore." Lex opened the door with a grimace. *A little sore? Jeez. I ache all over.*

Wonder if I could talk Amanda into a massage tonight? She smiled to herself as she stepped into the hallway with Lester behind her. *Oh, yeah.*

The cook patted Lex gently on the back and stepped around her. "I'm gonna go hunt down Ronnie and make sure he's okay." He limped down the hallway to the kitchen.

"Lex!" Amanda rushed from the sitting room and wrapped her arms around the startled rancher. "Are you all right?" She pulled back slightly to study the older woman's face. "You look a little pale."

The rancher gently grasped the small hand that was checking her forehead. "I'm just fine, love." She put her sore arm around Amanda's waist and continued to walk down the hall. "Did you two get everything done while I was gone?"

"Yes, we did. And we heard from Gramma, too." *Don't try and change the subject with me, Lexington Marie. I'll find out sooner or later,* she thought to herself. Amanda sighed at the obvious diversion, but allowed Lex to lead her to the kitchen. "They should be here in a couple of hours with Jeanne and Frank."

"Great." Lex inhaled deeply at the kitchen doorway. "Mmmm. It smells great in here," she complimented Martha, who was handing Ronnie a stack of plates. "Looks like you've drafted some more help, Martha." She waved at the young man as he made his way into the next room. "Hi there, Ronnie."

"Hi, Ms. Walters. You doing okay?" Ronnie asked as he carried the plates past her into the next room.

The tall woman favored him with a gentle smile. "Yep. Just great. Thanks for asking."

The housekeeper looked up and smiled warmly at the couple standing in the doorway. "I'm glad you're doing all right, honey, but you look completely worn out. Why don't you go upstairs and lie down for a little while?"

Lex was about to argue when she felt the arm around her squeeze slightly. "Sounds like a good idea. Guess I'll see you all in a bit." She looked down at Amanda and winked. "Wanna help me up the stairs?"

"Of course. I'd hate for you to strain yourself." Amanda grinned at Martha and escorted the rancher from the room.

Lester and Martha both smiled as the couple left. The housekeeper sat down at the table across from the old cook. "Okay. It's just you and me now. Tell me what happened."

"Not a whole lot to tell. Miz Lex asked me about her granddaddy, and I said that he was still around. Next thing I knew, she turned white as a sheet and hit the floor like a rock. Scared me half to death," the old man sighed. "Ronnie walked in about that time and took off like his tail was on fire."

Martha shook her head and sighed. "My poor Lexie. This has all been such a terrible shock for her."

Ronnie came back into the kitchen and stood next to the table. "I set the table, ma'am. Is there something else that I can do for you?"

Martha smiled at the earnest young man. "No, honey. I think you've taken care of everything. Why don't you go into the den and watch a movie? I know that Lexie wouldn't mind."

"Okay, Ms. Rollins. But you come and get me if you need anything done, okay?" Ronnie took off out of the kitchen with a large grin.

Lester chuckled. "That boy never walks anywhere." He sobered and looked at the housekeeper. "I had no idea that the boss didn't know about her grandparents. I just assumed that her old man poisoned her mind against them like he did Hubert's."

"What do you mean? And, forgive me for asking, but how do you know them so well?" Martha refilled both of their coffee mugs from the carafe that sat by her hand.

"Oh, yeah. I reckon we don't run in the same social circles, do we?" The old cook scratched his chin thoughtfully. "Well, it's kinda a long story, but if you're interested..." At Martha's encouraging nod, he continued. "Me and Travis grew up together. We've been good friends for close to sixty years now. He went on to college and made a name for himself in oil exploration, while I went and worked in the oil fields." Lester winked slyly at the smiling housekeeper. "I wanted to make quick cash to spend on the ladies, and Travis decided to go the safer route and build his money slowly."

Martha laughed. "That sounds about right. So you two have kept in touch for all these years?"

The older man nodded. "Yep. When he found out that the ranch needed a cook right after little Victoria got married, he asked me if I would take the job. It made him feel better knowing that there would be someone here to kinda look out for her." Lester tried to unobtrusively wipe a tear from his eye. "When she passed away, he and Melanie tried to get custody of the children—especially young Lexington and Louis. But their daddy fought back, and used Hubert's nasty temperament against them. He and the boy told them that none of them wanted anything to do with their grandparents and to leave them be."

"That's horrible," Martha shook her head sadly, "but why didn't they try to reach Lexie once her daddy left? Surely they thought she'd at least see them."

"Well, they did. Sorta." Lester fiddled with the box that he had laid on the table. "They actually phoned out here not long after Rawson took off, but Hubert was still living here at the time."

Martha's eyes widened. "Oh, no."

Lester nodded as he moved his coffee mug back and forth, leaving a small ring of condensation on the table. "Yep. Hubert told Melanie that they had no use for either her or Travis, and to never bother them again. She was really broken up about it." He trailed his fingertip through the water, leaving a small squiggle design behind. "So me and Travis exchange letters about once a month, and I keep him up to date on the things around here and how young Lex is doing. He was really upset after her accident last week. Told me to call him immediately if she got put in the hospital, and he'd be right down." He looked up sadly. "I'm just so damned sorry that I didn't tell the boss about them sooner. I shoulda known it was all Hubert's doing."

"That's horrible. Going through life thinking that your grandchildren want nothing to do with you. And dear Mrs. Edwards passing away before knowing any different. It's so tragic." The housekeeper brushed a sympathetic tear from her own cheek. "You say that Mr. Edwards is still interested in Lexie?" When the old cook nodded, she smiled as a plan formed in her head. "And you know how to get in touch with him?"

Lester chuckled. "Yep. He's living just north of Dallas right now." He patted the box on the table. "I figured that she might be a little uncomfortable calling Travis on the phone, so I thought I'd give her something that she could use to get to know him first."

* * * * * * * * * *

A couple of hours later, upstairs in their room, Amanda woke to find the tall woman wrapped snugly around her. Lex normally would sleep on her back and pull the blonde close to her, but today she had a death grip on her young lover. *She was a lot more upset than she wanted anyone to know,* Amanda thought as she gently played with the long dark hair that was splayed across her body. The older woman's head was pillowed on her stomach, and her long arms were wrapped tightly around Amanda's body. A quiet knock at the door caused Amanda to look up.

Martha had stood outside the door for several moments, debating with herself as to whether or not she should wake the women inside. She knew that Lex needed all the rest she could get, but Amanda's family had just arrived, and she thought that the younger woman would want to come downstairs to visit. The housekeeper knocked lightly on the door before opening it slowly. "Hi there, honey," she whispered to Amanda, who waved her into the room.

"Hi, Martha. Guess we were both kinda tired." Amanda was thankful that they were too tired to have done anything intimate earlier and were both sporting their usual choice of sleepwear. Lex had on a dark gray tee shirt and black Garfield boxer shorts, and Amanda was wearing a deep blue tee shirt that also belonged to Lex. She looked at the alarm clock and gasped, "Oh, no. I'm so sorry. I was supposed to help you with the dinner preparations. Why didn't you wake me sooner?" She was about to climb out of bed when the housekeeper waved her hand.

"No need, sweetheart. Lester is still pretty handy in the kitchen, and we got everything taken care of. Besides," she winked, "someone had to take care of Lexie, right?" She almost burst into laughter when the dark-haired woman squeezed Amanda tighter and mumbled in her sleep. "I wouldn't have disturbed you now, but your family is downstairs. I thought you might want to visit with your sister for a bit."

Amanda nodded. "I do, thanks. Let me just wake Lex up, and we'll be downstairs in a few minutes, okay?"

Martha smiled as she walked back to the door. "Sure thing, dear. I'll let everyone know that you're on your way." She closed the door behind her.

The young woman directed her attention back to the sleeping form holding her tight. *I really hate to disturb her when she's sleeping this well. Maybe I can sneak out and let her rest for a little while longer.* Amanda tried to scoot sideways slightly, but the rancher maintained her iron grip.

"Mmm...no..." Lex mumbled. Her breath tickled Amanda's exposed stomach where her shirt had ridden up, causing the blonde to giggle slightly.

"Oh, God." Amanda tried to keep from waking her lover. A light kiss near her belly button let her know that she was unsuccessful. "Lex?" She giggled as the dark-haired woman raised her shirt higher and nibbled a path up from her stomach.

Blue eyes sparkled with love for the young blonde.

"Hi there." Lex's voice was deep and slightly scratchy with sleep. "You planning on going somewhere?"

Amanda sighed as she ran her fingers through the tangle of dark hair. "Unfortunately, yes. My family arrived a little while ago, and I thought I'd go downstairs and visit." She looked at the clock on the bedside table. "We've been up here for almost three hours, honey."

"Wanna go for four?" Lex teased as she rose up slightly to give Amanda a kiss. "Who says we have to be sociable, anyway?" she asked after she drew back.

"You don't know how tempting that offer is." Amanda bent down and gave the rancher another, much longer kiss. "But," she sighed, "Martha has already been up here once, and I really don't want to give her any more ammunition for teasing." The housekeeper's favorite pastime was causing Amanda to blush, and the young woman really didn't want to provide her entire family with hours of sport, either.

Lex rolled over and chuckled. "Probably a good idea. Although, if Charlie does what I think he's gonna do, we're going to have the upper hand today." She sat up and stretched her arms over her head. "Ugh."

The smaller woman quickly snuck under Lex's arms and squeezed the rancher tightly. "Mmm." She kissed the tan throat under her lips. "What is Charlie going to do?" She smiled as she felt warm hands travel up the inside of her shirt.

"Well, he...aaah..." Lex squirmed as Amanda reciprocated. Teasing fingers found her most sensitive spots. "Amanda. Damn, woman. That tickles." Lex quickly rolled so that she could pin the blonde to the bed. "Do you really want to play this game right now?" the rancher whispered, as she leaned over Amanda. She held the younger woman's arms above her head with her left hand. "Because I know a few spots that could make you squeal." Lex leaned down further and nibbled on an accessible earlobe.

"Lex," Amanda pleaded. "Please. My family is downstairs." She remembered the last time they got into a tickle fight. Martha had heard her scream and burst into the room wielding her broom, much to the rancher's delight. "You wouldn't..." Her eyes widened as the older woman got a diabolical grin on her face. "Umm, please?" she begged sincerely.

The blue eyes softened as Lex released her hold. "I shouldn't let you get away with this, but I will." The rancher climbed off of Amanda and chuckled. "This time." She pulled the younger woman into her arms and hugged her. "C'mon, before your sister comes up here looking for you."

****

The dinner was certainly a rousing success, Martha noted happily as she looked around the table at the empty plates. The housekeeper sat between Frank and Charlie, and she exchanged an amused glance with Anna Leigh who was directly across from her. Lex sat at the head of the table with Amanda and Jeannie on either side of her, arguing good-naturedly back and forth. She was trying to follow the conversation between the two sisters over who destroyed whose doll years ago.

"Are you denying that you completely hacked off her hair?" Jeannie asked her sister. "She looked like a blasted GI Joe when you got through with her."

Amanda waved her fork at the auburn-haired woman. "It wasn't that bad. Besides, it was the only way I could get the gum out." She took another bite of the pumpkin pie that Anna Leigh had brought. "It didn't hurt her any. Not like what you did with my Jane and Johnny West dolls that Uncle Morris bought me at that garage sale." The ten-inch dolls were dressed with molded on turquoise western clothes. Amanda loved them and played with the already worn dolls for hours, much to her mother's distaste.

Jeannie grinned at Lex, who was watching them with an amused look. "Oh, I dunno. Seems to me that it was rather prophetic, don't you think?"

"What do you mean by that? You ripped their heads off and switched them, then glued them so I couldn't change them back. Johnny West was the first cross-dressing action-figure in California." Amanda noticed where her sister's attention was directed. "Why?" She looked at the rancher and giggled. *She's got a point. I did find my very own action figure.*

Lex looked at Jacob for an explanation. The older man shrugged his shoulders and watched as both of his grand-daughters laughed hysterically. "I have no idea, Lex." Just as the two women would get their mirth under control, one or the other of them would glance back up at the dark-haired woman and start all over again.

"How does she look in turquoise, Mandy?" Jeannie gasped out between giggles.

This caused Amanda to break out in laughter all over again. "Lex...turquoise..." she began, then chortled hyster-ically once again.

"Okay children," Lex sighed and looked at the other people at the table. "Does anyone know what is wrong with these two?" She watched as her partner reached out with one hand and grasped her arm. "What?"

"Sorry." Amanda rubbed the rancher's arm gently. "It's just that..." She giggled again.

Anna Leigh smiled at Lex's raised eyebrow. "Let me see if I can shed some light on the subject, while Amanda and Jeannie clear the table." She gave each woman a look that caused them both to stand, still giggling, and to carry plates into the kitchen. "When Mandy was about, oh, eight I guess, her mother's brother Morris took the girls for a drive while Elizabeth had some silly tea party or some-thing." The look on her face clearly illustrated what she thought about that. "Anyway, they happened upon an estate sale, and Morris decided to stop and let the girls look around. Jeannie found this beautiful wind up merry-go-round, and asked Morris if she could have it. Of course he said yes—that man just adored the girls," she sighed. "Sorry. So he told Mandy to pick out something too. She found these old dolls, similar to Barbie dolls. They had these blue bodies that were supposed to be denim clothes, and were dressed western style."

Lex suddenly realized where this was all going. "And Jeannie switched the heads on the boy and girl dolls?"

"Oh, yes. It was quite funny. But Elizabeth noticed little Mandy playing with a woman doll that had the body of a man, and I believe she threw it away. She was already upset because the toys were used—let alone not in perfect condition."

"That's a shame. It sounds like Amanda really enjoyed them." Lex felt a pang of regret for not knowing her friend then. *I would have found her more dolls, if that's what she wanted,* she vowed. *Hmm. I wonder...* "I don't mean to upset you, but why do you look so sad when you talk about Morris? He sounds like a great guy."

Jacob patted his wife's hand and addressed the rancher. "Morris has been disowned by the Kingston family, including his sister—Elizabeth."

The rancher shook her head. "Why? Is he a mass-murderer or something?" She was slightly confused by the sad looks on the older couple's face.

Frank, who had been listening to the entire conversation, finally spoke up. "Worse. At least in their eyes. He's gay," he uttered quietly. "He brought his...umm...significant other to Mandy's graduation. There was a nasty fight, and he was kicked out of the family." He looked up at Lex with a pained expression. "Mandy was devastated. As far as I know, she hasn't heard from him since. No one has, I guess."

"That's not entirely true, Frank." Anna Leigh spoke up with a proud smile. "We hear from him every now and then. I think he's somewhat adopted Jacob and I. He and..." She paused and looked at Jacob.

"Kevin, isn't it?" her husband offered.

Anna Leigh nodded. "Right. Thank you, darling. They send us cards on all the major holidays. We've been trying for years to get them to come down and visit." She gave

Lex a serious look. "Maybe if he realizes that he'd be welcome, we could get them both here for Christmas."

Lex grinned. "Sounds great." She heard the sisters,
still laughing, make their way back from the kitchen.
"Let's just keep it a secret though, okay?" Nods from
around the table answered her.

"Hi, Slim." Jeannie walked into the room and wrapped
an arm around the rancher's shoulders. "Sorry to be such a
ninny." She placed a kiss on the stunned woman's cheek
then grabbed a few more dishes from the table. "But knowing how fond of that damned doll Mandy was..."

Amanda stepped in behind her sister and dropped into
her startled lover's lap. "She's right. I loved that doll." She
placed a quick kiss on Lex's nose. "But I've got the real
thing, now."

Lester, who was at the other end of the table, laughed
and slapped Charlie on the arm. "Ain't that a hoot? Little
Lex being a doll?"

The sheriff chuckled and nodded. "You got that right."
He reached under the table and clasped Martha's hand.
"She really is though, isn't she?"

"Darn right." Martha squeezed his hand and smiled.
She started to get up, but was stopped by the rancher's
raised hand.

"Don't even think about it. We'll take care of the
cleanup." She raised an eyebrow at Amanda and the young
woman climbed off of her lap.

Ronnie jumped up, glad to have something to do. "I'll
help," he offered.

Martha looked across the table and smiled at Anna
Leigh. "I guess this means the rest of us can go relax in the
den." She began to stand, but was startled when Charlie
solicitously pulled her chair back for her. "Thank you,
honey."

"Any time, sweetheart." The sheriff nervously reached
into the right pocket of his pants. *The ring is still there.
Now I just gotta figure out the best time to...*

"Charlie? Are you okay?" Martha was concerned by

the faraway look in the lawman's eyes. "You look a little distracted."

Charlie snapped back to the present. "Huh? Oh, yeah. I'm great." He gave the worried woman a smile. "Why don't we get out of the way so the kids can clean up?"

Frank stood up and grabbed the nearly empty turkey platter. "That's a great idea. It won't take us any time at all, and then we'll join you."

Lex smiled at the housekeeper. "You're outnumbered, Martha. Go relax for a change, and let us take care of everything."

"You go with them, honey. There are plenty of us to handle the dishes and such." Amanda rubbed Lex's back with one hand. "No sense in you overdoing it." When she saw the rancher's mouth open to argue, the blonde covered her mouth with her hand. "Please? For me?" she added in a soft whisper.

Blue eyes softened and crinkled into a smile. When the small hand was pulled away, Lex grinned. "For you." She winked and followed Anna Leigh and Jacob from the room.

Amanda watched as Lex left. "That was way too easy," she murmured.

"You think she's up to something?" Jeannie asked from behind her. "She did give in pretty quickly. C'mon. Let's get everything cleaned up so we can find out what Slim has up her sleeve." The older woman swatted her sister on the rear.

"Hey!" Amanda squealed. She turned around and chased her sister back through the mudroom. "I'll get you for that."

Chapter
12

Lex closed the front door with a heavy sigh. *God, it's been a long day.* She had just returned from dropping off Lester and Ronnie at the bunkhouse, tired from fighting the heavy sleet that had begun to fall on the way back. She had spent the entire drive talking to Lester about her family.

"So, Lester," Lex had to drive slowly in deference to the heavy sleet, "tell me about my grandparents." She glanced in the rear view mirror at Ronnie, who was listening to the handheld cassette player that Amanda had given him. He was silently nodding his head to the music coming through the headphones, oblivious to the conversation in the front seat of the jeep.

The old man chuckled. "Well. I don't rightly know where to start. And I don't think that we have that much time." Lester met the rancher's serious eyes. "But I'll be more than happy to answer any questions for you." He was still feeling guilty for not mentioning the Edwards sooner.

Lex grimaced as the jeep hit a patch of icy mud, and she fought to keep the old vehicle on the road. "Anna Leigh told me that Mr. Edwards, my grandfather, almost

*disowned my mother when she married Dad. Is that true?"
What kind of man would desert his only child just because
of who she married? I'm not sure he'd want to have anything to do with me.*

"Not really." *Lester knew exactly what the young
woman was thinking.* "Travis adored little Victoria. He
wouldn't have done anything to jeopardize their relationship."

"Then what?"

Lester sighed. "I reckon someone overheard him when
he told her that her husband would never be welcome in
their home. Believe me, he regretted that almost the instant
he said it. But Travis is a proud man, and doesn't back
down very easily."

Lex exhaled heavily. "I wonder why? I know that Dad
is not the classiest guy in the world, but surely they didn't
hold his job against him."

"Hell, no. Travis didn't care what the man did for a
living. Truth is, he'd rather she hooked up with someone
who did an honest day's work." *The old cook scratched his
beard thoughtfully.* "I think that it was the fact
that...umm..." *He paused, too embarrassed to continue.*

"What?" *Lex turned to look at the suddenly silent
man. The jeep hit another patch of ice, and she wrestled
the steering wheel to keep it steady.* "Damn! This stuff's
getting worse."

A loud chuckle answered her. "Sure seems like it,"
Lester commented as he braced himself against the dash.
"You ain't fixin' to wrap us around a tree, are ya?"

*She steered into the skid and kept the vehicle on the
road.* "Not if I can help it." *They both heaved great sighs
of relief when the jeep steadied.* "You were about to tell me
what caused all the bad feelings between my grandfather
and Dad?"

"Oh, yeah." *Lester shook his head.* "They...umm...had
to get married." *He blushed slightly.* "Travis was livid, to
say the least."

"Had to? What do you...?" *Lex nearly drove off the*

road. "*She was pregnant?*" Damn. No wonder they never got along. "*They were forced to get married because she was going to have a baby?*"

Lester looked at the young woman. "*Not really forced. Just had to hurry, that's all.*" *He patted her gently on the shoulder.* "*Your daddy was plumb crazy about Victoria. He was thrilled when he found out that she was carrying his child.*"

That's so hard to believe. I don't think I can ever remember seeing Dad smile, much less happy. "*So it was more of an issue of honor, than anything else?*"

"*Rawson upset Travis because he was so happy about Victoria's condition. He thought that your father must have taken advantage of her and gotten her pregnant to get at her money,*" *Lester explained.* "*That made your daddy mad, and pretty much started the whole feud.*"

Lex pulled the jeep up in front of the bunkhouse in relief. God. I thought we'd never make it. "*So my grandfather isn't too bad of a guy, then?*" *she turned and asked Lester.*

He laughed. "*Travis is one of the best fellas I've ever known. I'd do anything for him, and have. The stuff in that box should help you understand him and Melanie more than the ramblings of an old man like me.*" *Lester turned around and poked Ronnie, whose eyes popped open. The young man pulled off the headphones and smiled.* "*You 'bout ready to go inside, boy?*"

"*We're here?*" *Ronnie stuck the stereo in his coat pocket.* "*Yes, sir. I'm ready.*"

"*You wanna bunk down with us tonight, boss? I'm a little worried about you trying to get back with the way the roads are getting.*" *Lester studied the rancher carefully.* She's looking a bit pale, too. "*How about it? I'll even let you beat me at poker.*"

"*Yeah, right. You couldn't even beat me if you cheated—which I think you've done on more than one occasion.*" *Lex shook her head.* "*I'd better get back to the house, though. I want to make sure none of our guests try to drive home in this weather." She leaned tiredly against the steering wheel. "Just radio if you need anything. I'll keep a handheld nearby until we can get someone out to check the phone lines."*

Lester climbed slowly out of the jeep and pulled Ronnie out behind him. "You be careful driving back, boss. I've already bought your Christmas card, and I don't want it to go to waste."

Lex laughed. "Don't worry, Lester. I plan on being around for a long time. Now get inside before you freeze to death." She watched fondly as Ronnie walked closely behind the old cook to make sure he didn't slip and fall. He's a good kid. I'm glad he's here to watch out for Lester. Lex shook her head and threw the jeep into reverse, which caused the vehicle to slide sideways and almost hit the nearby corral. "Damn!" She edged it back slowly to the main road and drove very cautiously back to the ranch house.

Lex rubbed her eyes tiredly. *I'll have to have Amanda sit down with me when I go through that little box. It sure was nice of him to leave it behind for me.* She could hear laughter in the den where Amanda was entertaining her family with stories of her life on the ranch. Lex hung up her drenched duster and hat, then peeked into the brightly-lit room.

"So Lex tried to sneak back into the house, looking like some sort of bog monster or something." The blonde woman stood in the center of the room, gesturing wildly with her hands.

Martha laughed. "She looked so pitiful, especially with the clumps of mud and twigs all over her." She shook her head regretfully. "And those socks. I had to throw them out—not even bleach helped."

"It wasn't that bad." Lex walked slowly into the room and tried to ignore the amused looks she received from around the den. Everyone was laughing except for Charlie, who was staring blankly into the fire. *Poor guy. He'd bet-*

ter pop the question soon, or he's gonna go crazy. "I hope you all are very comfortable where you are," the rancher drawled, "because the weather has gotten really nasty, and I'm not about to let anyone drive home in it." She stepped over to the fireplace and stood close to the fire, rubbing her hands briskly to warm them.

Amanda made her way across the room to stand next to the tall woman. "Are you okay, honey? Maybe I should go get you some coffee or hot chocolate." She rubbed Lex's back. "Good thing we've got that second guest room upstairs now, huh?" With her help and support, Lex had boxed up the mementos in Louis' room. The rancher had given most of his clothes to Ronnie, and sold off the furniture. Amanda had been in charge of redecorating, and had given the room a completely different look—much to her lover's pleased surprise.

"Yep. Shall we give the new room to your grandparents?" Lex asked with a smile. If she knew her friend like she thought she did, Amanda and her sister would spend half the night up chatting anyway. *Might as well put her and Frank across the hall so they won't have so far to travel,* she mused.

Charlie stood up nervously to address the room. "Well, since we're all here for the night, I've got an announcement to make." He looked over at Martha fondly. "More like a request, I guess. Since we're all practically family anyway." The sheriff took a couple of steps and dropped to one knee in front of the shocked housekeeper. "I'd like to take this opportunity to ask Martha to become my wife." Charlie took her smaller hands in his and brought them to his chest. "Sweetheart, I've loved you for longer than I can even remember. I'm not trying to take you away from here, but I think it's about time that you started thinking about yourself. Will you marry me?" He reached into his pocket with one hand and pulled out a ring and slid it on Martha's finger.

"I...uh..." Martha stammered uncharacteristically. The gold ring had two large diamonds offset by four smaller diamonds on each side. The two rows of gems sparkled brightly on her hand.

Lex grinned at the housekeeper's discomfort. "The proper response is yes," she teased.

Martha looked over at Lex with tears in her eyes. *She's right. I think that my little Lexie is in good hands now.* She glanced over at Amanda and smiled and then looked back at Charlie. "Yes." She pulled the lawman up off the floor. "Get off your knees, you crazy old man and come here."

"Y...y...yes?" Charlie seemed to have caught her stammer as he stood with her and was pulled into a strong hug. "You mean it?" He picked Martha up and swung her around the room. "All right!"

The rancher watched happily as the couple sealed their engagement with a kiss. *'Bout damn time. I wonder how quickly we can get the wedding together?* She looked over at Anna Leigh and Jacob, who gave her a thumbs up. *Bet I'll have plenty of help in that department.*

Once the happy couple broke apart, Jacob stood up and cleared his throat. "Congratulations, you two. I know this is rather sudden, but do you have any idea what kind of wedding, or where you want it to be held?"

"Wedding?" Martha and Charlie both asked together. "I figured we'd just go down to the Justice of the Peace and have it done," Martha answered, then looked at Charlie. "Right, honey?"

"Absolutely not," Lex practically yelled, which caused the entire room to fall silent.

Amanda clasped her arm lightly. "Lex, what are you saying?" *She can't be against them getting married. We've talked about this. What's going on in that head of hers?*

Lex gently shook off Amanda's hand and stepped towards the older couple. "I will not stand by and let you do this." She took Charlie's hand from Martha's and pulled him to her.

"Lex." Amanda started to her friend, but was halted by Lex's raised hand. "What...?"

"Shhh." The dark-haired woman waved her partner

off. Lex looked deeply into the old lawman's eyes. "I will not let two of the most important people in my life go to the damned Justice of the Peace to get married." She pulled Charlie to her and hugged him tightly. "Congratulations, Uncle Charlie," she whispered into his ear. Lex leaned back and looked at Martha. "It doesn't have to be a large ceremony, but you've got to let us do this for you, please." She nodded at Amanda, who gestured to Jeannie and they both sneaked quietly from the room.

"You little brat." Martha stepped over to where Lex stood and slapped the tall woman on the shoulder. "I ought to tan your backside for scaring poor Charlie like that." She wrapped her arms around Lex and pulled her into a bone-jarring hug. "Did you know he was going to do that?"

The rancher kissed the top of Martha's head. "I thought he was, just by the way he'd been acting all day." She looked down into the older woman's brown eyes. "I'm just so damned happy that you finally said yes. I know you two are going to have a lot of good years together, Mada." Lex felt the need to call the older woman by the name that Louis had given her all those years ago. "It'll be nice to have a real father figure around here again." She remembered the talk that Charlie had with her recently.

Lex had called the sheriff at home to make sure he would be at the ranch for Thanksgiving dinner. She wanted to give him a personal invitation, so that Charlie would realize how welcome he would be.

"This is Sheriff Bristol," Charlie answered the phone in his usual official tone.

"Hello, Sheriff. I need your help," Lex whispered, trying to keep the laughter out of her voice.

He sat up in his chair, suddenly alert. "What seems to be the problem, Miss...?" The voice was too quiet to recognize.

"There's this woman..." Lex paused dramatically.

"Yes? What's wrong?" Charlie asked anxiously.

Lex had to cover her mouth to stifle a giggle. "She's

expecting..."

Charlie grabbed a notepad and pen. *"Is she in labor?
Have you called an ambulance? What's the matter?"*

*"She's expecting to see you Thursday for dinner. You'd
better not be late."* She couldn't control herself any longer,
and laughed out loud.

"Lex?" Charlie dropped his pen and shook his head.
"What am I gonna do with you, girl?"

The rancher continued to laugh. *"Gotcha, Uncle
Charlie."* She couldn't explain it, but for some reason
lately she had begun to call him *"Uncle"* again. He didn't
protest, so Lex didn't really think that much about it. She
sobered for a moment. *"Seriously, I just wanted to make
sure that you'll be here for Thanksgiving dinner."*

The sheriff smiled. He remembered fondly when Lex
would call his office for a prank. Guess she's never out-
grown that. *"Martha made it pretty clear last night that
I'm supposed to be there."* He blushed when he realized
how that sounded. *"I mean, when I dropped her off last
night."* Charlie had driven her home after their usual Saturday night movie date. *"So don't worry, I'll be there."*

*"You know, it would be a lot easier on you if you lived
closer to the ranch,"* Lex mentioned matter-of-factly. *"Like
in a certain little cottage?"* she hinted.

"Umm...well..." the lawman stammered, at a loss for
words.

Lex laughed again. *"C'mon, Uncle Charlie. Would it
be so horrible? I think it's about time that you two settled
down, don't you?"*

Charlie sighed. *"I asked her again about three months
ago, honey. She still said no."* I'm beginning to think that
it's time to give it up. She'll never say yes.

"Do you have a ring?" Lex asked, trying to get him
out of his mood.

*"Yeah. For all the good it'll do. Might as well return
the damned thing,"* he mumbled.

The rancher chuckled. *"Don't send it back just yet,
Uncle Charlie. I have it on good authority that a certain*

lady would be really receptive to the right question, now."

"She's said something to you?" He sat up suddenly.

"Not to me, no."

The sheriff slumped in his chair again. "Then what makes you think...?"

Lex lowered her voice slightly. "A little bird told me." She looked up to make certain her office door was closed. "She was talking to Amanda yesterday, and told her she finally felt good about where I was in my life." She paused for a moment, having to blink away the sudden tears in her eyes. "I'm sorry, Uncle Charlie. If it wasn't for me, she would have accepted your proposals years ago, I'm sure."

"Don't apologize, sweetheart. We've both been worried about you. Neither one of us would have been comfortable with you living out there all alone." Charlie felt the weight of the young woman's guilt. "Martha would never think of leaving you like that."

"I'm hoping that won't happen." When Lex heard Charlie stop breathing, she continued in a rushed voice, "I hope that YOU'LL move into the cottage. It would be great to have you around more."

Charlie released the breath he had been holding. "I'd love that, honey. Especially since I never want to take Martha away from her home, or her family."

She looked at the picture of the older couple that she kept on her desk. It had been taken last Fourth of July, and they were wearing matching red, white, and blue shirts. "Good. It's settled, then. Why don't you ask her again? I bet you'll get the answer you've always wanted." She picked up the photo and studied it fondly. They were standing side by side—Charlie's long arm draped protectively across the housekeeper's shoulders. Both were smiling happily for the camera, and at the tall woman who stood behind it.

.   "I just might do that, honey," Charlie agreed. "I'll see you Thursday, all right?"

Everyone's attention turned back toward the doorway

when Amanda bustled in with a large wooden tray, eight glasses carefully balanced on it. Jeannie followed closely behind with a bottle of champagne nestled in a bucket of ice. Both women were smiling broadly.

"Here we go," the blonde cheerfully announced as she set the tray down on the coffee table.

Martha was stunned. "Where did that come from?" She looked from Lex to Charlie, then back to Amanda. "I know I would have noticed something like that in my kitchen."

"We had it hidden in our room," Lex informed her with a satisfied smirk. "I thought that we'd find some use for it even if Charlie chickened out." She playfully poked the older man in the ribs. "Right?"

Charlie blinked and shook his head. "Me? Chicken out?" He accepted a hearty handshake from Jacob. "Perish the thought. I decided earlier that if she said no, I'd just keep asking her today until she agreed."

"Good for you, Charlie. May you both have all the happiness you deserve." Jacob pulled his wife to him with one arm.

Anna Leigh looked at Martha, who stood with Amanda and Jeannie. "That's right. Although I've only known her through my association with Lexington, I feel that Martha is a wonderful woman." She smiled as she watched the housekeeper play with her new ring. "Congratulations, Charlie."

Lex waited until everyone had a glass of champagne, then raised hers in a toast. "Martha. Charlie." She smiled lovingly at the couple. "We may not be related by blood, but as far as I'm concerned, you two have been the most wonderful parents that any person could ever hope to have. Here's wishing you a lifetime of happiness together."

Everyone around the room raised their glasses with murmured words of encouragement. Charlie grinned as Martha blushed. "Thank you, Lex. Everyone. I know I speak for Martha too when I say that you have always been the best daughter we could ever have asked for."

"That's right, honey. I've always been proud of you."

The housekeeper stepped away from her fiancé and embraced the now-blushing rancher. Martha leaned back and looked deeply into Lex's eyes, noticing with a tiny smile the unshed tears. "But don't think for a minute that you'll be able to get rid of me easily. I'd still like to take care of the ranch house, if you'll let me."

"Let you? My God, Martha, I don't think this ranch could survive without you." Lex saw the smile of agreement on Amanda's face. "But I think we can handle it for a couple of weeks while you are on your honeymoon."

Charlie and Martha both paled. "Honeymoon?" they choked out together.

Amanda laughed as she stepped forward. "Don't worry about it, you two. You have plenty of time to be nervous later." She turned them towards the doorway. "I'm sure you have lots to discuss, so why don't you go on to the cottage and we'll see you both tomorrow?"

"You little sneak," Martha whispered in the younger woman's ear. "Not known for your subtlety, are you?" She playfully swatted Amanda on the rear before walking through the doorway. "Goodnight, everyone." The housekeeper grabbed Charlie by the arm and led the blushing lawman out of the room.

"They're just too cute," Jeannie chuckled. She stepped over to Lex and wrapped an arm around the rancher's waist. "So, Slim, you're looking a little pale. Maybe you should head off to bed, too." She winked at Amanda. "What do you say, little sister? Need some help?"

Lex rolled her eyes. "Lord help me," she muttered, "I'm surrounded." She looked over at Frank, who was trying to control his laughter. "Aren't you going to help?"

The big man shook his head. "I think that the two of them could handle you just fine, Lex. Besides," Frank stepped closer until he was face to face with the tall woman, "I didn't think I was your type." He quickly jumped away before Lex could grab him. "What?" he asked innocently.

Jeannie pulled the rancher into a protective hug.

"C'mon, Slim. He's just jealous because you have two women, and he doesn't." She winked saucily at her husband.

"You kids are all crazy." Jacob shook his head at the antics of the group in front of him. "Peanut, why don't you point me in the direction of our room, and we'll get out of your way?"

Amanda stepped between her grandparents and linked arms with them both. "You're never in the way, Grandpa. But if you're ready to call it a night, then I'll show you to the new guest room." She turned to call over her shoulder as they started for the doorway. "Lex? Why don't you drag my goofy sister and her brave husband along?"

"Brave?" Lex smirked at Frank, who was backing away from her slowly. "More like intelligence impaired, if you ask me." She watched in appreciation as Amanda escorted the Caubles from the room. *Mmm. Nice. She's got the cutest little...*her thoughts were interrupted by a grumble from beside her.

"Hey. Did she call me goofy?" Jeannie blustered. "I ought to..." She started to chase after her sister, but was grabbed from behind. "Oof!" A strong hand took a firm grasp on her belt.

Lex pulled the feisty woman back. "Hold on there." She looked over at Frank, who stood by the door. "Why don't you come over here and take your wife?"

"Don't look at me. She's your problem now," Frank laughed as he left the room.

Jeannie looked up at the dark-haired woman innocently. "Make you a deal, Slim."

"Hmm?"

"You don't kill my husband," the smaller woman traced a pattern on Lex's arm, "and I won't attack my sister. Deal?"

The rancher laughed. "Deal." She wrapped an arm around Jeannie and led her from the room. "But we don't have to let them know that, right?"

* * * * * * * * *

"I can't believe you did that to poor Frank." Amanda was curled up beside Lex in their bed a couple of hours later. "The poor man almost swallowed his tongue." She ran a light fingertip down the dark-haired woman's chest.

Lex chuckled as she reached over and switched off the bedside light. "Served him right." She pulled Amanda close to her and kissed the blonde head. "You looked a little rattled yourself."

The rancher and Jeannie had unintentionally found a way to get back at their respective partners. They had stepped into the guestroom arm in arm, and saw Amanda sitting on the edge of the bed next to Frank. Jeannie had taken one look at the scene and practically come unglued. "I can't believe it. Mother was right. You've always been after my husband."

Lex followed Jeannie into the room, her face dark with fury. She walked over to where Frank stood and jabbed a finger into his chest. "Is that right? Are you trying to take Amanda away from me?" She saw the big man pale slightly.

"Stop it!" Amanda jumped between the two and quickly pushed Lex away from her brother-in-law. "What's gotten into you both?" She was about to continue when Jeannie collapsed onto the bed in laughter.

"Oh, God. You should see the looks on your faces," the auburn-haired woman chortled. "Slim, you play the jealous lover quite well." She squealed when her sister jumped on top of her, tickling her unmercifully. "Aaaah! Mandy, stop it. You're gonna make me pee my pants."

Amanda straddled her sister and worked furiously on the older woman's ribs. "I can't believe you did that." She stopped her torture long enough to look over her shoulder at the tall woman still standing behind her. "And you."

"Now, sweetheart," Lex raised her hands palms up, as she backed away slowly, "it wasn't my idea, but," she grinned wickedly, "you gotta admit, we got you pretty

good." When she saw the look in Amanda's eyes, she looked at Frank for help. "You want to hold her back long enough so I can make a break for it?"

Frank laughed at the look on the rancher's face. "After you almost made me mess my pants? I don't think so." He saw the gleam in the blonde's eyes. "You'd better run now, my friend."

The young woman was about to leap from the bed when her sister wrapped her legs around her small waist. "Go ahead, Slim. I've got you covered," Jeannie yelled. She laughed as her sister turned and continued her tickle attack. "Aaah!"

Amanda kissed Lex on the throat gently. "That was so evil. But funny." She reached up and ran her fingers through the dark hair. "How are you feeling, honey? You looked pretty worn out earlier."

"I'm okay. Just a little tired, I guess. Been a long day." Lex captured the hand and brought it to her lips. "The dinner turned out well, don't you think?" She kissed Amanda's palm, which caused the younger woman to moan slightly.

"Mmm. God. When you do that..." Amanda squirmed even closer and burrowed her head into the older woman's chest. "What was the question again?"

Lex edged her other hand up under the back of the younger woman's shirt. "Hmm?" She gently massaged the soft skin. "Question?" Her own thoughts were clouding over due to the attention her chest was getting from Amanda's lips.

The blonde unbuttoned Lex's nightshirt, leaving a trail of kisses in the wake of her fingers. Amanda smiled as the dark-haired woman moaned and arched up into the contact. "You like that?" she whispered.

"Uh-huh." Lex pulled Amanda's tee shirt over the blonde head. "Sure do." She rolled them over so that Amanda was below her. "C'mere."

* * * * * * * * * *

"Look at this, honey." Amanda handed Lex a small photograph that looked as if it had been taken at a zoo. There was a young girl about three years old being held in front of some sort of fenced off pit. The gentleman holding her appeared to be in his late forties or early fifties and was smiling broadly. They looked very much alike, with their dark hair and light colored eyes. "I think this may be you with your grandfather."

Lex accepted the photograph gingerly. She turned it over and saw in neat writing, *Lexie and Travis 1975*. "You're right." She turned the picture back over and studied it carefully. A small frown crept onto her face. "I just wish I could remember him."

Amanda rubbed her hand across the taller woman's back in a comforting motion. "I know, love." She scooted the small box that lay opened between them on the bed out of the way, and moved closer to Lex. The rancher had awakened her with gentle kisses earlier, and then at Amanda's insistence tiptoed downstairs to get the mysterious box that Lester had left behind.

"It's just so strange," Lex murmured, still looking at the photograph. She also had a letter that Travis had written around that same time. "Could you...?" Lex handed the letter to Amanda to read.

"Sure, honey." Amanda accepted it. *"My friend, I hope that things are going well for you at the ranch. Melanie and I finally talked Victoria into allowing us to take little Lexie overnight back up to Dallas. We had promised her a trip to the zoo, and as the enclosed picture suggests, we made good on that promise. What a wonderful child she is! Smart and beautiful just like her mother, although I can see a streak of stubbornness that could only come from Rawson. As you know, there are no such personality quirks like that on our side of the family.*

"Have I properly thanked you for taking that position at the ranch? We are forever in your debt, my longtime friend, for giving us some peace of mind while our little

girl is marooned out there in the middle of nowhere. She did promise not to give you away to Rawson, but more out of respect for your position than anything else. I did let it slip that since you had been injured in that accident in the oil fields, you needed the stability of the job you now had. Please forgive an old man for a minor untruth, if you will. Victoria thinks of you as an uncle, as she should. You have always been a brother to me, ever since we were five and chasing the little girls together.

"*I'm sorry to cut this note so short, but Melanie just came in with exciting news. Our little Victoria just called, and she is expecting another child! God forgive me for say-ing so, but I hope this next child has Lexie's personality, and not Hubert's. That boy is so much his father's son. It's a shame, too. We've tried to get him to warm to us, but he is quite hateful towards us both. I can handle it, but I hate to subject my dear Melanie to his childish tirades. Well, I'll sign off for now. It seems our daughter wants us to visit the ranch next weekend, to share in her happy news. So I will see you then, my good friend. Sincerely, Travis.*"

Lex continued to study the photograph as Amanda's voice trailed off quietly. "This must have been one of the last times I actually saw my grandparents." She closed her eyes as she tried to remember the past.

"Honey?" Amanda put down the letter and touched Lex's cheek. She waited until the blue eyes opened and tracked to hers. "Are you all right?"

"Yeah." Lex studied Amanda's face and smiled. "You think he would mind a phone call from me sometime?"

Amanda smiled back at the rancher and hugged her tight. "I think he'd love it, Lex. Just like I know he loves you."

The rancher buried her nose in the blonde hair and took a deep breath. "I hope so. But I at least want him to know that he's welcome here, no matter what my father or brother may have told him at the time." She felt the younger woman's arms squeeze around her tightly.

"He'll know, honey. And I'm sure he will be thrilled to

finally get to know his granddaughter again after all these years." Amanda leaned back slightly so that she could look into Lex's eyes. A strong gust of wind blew against the house, whistling shrilly. "But, do you think we can stay up here for a while and snuggle? It's still really early, and I don't want to get out of this warm bed just yet." Amanda shivered as she heard the sound of sleet beating against the windows.

"I dunno. What's in it for me?" Lex teased. She really had no desire to get out of bed either, but the opportunity to tease her lover was just too tempting to resist. "There's probably a lot to do around here, with the weather being bad and all," she remarked dryly.

The blonde snorted. "Yeah, right. I can tell by the look on your face that you're just as comfortable here as I am." She reached up under Lex's shirt and tickled the warm stomach.

Lex squirmed and chuckled. "Hey!" She started to reciprocate, but changed her mind and wrapped her arms tightly around the younger woman instead. "Okay, okay, you win." She scooted down until she was flat on her back, with Amanda draped across her chest. "We'll lie around until Martha drags us out of bed, deal?"

"Deal." Amanda raised up and kissed Lex passionately, until the world faded around them.

Chapter
13

"Morning, Martha. Charlie." Lex breezed in to the kitchen with a large smile. She kissed the housekeeper on the head and squeezed the sheriff's shoulder before joining them both at the kitchen table. Sometime during the early morning someone had slipped in the extra leaf to the table, which allowed six chairs to circle the oblong wooden structure. "Isn't it a beautiful morning?"

Charlie looked quizzically at his fiancée, and they both turned slightly to look outside. The heavy clouds darkened the morning sky, and driving sleet still beat heavily against the windows. "Uh, well," the lawman scratched his chin, "I suppose it's a beautiful day *somewhere*," he teased.

Lex followed their gaze and grinned ruefully. "Heh, oops. I didn't even notice the weather." She was about to say more when Amanda stepped into the room. Anna Leigh and Jacob flanked the blonde, and all three were laughing.

"You should have seen the look on Frank's face. It was priceless. Of course, mine probably looked just as shocked. Oh. Good morning, everyone," she cheerfully greeted as she walked over and sat in the rancher's lap, leaving more than enough room for her grandparents at the table.

Anna Leigh sat down next to Lex and patted her on the arm. "How are you feeling this morning, dear?"

"Pretty darned good, thanks for asking. Care for some coffee?" The dark-haired woman poured three more cups of coffee while Martha walked over to the stove.

"Thank you, Lexington." Anna Leigh accepted the offering gratefully. "What are your plans for today?"

The rancher looked down at her coffee mug, then back up to the faces around the table. "Well, I've got to take a quick run to the barn and check out the horses. After that, my day is pretty much free."

"Do you need any help? I'm sure there's more than enough of us around here to give you a hand," Jacob offered. "No sense in you having to do all the work alone."

Amanda nodded. "Grandpa's right, honey. A couple of us could go with you, and it wouldn't take very long at all." Another blast of cold wind rattled the kitchen windows. "Whoa." She shivered involuntarily.

Lex squeezed the younger woman's waist. "I really appreciate the offer, but there's no reason for anyone else to be out in that weather." When Amanda began to argue, Lex covered her mouth with a gentle hand. "Shhh. I'm the only one who has the proper gear to be out in that mess, and you know it, sweetheart."

"I guess," Amanda sighed, "but it doesn't mean I have to like it." She looked up to see the rest of the table smiling at her. "What?"

Jacob chuckled. "I'm sorry about that, Peanut. But you just look so darned cute when you pout like that." He exchanged knowing smiles with the rancher. "Okay, Lex, you win this one. How long will it take you?"

"Probably less than fifteen minutes, I'd guess. I should be back before breakfast is ready. Why?" Lex looked over at Anna Leigh, who had a devious grin on her face.

The older woman rubbed her hands together and laughed. "I thought you might enjoy a glimpse of Mandy's childhood, so I brought several picture albums with us."

She saw the horrified look on her granddaughter's face. "Don't worry, honey. I didn't bring any nudes."

"Gramma," Amanda huffed while Lex laughed. "I would hope not." She slapped her lover's shoulder. "Hush."

"I'm sorry, sweetheart," Lex continued to laugh, "but I had my heart set on some cheesecake pictures." She had to wipe tears of mirth from her eyes. "Maybe on a bearskin rug, or something?"

Anna Leigh considered for a moment. "Hmm, not with this particular set of albums, I don't think." She took pity on the blushing woman and sighed. "No, I'm afraid not, Lexington. But I'll see what I can dig up for Christmas."

Amanda buried her face in Lex's shoulder. "Oh, God. Just kill me now."

Lex rubbed her back comfortingly. "It's okay, love. I'm sure Martha has already shown you all of my embarrassing photos." She felt the younger woman chuckle. "I'll take that as a yes."

Martha spoke up from her position on the other side of the room. "Well, of course I did. We had to have something to do when you were out gallivanting around the ranch." She poured batter on the griddle that covered half the stovetop. "I hope everyone likes pancakes. I thought it would be the easiest thing to fix."

"Sounds great, Martha. How about if I help you out over there?" Jacob stood up and walked over to the stove. "I can flip the pancakes while you handle the bacon and sausage."

"Thank you, Jacob. I'd appreciate that." Martha moved over and allowed the tall man access to the griddle.

Charlie looked at the two people working at the stove, then back to Anna Leigh. "He cooks?"

"Goodness, yes," Anna Leigh exclaimed. "Jacob was actually accepted to a culinary school overseas. He's just so fond of carpentry, he only cooks for fun."

"And I can tell you from experience, the man is a wizard in the kitchen," Lex exclaimed to the astonished lawman.

The housekeeper snorted from beside the stove, trying to contain her laughter. "Oh, honey. Nothing against Jacob here, but to you, anyone that can boil water is a master chef." She shared a smile with the tall man at the stove. "The poor girl never could find her way around in a kitchen," she shared conspiratorially.

"Gee, thanks." Lex helped the blonde off of her lap. "I think I'll escape to the barn before she starts in with the embarrassing stories." She continued to hold Amanda's hand as she walked to the doorway. "Wanna help me find my hat?"

Amanda grinned. "Sure." She waved at the rest of the room before they left. "Be back in a second, everyone." She followed the rancher to the back door, where the heavy duster hung next to the battered hat. As Lex pulled on the dark coat, Amanda reached over to button it up. "Are you sure you don't want my help? It won't take me but a minute to change."

Lex smiled down at the small hands that worked the buttons on the heavy material. "No, sweetheart. Stay inside and visit with your family. I'll only be gone for a few minutes. You won't even miss me."

"Wanna bet?" Amanda lifted the black hat from its hook and placed it on her companion's head. "I miss you when I close my eyes and can't see you." She felt a gentle touch on her face and looked up. "But then I just think of you, and can see you in my mind and everything's okay again."

"That's beautiful, love." Lex leaned down and covered Amanda's lips tenderly with her own. She continued to kiss the younger woman for several moments until they both had to break away breathlessly. "Wow."

The blonde leaned her head against the rancher's chest. "Yeah. Wow." She squeezed Lex close and sighed. "God, Lex. I love you so much."

Lex buried her face in the blonde hair and breathed in deeply. "I love you, too." She pulled back and straightened

her hat on her head. "Now, go visit. I'll be back in a flash."
She reached into a pocket to pull out a pair of thick leather
work gloves, then slipped them onto her hands.

"All right. Be careful, Lex. That weather sounds
awful." Amanda stepped away from the rancher regretfully. "I'll keep your chair warm for you."

"Sounds great, sweetheart." Lex opened the back door
and gasped as a blast of cold air nearly took her breath
away. "Damn." She looked back at her lover, who wrapped
her arms around herself in an effort to keep warm. "Make
that ten minutes. It's too damned cold out there to goof
off." She winked and hurried out, quickly closing the door
behind her.

Amanda moved to the door to look out through the
glass panes. She watched with a small smile as the tall
form jogged to the barn, holding the hat in place with one
hand. "Hurry back, Lex. I miss you already," she murmured to the retreating figure.

* * * * * * * * * *

Lex allowed the barn door to slam heavily behind her
as she made her way into the darkened barn. *It's too warm
in here,* she worried. *Somebody left the thermostat on too
high when they were in here last. Wait a minute. I was the
last one in here, I think.* The rancher pulled her hat from
her head and shook the excess water from it. She moved to
the wall where the control was. Before she could reach for
it, the lights came on and partially blinded her. "What...?"

"Leave it alone," a deep voice commanded from
behind her, near the door.

The tall woman spun around quickly. "Who the
hell...?"

A man stood by the closed door holding a pitchfork
pointed to Lex. "Ain't this my lucky day?" he laughed. "I
was trying to figure out how to get to you, and you came to
me instead."

"Do I know you?" Lex began to step forward cautiously. "Wait, you're..." She stopped when the man jabbed at her with the pointed tool.

"Stay back." He relaxed a bit when the tall woman put her hat back on her head and held her hands out from her sides. "That's better. Now back up a little, closer to the wall."

Lex did as he asked. "Okay. Just take it easy." She leaned up against the wall, took a steadying breath and tried to think. *Stall, Lexington.*

* * * * * * * * * *

Amanda was on her way back to the kitchen when she saw Jeannie and Frank descending the stairs. "It's about time you two got down here," she teased as she grabbed each one by the arm and dragged the two of them into the kitchen. "Look who finally decided to grace us with their presence."

"Good morning, kids." Anna Leigh stepped over to the cabinet and refilled the carafe from the fresh pot of coffee. "Have a seat. Martha and Jacob are about to please our palates with a combined effort."

Frank sat down next to Charlie and shook his head. "What did she say?" he grumbled as Amanda sat a cup of coffee down in front of him. The big man rubbed his eyes sleepily.

"She said that..." Charlie started, but was interrupted when the phone rang.

"I'll get it." Amanda raced over and grabbed the phone. "Walters' residence, Amanda speaking." She listened for a moment, then turned solemn. "Okay, sure. Hold on just a minute, please." She waved the receiver at the still seated sheriff. "Charlie? It's for you."

The lawman rose and walked over to where the young woman stood. "Thank you, honey." He took the phone and leaned up against the cabinet. "This is Sheriff Bristol."

Everyone in the room quieted as the sheriff took the call. Martha noticed the grip Charlie tightened on the phone until his knuckles turned white. "Charlie?"

"You what?" Charlie ground out between gritted teeth. He didn't even flinch when Martha stepped over to him and rubbed his arm. "How could you lose track of him?" His entire body trembled slightly from the strain of controlling his temper. "Dammit, Jeremy! Just how incompetent are you? I thought you had him under surveillance."

Martha was beginning to worry about her intended's health. The lawman was a very unhealthy shade of red, and she had never heard him utter a curse word in all the years that she'd known him. "Charlie. Honey. Please calm down. You're scaring me." She watched as his eyes slowly tracked to hers, and noticed a look of dread on his face. "What?"

Charlie placed a fingertip gently on the housekeeper's lips to silence her. "All right. I want you to get every available man on this right now. Send a couple out here to the ranch. I want that son of a bitch found yesterday, you got that?" He closed his eyes momentarily and took a deep breath. "I'll be expecting your full report on my desk by the time I get back to town." The sheriff slowly placed the phone back on its cradle and faced the rest of the room. "I've got some good news and some bad news, folks."

Amanda looked down at her trembling hands. *Why are my hands shaking?* She waited until Martha guided the lawman over to the table and sat down next to them. "What's wrong, Charlie?"

"I now know who was behind Lex's accident last week." Charlie scrubbed his hands over his face. "He just recently got out on bail, but I had my best deputy on him every second of every day. And I didn't think he'd be stupid enough to try anything, so..."

"Who?" Martha asked, rubbing her hand across the weary man's shoulders. "Out on bail?" She paled. "You mean...?"

****

"Matt Sterling?" Lex shook her head with a disgusted sigh. "So, someone actually posted your bond?" She reached to unbutton her coat. *Damn, it's hot in here. He must have cranked the blasted thermostat up to eighty degrees.*

The man limped forward slightly. "Hold it!" He jabbed his makeshift weapon at the rancher again. "What do you think you're doing?"

Lex sighed. "I'm unbuttoning my coat, since it feels like the damn tropics in here." She raised an eyebrow at him in question. *Forget it, asshole. I'm not afraid. I've had steaks tougher than you.*

"Go ahead, slowly." Matt watched as Lex slowly opened her coat. "Might as well take it off, you're not going anywhere for a while." He considered for a moment. "At least until I can figure out what I want to do with you."

"Okay." Lex removed the coat and dropped it carefully to the ground. She backed up to the wall again and gestured to the thermostat. "Mind if I turn that thing down? You're gonna make my horses sick if they get too warm." She waited until he nodded before she adjusted the temperature. "Thanks."

Matt leaned back against the door and shrugged. "Yeah. I was getting kinda hot, myself." He thought about her earlier question. "For your information, Miss High and Mighty rancher, I'm an important guy. My new boss paid my bail and even found me a place to stay."

The rancher nodded. *Keep him talking, and maybe I can get him relaxed enough to get that pitchfork away from him.* "Really? And just who is your boss?"

"Oh, yeah. Like I'm stupid enough to tell you." He waved the tool in her direction again. "But then again, who are you going to tell?" he laughed. "So, how are you feeling after your little jump from that drop-off? I loved the sound your head made when I whacked you with that log, you know."

"It was you?" *Damn. he's a head case. Gotta keep him talking.* Lex nodded. "Why did you do it?" She unconsciously reached behind her head and felt the healed wound. It took her a lot of convincing to get Amanda to remove her stitches last night. *But it was fun paying the doctor bill.* Lex noticed that he was still limping. "How's the leg?" She knew it was probably dangerous, but she wanted to keep Matt's attention on her, and not on the fact that there was a house full of people nearby. *Especially the local sheriff.*

He leaned a little heavier on the door. "Like you care. It's your damned fault that stupid deputy shot me."

The rancher shook her head. "Oh. So I forced you to break into my house? You're lucky that *I* wasn't the one who shot you." *What a dipshit. I do believe that Ronnie got ALL the brains in the family.*

"Shut up." Matt jumped away from the door and stalked menacingly towards Lex with the pitchfork. "Just shut up!" he screamed as he came at her.

****

Charlie nodded wearily. "Yeah. He's that worthless piece of trash that broke in here just a little over a month ago. He's out now, and we can't find the sorry..." He looked at Amanda, who had gotten very quiet. "Sweetheart, we'll find him. He's probably hiding in a cheap motel room somewhere by now."

"Who posted his bond?" Jacob asked. "He may still be with that person."

"We thought of that. Unfortunately, the bond was paid in cash, and the person used an assumed name." *And poor Naomi is ten years past retirement now. It's going to take a while to get a good description of whoever actually paid the bond.* Charlie stood up quickly. "I need to get back to town and head up the search." He gave Martha an apologetic smile. "I'm very sorry, sweetheart."

Martha enveloped the thin man in a strong hug. "Don't you dare be apologizing for doing your job." She exhaled heavily. "We'll get through this, honey. We always have."

Anna Leigh and her husband exchanged worried
glances. Jacob turned off the griddle on the stove, then
went over to where his wife sat. Wordlessly, she stood, and
he took her place in the chair. The gentle man wrapped his
arms around Anna Leigh as she perched on his lap, and
they held each other as they continued to watch the drama
unfold in front of them.

"I hate to sound paranoid, but what if he's somewhere
around here? I mean, he's already tried to hurt Lex once,
right?" Frank asked everyone.

Jeannie shook her head. "You're right, honey. You *are*
being paranoid. Just look at the weather." She pointed to a
nearby window. "Even if he is out to get Lex, he wouldn't
be foolish enough to be out in this, right?"

"Unless he's been here since *before* the weather got
bad," Amanda murmured. She looked over at the clock on
the wall. *It's been twenty-five minutes since she left for the
barn.* "Oh God."

Charlie turned around to faced her. "What is it?" He
kept one arm wrapped around Martha to comfort the housekeeper.

Amanda bit her bottom lip. "The barn." She looked
around the room anxiously. "It would be a perfect place to
hide."

"You've got to be kidding. It's too damned cold out
there, even if you were under some sort of cover." Frank
dismissed the idea with a derisive snort.

"No, she's right," Martha said thoughtfully. "When
Lexie decided to change the ranch over to raising horses,
she renovated the barn and added a climate control thermostat." She glanced at the clock. "And, it's been close to
half an hour since she left."

"That does it." Charlie kissed Martha on the cheek.
"I'm gonna go check out the barn." He started for the door.

Frank stood up. "Let me get my coat and I'll come
with you."

The sheriff shook his head. "I can't allow that, son.
It's probably nothing, but I can't put a civilian into any

kind of a dangerous situation."

"I appreciate what you're saying, Sheriff," the big man stood next to Amanda and put his arm around her, "but, Lex is family, and I can pretty much take care of myself." He looked at Martha who smiled at him with relief. "Does Lex keep any firearms in the house?"

Amanda answered him. "Yes. She has a gun safe in the office." She gave Charlie an apologetic smile, then looked back up at her brother-in-law. "C'mon. She gave me the combination when I moved in." *And showed me how to load and fire all the guns in there,* Amanda shivered in remembrance.

"I'll come with you. Might as well take something besides my revolver." Charlie started after them, but stopped and turned back around. "Martha, could you call the office and tell them what's going on? There should be a couple of cars here in about half an hour. I want them to know what to expect."

Martha nodded. "Will do, Charlie." She crossed the room quickly and wrapped her arms around his neck. "Now you be real careful out there, you hear me?" she whispered as she looked into his eyes.

The lawman smiled. "Don't you worry, sweetheart. We're probably over-reacting, and Lex is more than likely playing with her darned horses—but I'll be careful any-way." Charlie kissed her on the forehead and hurried from the kitchen.

* * * * * * * * * *

Lex braced herself when the crazy man charged her. She waited patiently, but he stopped a few feet away, breathing heavily. *What the...? I swear, this guy is defi-nitely not running on all cylinders.* She watched as he fought to get his emotions under control.

"Oh, no. That would be too easy." Matt stepped back a few paces. "I'd like nothing better than to stick you with this and watch you bleed, but I don't think I'm gonna do that just yet." He limped backwards until he could sit on a bale of hay.

"Okay. So what exactly is it that you want from me?" Lex shifted her weight around a little bit. Her back had not completely healed from the fall, and standing in one place for a prolonged period of time caused it to stiffen up. She casually looked down at her watch and noticed with some surprise that she had been gone from the house for over thirty minutes. *Amanda's probably going crazy by now. She always panics when I'm gone longer than I say. God, I hate doing that to her.*

Matt laughed. "Want from you? Damn. That's rich." He shook his head and continued to chuckle. "You've completely ruined my life. You turned my little brother against me, and you have the nerve to stand there and ask what I want from you?" He stood up again. "Maybe I just want you to apologize for taking everything away from me."

The tall woman took a step away from the wall and tried to stretch her now aching back. "You came out here in the middle of a winter storm and hid in my barn, just to get an apology from me?" Lex took a step towards the erstwhile rustler. "All right. I'm sorry."

"You are so full of shit, you know that?" Matt's face reddened in anger. "Like I would accept an apology from you. And I didn't mean to hide in your damned barn, but my car slid off the road last night, and I couldn't get it out of the ditch." He jabbed the tool in Lex's direction. "So don't be giving me no fake apologies, all right? I'm not stupid."

Lex raised her hands in a placating gesture. "Right. Okay." She continued to watch for an opening to get the weapon away from the increasingly unstable man. "No more apologies."

He moved forward another step. "You're still doing it. Treating me like an idiot." Matt was less than five feet away from the rancher now. "I'm so damned sick and tired of you people acting like you're better than I am. First my boss, and now you. I'm not going to take it any more, you hear me?" He poked Lex in the stomach with the pitchfork, causing her to take a step back to keep from being hurt.

"Hey!" Lex watched carefully as he pulled the make-shift weapon back. *If he comes at me again, I'm going to have to try and grab it before the moron gets in a lucky shot and turns me into a sieve.*

"That's right. I'm in charge now." Matt pulled the pitchfork back and spun it around. He grabbed the prongs and swung the tool like a baseball bat, slamming it at the rancher's right side. "How's that feel, huh?"

Not prepared for the attack, Lex felt the wooden handle connect with her ribs. She moved with the blow to lessen the impact. "Like you're a damned Little Leaguer just learning to swing," she taunted. *If I can get him to swing at me like that again, I can get it away from him.*

Matt exploded in anger. "You bitch." He pulled the tool back for another blow. "I'll give you a practice swing."

****

Charlie checked the rounds in the shotgun again before turning to Frank and Amanda. He had quietly donned his duty belt and wore his badge on his dark denim shirt. They were all standing by the back door while Frank buttoned up his coat. "Okay. I'll go around to the back entrance to the barn, and you take up your position by the main door. Once I get a look inside, I'll radio you if I want you to go in. Got it?"

"Got it." Frank nodded seriously. He looked at Amanda's worried face. "Lex will probably jump out of the barn and kick both our butts, you know that?"

Amanda forced a smile to her face. "Probably. Or she'll beat you back to the house." She felt a sick feeling in the pit of her stomach. *But I don't think so. She wouldn't stay out this long without calling.* "Wait. We could contact the barn with the intercom." The old intercom system was rarely used any more, since it depended on whoever was at the other end to open up the line to communicate. Amanda had used it on occasion to startle her companion for fun.

"Damn. Why didn't I think of that?" Charlie grinned and shook his head. "Good idea, honey. Let's go." He allowed Amanda to lead the three of them back into the office, where the intercom box was positioned on one wall.

Looking at the small box on the wall, Frank shook his head in amazement. "How many gadgets does she have?"

"Not that many and she really doesn't like this one, because it's so old." Amanda smiled at the two men. "Lex says that every time this thing buzzes in the barn, it's so loud that it scares her to death." She reached up and pushed a brown button and held it in for a couple of seconds. "We'll probably hear a loud bit of cussing any second now."

She waited for a moment and then pushed the button again. "Maybe she's already on her way back to the house," Amanda theorized, but felt doubtful. *Or maybe she can't answer it. God.*

"It could be down because of the weather." Charlie patted the young woman's shoulder sympathetically. "We'll head down to the barn and see what's taking her so long, okay?"

Frank nodded in agreement. "He's right. As bad as the weather has been, the line could have gotten icy and broken." He pulled Amanda close to him as they turned and left the office. "Don't worry, Mandy, everything's going to be just fine."

They walked back down the hallway and met Martha and Jeannie at the back door. The housekeeper looked upset, and the younger woman stood next to her with an arm around her waist. "Charlie, I hate to bother you before you go out, but I just talked to Lydia at your office. She said to tell you that only one car was coming out here because Councilman Alders heard about it on the radio and threw a big fit."

"Dammit!" The sheriff shook his head angrily. "Worthless politicians. I swear a dung beetle would turn up its nose at him." He looked at the women with a sheepish grin. "Sorry about that, ladies. It just sticks in my craw to have to put up with the likes of him." Charlie looked over at Frank. "You ready?"

"Yep. Let's go." The big man winked at his wife and followed the lawman through the back door. "Damn, that wind's cold." He quickly slammed the door behind them.

Amanda stepped to the closed door and moved the curtain that covered the small windows. "I think the sleet is letting up some," she commented quietly.

"C'mon, honey." Martha pulled the blonde away from her post at the door. "Let's go make sure Anna Leigh and Jacob are doing all right in the kitchen."

* * * * * * * * *

Lex tried to grab the handle of the pitchfork before it hit her again, but her right arm was in no shape to make the difficult move. She felt the blow more intensely this time as it hit the same spot on her side. With a pained grunt, she dropped to her knees and rolled to her left. *I've got to get that damned thing away from him before he does some serious damage.*

"Stay still," Matt screamed, as he reversed his hold and now held the tool by the handle once again. He jabbed at the rancher, who rolled out of the way and kicked his legs out from under him. "Aaaaaaah! Damn you."

"What's the matter, did that hurt?" Lex taunted him after she kicked the man in his healing leg. She felt a grim satisfaction when he fell to the ground in agony. Lex was having trouble moving as well; her back and right arm were both protesting their mistreatment. She lay on her back for a moment to catch her breath.

Before she could get up, Matt discarded the pitchfork and sat on her chest. He grabbed her around the throat with both hands and began to squeeze. "You bitch," he panted. He pulled her head up slightly and began to shake her. "I'm gonna finish you."

Lex grabbed his wrists with both hands, frantically trying to pry his fingers away. A loud buzz echoed through the barn at that moment, which caused Matt to loosen his grip in confusion. Another buzz caused him to look away for a split second. It was just the break the rancher needed, and she slammed her head into his face, hard.

"Aaaah! My nose!" he screamed and fell back, clutching his now bleeding face. He rolled over onto his side and whimpered.

The rancher gasped and pulled air into her burning lungs. She rolled into a sitting position and rubbed her throat with one hand. "Bastard," she choked out. Lex blinked several times as she tried to get her eyes to focus. *That was close.*

Matt wiped his bloody face on his sleeve and looked around for the pitchfork. His eyes were quickly swelling shut, so he ran his hands around the barn floor aimlessly.

"Oh, no you don't." Lex rolled to her knees and crawled after him. "I'm not finished with you yet." She grabbed his leg and pulled.

"Let go of me, dammit." Matt kicked back at the rancher. He smiled to himself when he felt his foot make contact and heard a grunt.

Lex's head snapped back from the blow as the man's heel connected with her forehead. *That's gonna leave a bruise,* she thought. "Come here, you little shit." She pulled at his leg again, flipping Matt over onto his back. "Now I've got ya." The angry woman quickly straddled his body and easily slapped his hands away. She blocked a punch and slammed her fist with determination into his already bloody face. "That's for slapping Ronnie." Lex pulled back her fist to hit him again when she felt a strong hand grasp her shoulder.

* * * * * * * * *

Charlie stood at the back door to the barn. As the rain and sleet continued to beat down, he pulled the radio from his coat pocket and put it to his lips. "I'm in position, Frank. Everything clear on that side?"

"All quiet. Do you want me to go in?" Frank's voice asked on the radio. The ex-football player stood to one side of the main entry of the barn. He put his ear up to the door and tried to hear if anything was going on inside.

"No. I want to try and peek inside first. But be ready just in case," Charlie advised him quietly. He slowly opened the door a couple of inches and peered inside the barn. Two figures were scuffling across the floor. "Let's go in, Frank. Looks like Lex is in trouble." He quickly pocketed the radio and stepped into the barn. Across the room he could easily make out the tall woman's figure as she grabbed the other person and flipped them onto their back. *Maybe she doesn't need any help after all,* he observed wryly.

Frank swung the barn door open and rushed in. He saw Lex roll the other person over onto their back and climb onto the man's chest. *At least I think it's a man,* he thought. *What the hell happened to his face?* Before he could get to them, Lex had pulled back her left arm and punched the screaming man in the face. He set his gun down by the doorway and rushed over to where the two combatants were still going at it.

The sheriff nodded at Frank. "Go ahead, son. You're a lot stronger than I am." He stood back as the big man attempted to pull the rancher off the bloodied form underneath her. He watched the scene with relief. *Should have known she'd have everything under control. That's my girl,* he thought proudly.

"Lex. That's enough," Frank yelled as he grabbed her shoulders. He pulled at her ineffectually. *Damn, she's strong.* "C'mon, let go of him, Lex."

"What?" Lex spun around and threw a punch at her friend. "Frank?" Once she recognized the man standing over her, she allowed him to pull her to her feet slowly. "Sorry about that."

Frank grinned at her. "No harm done." *Thank God she*

didn't connect with that punch. I'd probably have ended up with a black eye, at least.

A loud moan brought their attention back to the man lying on the floor of the barn. "Ooowww." Matt started to get up, but was rolled over roughly by Charlie. "Hey, watch it. That crazy broad tried to kill me," he whined as the sheriff cuffed his hands behind his back.

"Shut up." Charlie looked back up at Lex. "Are you okay, honey?" He noticed that the tall woman was leaning against Frank rather heavily. Lex had bits of mud and hay on various parts of her body, and he could see a bruise forming in the middle of her forehead.

Lex ran a hand through her hair to get it out of her eyes. "Yeah, I'm okay. Just a little sore." She flexed her left hand. "Nothing broken." She smiled at the lawman. "Don't take this the wrong way, but what are you guys doing here? And what's with the guns?" The tired woman allowed Frank to help her to a bale of hay to sit down. "Thanks."

"No problem." Frank squeezed her shoulder gently and walked over to help Charlie lift the whining man off the floor. "Oh, quit your bitching," he grumbled to Matt, "or, I'll turn her loose on you again." He looked over at the sheriff. "What are we gonna do with him?"

Charlie laughed. "We'll bring him up to the house and let one of my deputies take him back to town when they get here." He looked over at Lex with a worried expression. "You think you can make it back to the house, sweetheart? I'll tell you everything when we get there, okay?"

The rancher stood up stiffly. "Sounds good." She reached down and picked up her hat. "Let's go. I'm starving."

Chapter
14

Later that afternoon, Lex was upstairs with Amanda, as she allowed the younger woman to see to her various cuts and bruises. They had just recently retired to the bedroom, having waited downstairs until the deputies arrived to remove their unwelcome guest. Amanda's family left shortly after everyone else, and Martha had chased the younger women upstairs to make sure Lex got cleaned up. Now the rancher sat on the edge of the bed, fresh from a hot bath and wearing only a dark green towel that was wrapped around her body. She held the towel open, so that her friend could tend to her injuries.

Amanda was on her knees next to the bed, carefully rubbing Martha's homemade salve on her lover's side. "At least nothing's broken this time," she murmured quietly as her hands shook.

"Yeah. I'm just glad it was my right side instead of my left." Lex looked down and saw the trembling hand. "Hey." She grabbed the hand gently to still its progress. "C'mere." She pulled her friend up so that she could look into Amanda's eyes. "It's okay." Her heart nearly broke at the pain reflected in the green eyes.

"When will it end, Lex?" Amanda asked. "How much

more do we have to go through to finally be happy?" *Why can't they just leave us alone?* She felt tears well up in her eyes.

Lex used her thumb to wipe a tear that fell from Amanda's sad eyes. "I am happy, sweetheart." She pulled her lover into her lap. "I've never been more happy in my life than I am right this second." The dark-haired woman caressed the soft cheek of her companion. "I would gladly go though everything again, just for the opportunity to be here with you right now, like this."

Amanda took a deep breath and smiled. "I feel the same way. It's just that I'm tired of seeing you hurt. And we don't even know who put him up to all of this."

The captured man sat in the den scowling quietly. He refused to tell who had paid his bail and who his boss was. Nothing anyone said to him could get him to change his mind. Matt sat unhappily with his back against the wall and glared at Lex, mumbling under his breath. He continued to threaten the rancher, even as the sheriff advised him of his rights.

"I know my rights, old man," Matt grumbled. "And, once my boss finds out about all of this, you're all gonna pay for what you've done." He tried to look menacing, but failed. His nose had swollen up to three times its normal size, and both eyes were swollen and black. The hapless rustler looked more comical than scary.

Lex laughed from her position by the fireplace. "We're scared, Sterling. Face it. Your boss will leave you dangling in the breeze, and you're going to spend the rest of your life in jail." She stood and crossed over to where he sat on the floor. "Now make it easy on yourself and tell the sheriff what you know."

Matt glared up at the tall woman. "I don't know nothin'." He lowered his gaze and stared at his muddy boots.

"That much is obvious," Lex muttered. She shook her head and walked back over to the fireplace to sit next to

Amanda.

The rancher smiled at her friend. "We will. He's too stupid to hold up under any type of real interrogation. But, I honestly don't think he knows who it is." She pulled Amanda close and squeezed her tight. "Let's not worry about him right now."

"You're right. It's not that important." Amanda pulled back slightly to look closely at Lex's face. She ran her fingertips gently over the taller woman's forehead. "Are you sure that you're all right? That's a nasty looking bruise."

"I'm fine, sweetheart. Just ask Martha. I have the hardest head around." Lex grinned and kissed her friend on the tip of her nose.

Amanda tried to stay serious, but failed miserably. *She just looks so darned cute when she grins at me like that.* "That's not funny. You could have been seriously hurt." She looked down again at the discoloration that covered Lex's side, touched the area softly, and sighed. "You're a walking bruise, love."

Lex reached down to capture the small hand and brought it to her lips. She kissed the delicate palm and brought it to her cheek. "It doesn't hurt at all." She waited until Amanda's eyes met hers. "You are so beautiful, did you know that?"

"Uh, no." Amanda blushed and looked down at the bedspread. "I never really thought about it." She felt the rancher's other hand cup her chin gently and raise her head. "What?"

"Sweetheart," Lex studied the younger woman's face intently, "you are. In so many ways." She trailed a fingertip down Amanda's jaw line and slowly across the blonde's throat. "Have I told you today how much I love you?" she asked quietly.

A small chill chased down Amanda's back as Lex traced a gentle pattern down her neck. "Mmm. Yes. I believe you have." Her breathing quickened as long fingers deliberately unbuttoned her shirt.

The rancher undid each button slowly, smiling at the

effect her touch had on her lover. "You have the most beautiful skin, Amanda," she marveled in a low voice. Lex opened the oversized denim shirt that the younger woman wore. *She looks better in my clothes than I do.* Her other hand reached behind Amanda to keep her from falling back. Once the last button was undone, Lex carefully peeled the shirt back off of her companion's shoulders. "I said it once, and I'll say it again. Beautiful." She leaned down and kissed the blonde thoroughly.

Amanda reached up and tangled her hands in the dark hair. "Yes." she moaned when Lex finally pulled away from her mouth. "God, Lex." She felt her entire body tremble as the rancher blazed a trail of kisses down her throat. The shirt was carelessly tossed to the floor as Lex shifted slightly and turned to place Amanda on the bed. Warm hands quickly removed the blue lace bra that had been a recent gift from the dark-haired woman.

"Stunning." Lex leaned over Amanda and smiled. Her blue eyes sparkled with the overwhelming love she felt. She bent down and kissed the blonde again as her free hand mapped a course along the petite body. "I love you so much, Amanda." Her hand continued its path down the toned abdomen, until she reached the clasp on the younger woman's jeans. "I think you're overdressed, sweetheart," Lex whispered in her lover's ear right before she nibbled on it.

"Oooh." Amanda's eyes closed when she felt the warm breath on her neck. "I love you too, Lex." She was barely able to speak as she felt her jeans being removed. "Oh, God," she mumbled when the rest of her clothes were expertly stripped from her body. Gentle lips kissed down her neck again as Lex's hand continued to explore.

Lex felt Amanda's body arch upward in response to her questing hand. "I love the way your skin feels, sweetheart." The rancher enjoyed talking as she touched her lover. She could always depend on Amanda to react to her words, as well as her touch. When she found a particularly sensitive spot, the blonde used the grip she had on Lex's hair to pull her more tightly to her body. "I'm here, love," Lex whispered in Amanda's ear.

Small hands quickly discarded the towel from the rancher's body. "I need..." Amanda demanded in a soft voice. "Lex. Please." She almost cried with relief when she felt Lex's bare skin touch her own. "Yesss." The cold chill of the room was banished when Amanda finally pulled the long body down on top of her own. "Mine," she murmured, and then there were no more words needed as they shared their love.

* * * * * * * * * *

A quiet knock on the door caused Amanda to wake from a very pleasant dream. Still smiling, she opened her eyes and glanced at the clock on the nightstand. Her eyes popped open fully when she saw that it was almost seven o'clock in the evening. *Oops. Lex is gonna kill me for letting her sleep this late.* She looked over at her slumbering companion and smiled. *Too bad. She needed it.*

The door opened slightly, and Martha's graying head poked in. She looked over at the bed with a fond smile, then stepped into the room when Amanda waved her in. "Hi, honey," the housekeeper greeted quietly. She glanced down at the bed where Lex lay on her stomach sound asleep. "How is she?"

"Not too bad, actually." Amanda sat up and ran her fingers through her hair. "Her back was bothering her earlier so I gave her a massage after she soaked in the tub. I think that really helped."

"That's good to hear. I wouldn't be up here bothering you right now, but Charlie just called. They've finished questioning that hateful man that Lexie caught in the barn." Martha sat down at the foot of the bed. "Charlie wants you to call him at the office as soon as you can, because he and the prosecutor have some questions for you."

Amanda's brow wrinkled in confusion. "For me? I'm

afraid I don't know much. Are you sure they don't want to talk to Lex?"

Lex groaned and rolled over onto her back. "Martha?" She blinked several times and smiled sleepily. "What time is it?"

Martha reached over and squeezed Lex's leg. "Almost seven. I thought that you might want to eat dinner since you didn't eat much lunch." She was privately worried about the rancher's health, because the young woman barely touched her lunch and then slept the afternoon away. *That's not like my Lexie at all. Maybe I should call Dr. Anderson to come and take a look at her.* The house-keeper stood and walked around the bed to stand next to her charge. "How are you feeling, honey?"

"Hungry, now that you mention it." Lex started to sit up then realized that she had nothing on. *I knew I forgot to do something before I fell asleep, but I was so damned relaxed after that massage I couldn't keep my eyes open.* Mentally shrugging and figuring that Martha had seen her naked before, she sat up and tucked the sheet and com-forter under her arms. She looked over at Amanda as the blonde slipped from the other side of the bed. *When did she...?* "I guess we'll be down in a minute."

Amanda chuckled at the perplexed look on the rancher's face. She had pulled on her long tee shirt after Lex had nodded off in case she had to get out of bed. She reached over for her robe and slipped it on. "I'm going to brush my hair and wash my face while you two visit for a minute." She winked at Martha and stepped into the bath-room.

"Do you want me to bring your dinner up here, Lexie?" Martha sat down next to the still groggy woman. She reached over and brushed the dark bangs out of Lex's eyes. "Looks like it's about time for another trim, sweet-heart." She purposely stayed silent about the ugly bruise on the young woman's forehead.

"Again? Didn't you just cut it last month?" Lex saw the brown eyes across from her cloud in concern. "It doesn't hurt, you know," she smiled at the older woman, "and we'll come downstairs for dinner. There's nothing wrong with me, Mada." She clasped the housekeeper's hand and squeezed it gently. "I wouldn't have slept so long, but you know how I am after a long soak."

Martha laughed, relieved to see that Lex was indeed all right. "Did you fall asleep in the tub again, honey?"

Lex shook her head and grinned. "Almost. But Amanda made me get out and go to bed." *Yeah. She really forced it on you. What a mushball. Nothing like the promise of a massage to make me hop out of the tub.* She had argued with the younger woman about the need for a massage. *Heh. Although I thought I provided her with pretty convincing evidence that there was nothing wrong with me.* A small chuckle escaped her at that thought. Lex was certain that after they had made love Amanda would want to just curl up together and sleep. Despite being worn out, the younger woman had insisted on giving the rancher the promised massage anyway.

"What's so funny, dear?" Martha was charmed by the look on Lex's face. *I bet anything I know who's on her mind.* She shook her head and stood up. "Never mind. I don't think I want to know." Martha leaned down and kissed the top of Lex's head. "Hurry up and get yourself downstairs before dinner gets cold."

The dark-haired woman smiled at the woman who had raised her with so much love and care. *I couldn't have picked a better mother. I really do need to do something for her.* "Yes, ma'am. Should I get dressed, or do you want me to wear what I have on?"

The housekeeper was almost to the door when she turned around. "I've seen you in your birthday suit all your life, Lexington Marie. It won't matter to me one bit." She put her hands on her ample hips and gave the younger woman a stern look. "But if you catch cold from running around in your altogether, don't come crying to me to wipe your nose." She shook her head at the laughing rancher and left the room with a haughty air.

Amanda stepped out of the bathroom. "What's so funny?"

"Martha's full of herself today, that's for sure," Lex laughed as she tossed the bedcovers aside and slowly climbed out of bed. "Damn!"

Amanda hurried over to where the rancher stood by the bed. "What's wrong?" She reached for Lex but her hands were gently batted away. "What?"

Lex grabbed the younger woman and pulled her close. "It's damned cold when you get out of bed with no clothes on." She untied Amanda's robe and stepped closer, pulling the robe closed around them both. "Ah, much better."

"And how do you propose that we get downstairs for dinner?" Amanda asked, wrapping her arms around the bare body against hers. "Could be tricky."

"But definitely fun," Lex teased. She was leaning down to kiss Amanda when a voice called from the hall- way.

"Don't be in there playing kissy-face all night, girls. I'm an old woman, and I need my rest." They could hear the housekeeper's laughter trailing in her wake as she descended the stairs.

Lex looked at her lover and sighed. "She can be such a smart ass at times." She regretfully stepped out of the ter- rycloth cocoon and bent over to pick up her sweat pants.

The blonde giggled. "Must be where you got it, then." She quickly stepped over to the dresser and pulled out a sweatshirt. She didn't see the pillow that flew across the room and whacked her in the back of the head. "Hey!" Amanda turned around to see Lex standing by the bed, wearing sweat pants and nothing else. *Oooh Nice. National Geographic, eat your heart out.*

"What are you grinning at?" Lex asked as she stood there with her hands on her hips. "Haven't you ever seen a half dressed woman before?"

"Not that looks quite that good," Amanda answered. She continued to smile as she brought the tall woman the sweatshirt. "I suppose I should let you get dressed before you catch a cold."

"Gee, thanks." The rancher pulled the shirt over her head gingerly. *Still a little sore, but nothing too bad.* She was in the process of pulling the shirt down when cold hands lay flat against her belly. "Aaah! Damn, Amanda, your hands are cold." She batted the offending appendages away and finished dressing.

The blonde grinned. "Serves you right for hitting me with that pillow." Amanda wrapped her arms around the tall woman and squeezed gently.

Lex happily returned the hug. "C'mon, cute stuff, let's go downstairs before Martha comes back up here to harass us." She pulled away, but kept one arm around her love and escorted her out of the room.

* * * * * * * * * *

"Hello? This is Amanda Cauble. I'm calling for Sheriff Bristol." Amanda sat at the desk in the office with Martha and Lex close by. Actually, Lex was more than close by—she was sitting in the desk chair with the petite blonde in her lap. She had her arms wrapped around Amanda, her chin resting lightly on her friend's shoulder. Martha, at both women's insistence, sat in the soft leather chair on the other side of the desk.

"This is Sheriff Bristol," Charlie answered, picking up the line with a weary sigh. "Amanda? Thanks for calling. I've got the county prosecutor here with me—Mr. Robert Campbell. Do you mind if I put you on speakerphone?"

Amanda took a deep breath. "No, not at all. Lex and Martha are here with me. Do you mind if I use the speakerphone, too? They may be able to help."

Charlie chuckled. "Not at all, honey. That's a good idea."

She heard a click and then the slight noise as the sheriff settled his weight in a chair near the phone. Lex loosened her grip enough so that Amanda could press the speaker button on the phone. "Hey, Charlie." The rancher was not one for formalities. "Mr. Campbell? I don't believe we've met. I'm..."

A deep rich voice interrupted her. "Ms. Walters. I've heard a lot about you. Although Sheriff Bristol here says that most of it is not entirely true." Robert Campbell chuckled. "It seems our prisoner claims your attack on him was unprovoked." The tone of his voice expressed what he thought of the accusation.

"I wouldn't quite say unprovoked, Mr. Campbell. The man came at me with a damned pitchfork." Lex felt Amanda stiffen and saw the housekeeper pale. *Damn. I gotta learn to think before I speak.*

"I know, Lex." The prosecutor paused. "May I call you Lex? Charlie has told me so much about you, it seems as if I already know you."

Lex laughed. "That's fine. Just don't believe everything you hear from him. The man tends to exaggerate." She winced as Amanda pinched her leg. "Umm. Sorry about that. Do you want to go ahead and tell us what this call is all about?"

Charlie took a deep breath and shuffled papers. "Amanda, from what you told me the other day, a former employee of your father's contacted you last week. Is that correct?" The sheriff was certain of the information, but he wanted Amanda to verify it for the prosecutor.

"Yes, Mark Garrett used to work for my father. He quit and came to Somerville to find a house and to settle his family here. Remember that I told you he brought flowers to my grandparents' house when he found out about Lex's accident? Is something wrong?" Amanda felt Lex's arms tighten around her reassuringly. "Is he okay?"

Robert Campbell answered her question. "We're not sure, Amanda. He seems to have disappeared."

"I don't get it," Lex interrupted. "What does Mark Garrett have to do with all of this? And, why all the concern over his whereabouts?"

"He fits the description we got from Matt Sterling of the man who posted his bond," the prosecutor intoned.

"And, we checked with the clerk who accepted the bail money. She's pretty sure that a man with his build and coloring gave her the cash."

Amanda gasped. "Why would someone who *used* to work for my father post bail for someone he doesn't even know? What's Mark's connection in all of this?" *Oh, no. I should have listened to my instincts after he brought the flowers.* She didn't want to think of those possibilities right now. *If my father is responsible for almost killing Lex, I don't know what I will do.*

"Let's not go jumping to conclusions before we have the facts, okay? Amanda, we don't know for sure if Mr. Garrett is involved and we certainly have no reason to believe that he still works for your father. But, we did want to talk to you and see if he had contacted you since we talked last. Maybe left an address or phone number with you to reach him?" Charlie knew how hard this must be on the young woman.

Worrying about how Amanda must be feeling, Lex decided to end the conversation as quickly as possible. "Mr. Campbell. Charlie. If we hear from Mark or find out anything else, we'll be sure to give you a call." She looked over at Martha who had a concerned look on her face. "Is that all for now? I'm really not feeling one hundred percent just yet, and would like to get some rest."

"Of course, Lex. I'm sorry we had to bother you after the day you've all had. Amanda," Mr. Campbell sounded sincere, "thank you for your time. I'll leave my home number with Charlie. If you need anything, please don't hesitate to call."

Charlie cleared his throat. "I'm sorry about all of this, honey. But when Sterling told us who had posted his bond, I remembered the conversation that you and I had, and that you were a little leery of how he knew about Lex's accident. I doubt that he has any ties left to your father, but we wanted to cover all our bases."

"That's all right, Charlie. I understand." Amanda felt a knot of dread in her stomach. "If I can think of anything, or I hear from him, I'll let you know immediately."

"I know you will, sweetheart. Now don't you worry about a thing. I'll call you as soon as I find out anything, okay?" Charlie's heart broke at the pain these accusations would cause the young woman. He had already become quite attached to her, and considered Amanda family.

Lex could almost feel her friend's upset. "Thanks, Charlie. And we hope to see you out here for dinner tomorrow night. No excuses, all right?" She looked over at Martha, who gave her a grateful smile.

The sheriff laughed. "Okay. I know when I've been beaten." He looked over at the prosecutor. "Mind if I bring a guest?"

Martha finally ended her silence. "Only if it's Mr. Campbell. I know he's new in town, and it's about time we get the chance to meet him."

"You win, sweetheart," Charlie laughed. "We'll see you all tomorrow night." He recradled the receiver and turned to the other man in the room. "I hope you don't have any plans, because my Martha doesn't take no for an answer."

Robert shook his head. "Nope. My wife and daughter won't be here for another week at least, so I'm all yours."

Amanda disconnected the call and sat quietly on her friend's lap. *Does Mark still work for my father? Could they both be involved in what happened to Lex? What am I going to do if any of this is true? How can I possibly face Martha or Lex?*

Lex could feel the struggle her friend was going through. "Amanda? Sweetheart." She saw Martha nod and leave the room. "Talk to me."

"What's there to talk about?" Amanda allowed the rancher to turn her around so that they were looking eye to eye. "You heard what they said."

Lex nodded. "Yes. I heard that a man who's afraid that he would spend the rest of his days in prison made some accusations." She ached for what her friend was going through. "But, until they are proven in court, they're just that. Accusations."

The younger woman bit her bottom lip in thought. "But what if..."

"No what ifs. We'll wait to see what happens." Lex covered Amanda's mouth with her hand. "And, if the worst is true, then we'll get through it. Together." She removed her hand and kissed the blonde gently. "You and me. Together, we can handle anything." The rancher smiled. "I love you, Amanda. Nothing or no one can change that. Ever."

"Always and forever," Amanda whispered, as tears of relief filled her eyes.

"Always and forever," Lex assured her. "Until the end of time, my love."

Amanda smiled. "Thank you." She took a deep breath and gathered her wits about her. "But, now I think I need to call my father and see what he has to say about this whole mess."

Chapter
15

"Why don't we just spend the night at my grandparent's house, and then come back in the morning?" Amanda suggested. "You said that you didn't want to drive home after dark because of the ice on the roads. This way, we can shop until the stores close." She also wanted a chance to talk to her grandparents before she called her father. Amanda was hoping Anna Leigh and Jacob could help her with what she believed would be a very difficult phone call. *I hope that he had nothing to do with Mark posting the bail for Matt Sterling—but it's too big a coincidence to ignore.*

They had gotten up early to go into town to do their Christmas shopping at Lex's insistence. Amanda had tried to get her to reconsider because of the previous day's activities, but the rancher refused.

Lex was lying in bed on her left side with her head propped up on one hand. She studied the young woman beside her who was still sleeping peacefully. With a mischievous smile, she ran a light fingertip across one side of the blonde's cheek. Amanda murmured and rolled over onto her side, facing the rancher. Lex paused until her companion had settled down again, fast asleep. Charmed by the innocent smile on Amanda's face, she brushed the hair away from the younger woman's face and leaned over to place a tender kiss on her brow. "Amanda?"

"Mmm." The blonde scooted closer to Lex and buried her head in the rancher's nightshirt. Still asleep, she tangled their legs together and sighed happily.

"C'mon, sweetheart." Lex rolled over onto her back, carrying her lover with her. "Time to get up." She rubbed Amanda's back with her hands in a comforting manner.

Amanda stirred once again. "No. Comfy." She wrapped her arms tightly around Lex and snuggled even closer. "Too early."

The rancher chuckled and returned the squeeze. "I thought that you wanted to go Christmas shopping?"

"No. Wanna snuggle," Amanda grumbled petulantly. She raised her head until she could see Lex's face. She studied the older woman carefully. "You had a pretty exciting day yesterday. Why don't we just give the shopping a miss? We can go next weekend."

"YOU don't want to go shopping?" Lex put a playful hand against Amanda's forehead. "Funny, you don't feel like you have a fever." She grinned when her hand was casually slapped away. "Seriously, sweetheart, I feel fine. Don't let what happened yesterday influence your decision, okay?"

The blonde continued to watch Lex's face for any sign of pain or fatigue. She does look good, but... "I just don't want you to wear yourself out for something as minor as a shopping trip."

Lex shook her head. "There's nothing wrong with me, Amanda. As for what happened yesterday, I promised you a month ago that we would go Christmas shopping today." She leaned up enough to kiss the younger woman gently. "And no two-bit cattle thief is going to make me break that promise."

She's so darned stubborn, Amanda remembered with a

fond smile. The petite blonde sat on the bed, to untie a serious knot in the laces of one of her sneakers. "How on earth did I manage to do this?" Amanda continued to work unsuccessfully at the laces. "Crap."

· Lex stepped out of the bathroom wearing only her jeans, a sexy satin bra and a towel around her neck. "Umm. That's kinda my fault, sweetheart." She walked over to the bed and took the white leather shoe away from her friend.

"Your fault?" Amanda watched in amusement as Lex fought with the shoestring. "How do you figure that?"

"I couldn't find mine." The rancher walked over to the dresser and picked up a small pocketknife.

"Oookaaay." Amanda drew out the word in confusion. "Not that I mind, honey, but your feet are a little big for my shoes."

A dirty look answered her. Lex sighed. "I didn't try to wear them. Dr. A told me that trying to tie shoes with one hand was a good exercise to rebuild the strength and dexterity in my arm and hand." All of her other injuries were almost healed, but Lex was still having trouble with her right arm. Dr. Anderson had assured her that it would heal completely, but the stubborn woman was impatient and ready for it to be back to normal. She opened the knife and started to use it against the knot.

"Hey. Don't." Amanda jumped up from the bed. Before she could cross the room, Lex tossed her the shoe. "Oh. Thanks." She sat back down on the bed and slipped the sneaker on. "So, do you want me to call Gramma and see if they mind us staying with them tonight?"

"Sure. Maybe we can talk your grandfather into cooking stir fry." Lex wandered into the closet. "Have you seen my blue shirt?" she called from inside.

The question caused Amanda to sigh and get off the bed. "Can you be a little more specific, honey?" She poked her head into the closet. "I swear you have nothing *but* blue shirts."

The rancher grabbed Amanda and pulled her the rest of the way into the closet. She wrapped her arms around the smaller woman and grinned. "Gotcha."

"You sure do." Amanda smiled happily.

"Can I keep ya?" Lex leaned down until their breaths mingled. She watched as the green eyes below her closed dreamily.

"Uh-huh." A barely heard whisper was her answer.

"Amanda?" Lex dropped her voice to a sexy murmur.

Amanda swayed slightly in her lover's arms. "Mmm?" Her eyes were still closed, and her breathing quickened.

"Where's my blue flannel shirt?" The quiet question sounded almost erotic.

"Oooh, you." Amanda swatted her on the shoulder. The younger woman leaned her forehead onto Lex's chest and sighed. "You are such a brat." She pulled back slightly and looked up into blue eyes that sparkled with mischief. "I think Martha did laundry yesterday, so it's probably in the utility room."

Lex smiled broadly. "Great. I'll just go downstairs and..."

"I don't think that you're quite dressed to be running all over the house," Amanda observed. "Why don't you get your boots on, and I'll run and grab your shirt?" She reached up and ran a finger down the strap of Lex's dark blue satin bra. One of the first things Amanda had done when she moved in, was to buy the rancher colorful satin undergarments. "I really like this one on you." She looked up and smiled. "Brings out the color in your eyes."

The eyes she mentioned rolled in wry amusement. "If you say so. It is really comfortable, though." Lex leaned down and placed a quick kiss on Amanda's lips. "Thanks."

Amanda frowned. "You call *that* a thank you? I've gotten better thanks from...umph." Her good-natured protest was cut short when Lex kissed her deeply. "Mmm." She stretched up and wrapped her arms around the dark head as she felt warm hands gently grasp her hips.

The closet door opened wide, and a small hand reached in to switch on the light. "I swear, I find you two in the craziest places," Martha teased. She enjoyed the deep blushes that both women suddenly wore. *I just love getting them like this.*

"I was just looking for my blue flannel shirt," Lex stated matter of factly. She slowly pulled away from Amanda and tried unsuccessfully to take the handful of clothes from the housekeeper. "You didn't have to bring these up, Martha. We're perfectly capable..."

"I know, honey. But I figured that you'd forgive an old woman her little habits." Martha took the clothes and hung them in their proper places. She kept one out and handed it to the tall woman. "Here. Although I think it's about time to retire this one to the rag box."

Lex pulled the garment to her chest protectively. "No. This is my favorite shirt." She quickly slipped the shirt off the hanger and put it on. "And you're *not* an old woman."

"Do you think that we could finish this conversation in the bedroom?" Amanda asked as she gestured to the doorway. "I'm for togetherness as much as the next person, but even I have my limits."

Martha backed out of the closet and waited until both women joined her. "That was a little silly, wasn't it?"

"It was different, that's for sure." Amanda stepped over to button Lex's shirt. The rancher started to argue, but shrugged her shoulders at Martha and allowed Amanda to continue her pampering.

The housekeeper had to bite the inside of her cheek to keep from laughing out loud. *They are just too cute together.*

"We've decided to stay in town overnight after we get through shopping," Lex informed the older woman. "Do you want to come with us?" She gave Amanda a grateful smile and crossed the room to retrieve a pair of socks from the dresser.

"No thank you, honey. Charlie is driving out tonight, and we're going to watch movies." Martha watched in amusement as Amanda packed a small bag. "I thought you both had clothes there."

Amanda nodded. "We do, but I like to pack a few

extras just in case of an emergency." She waved in Lex's direction. "You know how some people always seem to get dirty, no matter where they go."

Martha laughed. "I know that all too well." She waved off a glare from Lex. "Don't you be looking at me like that, Lexie. It's true and you know it."

Lex shook her head. "I'm not that bad, Mada." A poke in her arm made her turn her head. "What?"

"Nothing." Amanda smirked. "I've got our bag all packed, honey. Are you about ready to go?"

"Now you wait just one dadblasted minute. You're not going anywhere until you both have had a decent break-fast." Martha had her hands on her hips and a no-nonsense look on her face. "Lexie, you're going to start taking better care of yourself or I'm gonna sit on you and force you to relax." She pointed an accusing finger at the dark-haired woman then turned and stomped to the bedroom door. "Well?"

"We'll be right down, Martha," Amanda answered. She looked over at the rancher, who stared at the housekeeper in confusion.

"Right." Lex nodded. She watched as Martha left the room then turned and faced Amanda. "What did I do?"

Amanda crossed the room to where Lex stood. She wrapped her arms around the tall woman and squeezed. "I don't think you did anything, love." She looked up and saw a flash of hurt quickly race across Lex's face. "Honey, she's just worried about you. The last couple of months have been really hard on her." Amanda rubbed her hands across Lex's back in a comforting gesture. "C'mon, let's go eat and then hit the road. I've got a lot of shopping to do."

The rancher sighed. "I'm going to regret this, aren't I?"

"Probably." Amanda stepped back and gave the tall woman a gentle pat on her side. "But I promise to make it up to you tonight." She winked and walked to the doorway with Lex closely on her heels.

"Wait for me." Lex chased after the blonde wearing a very large, happy smile on her face.

* * * * * * * * * *

Lex's large green truck pulled slowly into the driveway and parked beside Jacob's Suburban. She turned to her companion and released a heavy sigh. "Are you sure that we left anything at the mall for anyone else to buy?" She could barely see through the back windows of the vehicle due to all the packages that were piled in the back seat.

"It's not that bad." Amanda reached over and clasped the older woman's arm. "But you look completely beat, honey. Why didn't you tell me that I was wearing you out?" *Although I'm feeling a bit tired, too.*

Lex grinned evilly. "You'll *never* hear me complain about that."

The blonde flushed darkly. "Oh, boy. I can't believe I walked right into that one." She lowered her head and tried to ignore her heated face.

"Heh. You're so cute when you blush." Lex covered Amanda's hand with her own. "But seriously, love. I'm fine." She looked past Amanda through the window. "Looks like our welcoming committee is here."

Bounding up to the truck were Frank and Jeannie. The auburn-haired woman was draped over her husband, piggy-back style. Once they got close to the truck, she reached out and rapped on the window. "You two gonna sit in there all evening, or are you coming inside?" Jeannie couldn't understand why her sister blushed and covered her face with her hands. "What?"

Lex patted her friend's arm and opened the truck door. "C'mon, beautiful. Let's go see what Jacob's got cooking." She winked at Amanda and climbed out of the vehicle. The rancher stepped around the truck and opened the passenger door. She paused when her friend stumbled from the vehicle. "Amanda? Are you okay?"

"Great. Just great," Amanda sighed and allowed Lex to

help her from the truck. She reached over and tweaked her sister's nose gently. "What are you two doing chasing around outside like a couple of teenagers?"

Jeannie playfully swatted the offending hand away. "Waiting for you guys, of course." She looked over at Lex, who had pulled a small duffel bag from the back seat of the truck. "How are you feeling, Slim?"

"A little tired." Lex closed the door and put her right arm around Amanda's shoulders. "Remind me to never offer to take Little Miss Bargain Hunter here to the mall Christmas shopping again, okay?"

Frank looked at the tall woman with a new respect. "Good lord, Lex. No one in their right mind would be that brave." He quickly spun around and walked back to the house.

"Giddy-up." Jeannie gently kicked her husband's thighs with her heels. "Better watch it, handsome. My sister has that look on her face."

"Oh, no." Frank galloped comically up the steps. "Anything but the Look." He raced into the house with a laugh.

Amanda watched her brother-in-law run into the house with Jeannie hanging onto him for dear life. "Those two are crazy." She snuggled up against Lex as they walked slowly to the house. The blonde looked up and noted the dark circles under her lover's eyes. "Are you sure you're okay?" *She's probably exhausted, but I bet I'll never hear about it from her. I'm feeling a little run down myself. I hope I'm not coming down with something.* She inhaled heavily.

"I'm all right, love. How are you feeling? Maybe we can sneak a nap before dinner." Lex felt the fatigue pull at her. *And I love the idea of snuggling up with her. God, I've completely gone off the deep end. World class mushball.* She waited for the blonde to step into the house and then closed the door behind them. *I hope she's not catching something. It sounds like she's having trouble breathing.*

"I'm fine, Lex. Too many pine-scented candles in the

mall, I think." Amanda stepped into the entry hall of the large house.

The mall was full of people, which was normal for the time of the year. It seemed like every shop had candles or incense burning. Even Amanda, who normally enjoyed the scents, had waved her hand in front of her nose. "This stuff is overpowering, isn't it?" she asked her companion.

Lex rubbed her nose with one hand. "You could say that." She looked over at Amanda, who cleared her throat. "How about if we get something to drink, and take a break over there?" She pointed to a large open area that had several benches and indoor trees.

"That sounds wonderful. My feet are beginning to complain," Amanda admitted. "Why don't you take the bags and sit down, and I'll go get the drinks?"

"Nah. MY feet are fine. YOU take the bags, and I'll fetch the drinks." Lex handed her packages to her friend and walked away before Amanda could argue.

The blonde stared after her friend. I can't believe I let her win. *She smiled thoughtfully.* Yes I can. She's just so darned cute when she wins.

The rancher stepped up to a nearby refreshment cart. She smiled at the young woman working behind the counter, who was frantically trying to keep up with the orders. When the teenager looked up and saw Lex, she stopped what she was doing and returned the smile.

"Hi. Umm. Can I help you?" The young girl's eyes never strayed from Lex's.

"Hello. I'd like two large Dr. Peppers, please." Lex was shoved from behind. She turned around and glared at the teenaged boy behind her.

The boy stared up at her defiantly. "What?" he snapped.

"Don't push your luck with me, boy; I'm not in the mood." Lex sharpened her glare, which caused the young man to turn away.

The girl behind the counter smiled. "He's been here

several times today, harassing folks. Thank you. " She gave
Lex *two Styrofoam cups filled with soda.* "You have to get
the lids on the counter there beside your left hand, I'm
afraid. I don't have room for them back here." She winked
at the tall woman. "I get off in about an hour and a half, if
you're interested. "

Ooh, boy. Jailbait. My favorite, *Lex winced to herself.*
"*Umm, thanks, but I can't. My girlfriend is sitting over at
the atrium, and she's the jealous type.* " Lex winked at the
girl. She left the cups on the sideboard momentarily and
grabbed a couple of lids and straws. "Thanks again. "

*Covering the drinks, she looked around and noticed
the teenaged boy had disappeared.* Good. Maybe he'll
leave that poor girl alone. *The rancher picked up the
drinks and made her way back over to Amanda, who was in
an animated conversation with an elderly woman.*

"*And I told that clerk that I could get the same pair of
gloves at the discount store downtown for half that price.
And do you know what she told me? She said that maybe
I'd be better off buying from there, since it's apparent that
I have no taste.* " Amanda shook her head in disgust.

The older woman laughed. "Those folks in that store
always think that they're better than anyone else. Still, I
figured THEY'RE the ones having to work there, and I'M
the one that's shopping, so I think that makes me a little
better." She looked up and saw a tall woman smiling down
at them. "Oh my, you're a tall one, aren't you?"

Lex chuckled and handed Amanda her soda. "So I've
been told, ma'am. Would you like a drink?" She offered the
other drink to the older woman.

"*Oh, honey, you don't have to do that. I can get my
own,* " the elderly woman demurred, but gratefully
accepted the cup. "What about you?"

"*I'll just go grab another one. I've got a friend working at the drink stand, so it won't take but a second.* " She
winked at Amanda and walked back over to the refreshment
booth, much to the delight of the young girl working
behind the counter.

"Mandy. Lexington. It's great to see you both again." Anna Leigh rushed from the den and wrapped her grand-daughter in a bone-jarring hug. "I know it was only yester-day, but it seems like forever." She pulled away from Amanda and studied the tall woman standing quietly nearby. "You look horrible, honey." *And my granddaughter doesn't look much better. I think it's time to get tough with both of them.*

Lex allowed the older woman to pull her into a gentler embrace. "I'm all right, Gramma." She didn't think that she would feel comfortable using the name bestowed upon Anna Leigh by Amanda, but it slipped out quite easily. *I must be tired.*

Anna Leigh beamed with happiness at the name. "I don't think so, Lexington. You're pale and look like you're about to fall over." She looked over at her granddaughter, who stood between Jeannie and Frank. "Honey, why don't you help Lexington upstairs and rest a bit before dinner? It's still about two hours away." The ringing of the tele-phone interrupted the young woman's answer.

"I've got it!" Jacob called from the den. A moment later he stepped from the room with a serious look on his face. "Hello, girls." He noticed the look of exhaustion on the tall woman's face. "I hate to bother you Lex, but Rev-erend Nelson is on the line. He's returning the call I left for him the other day."

"Maybe I should just take the call for you, honey." Amanda stepped over and wrapped her arm around the rancher's waist. "There's really not much you need from him now anyway, is there?"

"No, but since he's nice enough to return the call, the least I can do is talk to him." Lex squeezed Amanda gently and led her into the den. "Thank you, Grandpa." She stopped and kissed the older man on the cheek. When Amanda had told her how happy the older couple was that Lex called them by more familiar names, the rancher had vowed to herself to try and continue the practice. *They've done so much for me; I'll gladly do it for them if it makes them happy. Besides, I like having them as grandparents.*

Jacob grinned. "Any time, sweetheart. The rest of us will be in the kitchen when you get finished." He walked over to his wife and pulled her close. "Shall we, my love?" They walked into the other room with a smiling Jeannie and Frank close behind them.

Lex walked over to the desk and picked up the phone as she sat down. "Hello? Reverend Nelson?" She waited for Amanda to sit down in her lap before she continued. "Thank you for returning our call."

The voice on the other end of the line was that of a much older man, deep and resonant. "No problem at all, young lady. I don't know the Caubles that well, since they don't attend our church, but I've made their acquaintance. Jacob has done some very fine work for us in the past." He cleared his throat and continued. "Now what is it I can do for you, my dear?"

"I'm trying to get some information on my grandparents. Mr. and Mrs. Cauble tell me that you performed my parent's marriage ceremony, and may remember something that might help."

"Of course. Just who were your parents? I'll see what I can do." Reverend Nelson felt a kernel of pride that they had thought to come to him to help.

Lex shook her head. "I'm sorry. That was terribly rude of me. My name is Lexington Walters. My parents were Rawson and Victoria Walters, and their ceremony was held about thirty-six years ago."

The older man was struck speechless momentarily. "Walters?" he asked when he got his voice back. "You're the young woman who runs that ranch, aren't you?"

"Yes sir, I am." Lex shrugged slightly at the questioning glance she received from Amanda.

"What do you want from me? Your kind of people is not natural," the reverend blustered.

The rancher felt a pang of hurt. "What do you mean, my kind?" she asked quietly.

"Godless heathens, the whole lot of you. Flaunting

your perversity in front of all decent folks." He paused for a minute. "Why do you want to know about the Edwards? They were upstanding god-fearing people. I heard that Mrs. Edwards passed on recently, probably from the shame of knowing how truly sick her granddaughter is." He took a breath and spoke in a quiet tone, "Give up your ungodly ways and come to the church. We can help you, young woman."

Amanda saw the hurt on her lover's face and gently took the receiver away from Lex. She cleared her throat and drew in another heavy breath. "Reverend Nelson?" She had heard the question that Lex had asked him and had a pretty good idea what he had said. "My name is Amanda Cauble. I'm Jacob and Anna Leigh's granddaughter." She fought back a yawn. *Must have been all that walking in the mall. I'm pooped. Lord, I hope it's not a cold. It's getting hard to breathe.*

He took a deep breath and sighed. "Amanda. It's good to meet you. Don't tell me you're a friend of hers."

"Actually, I'm more than just Lex's friend, sir. I happen to love her very much." She could hear the reverend take a breath to speak. "Just a minute. You are supposed to preach love and forgiveness. What gives you the right to judge anyone? The last I heard, that wasn't your job."

"Now you listen to me, young lady," he retorted in anger.

"No. You listen to me. I've had it with people who think they're better than anyone else, just because they have money, or a nicer house, or they go to a certain church. It's wrong. You're wrong. Thank you for your time." Amanda hung up the phone with a sharp exhale. "I hate hypocrites."

Lex smiled tenderly at the young woman sitting in her lap. "You are amazing." The upset that she had felt at the clergyman's words faded quickly. "I love you so much, Amanda."

The blonde leaned over and kissed Lex on the forehead. "I love you too, honey. Why don't we sneak upstairs and take a quick nap? All that righteous indignation can wear a girl out."

"Sounds like a really good idea." Lex allowed her friend to climb off her lap and lead her from the den. She watched as Amanda climbed the stairs. *Hmm. You know, suddenly I'm not quite as tired as I was a few minutes ago.*

"Don't even think about it," Amanda called over her shoulder. "We're going to rest." She missed a step and stumbled slightly. "Oops."

The rancher sighed as she helped steady her friend. *How does she do that? I can never get away with anything.* "Right. Rest. Gotcha."

* * * * * * * * * *

Charlie looked up as the prosecutor entered his office. "Well? Did you get any more information out of him?" Robert Campbell had spent the entire morning talking to Matt Sterling, trying to pry the name of the man's employer from him.

"Finally." Robert sat down across from the sheriff and loosened his tie. "I at least have a lead on where he was staying. It seems that he was evicted from his apartment a few months ago." He pulled out a notepad and flipped through several pages. "He bragged that his boss was so impressed with him, that he was furnished with a fancy condo where he said, 'You can walk to the store and get beer and cigarettes.' I've got a couple of men checking out the condominiums that have short-term leases available; so, hopefully, we should hear something later today."

"That's good news. I'm not going to rest until we find out who's behind this whole mess." Charlie closed the file he had been reading and rubbed his eyes. "I'm worried that they'll try again. Lord knows that Lex has been through enough lately." *Not to mention my poor Martha. She tossed and turned all night last night.*

Robert shook his clean-shaven head. The handsome African-American was in his late thirties, and looked more like a model than an attorney. "I really don't think that's the case, Charlie. I finally got Sterling to admit to the assault on Ms. Walters." *The idiot practically bragged about it.* "He was rather proud of himself since he was able to trick her into going near the ledge. He then, and I quote, 'Whacked that dyke bitch good. I thought I killed her.' Later during the interrogation he told me that his boss had read him the riot act for the attempted murder. Now he's afraid, because he tried again. But I still can't get him to give up the person he's been reporting to." He flipped forward a few more pages in his notebook. "He was supposed to just keep an eye on Ms. Walters and her friend—not take any action against them. So I don't think that there's any danger of someone else following in his footsteps." Robert looked up at the lawman, who had grown very quiet. "Do we have any more information on the guy who posted his bail? How did we get a positive identification if no one actually knew who he was?"

The sheriff stopped rubbing his eyes and smiled grimly. "That's the good thing about small towns: a stranger sticks out like a sore thumb. The town gossips had already spread the word that he was here." He blew out a disgusted breath. "Hell, I've never met Mark Garrett, but after getting the description from Naomi, I knew exactly who had posted Sterling's bond."

"Still no word on his whereabouts? I think that if we could find him, we could get the name of the person behind it all." The prosecutor looked at his watch. "Damn." He looked back up at the sheriff. "I've got an appointment to look at a house. Are we pretty much done here?"

"Yeah, I think so. You've decided to move to Somerville, then?" Charlie smiled sincerely. At the younger man's nod, he continued, "It's a nice little town, most of the time."

The prosecutor returned Charlie's smile. "I know and even though most of my work will be in the outlying areas, I really feel more comfortable about relocating my wife and daughter here. The schools are good, and there's not much crime."

Charlie nodded. "That's true. Well, most of the time, anyway. This mess with Sterling is about as bad as it gets around here."

"It will be all right, Sheriff." Robert stood up and brushed off his slacks. "I'm going to talk to the judge before I leave today, and make sure that Matt Sterling stays in custody this time. He's too dangerous to Ms. Walters to be allowed out on bond."

"Thanks, Robert. I'd say something, but since I'm more or less family, my argument wouldn't hold much water." The sheriff stood up and offered his hand over the desk. "I'm sure glad that you're on this case, young man. Makes me breathe a little easier knowing that you're here."

The prosecutor shook the older man's hand. "My pleasure, Charlie. My uncle has told me nothing but good things about you, and about Somerville." His uncle ran a barbershop in the downtown area for over forty years. Harrison Campbell had been trying for quite some time to talk his oldest nephew into settling down away from the big city. When Robert's daughter got into the wrong crowd at her junior high school, the lawyer had accepted a position as a county prosecutor and decided to move his family to the quiet and friendly community of Somerville with the hope of straightening her out.

The sheriff laughed. "Just don't believe everything that Harry tells you. He hears all the good gossip almost before it happens. Sometimes I think he tends to add a little bit extra to the retelling."

"Don't worry, I've always taken whatever he said with a grain of salt. Sometimes I think that the only reason Uncle Harry ever opened a barbershop was so that he could hear all the news before anyone else. He's always been a nosy old guy." Robert checked his watch again. "I'm going to stop by the judge's office on my way out. What are your plans for the rest of the day?"

Charlie turned serious. "I'm going to wait around a bit and see if we get any information from the investigators that are still out in the field. Hopefully we'll hear something soon about where Sterling was staying." He looked down at his desk for a moment and smiled a little. "Then I've got a date to watch movies tonight with my beautiful fiancée."

"Sounds like a plan, my friend. You've got my cellular phone number in case you hear anything, right?" Robert walked to the door and opened it. "Give my best to your lady, and tell her I look forward to meeting her."

"Will do, Robert. I'll let you know the moment I hear anything. And don't forget the dinner invitation. Martha's one of the best cooks around." Charlie waved to the prosecutor as the younger man left his office. He was about to pick up the phone when it rang, startling him. "This is Sheriff Bristol." Since it was Saturday, the main phone was forwarded directly to an answering service. *Someone must be calling the private number.*

"Charlie. Thank goodness I've found you." Martha sounded upset and out of breath.

He stood up quickly, almost knocking over the chair behind him. "Martha? What's wrong, sweetheart?"

The housekeeper took a deep breath to settle her nerves. "I hate to bother you, but I can't seem to get in touch with Lexie. Could you come on out to the ranch right now? We're having a problem with young Ronnie. He overheard one of the hands talking about what happened here yesterday."

"I'm on my way, honey. Just sit tight." Charlie hung up the phone and grabbed his Stetson from the coat tree in the corner. He slammed the hat on his head and raced from the office.

Chapter
16

Lex woke up covered in sweat. *Damn. Feels like I'm lying too close to a fire, or something.* She felt the smaller body next to hers shiver. *What the...?* The rancher pulled back the covers and saw that her companion was huddled up beside her, trembling violently. "Amanda?"

No answer, just another hard shudder.

"Amanda." Lex tried to roll the younger woman onto her back. "Sweetheart, can you hear me?"

A strangled gasp was Amanda's only response.

"C'mon, baby. Wake up for me," Lex pleaded in a worried tone. She could feel the heat radiating from the feverish body next to her. "Oh, God." The dark-haired woman leapt from the bed in a panic. "Okay. I'll go downstairs and get your Gramma. She'll know what to do." Lex rushed to the door, then paused in afterthought as she looked down at her nude body. "Shit."

They had taken a short nap before dinner, and after the meal had declined Frank and Jeannie's invitation to go out dancing. Lex was still tired, and Amanda had been unusually quiet throughout the entire meal. The blonde had quickly bid her sister and Frank goodnight, then led the rancher upstairs. Within minutes, both women were

undressed and in bed asleep, which accounted for her cur-
rent lack of attire.

Lex quickly grabbed the nearest clothes and put them
on. She tried one more time to rouse her lover. "Amanda?"
She gently shook the trembling woman's shoulder. Amanda
did not awaken in response to her touch, just rolled over
into a fetal position and continued to shiver.

Her concern turning to fear, Lex grabbed a nightshirt
from the nearby dresser and quickly clothed her friend.
"Hold on, baby. I'm gonna get you to the hospital." She
wrapped Amanda in the quilt from the bed and picked her
up. Ignoring the protest from her still-healing back, Lex
pulled the shuddering woman close and carried her down
the flight of stairs.

The rancher paused at the foot of the steps and shifted
her precious cargo. She looked around anxiously and spotted a weak light coming from the den. Heading in that
direction, she stopped in her tracks when a faint voice
spoke.

"Lex?" Amanda's eyes opened slightly. She blinked
several times and tried to focus. "What's happening? I'm
so cold," she rasped out quietly.

"Shhh. You're really sick, sweetheart. I'm gonna get
you to the doctor." She watched as the glassy green eyes
closed involuntarily. "You're gonna be all right," the
rancher mumbled, more to herself than to the woman
unconscious in her arms. She kissed the heated forehead
and stepped into the den. "Anna Leigh. Jacob," Lex was
close to tears, "I need your help."

The older couple was snuggled together on the sofa in
front of the flickering fireplace. When the dark-haired
woman appeared in the doorway, Anna Leigh turned
around and gasped aloud, "Lexington? Dear Lord." She
jumped to her feet and rushed to the rancher's aid.

Jacob followed his wife to the standing woman.
"What's the matter, honey?" He saw that Amanda's face
was flushed and her eyes were closed. "Never mind. I'll go
get the Suburban warmed up." He hurried from the room

without another word.

Anna Leigh touched Lex's arm. "Sweetheart, why don't you bring Mandy over here to the sofa?"

The tall woman continued to stand and looked down worriedly at the frail bundle in her arms. "She's burning up," she murmured with tears in her eyes. "I don't know what to do. We've got to get her to the hospital."

"Okay. I've brought the truck around to the front of the house," Jacob broke in breathlessly. "Let me help you there, Lex." He reached carefully for his granddaughter.

Lex pulled Amanda closer to her. "No. Please." She allowed Anna Leigh to put an arm around her shoulder.

The older woman gave her husband a knowing look. *Let's not argue with her. We need to get Mandy to the hospital.* She smiled a little when he seemed to read her mind.

Abandoning his effort to relieve her of Amanda's weight, Jacob moved to the other side of Lex and helped her navigate to the front door. "I'll help her get Mandy into the truck, love." He looked down at the rancher's bare feet and legs. She had rushed out of the room in her boxer shorts and tee shirt. "Why don't you run upstairs and grab some of Lex's clothes?"

"Good idea, darling. I'll be right there. And I'll leave a note for Frank and Jeannie so they'll know where we went." Anna Leigh patted Lex on the shoulder and hurried up the stairs.

* * * * * * * * *

Oblivious to the stares she received, Lex paced up and down in the waiting room. "What's taking them so damned long?" she grumbled, as her bare feet rapped out a steady beat on the tile floor.

"Lexington, please come over here and get your clothes," Anna Leigh requested for the tenth time. "You're not going to do Mandy any good if you catch pneumonia." She was worried about her granddaughter's friend. The tall woman seemed completely lost without Amanda nearby to anchor her. Anna Leigh looked up as her husband stepped back into the waiting area.

Jacob quickly covered the distance from the door and sat down next to his wife. They were at Parkdale General Hospital instead of the community hospital, because the facility was newer and much bigger. All of them had agreed that the extra thirty-minute drive would be well worth the time since the staff was larger, and the hospital was more up to date. Now he was regretting the decision. *I don't know any of the people here, and they all seem so...impersonal.* "I checked with the nurse at the admitting desk. Still no word on Mandy's condition, but she did tell me that the doctor was in with her now." He watched as Lex continued to pace and sometimes exchange dirty looks with the other people in the room. Jacob pulled his wife close and studied the rancher. She was still wearing her boxer shorts and tee shirt, and carried around the boots and socks that Anna Leigh had brought for her. "Still can't get her to calm down or get dressed, huh?" he commented worriedly.

"I'm afraid not. I can't get much of a reaction at all from her." A sudden inspiration caused Anna Leigh to shake her head. "I don't know why I didn't think of it before." She patted his leg and stood up. "I'll be right back, love. I'm going to go make a phone call." Anna Leigh left the room before her husband could ask where she was going.

The older man stood up and walked over to where the distraught woman was standing. Lex was staring out the window into the evening gloom. Small crystals of sleet slashed against the glass, and Jacob felt a sympathetic chill run down his spine. "Lex," he cautiously placed a hand on the rancher's shoulder, "come away from the window, honey." He felt her shiver as a blast of cold air rattled the window.

Lex turned away from her vigil and stared at the handsome older man. "What?" She looked at the closed door. "Has the doctor been in yet?"

"No, sweetheart. Not yet." Jacob put an arm around Lex and gently led her to a nearby chair. He grabbed an abandoned blanket from another chair and wrapped it around the dark-haired woman's shoulders. "You're like a block of ice, Lex. Why don't you let me get you a cup of coffee?"

"No, thank you." Lex shook her head, but didn't take her eyes from the door. *What the hell is taking so long?* She jumped to her feet as the door opened, but wearily sank back down when Frank and Jeannie burst into the room.

The small auburn-haired woman quickly scanned the room. When she spotted Jacob and Lex, she grabbed Frank's arm and dragged him across the waiting room. "Grandpa. Lex." Jeannie stepped into her grandfather's open arms. "What on earth happened?"

Jacob held the young woman close. He glanced down at Lex, who stared at the door. "Your sister developed a rather high fever after you left the house this evening," he murmured quietly so as not to upset the rancher with the reminder. "Lex brought her downstairs, and we rushed her here."

"Damn." Frank sat down next to Lex and put a gentle hand on her leg. *That explains why Lex looks as if she jumped right out of bed.* "Hey there. Can I get you anything?" He watched as the blue eyes slowly tracked to his face, and blinked.

"Frank? Amanda's sick." She bit her lip as tears welled up in her eyes. "I couldn't get her to wake up." Lex took a deep breath to try and calm herself.

Jeannie pulled back from her grandfather's embrace and looked around the room. "Where's Gramma? Has she gone to call Mother and Father?"

"I'm not sure, honey. She did say she was going to make a phone call, but I don't know to whom." Jacob looked up as the door opened.

A dark-haired man wearing a white lab coat walked purposefully into the room. He glanced down at the clipboard in his hand and looked around the waiting room. "Are there any relatives of a Miss Amanda Cauble here?"

Jacob made his way over to the smaller man. "I'm her grandfather, Doctor...?"

"Barnes." The weary doctor looked up into the older man's concerned eyes. "Why don't we go into the consultation room, and I'll brief you on what I know."

"How's my granddaughter, Dr. Barnes?" Jeannie, Frank, and Lex had joined Jacob. "Can we go in and see her now? Is she going to be okay?"

The doctor looked at the anxious faces surrounding him. "She's resting comfortably for now. But I really need to get some information from you first." Dr. Barnes consulted his clipboard again. "Has Miss Cauble complained of difficulty in breathing, or had any problems with coordination?"

All faces turned to Lex. "You've been around her more than the rest of us lately. Has Mandy mentioned anything like that to you?" Jeannie asked the tall woman. "She did seem rather quiet at dinner this evening."

Lex shook her head. "No. She hasn't said anything to me, although she seemed more tired tonight than usual. What's wrong with her, doctor?"

"As I said before, I really want to talk about her condition privately. Let's go into the consultation room." The doctor opened the door and began to usher the group out with him.

Jacob stopped suddenly. "Wait. My wife. She's gone to make a phone call." He didn't want Anna Leigh to come back and see her family missing.

"I'll wait for her, and then we'll both join you," Frank volunteered. He wanted to know what was wrong with Amanda too, but felt that it was more important for the others to receive the information as soon as possible.

Dr. Barnes nodded. "Very well." He looked at the three remaining people. "You all *are* immediate family, correct?" All but the tall woman nodded. "Who are you in relation to the patient?"

"I'm, uh..." Lex looked at Jacob with confusion. *What the hell am I? Friend? Family? Significant other? Damn.* "She's my...uh...we're..."

"Never mind. If you're no relation to Miss Cauble, you'll have to stay here. Immediate family only." He ushered Jacob and Jeannie from the room.

Jacob could be heard arguing with the doctor as they walked down the hallway. "You had no cause to treat her like that. Lex is a part of our family, too." The doctor's reply couldn't be heard.

Lex stood there and stared at the closed door. She felt Frank's strong hand clasp her shoulder gently. "C'mon, Lex. We'll wait for Anna Leigh to get back, and then she'll find out what's going on for us."

* * * * * * * * * *

Charlie pulled his cruiser up to the front entrance of the ranch house. He noticed that two old trucks were also parked nearby. *Those are the trucks that the ranch hands use. I wonder what on earth is going on?* Before he could finish climbing the steps, the front door opened and Martha bustled out.

"Thank goodness you're here." She rushed to the lawman and enveloped him in a fierce embrace. "Ronnie's in the den. He's really shook up, too. Lester and Roy are with him now, and I can't seem to get in touch with Lexie. There's no answer at the Caubles', and I get the voice mail message when I call her cell phone."

"Calm down, sweetheart. Everything's going to be okay." Charlie rubbed her back and then pulled away slightly. "What seems to be the problem? You said on the phone that Ronnie found out about his brother and became upset. Does he blame Lex for Matt being back in jail?"

Martha allowed her fiancé to lead her back into the house. "No, he somehow feels responsible for what his brother has done, and is trying to leave the ranch." She stopped when she heard several loud voices coming from the den.

"Now just calm yourself, son," Roy's deep voice rumbled. "No sense in you getting all upset."

"I don't deserve to stay here." The young man tried to race from the room, only to run into Charlie in the hallway. "OOOF." Ronnie stumbled back and then paled. "Sh...Sheriff Bristol?" He looked at Martha, and then to Charlie. "I guess you're here to take me back to the detention center, aren't you?" He raised both hands up in front of his body. "Might as well put the handcuffs on me. I'm no better than my brother."

The lawman shook his head and was about to speak when Martha stepped between them. "Now you wait a cotton-pickin' minute. Don't you dare compare yourself to the likes of that man." She reached out and grabbed the teenager's shoulders and pulled him to her gently. "My Lexie would be the first to tell you that you can't judge a person by their family." She felt Ronnie's arms wrap around her body as the young man buried his face in her ample chest and began to cry. "It's all right, honey. This is your home now. No one's going to send you anywhere, I promise."

Charlie watched with pride as his wife-to-be comforted the upset boy. *She's so good with kids. It's a shame she never had any of her own. Well, I should take that back. Lex is more like her own than anyone could ever be. And she's done a fine job with her.* He motioned for the other two men to join him in the hallway.

Lester smiled at the scene as he passed. "Sorry you had to make the trip out here for nothing, Charlie." He led the other two men down the hall to the kitchen. "Might as well make some fresh coffee, right?"

"Sounds good to me," Charlie acknowledged. "And I was about to drive on out here anyway."

Roy laughed. "That's right. I hear that congratulations are in order." He slapped the lawman on the back good-naturedly. "You're not planning on taking Martha away from the ranch, are you?"

Charlie shook his head and sat down at the kitchen

table. "Like I ever could." He saw the relief cross the foreman's face. "Are you kidding me? I'll have to tie her up
and kidnap her just for the honeymoon."

"Don't we know it? I'll bet that..." Lester's remark
was cut short by the ringing of the nearby phone. "Let me
get that." He limped over to the cabinet and picked up the
receiver. "Rocking W ranch, Lester here."

"This is Anna Leigh Cauble. Is Martha available?"
The older woman's voice conveyed that she was somewhat
upset.

Lester looked at the phone in his hand. "Mrs. Cauble?
Is everything okay?" He covered the mouthpiece with his
hand and raised his eyes to the other two men. "Go get
Martha—it's Amanda's grandmother."

"I'll get her." Roy jumped up and hurried from the
room.

The sheriff stood up and accepted the phone from
Lester. "Anna Leigh? This is Charlie. Is everything okay?"

Anna Leigh sighed heavily. "Charlie. I'm so glad
you're there. We're at Parkdale General."

"Hospital? What happened?" Charlie heard footsteps
and then felt Martha lean up against him. "Martha's here,
Anna Leigh." Neither noticed as Lester limped quietly
from the room to give them privacy.

She breathed a heavy sigh of relief. "Great. Can you
bring her up here? We brought Mandy in over an hour ago,
and poor Lexington is beside herself with worry." *Poor
girl. I think she really needs Martha right now.*

Martha allowed Charlie to hand her the phone. "Did I
hear something about a hospital? What's going on, Anna
Leigh?" She felt her fiancé wrap a comforting arm around
her.

"Mandy seemed to develop a very high fever this
evening after they went to bed, and we rushed her to
Parkdale General. We're now waiting on word from the
doctor. Could you possibly come up here and help us with
Lexington? I'm afraid she's not taking this whole situation
very well."

"Of course. We'll leave right away." Martha smiled at Charlie's agreeing nod. "Is there anything we can bring?"

Despite the gravity of the situation, the older woman almost laughed. "Well, you might want to bring Lexington a change of clothes. She's pacing around here in her pajamas, and I can't get her to put on the jeans and shirt I brought."

"Don't tell me she's wearing a pair of those cartoon shorts and a tee shirt?" Martha closed her eyes in resigned disbelief. *I swear that girl is gonna be the death of me yet.*

Anna Leigh chuckled at the tone in the housekeeper's voice. "I'm afraid so. Everyone in the hospital has seen the Grinch in all his glory."

Martha groaned. "Dear lord, not those. Okay, then. We're on our way, honey." She paused for a moment and turned serious. "My prayers are with you and your family. I know that Amanda is going to be just fine."

Anna Leigh took a deep breath and smiled into the phone. "Thank you, Martha. I'll see you both in a little while."

The housekeeper hung up the phone and looked up into the worried eyes of her intended. "Poor little Amanda's sick, and our Lexie needs us."

"Let's get going, then." Charlie kissed the top of Martha's head and led her from the kitchen.

* * * * * * * * *

Dr. Barnes waited until Jacob and Jeannie were seated in front of his desk before he spoke. When the older man opened his mouth, the doctor raised a hand to forestall him. "Please, Mr. Cauble. We've been over this half a dozen times. Hospital policy states that if a person isn't related to the patient, we cannot release information to them."

"I can appreciate that, Doctor. But what I don't appreciate is the manner in which you dismissed Lexington. She's as much a part of our family as I am." Jacob smiled as Jeannie nodded in agreement.

"That may be true, but policy is policy." Dr. Barnes had worked two double shifts in a row and was completely exhausted, and less than empathetic. He flipped through the notes on his clipboard. "Let's just get a few questions out of the way. Then we can worry about my manners, or lack thereof." The pair across from him looked disgruntled, but nodded. "Please don't take any of these questions personally. I'm trying to help Miss Cauble, so I'll need you to be as truthful as possible."

Jeannie looked questioningly at the physician. "Believe me, we'll do everything we can to help my sister."

"Thank you." Dr. Barnes consulted the papers in front of him. "Does Miss Cauble use drugs, even recreationally?"

"WHAT?" Jacob jumped to his feet. "Are you out of your mind?"

"Grandpa, please." Jeannie grasped his arm gently and pulled him back down to his chair. "No, she never has."

A timid knock at the door caused all three heads to turn in that direction. Anna Leigh poked her head in and smiled slightly. "I'm terribly sorry I'm late. The nurse at the front desk told me where to find you." She noticed the upset look on her husband's face. "What's wrong?" The small woman stepped the rest of the way into the room and stood next to Jacob.

He pointed a shaky finger at the startled doctor. "This man insinuated that Mandy is on drugs." Jacob glared at the seated man.

"Mr. Cauble, I wasn't insinuating anything. Due to the nature of my patient's illness, I had to ask that question." He waited until everyone was seated again. "We can rule out drug use, then." Dr. Barnes spoke more to himself as he wrote something on the clipboard. "Did I hear you correctly, that she spends most of her time with that woman in the lobby?" he asked the concerned people in front of him.

"That's right, Doctor. Amanda has been living at Lex's

ranch for over a month now," Jeannie offered helpfully.

Dr. Barnes continued to write, as he mentally braced himself for the next question. "How well do you all know this woman? Does she have a history of drug use?"

Anna Leigh couldn't help herself. She laughed. "Good Lord, no." She patted her husband's arm to keep him calm. "I've known Lexington for most of her life. She's the most anti-drug person I have ever met. Why all the questions about drug use?"

"After running several tests, we've concluded that Miss Cauble's illness was brought on by barbital poisoning." Seeing the blank looks on everyone's faces, he continued. "This is something that cannot be accidental."

Jacob felt his wife's fingers dig deeply into his arm. "Poisoned?"

"Is she going to be okay?" Jeannie asked shakily.

"We hope so. The next twelve hours are crucial. Once she gets past that, she should be fine."

"How could she have come in contact with this? Are you sure it wasn't somehow an accident?" Anna Leigh questioned. *Why would anyone want to hurt Mandy?*

The doctor set his pen down on the desk with a weary sigh. "I'm afraid not. This had to be administered either orally or by injection. From the traces we found in her bloodstream, she was given a very large dose. Today."

* * * * * * * * *

Frank watched as Lex tossed the blanket from her shoulders and paced the waiting room again. *She looks like hell.* He stood and tried to keep up with her. "Lex, why don't you get dressed, and we'll go get some coffee? I'm getting cold just looking at you." It was true. The waiting room felt like it was about sixty-five degrees, and the sleet slamming against the windows made it feel even cooler.

"Why won't they tell us what's wrong with her? They won't even release the damned room number to me—just that she's in intensive care." Lex ran a nervous hand through her disheveled hair. She stalked over to the window and peered out at the late night gloom.

Frank stood behind the tall woman and put his hands on her shoulders. "I'm sure it's just a precaution. She going to be fine—you've got to believe that." Neither one of them heard the door open behind them.

Martha stood inside the doorway holding a small suitcase. "Lexington Marie Walters. You get yourself over here and put some clothes on this instant."

Spinning around, Lex almost knocked Frank down. "Mada?" she murmured and rushed forward as tears spilled down her cheeks.

Martha crossed the room to meet Lex halfway and gently embraced the distraught woman. "It's going to be all right, baby. I'm here now." She dropped the suitcase behind Lex and held the tall woman tight. Allowing the rancher a few moments to get herself together, she then pulled back a little and gave Lex a no-nonsense look. "Now, you're going to put some clothes on and go wash your face."

"But what if..." Lex argued, until her mouth was covered with a small hand.

"No arguments, Lexie. Charlie and Frank can wait here while we get you presentable. You don't want Amanda to see you looking like this, do you?" The housekeeper wiped at Lex's face with a cotton handkerchief.

Lex smiled slightly. *She always seems to have one of those things stashed somewhere. I don't know where they come from.* "No, Mada. You're right. I'm a mess." She gently took the handkerchief away from the smaller woman and dabbed at her eyes. "C'mon, let's get this over with before the doctor comes back." She kissed the graying head beneath hers and bent down to get the suitcase.

"I'll get that for you, sweetheart." Charlie picked up the overnight traveling case.

"Thanks, Uncle Charlie." Lex wrapped her arms around the lanky sheriff and squeezed. "I really appreciate you both coming."

The lawman cleared his throat and returned the hug. "No place I'd rather be than here with you, honey." He rubbed her back comfortingly then took a step back. "You two go take care of business, and I'll stay here with Frank. We'll send word if the doctor comes back before you do, okay?"

The dark-haired woman nodded. "Please, do." Lex took the suitcase from Charlie and kissed his cheek. "Thanks again. I don't know what I'd do without you both." She allowed Martha to lead her from the room.

Charlie watched her leave with a sad look on his face. *Wish I could take that hurting look away from her.* He looked over at Frank, who was also watching the tall woman as she left the room. "Have you heard anything at all?"

Frank shook his head. "No. Not a damned thing." He stood up and stretched. "It's been several hours since they brought Mandy in. The doctor came to get Jacob and Jeannie about twenty minutes ago." He looked at the sheriff with a grim smile. "I thought we were going to have a fight on our hands." He brushed off the front of his jeans and sat back down.

"A fight? Did Lex do or say something?" Charlie dropped down next to the brawny man. "I know she's not the most patient person in the world, but..."

Frank shook his head. "It wasn't her. Jacob got upset when the doctor refused to allow Lex in the consultation room with them. He claimed that he could only talk to the immediate family."

The older man sighed. "Damn. I'd forgotten all about that rule. No wonder Lex looked so upset when we came in. I'm just glad that Anna Leigh thought to call us."

"She called you? I was wondering how you two heard about this so quickly." Frank stretched out his long legs. "I keep debating with myself on whether or not to call Amanda's parents. I honestly don't know if they would even care."

The door opened and Anna Leigh bustled through it,

looking around anxiously. She saw the two men sitting down nearby and rushed over to them. "Charlie. Thank goodness you could make it. Where's Lexington?"

Charlie and Frank had both jumped to their feet as the small woman came into the room. "Martha took her to get cleaned up and dressed. Is something wrong?" The sheriff felt a knot of apprehension build in his stomach.

"Not with Mandy. Although they said that the next twelve hours are crucial. We need to find out exactly where they were today. Mandy has been poisoned." Anna Leigh looked around the room. "While we were in there with the doctor, a nurse came in with the most disturbing news."

After Dr. Barnes dropped the bombshell about Amanda's poisoning, he sat back to allow the family time to adjust to the news. He was about to go over the young woman's condition when a knock at the door interrupted him.

A slender blonde nurse entered the room. "I'm sorry to disturb you, Dr. Barnes, but Dr. Sanderson thought you should read this." She handed him a clipboard, then quickly exited the room.

"Thank you, Francis," he called after the woman. After reading for a few moments, Dr. Barnes looked up at the people seated across the desk. "You're from Somerville, isn't that right?"

"That's right," Anna Leigh answered, and then looked at her husband in confusion. "What does that have to do with Mandy's condition?" she asked quietly.

The doctor looked up from the notes with concern. "It appears that an elderly woman was brought into Somerville Community Hospital earlier this evening with the same symptoms as your granddaughter."

"An elderly woman? Do you think that she may be able to tell us how Mandy was poisoned?" Jacob asked expectantly. "It's too much of a coincidence to ignore, isn't it?"

"You're right. But I'm afraid she won't be able to help us. The woman died this evening before she was able to tell

anyone anything," the doctor related quietly. "We need to find out where Miss Cauble has been today—it's the only way we can figure out how it happened, and possibly keep others from being exposed to the poisoning agent."

Anna Leigh stood up. "I'll go get Lexington. They went shopping today, and she would be able to answer your questions better than we can."

Dr. Barnes stood up as well. "That's a good idea." He looked at Jacob with a small smile on his face. "It would also give me an opportunity to apologize to her." He stepped around the desk and headed for the door. "If you'll excuse me, I'm going to go check on my patient. I also have to contact the authorities and notify them of the latest development." He left the room quickly.

"Are you saying that someone else was poisoned too?" Charlie immediately changed from concerned family member to sheriff. *I'd better make some phone calls.*

Anna Leigh nodded. "That's what the doctor told us. And now he wants to talk to Lexington to find out where they were today."

The door opened and Lex stepped inside. She was wearing her usual denim shirt and jeans, and a pair of comfortable-looking boots. Martha had also braided her long hair in one long plait, and it dropped casually down her back. She was followed by Martha, who looked quite upset. "Lexie, please calm down. I'm sure that Charlie can get to the bottom of this in no time." Martha looked up and saw Anna Leigh approaching. "Has there been any word?"

"Not yet. But the doctor has gone back in to check on Mandy now." Anna Leigh crossed over to Lex and gently touched her arm. "What's wrong, Lexington?"

Lex had to stop herself before she shook off the light touch. "It's bad enough that they won't tell me what the hell is going on, but now there's a couple of policemen who want to talk to me about Amanda." She looked over at Charlie with tears of frustration in her eyes. As much as she hated asking for help, the lawman's presence would be a great comfort. "Can you go with me, Uncle Charlie? I could really use the moral support."

"That's a good idea, honey. I need to talk to them anyway." The lawman wrapped an arm around Lex's shoulders. *How can anyone so strong suddenly look so frail? Poor Lex. Looks as if she's about to collapse.* "C'mon, sweetheart. Let's go see what they want." He nodded at Martha, who returned the look. *They'd better be easy on her. I don't think she can handle much more right now. Although I'd feel better if she had a lawyer with her, not just me.*

"Do you want me to go with you?" Martha asked.

The rancher looked at the housekeeper with a sad look. *If for some reason they arrest me, I don't want her to witness that. It would just about kill her.* "Umm. Would it be okay if just Charlie went with me?"

"That'll be fine, Lexie. I'll just wait here with Anna Leigh, okay?" The housekeeper patted Lex on the back as they walked by. "If you need me, just holler." She knew that the young woman was having problems coping, and realized that being the focus of a roomful of people would be too much for her.

****

After a short foray down the corridor, Lex and Charlie stepped into the small room and looked around. The doctor's consultation room was furnished with a cheap formica-topped desk and several uncomfortable looking chairs. Two men in suits stood up as they entered. The older one was a tall blonde with a crew cut. The shorter, stockier of the two had loosened his tie, and his dark hair was damp with perspiration. Both looked uncomfortable in their dark suits.

The shorter of the two men came forward and offered his hand. "I'm Detective Weingart, and this is Sergeant Byers." He motioned to the taller man who waved the two people inside. "Thank you for taking the time to talk to us,

Ms. Walters. This is not an interrogation. But if you'd feel more comfortable with a lawyer present, we can wait." At the negative shake of her head, he continued. "We know what a trying time this is for you since your...friend...is so ill. Please, have a seat, and we'll try to make this as quick as possible." The detective looked speculatively at Charlie, who was still wearing his sheriff's uniform. *Great. A small time sheriff trying to play cop. Just who we need under- foot.* Suppressing a sigh, he offered his hand. "I'm sorry. I don't believe we've met."

Charlie stepped forward and shook the man's hand. "I'm Sheriff Bristol from Somerville." He gently guided Lex to a nearby chair. "I hope you don't mind if I sit in." *Although I'm not about to leave. I don't like the way the short guy is looking at Lex. He's going to be trouble, I'll bet.*

The sergeant reached over and shook Charlie's hand also. "Not at all. We were just hoping that Ms. Walters could help us figure out how Miss Cauble was poisoned."

"Poisoned?" the dark-haired woman gasped, missing the edge of the chair and falling to the floor. She didn't even realize when Charlie helped her up and into the chair. "Did you say that Amanda has been poisoned? How in the hell did that happen?"

"That's what we'd like to know. Was she with you at all times today? Did she come into contact with any strang- ers or suspicious persons?" the blond, crew-cutted man asked. He consulted an open folder that was lying on the desk.

"We were together all day today. I promised to take Amanda Christmas shopping at the mall, and we spent the entire day there. We never left each other's side." Lex frowned in deep thought. "Wait. I did leave her at the atrium while I went to get us something to drink, but she really wasn't out of my sight."

The sergeant wrote furiously in the folder while the detective circled the desk and sat on the corner closest to Lex. "You both had something to drink at the mall?" He looked down at the upset woman. "How do you explain that Miss Cauble became ill, while you appear to be in good health?"

Charlie stepped forward and got between the detective and Lex. "I don't think I like your insinuation, Detective. Just what is it you're trying to say?"

"We're not insinuating anything, Sheriff. We're just trying to find out how Miss Cauble could have been exposed to the poison." Detective Weingart stood firm. He didn't like the attitude of the old man or this woman. *She's Miss Cauble's "special" friend. Disgusting.*

Lex stood and put a reassuring hand on Charlie's shoulder. "It's all right. I want to get to the bottom of this as much as they do." She guided the sheriff into a nearby chair and stood over the still seated detective. "We ate the same foods, drank the same drinks..." She stopped as a thought occurred to her. "Damn."

Sergeant Byers looked up from taking notes. "What is it, Ms. Walters?"

"I'm not sure, it may be nothing, but..." Lex's brows were creased in thought.

Detective Weingart crossed his arms across his chest. "Why don't you let us be the judges of what's relevant, and what isn't. Just spit it out." *Smartass dykes. Think they're better than men.*

The rancher ignored him and spoke directly to the sergeant. "I bought a couple of drinks from this little stand in the mall. There was this obnoxious teenaged boy behind me, pushing people around and just being a general nuisance. When I turned back around from getting lids for our drinks, he had disappeared."

"And you expect us to believe that a teenage boy is responsible for something as devious and well-planned as this poisoning obviously was? How was he supposed to know which drink belonged to which person?" The detective snorted in disgust. *Save me from amateurs.*

"I don't know. But that's the only." Lex paused in mid-sentence. "Wait. I forgot. I didn't drink mine."

Detective Weingart pointed an accusing finger at the rancher. "So you admit that you didn't have the same drink." *I've got you now. Probably had a little lover's quarrel and wanted to get back at her. I'll bet Miss Cauble was going to dump her for a man, and she lost it.*

"If you'll just shut your damned mouth for half a second, I'll finish telling you." Lex glared at the pudgy man. When he leaned back a bit and nodded, she continued. "Amanda was talking to an elderly lady when I got back to where she was sitting in the atrium. I gave Amanda one of the drinks, and offered mine to the other woman because she looked as if she needed it."

The two policemen looked at each other in silent communication. "That certainly explains a few things," the tall man murmured to his partner.

"Explains what?" Irritated, Charlie stood up again. "Are you about through giving Lex the third degree? I don't appreciate you treating her as if she was some sort of criminal." He quieted when Lex put a hand on his arm. "I'm sorry, honey, but I can't stand by and watch them treat you like this."

Lex smiled gently at the older man. "I really appreciate your concern, Uncle Charlie, but these guys are just doing their job." *Although, "chubby" over there is beginning to get on my nerves. I hope they're not trying to play good-cop, bad-cop.* She almost laughed out loud at that thought. *Too many reruns of* Miami Vice, *I'll bet.* She looked back at the officers and posed Charlie's question again. "What exactly does this explain?"

Detective Weingart looked over at his sergeant, who shrugged. "We received a report from Somerville Community Hospital some time ago. An elderly woman was admitted earlier this evening with the same symptoms as Miss Cauble."

"Elderly woman? Oh, God." Lex paled and sat back down in her chair. "How is she?"

"She passed away about three hours ago," Sergeant Byers advised sympathetically. *Poor woman. First her friend is poisoned, and then she finds out that her act of kindness killed an innocent bystander.*

The dark-haired woman closed her eyes and slumped in her chair. "She's dead because of me." Charlie's comforting hand on her shoulder almost did her in. "What about Amanda? Do you know if she...?" *I couldn't survive if I lost Amanda. God.*

"Mrs. Carruthers had a history of heart problems. Her family said that she had been complaining of chest pains for the past week or so. We're fairly certain that the poison just sped up the inevitable," the sergeant explained. *She's got enough to worry about without assuming the guilt for the old woman's death. Maybe I can make her feel a little better.* "Just as an added precaution, we've assigned an officer to Miss Cauble's room. We don't want whoever slipped the poison to her to try and finish the job." *I don't think that's going to happen, but better safe than sorry.*

"I don't think Amanda was the target, gentlemen." Charlie squeezed Lex gently on the shoulder again. "Why don't we let Lex go back to the waiting room, and I'll be more than happy to brief you on the events before today. It's a rather long and complicated story."

"I don't know," Detective Weingart demurred. "I think that I'd like Ms. Walters to come down to the station for further questioning. I want to make sure that we have all the details correct." He practically glared at the seated woman. *Teach her to take an attitude with me.*

Lex stood up and challenged the red-faced policeman with a defiant look in her eyes. "Then you're gonna have to arrest me, Detective, because I'm not leaving this hospital any other way. Now if you'll excuse me, I need to go check on my friend." She turned and stalked from the room.

The stocky detective jumped to his feet and started for the door. "She wants to be arrested, I'll be more than happy to oblige her."

"Hold it, Barry. Let her go," Sergeant Byers ordered. "I'm sure that Sheriff Bristol can answer any questions we may have." When Charlie nodded, he motioned for the detective to sit back down. "Now why don't you start at the beginning, Sheriff?"

* * * * * * * * * *

Mark Garrett sat in a hotel room about four blocks away from Parkdale General. He had been parked outside the Caubles' home earlier to see if his plan had worked, but had been horrified to see Lex carry an unconscious Amanda to the Suburban. Now he was determining the need for damage control. "Hello. I would like to check on the condition of a patient that you have there."

"Yes, sir. And what is the name of the patient you are inquiring about?" the nurse asked pleasantly.

"Amanda Cauble." Mark crossed his fingers. *Please let her be okay. I'll be in so much trouble, otherwise. Stupid teenager. Can't depend on anyone to do anything right.*

The nurse paused for a moment. "Umm, let me check. Will you hold for a moment, please?" Loud classical music played on the line as she put him on hold.

Mark quickly slammed the phone down. "Dammit." He jumped up from the edge of the bed and paced the small room. *They must have figured out what happened. That stupid kid was supposed to drug both cups then make sure that Amanda DIDN'T drink hers.* He checked his watch and sighed. *Midnight in Los Angeles. Damn. I really do not want to make this phone call.* With slumped shoulders, Mark sat back down on the bed and dialed a number from memory. After several rings it was finally picked up.

"Yes?" A slightly breathless voice answered.

"It's me." Mark knew that no other identification was necessary.

"Where in the hell have you been? I've been waiting by this phone for hours," the voice berated. "I called your hotel last night, and they said that you had already checked out. What's going on down there?"

The weary man wiped a hand over his face. "Everything kinda fell apart. I had to go into hiding."

The person on the other end of the phone sighed heavily. "It has to do with that jackass you hired, doesn't it? I knew that he was too stupid to be trusted."

"Well, that's part of it." Mark leaned back on the bed and closed his eyes. *This is not going to be fun.* "He attacked Walters in her barn yesterday morning."

"You've got to be kidding me." Shocked, the speaker paused to reflect, then continued. "Well, was he able to do any damage? That would at least be some consolation."

Mark sighed. "Not exactly. She pretty much kicked his ass all over the place, even though she was still recuperating from his last mistake." He took a deep breath. "And, to top it all off, the sheriff is actually engaged to her housekeeper—so he had spent the night there at the ranch. Sterling never had a chance. He got hustled off to jail in a hurry."

There was another thoughtful silence on the phone. "This just keeps getting better and better." The sarcasm fairly dripped from the voice. "Thank God the idiot doesn't know much." A slight pause. "He doesn't know who I am, does he?"

"No. Of course not. That little voice-altering device not only made your voice indistinguishable, but scared the hell out of him," Mark assured his boss. "But, I have more bad news." He braced himself for the outburst that was sure to come. "I wanted to surprise you by getting Walters out of the picture but things didn't go quite as I had planned."

The voice turned icy. "What did you do?" *This will teach me to use amateurs instead of professionals when I want something done.*

He tried to soften the news. "It really was a great plan. Even if it didn't succeed, her reputation would be in question." *It would have looked like she overdosed on drugs. My plan was practically foolproof.*

"What...did...you...do?" Each word was bitten off sharply as the question was drawn out angrily.

"I paid this punk kid fifty dollars cash to dump some

drugs in her drink—he was supposed to put it in both cups and then whiz by on his skateboard to knock Amanda's out of her hand."

"Dear God. You don't mean that...?" Pain colored the voice. "Is she...?"

Mark sat up again. "She's alive. But Walters gave her drink to some old lady, and it killed her."

"You almost killed her? You stupid fool." Shaky fingers rubbed a suddenly pounding forehead. "Where is Amanda right now?"

"She's at Parkdale General Hospital. The last I heard, they had her in intensive care. But I can't call for any information. I think the cops know that she was poisoned, and are screening all incoming calls." Mark twirled the phone cord around his finger. "What do you want me to do?"

Silence.

"You still there?" he questioned cautiously.

"Yes, I'm here. Shut up for a minute while I think." *Incompetent moron. I should have just hired a professional to do away with that abominable woman when I had the chance.*

The exhausted man sat on the edge of the bed, waiting for a brilliant resolution for his problem. "Do you want me to..."

"No. You've done quite enough already. Just sit there quietly while I try to think. Wait. My other line is flashing. Hold on a minute." A quiet click, and there was silence on the line.

Mark sat patiently. Other scenarios kept running through his mind. *I don't know where everything went so wrong. If I weren't so afraid of going to prison, I'd shoot the bitch at point blank range.*

"I'm back." The voice sounded tired and upset. "That was my obligatory phone call notifying me of Amanda's condition. About time they called me, don't you think?"

"Maybe they were just waiting until they had something to report. How is she?" Mark really didn't care too much about her condition. He was more worried about what would happen to him if she died.

A slight silence, then a heavy sigh. "She's still in intensive care. The doctor said it would be sometime tomorrow before we know for sure if she'll pull through."

"Is there anything I can do?" he asked with fake concern.

"I believe you've done quite enough, Mark. Get yourself on the next flight to Los Angeles, and we'll find someplace for you to hide until this mess all blows over." Thoughts of a sudden car accident, or having the man disappear altogether flashed through the churning mind. *I can't allow him to be out running around. If they were to catch him, they'd have no trouble getting the little idiot to blab everything he knows to save his own skin.*

Mark nodded at the phone. "All right. I'll drive straight to the airport from here. I should be able to get a flight out in the next couple of hours."

"Actually, I think it would be better if you drove to Austin to catch a flight. I know it's a lot further for you, but the authorities won't be looking for you there." *And it's a long stretch of highway. Lots of construction. Anything could happen.*

"Good idea. I'll leave immediately." He was anxious to please his employer after the mistakes of the past week.

. "Now remember—keep as low a profile as possible. Fly back coach, and try to make yourself as invisible as you can. I don't want anyone to remember you. I'll have you booked on a flight out of the country when you get here. There will be someone to meet you that will have your itinerary."

Mark exhaled a sigh of relief. "Thank you. I know that I let you down, but if you'll just give me a chance, I'll make it up to you."

"I know you will." The voice was calm, almost soothing now. "None of this was your fault. Everything is going to work out just fine. Now hurry back. I've got an assignment for you in Great Britain that I think you'll enjoy."

"Thank you. I won't let you down," the happy man gushed. *I KNEW that I was special. This just proves it. A shame my worthless wife didn't seem to think so, but once I get settled overseas, I'll try to get custody of the kids.*

"Oh. Just in case. You don't have anything with you that could be traced back to me, do you? I'm a little concerned that you could be caught by a radar-happy trooper."

Mark thought for a moment. "Nope. Not a damned thing. But you don't have to worry. You can trust me," he assured his employer.

"I believe you. I guess I'm just a little paranoid." A nervous chuckle crackled through the line. "Hurry back, and we'll get you settled overseas."

"Great. I'm leaving right now." Mark hung up the phone with a satisfied smile. *Guess someone else will get to take care of that Walters woman. Oh, well.* He grabbed his suitcase and looked around the room. *No more backwater dives for me. Ritz Carlton, here I come.*

Chapter
18

Dr. Barnes strode into the waiting room where six faces turned to him anxiously. Charlie was the only person missing, as he was still in conference with the two police officers. The doctor walked over to where Jacob sat, flanked by his wife and Jeannie. "Mr. Cauble. I'm sorry it's taken me so long to get back to you, but I wanted to see how your granddaughter responded to the treatment before I spoke to you."

"How is she?" Anna Leigh asked, as she spared a glance at Lex and Martha, who were over by the windows. The dark-haired woman looked completely lost and alone, and it broke Anna Leigh's heart.

"She's stable for now. We have her on a respirator to help her breathe, so that her heart and lungs are not over-worked."

Jeannie squeezed Frank's hand. Her husband sat on the other side of her and pulled her close. "Can we see her?" she asked.

Dr. Barnes glanced over at the woman by the window. *Sometimes I really hate my job.* Responding to Jeannie's question, the doctor nodded. "Only for a moment, and not all at once." He turned to face Lex. "And I'm sorry, but

only family members are allowed into ICU." *Stupid rule—
she's obviously very close to Miss Cauble. Maybe I can do
something about that.*

The rancher nodded wearily. "I understand. Thank you
for all you've done, Dr. Barnes." Lex felt Martha put a
sympathetic arm around her waist. "If it's okay, I'll just
hang out here for a while."

"Certainly.   Thank   you   for   understanding,   Ms.
Walters." Dr. Barnes turned away from them and stepped to
the door, then spoke loudly to the family. "If you will just
follow me. She's in room two-thirty one of ICU. Right
down the hall from our supply office." He winked at Lex
and led the rest of the family out of the room.

Martha looked after them in surprise. "I do believe
that Dr. Barnes is human after all," she murmured to the
tall woman next to her.

"You've got that right." Lex smiled down on the older
woman. "I'm gonna give the Caubles some time with her
first, then I think Amanda is going to have a 'nurse' by her
side for a while." She kissed the top of Martha's head.
"Why don't you and Charlie check into a nearby hotel?
You look a little worn out." *More like a LOT worn out. I
keep forgetting she's not as young as she used to be. These
late hours can't be too good for her, or Charlie.*

"Good idea, sweetheart. We'll book several rooms
together so that everyone will have a place to rest up,"
Martha agreed. "That means you, too." She gave the
rancher one of her serious looks. "And before you give me
any trouble, don't bother. You're not too big for me to take
over my knee."

Lex rolled her eyes. "Yes, ma'am. Just call and leave
me a message at the nurses' station so I'll know where you
are." She pulled the short woman into a strong hug.
"Thanks for being here, Mada. I couldn't have made it
without you."

The housekeeper returned the hug. "Phooey. That's
what family is for, honey. Now don't be too late, all right?
You need your rest too, if you're going to be in any condi-

tion to do Amanda any good." She pulled away just as the door opened, and an exhausted looking Charlie stepped into the waiting area.

"Where'd everybody go?" he asked as he looked around.

"They've gone to see Amanda." Martha walked over to him and rubbed his arm. "Lexie is going to wait here for them, and we're gonna go get a few hotel rooms for us all."

Charlie looked over at Lex, who was leaning against the far wall with her arms crossed over her chest. "Are you sure that you don't need us to stay with you, honey?"

The young woman shook her head as she pushed away from the wall and walked over to the older couple. "I'm sure, Uncle Charlie. I really just need a little time by myself." She pulled the lawman into a strong embrace. "You take care of Martha for me, all right?" she whispered in his ear.

"You know I will, sweetheart." He pulled back and looked into her eyes. "You just call if you need us, and we'll be back here in a flash."

"I promise." Lex leaned over and kissed them both. "Now go on, before y'all collapse on me." She watched with a fond smile as the couple left the room. *There go the best parents anyone could ever ask for. I've certainly been lucky to have them.*

****

After looking in both directions, the tall figure stepped quietly into the empty corridor and stealthily approached the intensive care unit. Strong hands brushed down the front of the well-fitting scrubs before the desk and its attendant were broached.

The nurse seated behind the counter looked up from her paperwork and smiled at the new arrival. "You're a little early, aren't you? Shift change isn't for another forty-five minutes."

"Umm. Yeah. But I couldn't sleep, so I thought that

I'd just take a look around."

The young nurse nodded. "I know the feeling. We've got one new patient, and her family left a little while ago. It was really close for a while, but it looks like she's going to pull through just fine." She looked down at a chart. "I expect the doctor will take her off the respirator first thing in the morning."

Lex almost collapsed in relief. "That's great. I'll just go in and check on her, if you don't mind." Her entire body was screaming for her to race into the room, regulations be damned.

"Go on. I'll cover for you." The nurse nodded at the uniformed police officer standing by the entry door to the unit, and the tall woman passed through into the corridor housing the patient rooms, closing the door behind her. The nurse picked up the phone and dialed an extension. "Dr. Barnes? This is Nurse Hamil in ICU. I did as you asked. The dark-haired woman is in there now."

"Thank you, Shelly. Don't let anyone disturb her, all right? I think that she's the best medicine for our patient right now." Dr. Barnes smiled and hung up the phone.

Lex peered through the glass wall before reaching the door. *Room two-thirty one. But it's too dark to see any-thing.* She pushed the door open slowly and stepped in, allowing it to close quietly behind her. Blue eyes tracked to the bed on the other side of the room. It was tucked into the corner and was surrounded by several different machines. *Oh, God. Amanda.*

Amanda's small body was lying deathly still on the bed with several tubes running between her and the machines. The only sounds in the room were the thump and hiss of the respirator and the quiet beep of the heart moni-tor. Her upper body was slightly elevated, and her hair was in disarray and matted to her head.

"My poor love," Lex murmured quietly as she stood next to the bed. She pulled a nearby chair closer and sat down, her eyes never leaving the frail form. She reached over with a trembling hand and gently grasped the small fingers. "Oh, sweetheart. What have I done to you?" *None of this would have happened if you weren't with me. How will I ever be able to look into those beautiful green eyes again? WILL I ever be able to look into them?* Her other hand lightly brushed the blonde hair from Amanda's face. "I love you so much. Please don't leave me." She let her hand fall to the nearest shoulder and clasp it gently. Her dark head fell to the bed and she cried herself to sleep, never relinquishing the hold she had on her lover.

A soft pat on her shoulder caused Lex to bolt upright. "What?" She looked around in fear, only to be faced with the knowing smile of Dr. Barnes.

He chuckled at the way the rancher was dressed. The dark green garments flattered the dark-haired woman and fit her form as if they were made for her. *She could easily pass as a nurse or doctor, the way they fit.* "I'm sorry, Ms. Walters, although I do admit that you look right at home in those scrubs, we're going to have to ask you to leave." He saw the panicked look on her face and hastened to reassure her. "We need to move Miss Cauble out of ICU and into a private room."

"What time is it?" Lex asked, as she looked around, disoriented. *How could I fall asleep when I was supposed to be watching her?*

The doctor checked his watch. "About ten minutes after seven. It seems that Miss Cauble responded well to the medication during the night." *Not to mention the specialized care she received from her friend. I'm glad Ms. Walters could take a hint.*

Lex glanced over at the still form on the bed. She couldn't see any visible change in her friend from when she sat down next to her last night. *She still looks the same to me.* "Is she going to be all right?"

"Barring any complications, yes. She should even regain consciousness before too long." Dr. Barnes patted the tall woman on the shoulder gently. "Why don't you go get changed? We'll have her placed in a private room within another hour or so. Nurse Hamil is pulling a double

shift, so she'll be glad to let you know which room we put
her in."

"Thank you, Dr. Barnes. For everything." Lex shook
his hand and stepped back. She started for the door and
then turned back to look at the young woman lying on the
bed. "I'll be back in a few minutes, love," she murmured
softly, tears filling her eyes as she left the room.

* * * * * * * * * *

Jeannie walked into the hotel coffee shop where Charlie and Martha were having breakfast. The sheriff had a
serious look on his face, and the housekeeper was looking
down at a half-eaten plate of food. The young woman
stepped up to the table and smiled. "Good morning. I hope
you two slept a little better than we did last night."

Martha looked up and brightened. "Good morning,
honey. Why don't you sit down with us?"

"Thanks. Everyone else should be downstairs soon,
and then we can all go see Amanda. I called the hospital
earlier, and she's been moved to a private room." Jeannie
sat down and looked up with appreciation as a waitress
came over and poured her a cup of coffee. "Thanks."

"I'm sorry to hear you didn't sleep well. Were you
worried about your sister?" Martha asked sympathetically.
She was concerned about Lex. The rancher never came to
the hotel during the night, and never called. *I hope she's
okay. It's not like my Lexie to stay gone so long without at
least calling.*

The younger woman shook her head. "Not exactly.
Well, I mean I was worried about Amanda, but the most
upsetting thing was having to call my parents and let them
know what had happened. They didn't take it very well,
I'm afraid."

Charlie looked at Jeannie. "You talked to your folks
last night?"

"Yes." Jeannie nodded with a grim smile. "Dad complained that I waited too long before I called, and Mother

complained because I called so late in the evening and woke her up." She rolled her eyes.

"Are they on their way here to see Amanda?" the sheriff asked. After the information that he had received that morning, Charlie really wanted a chance to talk to Michael Cauble. *Especially after all the things that Amanda told me about him and Lex.* Thinking back to the earlier phone call, he listened with only half an ear to the conversation around him.

When the phone rang at six am, Charlie had feared the worst. He quickly reached over to grab the phone before it could wake Martha. "Hello?"

"Sheriff Bristol? This is Robert Campbell. I'm sorry to bother you, but late last night we found out where Matt Sterling had been holed up."

"Last night? Why wasn't I notified then?" Charlie whispered, somewhat upset. He sat up and turned on the light to find his glasses and a notepad.

Martha sat up sleepily. "What is it, honey? Is it Lexie?"

He turned to his fiancée and covered the mouthpiece on the phone. "No. It's Robert Campbell. He has some new information on the case for me."

"Oh, good." Martha nodded and then grasped his arm gently. "Do you want some privacy for the call?" She knew that most of the information that Charlie was given was confidential, and she didn't want to put him in an awkward position.

"No. It's all right, sweetheart." Charlie smiled at his intended. "You might as well get used to it, I suppose." He leaned over and gave Martha a quick kiss. "Go ahead, Robert."

The young prosecutor sighed heavily. "I know that you're out of town on a family emergency, but it may be somehow related. After we found the residence," he paused with a chuckle "it's actually more of a rundown duplex. Not a condo as the suspect had previously stated."

Charlie laughed. *"Sounds about right. But how does finding where Sterling stayed relate to what's going on here?"* He scribbled down a few notes while he waited for the younger man's answer.

"We were also able to obtain the phone records for the time he spent at the residence. It seems that Mr. Sterling received quite a few calls from a nearby hotel, as well as a couple from a Los Angeles exchange."

"Los Angeles? Were they all from the same number?" The sheriff turned slightly so that he could exchange glances with Martha.

Robert shuffled some papers. *"Yeah. All the same number. It's listed as a private office line for a large corporation. We're checking into it now to try and trace it back to an individual. But I thought that I'd let you know, since one of your earlier suspects in the attempted murder was in California."*

"Thanks. But I'm really hoping that it all turns out to be just a big coincidence." Charlie wrote a little more then closed his notepad. *"I really do appreciate you keeping me up to date, Robert. We'll be going up to the hospital shortly, so I'll call you from there if I uncover any new developments."*

"Sounds good to me," Robert agreed. *"I hope everything turns out okay for your family. Let me know if there's anything that I can do for you, okay?"* the prosecutor offered.

Charlie looked over at Martha and smiled. My family. I think I like the sound of that. *"Thank you, my friend. We're going to go find Lex this morning and try to get her to take a nap. I'm sure she spent the entire night up worrying. Let me know if you get any more information."*

The prosecutor exhaled heavily. *"Sure will. Talk to you later, Charlie."* He hung up the phone before the sheriff could say another word.

The sheriff looked back up at Amanda's sister. The young woman looked as if she had a bad taste in her mouth.

Jeannie shook her head. "I asked them if they'd be flying in to see Mandy. Father flatly refused because he didn't want to run into Lex. Mother said that as long as my sister was involved with 'that woman,' she wouldn't feel comfortable here either." She looked over at Martha sadly. "I'm sorry, Martha. I hope you realize that not everyone in my family feels the same as my parents do."

Martha patted the younger woman's arm sympathetically. "You have nothing to apologize for, honey. I'm just sorry to hear that your parents gave you such a hard time." She shook her head. "I can't believe that they'd leave their own daughter in the hospital hundred of miles away without trying to see her. Maybe they'll feel differently about it this morning."

"I doubt it. They were pretty upset when Mandy chose Lex over them," Jeannie explained.

"Just how upset were they?" Charlie asked. "Were they angry at Amanda, or at the situation?"

The young woman looked at the sheriff with a confused frown. "Well, they haven't disowned her or anything, so I suppose it's more the situation than anything else. Why?"

The sheriff smiled. "Just thinking out loud, that's all." He looked over Jeannie's shoulder to the door of the restaurant. "Looks like everyone's up, now." Charlie waved at the three people standing inside the doorway.

Jacob returned the wave and escorted his wife and Frank to the table. "Good morning, everyone." He held the chair for Anna Leigh and then sat down next to her.

"Good morning to you, too." Martha smiled warmly at the newcomers. "Would you like some breakfast? Charlie and I were just about to go over and check on Lexie. She never came to her room last night."

"You mean to tell me that Lex spent all night in that damned waiting room?" Frank asked incredulously. He sat down next to Jeannie and put an arm around her shoulders.

The housekeeper chuckled. "No, not in the waiting

room. She sneaked into Amanda's room and stayed with her all night, I'll bet."

Anna Leigh laughed in delight. "That explains why Dr. Barnes told us exactly where Mandy's room was. I was wondering why he would mention a supply room."

"Me too," Jacob agreed. "I'm really glad that Lex was there with Mandy during the night. It could only help."

Everyone at the table nodded in agreement. Charlie stood up and helped Martha to her feet. "I'm sorry to leave such fine company, but I really want to go check on Lex. I'm afraid she's asleep in a corner somewhere."

Martha laughed. "Knowing our Lexie, she's probably curled up somewhere near Amanda."

* * * * * * * * * *

She stared into the mirror and grimaced. *I look like hell. No wonder Dr. Barnes chased me out of Amanda's room.* Lex bent down and splashed more cold water on her face. "Martha is gonna kick my butt for sure," she mumbled as she looked into the mirror again. *At least my hair still looks halfway decent. I've got to remember to thank her for braiding it.* She rubbed her eyes then looked down at her watch, which had been a birthday gift from her lover.

Lex had been awakened by light kisses across her face. When she opened her eyes, she saw Amanda's beautiful face smiling down on her. "'Morning," Lex mumbled with a smile.

"Happy birthday, love," Amanda offered with a knowing smirk. She leaned down and kissed the dark-haired woman tenderly.

"Umm." Lex licked her lips as they broke apart. "Thanks. But how did...?" She paused. "Martha told, didn't she?"

Amanda nodded. "She sure did. But don't be angry with her, okay? It just came up in a conversation recently."

Yeah. A conversation that started, "Hey, Martha, when's Lex's birthday? I know it's sometime in November, but I don't know the exact day." *She smiled inwardly. "You should have been in the military, honey. Having your birthday land on Veteran's Day like that."*

The rancher rolled her eyes. "Oh, yeah. I'm sure I'd have been a great soldier. I take orders so well." She tickled the younger woman. "At least it's easy for me to remember—11-11-71. Guess 11 is my lucky number."

"Be thankful you weren't born right after New Year's. My mother has always whined about missing out on all the hoopla surrounding a New Year's baby," the younger woman sighed. "Only a couple of hours late, but to her it was such a big deal," she laughed. "Dad complained because I wasn't born in December. He had to wait another whole year to claim me as a deduction."

"I'm sorry to hear that, sweetheart." Lex commiserated, struggling up to a sitting position. "I don't really celebrate my birthday, but Martha usually makes me a cake and gives me a little something. I go along with her to make her happy." She saw a sad look cross her friend's face. "What's wrong?"

The blonde passed gentle fingertips across Lex's face. "Martha told me about your birthdays before." Amanda ran her hand through the thick dark hair. "I'm really sorry that there was never much to them. But I plan to make certain that from now on all of your birthdays are special."

Lex smiled tenderly as she captured the small hand in her hair. She brought it to her lips and held it there, waiting until Amanda's eyes were completely focused with hers. "As long as I have you with me, every day will be special, my love."

"You're sweet," Amanda whispered. "I love you so much, Lex." She opened her hand as the rancher kissed the palm. "Mmm."

"I love you, Amanda. You're the best birthday present that I could ever ask for." Lex's eyes opened wide when Amanda reached under a pillow and pulled out a fist-sized

box. It was wrapped with brightly colored paper and matching ribbon. "You didn't have to do that, sweetheart."

Amanda smiled happily. "I know that you don't like a big fuss, so I just got you a little something for now, and then a little bit more for tonight." She handed the package to the still-dazed woman. "Go on, open it."

Lex grinned as she looked at the package in her hand. "It looks almost too pretty to tear into," she murmured. She slowly peeled the ribbon away and set it aside carefully.

"C'mon, honey. Just open it," Amanda urged impatiently. She watched as her friend enjoyed the wrapped package like a small child on Christmas morning. It's probably the first gift that anyone besides Martha has given her in a long time. *She was charmed by the way Lex savored the moment, taking her time to unwrap the box.*

When the last of the paper finally fell away, Lex was left holding a blue box with the word Seiko etched in silver across the top. With shaky hands she opened the box to reveal a beautiful silver and gold watch. "Oh, Amanda." She pulled the watch from the package and held it up. "It's stunning."

Amanda released the breath that she had been holding in anticipation. "You really like it?" she asked.

"It's incredible." Lex started to put it on then noticed the back of the watch. Engraved? *She turned the watch slightly until the morning light from the windows reflected off its back.* I will always protect and cherish your heart— Love, Your Amanda. *Lex glanced up with tears in her eyes. "That's beautiful." She slipped the watch onto her left wrist and secured the clasp. "Perfect fit." Lex set the empty box down and framed the younger woman's face with her hands. "Thank you, sweetheart. I will cherish it as I do you. Forever."*

Amanda leaned forward to meet Lex halfway. "You're very welcome," she whispered just before their lips touched. "Just wait until you get your other present tonight."

Lex sighed and pulled her sleeve back down. *That had to be just about the best birthday that I've ever had.* She took another quick look in the mirror then turned and left the ladies' room.

"Ms. Walters." Nurse Hamil waved to her from down the hall. She waited patiently until Lex walked up to the nurse's station. "Good morning."

"Good morning, ma'am." Lex smiled at the older woman. "You've certainly put in a full day, haven't you?" She thought about the deception that she had played on the nurse last night. "I'm sorry about what I did last night. I really hope that I didn't get you into any trouble."

The nurse waved the apology off. "Don't worry about it, honey. Dr. Barnes had warned me that you would be showing up and told me to make sure you got in okay." She laughed at the surprised look on the tall woman's face. "It's okay. You weren't wearing any identification, so I normally wouldn't have let you in."

"I kinda wondered why it was so easy to get through." Lex grinned. "Well, anyway, I really appreciate everything that you've done for Amanda. She's very important to me." *That's an understatement. She's the most important thing in my life. She IS my life.*

"That's what we're here for, dear. Would you like to see her now?" The nurse patted Lex on the arm. "C'mon. She should be awake any time now." She grasped the rancher's forearm and led her to a nearby room.

Lex paused at the door, suddenly unsure. She was afraid of what she might find on the other side of the door. "It's okay for me to go in?"

The smiling nurse nodded. "Of course, honey. The doctor left a few minutes ago, and her family hasn't made it in yet." She leaned forward and whispered conspiratorially, "It's about an hour before visitors are allowed, but I won't tell if you won't."

"Okay. Thank you." Lex smiled at the smaller woman. "If anyone calls for me, will you...?"

"Sure. Now go on. She's probably awake already, and

wondering where you are." Nurse Hamil gently pushed the tall woman through the door.

After last night's shock, Lex was relieved to see that all of the machines were gone from Amanda's bedside. The only thing left was the intravenous drip that stood discreetly by the headboard. She stepped quietly over to the bed and looked down at her resting friend. "Hi, beautiful," Lex whispered. She reached down and brushed Amanda's bangs away from her eyes. "You sure gave us a scare, you know." The rancher looked around for a chair. Not seeing one, she decided to just stand by the bed. Her back still ached from carrying the smaller woman down the stairs the night before, but she was not about to leave Amanda's side. While one hand continued to comb through the blonde hair, her other grasped the small hand unencumbered by tubes. "I would give anything to see those beautiful green eyes again."

Almost as if she heard Lex's wish, Amanda's eyelids fluttered open. She blinked several times and finally was able to focus on the tall woman's face. Her mouth opened, but only a strangled gasp came out. She reached for her throat in a panic.

"Sshhh. It's okay, baby." Lex released her hold on Amanda's hand and poured her a glass of water from a nearby pitcher. "They had you hooked up to a respirator during the night. That's why your throat is so sore. Here. Take a sip or two." She helped the younger woman take a few small sips of water. "How's that?"

"Better," Amanda whispered with a grimace. "Still hurts, though." She looked up at her lover. "What happened? The last thing I can remember is going to bed after dinner."

Lex thought back to the frightening moment when she woke up with the feverish woman by her side. *God. I don't think I can go through that again.* Her eyes teared up, and she found it hard to breathe. "Well. I woke up, and you had a really high fever." Lex didn't realize that she'd sat down on the edge of the bed until she felt small fingers tangle with hers.

"Lex?" Amanda's voice was still raspy, but she was very concerned for her friend. The rancher's eyes had filled with tears, and they didn't seem to be focused on anything.

"I couldn't get you to wake up. You got so sick, so fast." Lex continued quietly. "We got you here, and they put you in Intensive Care." She choked back a sob. "Then they wouldn't tell me anything. I'm not family, they said."

"Honey," Amanda could see that Lex was on the verge of a breakdown, "it's okay." She coughed slightly, then allowed her lover to help her with the cup of water again. "Thanks."

The rancher put the cup away automatically, then ran her fingers through Amanda's hair, as if to reassure herself that the younger woman was okay. Her other hand continued to hold Amanda's tightly. "The police even questioned me. They said that you had been poisoned, and thought that I might have had something to do with it." Lex ignored the tears now trailing freely down her cheeks. "I did, you know."

Amanda shook her head. Her natural protective instincts leapt to her partner's defense. "No, you didn't. Don't say that." Belatedly, she registered what Lex had said. "Wait. Poisoned? Are they sure? Why would...?" She could feel Lex's anguish, and it tore at her heart.

"It's true. A kid slipped it into our drinks at the mall. He was probably trying to get at me." Lex sniffled and blinked to try and clear her vision. "It's all my fault. I killed her."

"Who, love?" The conversation was quickly tiring Amanda, but she fought the sleep that pulled at her. *She needs me. I don't think I've ever seen Lex so...lost.*

Lex looked down at their linked hands. "That old woman at the mall. I gave her my drink, and now she's dead." Her breathing quickened as she fought her emotions. "And I almost killed you."

Amanda pulled Lex forward until the older woman was

cradled against her chest. "Shhh. You did no such thing.
Whoever put that stuff in our drinks did that, not you." She
felt Lex tremble and then begin to sob. "It's okay, honey.
Everything is going to be okay." She looked past the
rancher when she heard the door open. Amanda raised one
hand from Lex's back and waved at her grandmother, who
nodded and stepped back through the door, closing it quietly behind her.

"I almost lost you," Lex murmured. She had both arms
wrapped tightly around Amanda as she continued to cry.
"Oh, God."

"Shhh." Amanda continued to rub her lover's back
comfortingly. "I'm fine, really. It's all going to be okay,
Lex." She looked at the tubes that ran down to her left
hand. *Guess it was pretty close. Poor Lex. But why would
someone try to poison...? Oh, no. That means that someone
else besides Ronnie's brother is after Lex.*

****

Anna Leigh looked at the people gathered in the hallway with her. "Why don't we all go get a cup of coffee in
the cafeteria? Lexington is with Mandy right now." She
saw knowing smiles all around. "From what I could see,
they both looked just fine."

"That's great news," Charlie exclaimed. "I'll even buy
the coffee." He took Martha's hand in his and led her down
the hallway.

Jacob looked at his wife, then at Jeannie and Frank.
"We should give them a few minutes alone anyway, don't
you think?" He reached for Anna Leigh's hand and followed the sheriff.

Charlie had only taken a few steps when his pager
went off. He looked down at the display and turned grim.
"Let me just make a quick phone call, and I'll meet you all
there." He leaned over and kissed the top of Martha's head.
"I won't be but a minute, sweetheart."

"C'mon, Martha. You can tell us some embarrassing

stories about Lex while we wait." Jeannie took the older woman by the arm and led her down the corridor.

The sheriff watched his friends leave as he made his way to the row of payphones nearby. He sighed as he picked up a receiver and dropped his coins into the phone. After he dialed, he waited impatiently while the phone on the other end of the line rang.

"Campbell here."

"Hello, Robert. I just received your page." Charlie pulled out his notepad.

The young man on the other end of the phone sighed in relief. "That was fast. Thanks for calling back so soon."

The sheriff clicked his pen and turned to a clean sheet of paper. "No problem. What's up?"

"I'm afraid you're not going to like it." Robert could be heard shuffling papers in the background. "We traced those phone calls that were made to Sterling."

"Great. Where did they come from?"

"We traced one number back to a local hotel, where a man fitting Mark Garrett's description had rented a room for the past two weeks. He paid cash, so we really have no solid proof that it was him." The prosecutor sighed wearily. "But it at least gives us a connection."

Charlie wrote for a moment, then stopped. "A connection? What sort of connection? We already knew that Garrett posted bond for Matt Sterling."

Robert paused for a moment. "We have a connection between Sterling and the person I believe is behind this whole mess. Seems his boss was calling from an office in his home."

"Really? Then we have a positive ID on the employer?" The sheriff continued to write furiously. "Do we have a name?"

The prosecutor paused a beat before answering. "The phone number was traced to a private office in the home of Michael Wayne Cauble."

Chapter
19

The receiver dropped from Charlie's fingers. He watched it swing back and forth for a moment before he put the phone back to his ear. "Is that a positive identification? Are we sure that the phone number is registered to Michael Cauble?"

"I'm afraid so. I personally ran the check three different times," Robert assured him. "I'd really like to talk to this man. Do you think that he'll be coming here to see his daughter?"

"I'm not sure. His oldest daughter called last night to notify him and his wife of Amanda's condition. Neither one of them seemed too concerned." Charlie put his notepad back in his pocket. He looked up as the door to Amanda's room opened and a very haggard Lex stepped out. "I've got to go, Robert. Page me if you get any more information, okay?"

The prosecutor released a tired breath. "You've got it. I'll talk to you later. Give my best to your family, Charlie."

Charlie hung up the phone and walked quickly over to Lex. "Lex? Are you okay, sweetheart?" He stepped up next to her as the tall woman turned and fell into his arms. "What's wrong?"

"Uncle Charlie." Lex buried her face in the older man's shirt and breathed in the familiar scent of his cologne. She cried with relief for a few moments, then pulled back, wiping ineffectually at her tears. "Sorry about that."

He pulled a handkerchief from his back pocket and used it to clean away the tears from her face as he asked, "What's the matter, honey? Is Amanda okay?"

Lex looked up at the sheriff with a relieved smile. "She's fine. I'm a basket case, but she's okay." She looked around the hallway and then back to him. "Where's everyone else?"

He wrapped his arm around her shoulders and led her away from the room. "They went to the cafeteria for a cup of coffee." Glancing down at the young woman, he observed, "You look like you could use a cup yourself, sweetheart."

"Yeah. I think I could. You buying?" She smiled up at the man who had always been there for her.

"Yup." Charlie continued to lead her down the hall. "C'mon. They probably make it nice and thick, just the way you like it."

Lex laughed. "Great. Think they'll just give it to me intravenously? I'm so damned tired that I don't think I could lift the cup." She gratefully accepted the sheriff's arm around her waist as they headed toward the cafeteria.

* * * * * * * * *

"You've got to be kidding me." Martha almost spewed coffee through her nose. "She didn't actually do that, did she?"

Anna Leigh nodded. "Took off all her clothes and raced through the front yard, right during shift change at the plant." She laughed with the others at the table. "I swear, the woman you know is not the same child I knew growing up. She was such a little exhibitionist as a toddler."

Martha shook her head. "That's hard to believe. Amanda gets embarrassed just talking about anything related to that sort of thing." She met the older woman's glance. "It embarrasses her to let me wash her underwear."

"That sounds just like my sister," Jeannie shared. "She turned into such a prude when she grew up. I was afraid she was going to die a virgin." She felt an elbow in her side. "What?" The auburn-haired woman glared at her husband. "Well? It's true."

Frank covered his face with one hand. "I can't believe you talk like this around your grandmother," he murmured.

Jeannie leaned over and whispered loudly in his ear, "She knows about sex. How do you think my dad got here?"

"Jeez." The big man blushed.

Lex sat down next to the red-faced man and leaned into him. "What's the matter, Frank? You look a little flustered." She nodded and smiled gratefully to Charlie when he set a cup of coffee down in front of her. "Thanks, Uncle Charlie."

"No problem, kiddo." The sheriff took his place next to his fiancée. "Hello there, beautiful. What are you folks jabbering about?"

"Just telling some old stories to pass the time. How's Mandy doing, Lexington?" Anna Leigh asked the exhausted woman. *She looks completely worn out. Poor thing.*

The rancher looked up from her cup of coffee. "She's sleeping right now. But she was feeling pretty good, other than having a sore throat from the respirator." Lex bit her lip to keep from crying. *She just looks so tiny and frail in that bed, all alone. I should have never promised her that I would go lie down for a while. I hate leaving her by herself. Damn.*

Jacob reached across the table and took Lex's hand in his. "I'm glad you were there for her, Lex, but you look like you're about to fall over." Out of the corner of his eye, he saw Jeannie quietly leave the table. "Why don't you go back to the hotel and get a little rest?"

"I promised Amanda that I would take a nap, but I didn't actually tell her I would leave the hospital." Lex quickly drained her coffee cup. "I think I'll go find a quiet corner in the waiting room to curl up in." She stood up slowly.

Martha stood up also. "I think that we can do better than that, Lexie." She smiled as Jeannie walked back into the room and gave her a thumbs up. The housekeeper was about to lead her charge from the room when a young nurse stopped them.

"Excuse me. Are you Ms. Walters?" She had been given a detailed description of the woman, but the lady that stood before her was more beautiful than the man on the phone had described.

"What's wrong?" Martha asked. She had one arm wrapped protectively around the rancher and wasn't about to let go.

Lex smiled faintly at the nurse. "I'm Lexington Walters. Is something wrong with my...friend?" She stammered a bit on the last word, unsure of how their relationship could best be described.

"Oh, no. Nothing like that. There's a phone call for you at the nurses' station. It's a Mr. Dempsey. He says that it's quite urgent."

The housekeeper scoffed. "That old geezer thinks that everything is urgent." She remembered when he would call the ranch all upset at the slightest rise or fall in the market. Joshua Dempsey had been Victoria's investment broker. When she passed away and left a large sum of her funds to Lex, he had stayed on to make certain that unscrupulous men, like her older brother, wouldn't take the young woman for all she had.

"How did he know where to find me?" Lex looked at Martha, who shrugged innocently.

"I wouldn't know. I called Roy before we left, so that he could keep an eye on the house for us. But he's the only one I told. I think that old man is psychic, or something."

She shook her head.

The rancher sighed. "Might as well go talk to him before he has a stroke." She smiled at the nurse. "Thanks for coming to get me."

"No problem." The young woman returned the smile before leaving the room.

Martha squeezed Lex gently. "Do you want me to talk to him and just take a message? You look like you're about to collapse, honey."

"No, I'll talk to him. I was supposed to call him earlier this week anyway." Lex turned slightly and looked down at the older woman. "When I finish with him, I'm gonna go hide somewhere and take a quick nap." She pulled Martha into a strong hug. "I'll see you later, okay Mada?"

"Sure, honey. But when you get through with Mr. Dempsey, stop by Amanda's room first. We've got a little surprise for you."

Lex looked down with a smirk. "You have something up your sleeve? Should I be nervous?"

"Nope." The housekeeper patted Lex gently on the side. "Now go talk to that old man before he calls out a search party."

"Yes, ma'am." Lex saluted Martha and left the room smiling. She hurried to the nurses' station. "I'm Lexington Walters. Did you have a call for me?"

The young nurse who had given her the message came up behind Lex and patted her on the back. "Here. Let me get that for you." She walked around the desk and picked up the phone. "Here you go." She handed the receiver to Lex and stepped back. "Just holler when you're done."

The tall woman nodded and smiled. "Thanks." She ran a hand over her face and spoke into the phone. "This is Lexington."

"Young lady, you're harder to find than a five-dollar call girl on a Saturday night," the old man the other end of the line teased. "I know you're busy, but I have to notify you of a problem with one of the companies that you are a major stockholder in."

"I'm sorry, Joshua. I should have called you sooner. What's going on?" Lex smiled gratefully at the young nurse when she was handed a pen and paper. She whispered her thanks to the smiling nurse, and began to doodle on the small notepad.

The old man took a breath and then coughed. He'd smoked two packs of cigarettes a day for over fifty years, and refused to give them up. "Well, it's actually an investment that your dear mother made, rest her soul. But the company's stock is dropping drastically, and I'm afraid that if you don't get out now, it could seriously hurt the sale price of your investment."

Lex nodded. She had always trusted the old man's business savvy—he'd never been wrong before. "Okay. What's the name of this business?" She listened for a moment and then wrote. "Cawkeen Enterprises? Did I hear that right?"

"That's right. I don't have too many particulars about it, but something happened to it recently and it's dropping fast." Joshua could be heard shuffling papers in the background. "If you sell now, you'll still be making a profit."

Lex thought for a moment. *Never heard of it. Oh, well.* "Go ahead and sell it all, Joshua. I trust your judgement." She scribbled down the name and put the bit of paper in her shirt pocket. "Thanks for calling."

Dempsey chuckled. "No problem, Lexington. I'll call you back next week to go over some new investment ideas." He hung up the phone still smiling. *That girl has as good a business sense as her mother.*

She hung up the phone and smiled at the two nurses. "Thanks again for the use of your phone." Lex turned and walked down the hallway to Amanda's room. She saw Charlie and Martha standing outside the door talking with Frank and Jeannie. "Hi folks. Did I miss anything interesting?"

"Hey, Slim. My sister was asking for you." Jeannie walked up to the tall woman and enveloped her in a hug. "I think she wants you to break her out of here," she whispered into Lex's ear. "I heard her arguing with Gramma. She's feeling a lot better, but the doctor refuses to release her."

"Damn." Lex pulled out of the embrace slowly. "I'll see what I can do." She reached for the doorknob and then stopped. "Maybe I should give your grandparents more time with her."

Jeannie laughed. "Maybe you should go in and save my grandparents." She winked at the others. "We could hear Mandy from here. I guess her throat is feeling better."

Lex looked at the smiling faces around her. "Okay. Wish me luck." She squared her shoulders and pushed the door open.

* * * * * * * * * *

He tossed the suitcase onto the bed and flipped it open. *Of all the days to give the servants the day off,* he thought angrily. *I hate having to pack my own bag. I always forget something.* The phone next to the bed rang several times before he sighed heavily and picked up the receiver. "Michael Cauble here."

"Mr. Cauble. Thank goodness I found you." The excited voice on the other end of the line practically yelled. "I thought you were out of town?"

"I was. Something unexpected came up. What's the problem?" Michael cradled the receiver between his shoulder and ear as he continued to pack the bag. *I really don't have time for his hysterics. Damned fool.*

The man paused for a moment. "Umm. You remember how your stock began to fall this past week?"

Michael stopped what he was doing. "Yes? You told me it would pick back up and not to worry about it." A small knot of apprehension formed in his stomach. "Why?"

"Well...umm..." The voice trembled slightly.

"Dammit, Craig. What the hell is going on?" Michael finished tossing clothes into the suitcase and zipped it shut. *I just get back, and now I have to find enough clean clothes to pack. Thank God I have a spare set of luggage.*

Craig coughed to clear his throat and to stall for time. "It seems like one of your major stockholders couldn't be so patient."

"What do you mean?"

"They sold their stock. And a couple of others must have gotten scared because they did the same," the frightened man almost whispered.

The executive dropped soundlessly onto the bed. "How bad is it?" he murmured.

His employee swallowed loudly. "Umm...well..." Craig stammered. "They'll probably freeze all your assets to pay off the stockholders. I'm afraid you've lost it all, Mr. Cauble."

"Everything?" Michael felt lightheaded. "Even the Swiss accounts?"

"Uh. Those were closed out a month ago, sir. I thought you had done it."

Michael closed his eyes. *Elizabeth. That bitch said that she'd take me for everything I had.* "Do you have any idea what caused the stocks to fall so rapidly?"

Craig breathed a sigh of relief. *At least he's not going to shoot the messenger. Thank God.* "There is a rumor making the rounds that you were going to sell the company to an overseas buyer that had a bad reputation on the market. Everyone believed it, sir."

"All right. Thanks, Craig." The beaten man leaned forward and cradled his head in his free hand. "I've got to go to Texas for a while, My daughter has taken ill. You can reach me at my parent's house." *I hope. Maybe I can mend a few fences while I'm there. Dad was right: a corporate merger does not a good marriage make.* He hung up the phone and stared unseeingly out of the bedroom window.

Michael had hung up the phone last night, angry with his oldest daughter. I can't believe she took so damned long to call us. How does she think that makes us look? He grabbed a decanter of scotch and walked out into the garden, dropping down under the large tree. Even at three o'clock in the morning, the temperature was not too uncomfortably cool.

Amanda. *He remembered small snippets from her childhood:*

A small, bright-eyed toddler climbing into his lap, wanting to "help Daddy work" at his desk.

A laughing ten year old following him around, carrying an old discarded briefcase full of pencils and notepads.

A proud young woman, who had doubled her college workload, in order to graduate early and join her father's business.

What have I done? *Michael remembered the hurt look on his youngest daughter's face when he dismissed her after graduation.* I've become exactly what I have always detested—a man who cares about nothing but status and money. *He took a long pull on the bottle beside him and closed his eyes.* "My God. My little girl." *Michael Wayne Cauble leaned back against the tree and, for the first time in his adult life, cried.*

Hours later, Michael woke up with the sun shining in his face. The hung over executive opened his bloodshot eyes and looked around. I hope it's not too late. *He struggled to his feet and hurried to the house.* "I'm going back to my daughter, if she'll have me." *He dropped the empty bottle in the kitchen trash as he walked purposefully up the stairs. And packed.*

A sound at the doorway caused him to turn from the window. "Michael. I thought that I had heard the phone. Who was it?" Elizabeth Cauble stood with her arms crossed over her chest.

He straightened and took several steps towards her. "You did it. I'm ruined." Michael walked over and picked the suitcase up from the bed.

"Where do you think you're going?" She held out an arm to stop him from passing her. "And what on earth are you talking about? What do you mean, you're ruined?"

"Several stockholders pulled out. I'm broke." He

laughed humorlessly. "Don't look so innocent. I knew you were up to something while I was out of town. I just never figured you to be this vindictive."

Elizabeth glared at her husband. "You've always been weak, Michael. I've tried to give you a backbone, but you're just like your father."

Michael shook his head sadly. "No. I'll never be half the man my father is." He set the suitcase down, pulled out his keyring and removed several keys from it. "You can have this damned mausoleum, Elizabeth. For years I've listened to you, and I became just as cold and calculating as you are." He handed her the keys and wiped his face with his sleeve. "I almost lost my daughter yesterday. I may have already lost her heart." Michael picked up the suitcase and started for the door.

"Don't you dare walk out on me. Not after all I've done for you," Elizabeth yelled.

He stopped and turned back around. "Done for me? What in the hell have you done for me?" Michael dropped the suitcase at the door and shook her head. "You've never done an unselfish thing in your life."

The enraged woman crossed the room and slapped him. "You ungrateful bastard. How dare you speak to me that way." Then Michael watched, spellbound, as Elizabeth's countenance changed from angry and imperious to soft and condescending. She took his hand and led him to the bed and sat him down. "I didn't ruin you. She did."

"Who?" Michael rubbed his cheek where his wife had slapped him. *What the hell is she talking about?*

"I tried to stop her, you know," she looked down at their linked hands, "but she has more lives than a cat."

Her husband jerked his hand out of hers. "What are you talking about?" Understanding dawned on his face. "You're talking about that Walters woman, aren't you?" Michael scooted away from the woman he thought he knew.

"Nothing can be proven, you know." Elizabeth smiled coldly and patted his leg. "And don't act so offended. You don't like her any more than I do. You're just too spineless to do anything."

Michael slapped her hand away. "Just because I don't like someone, doesn't mean I want any harm to come to them. What's the matter with you? Have you completely lost your mind?"

Elizabeth tilted her head back and laughed. "You fool. That woman is the one that ruined you. *She* was the major stockholder that sold you out." She shook her head. "She's probably sitting in a bar drinking beer with her redneck friends and laughing her head off."

"Do you actually believe that?" Michael asked. "As much as I dislike the woman, I can't believe that Amanda would have anything to do with someone like that."

"Oh grow up, Michael. Our daughter—both of them, actually—have been too influenced by those simpering fools that you call parents. It's a shame mine were killed in that car wreck all those years ago. They would have been excellent role models." She stood and paced the room. "I've done everything possible to secure our future and that country bumpkin ruined it."

Her behavior was scaring him. Michael stood up and caught her arm as she walked by. "Stop it, Elizabeth. You're acting crazy." He stopped and thought back to what she had said. "Secure our future? Just exactly what have you done?"

"Since you wouldn't do anything more than hire that worthless private investigator to dig up old history, someone had to take charge." She turned and gave him a disgusted look. "I sent someone to Texas to keep an eye on her."

"You did what? Don't tell me you had anything to do with her almost getting killed." He stepped away from her.

"Not exactly. But the moron that Mark hired..." Elizabeth was cut off by her now furious husband.

He stepped forward and grabbed her arm roughly. "I *knew it*. You slut. Garrett is your little plaything, isn't he?"

"Let go of me." She shook off his hand. "At least he

was man enough to take care of what I needed."

"My God. What haven't you done?" Michael stepped away from her. "Are you going to marry him after our divorce is final?"

She laughed mirthlessly. "Oh please. He was a good distraction, but hardly worthy of any long-term investment on my part." She sat down at the dressing area and picked up a brush. "I sent him overseas." Elizabeth looked at her husband's pale face in the mirror as she brushed her hair. "And as for a divorce. I'm not sure." She reached for her lipstick and applied it to her lips. "There's such a stigma attached to being a divorced woman. I don't know if I want that applied to me."

Michael walked over and stood behind her. "I can't stay married to someone who paid to have another person killed. How can you be so cold and calculating?"

"Don't be such a baby, Michael. I paid someone to keep an eye on her. *He* hired some inbred moron who had a grudge against her. It was his idea to push her off a cliff." Elizabeth sighed. "What's the big deal? She lived. Not that I was happy about that fact," she mumbled, almost under her breath. She met Michael's eyes in the mirror. "Since when have you gotten so attached to her? Why the sudden change in you, Michael?"

"Do you realize that I yelled at Jeannie last night for waiting so long to call about Amanda?" He dropped his gaze. "I didn't even ask how she was." He looked back up at his wife with tears of anguish in his eyes. "My little girl was lying unconscious in a hospital halfway across the country, and I was more concerned with appearances. Dear God. I've turned into your father." He turned away and walked to the door.

Elizabeth turned and glared at his back. "Just where do you think you are going?"

He bent down and picked up the suitcase again. "I'm going home, Elizabeth. And I'm going to beg my children for forgiveness and pray that it's not too late." He walked out the door without another word.

"We'll just see how welcome you'll be when your children find out that *you* were behind this whole mess," she murmured with a smile. "At least all the evidence will point to you."

Chapter
20

Lex opened the door and poked her head inside. Amanda was sitting up in the bed, her arms crossed stubbornly over her chest. *She looks a lot better and she's so cute when she's trying to get her way. I can never tell her no.*

"Just stay one more night, Mandy. The doctor wouldn't ask if he didn't have a good reason." Anna Leigh sat on the edge of the bed. "For goodness sake. You were in Intensive Care last night, and on a respirator. Give your body a chance to get over this, please?" *Where on earth does this child get her stubborn streak?* She glanced over at her husband's smiling face. *Oh, yes. Now I remember.* she smiled to herself.

"But I feel fine, Gramma. I just want to go home." *And snuggle up with a certain rancher.* The young woman sighed in defeat. She heard the door squeak and looked up with a smile. "Hi, stranger."

"Hey, sweetheart." Lex walked into the room slowly. *I feel like I went ten rounds with Mike Tyson, and lost. Every bone in my body aches.* "What seems to be the problem here?" She looked over and saw an empty bed near Amanda's. *Another bed? I bet that's Martha's surprise.*

Sneaky. She grinned inwardly.

Jacob met her halfway across the room and escorted the tall woman over to the spare bed. "Have a seat, honey. You look like you're about to fall over." He put his arm around Lex and felt her lean into him.

Amanda studied her friend carefully. *She looks worse than I feel. Maybe a good night's rest wouldn't hurt either of us.* She looked up at her grandmother's understanding face. "Guess one more night can't hurt." She winked at the older woman. *You win this one, Gramma. But only because I think that Lex needs the rest more than I do.*

Anna Leigh smiled at her granddaughter. "Thank you, dear." She looked over at her husband as he gently helped Lex to the other bed. "Why don't we let these two girls get a little rest and come back after lunch?"

"Good idea." Jacob bent down and picked up the tall woman's feet and swung them up onto the bed. He started to pull off her boots when Lex stopped him.

"Jake. Umm, Grandpa? You don't have to do that. There's nothing wrong with me." She smiled at the older man, who continued to work with her feet.

He removed the boots and set them quietly under the bed. "Nothing other than you're still recovering from a major injury, honey. Now just lie back and get some rest. You both could use it." He covered Lex with a blanket and patted her leg. "Stubborn kid." He walked to the door shaking his head.

Lex heard Amanda giggle. She turned her head and rolled her eyes. "Don't encourage him, sweetheart." She smiled at Anna Leigh. "Could you make sure that Charlie and Martha get a little rest today? I'm really worried about them."

"I'll be glad to, dear." Anna Leigh joined her husband on the other side of the room. "You two girls take it easy, and we'll see you this evening, okay?"

"Okay." Amanda smiled at the couple. "Thank Martha and Jeannie for me, will you? They've been really great." She nodded her head in Lex's direction. *This way I know she'll get some rest.*

Anna Leigh nodded. "I will. Please rest, Mandy." She grinned at Lex, who sat up in her bed with her arms crossed and a disgusted look on her face. "Take care, Lexington." She stepped out of the room, and Jacob quietly closed the door behind them.

"You are so cute when you pout," Amanda giggled, "but I think that you lost this round." She frowned as Lex climbed out of bed. "What are you doing?"

"This isn't gonna work." Lex crawled under the bed. She struggled for a moment, then stood up with a triumphant grin on her face. "There." Amanda's eyes widened as Lex slowly rolled the bed close to hers. When they were side by side, the rancher winked and crawled back under the bed to re-lock the wheels. "Much better." She climbed back up on the mattress and opened her covers to her friend. "Care to join me?"

"Sure." Amanda pulled her sheet and blanket loose on that side and scooted closer. She curled up next to her lover and sighed happily. "Mmm. Perfect."

"Yeah," Lex murmured, as her arms automatically wrapped around the younger woman. She buried her face in the blonde hair and closed her eyes. She felt her throat thicken with emotion. "God. I love you so much, Amanda."

Amanda could feel Lex struggling to maintain control. With her head on the older woman's chest, she could hear the pounding heartbeat and Lex's breathing hitch as she fought the urge to cry. "I love you too, Lex." She squeezed the rancher tighter. "It's okay, honey. I'm fine now."

Lex took a deep breath trying to calm herself. "That was too close. I almost lost you." She bit her bottom lip hard to keep from crying. *Don't you dare cry Lexington. She's been through enough without having to worry about you, too.*

"Nah. You can't get rid of me that easily." Amanda turned her head so that Lex would look at her. "You found me and I followed you home. And I'm not leaving you." She smiled. "That's what happens when you feed a stray, you know. They never leave."

The rancher laughed. "So that's all I have to do?" She hugged Amanda to her tightly. "Guess I'd better stock up on groceries, then." She fought off a yawn. "Damn. I can't believe I'm so tired."

"I don't know why..." Amanda played with the buttons on Lex's shirt. "Dr. Barnes told me that I had a private nurse all night last night," she teased. "I doubt that has anything to do with you being exhausted." She unbuttoned the shirt and slipped her hand inside. When she found only smooth skin, she paused. "I think that you forgot to put something on, honey."

"Nah...Martha didn't bring me one." Lex mumbled as her eyes closed.

The blonde's eyes widened. "Didn't bring you one? What did you wear to the hospital?"

One blue eye opened. "Umm." Lex bit her lower lip. "I was in a hurry," she tried to explain. "And it was the middle of the night, you know."

"Uh-huh." Amanda ran her hand down to Lex's stomach and patted it gently. "Just exactly what *were* you wearing?"

"My..." she grumbled under her breath. *God. How embarrassing.*

A light tickle on the rancher's ribs caused her to jump slightly. "What? I didn't quite get that," Amanda teased. *My God. She's actually blushing.*

Lex sighed heavily. *Busted. My reputation is shot. She'll never let me live this down. Oh, well. At least she'll get a good laugh out of it.* "My boxer shorts and tee shirt."

"Oh, lord. Not the ones you wore yesterday afternoon when we took our nap?" Amanda winced, then giggled.

"Yeah. The Grinch ones." Lex closed her eyes. *Just kill me now.*

Amanda buried her face in her friend's chest and laughed. "You ran around all over the hospital in your Grinch jammies and tee shirt?" Her laughter wound down, and she looked up at her sheepish lover. "Is that *all* you were wearing?"

Damn. "Like I said, I was in a hurry." Lex met the green eyes nervously. "I really didn't think about what I was wearing."

"You could have caught pneumonia, Lex. It's cold and nasty out there." Amanda raised a hand and touched the rancher's face gently. "Wait. You said Martha brought you some clothes? Why didn't my grandparents think about..."

Lex covered Amanda's mouth with her hand. "Your grandmother brought some stuff with us. I just didn't think about putting it on. And then Martha got here. I swear, I thought she was gonna pull a wooden spoon out of her pocket and whip me right there in the waiting room." She saw the younger woman smile from behind her hand. "It's not funny. Those two practically ganged up on me." She removed her hand when a small tongue licked it. "Yuck."

"Poor baby. Remind me to thank them later," Amanda teased. She saw that Lex was fighting sleep, and losing. "But for now, can you just hold me while we sleep? I'm a little tired, too." *Not really a lie. Although I feel a lot better than she probably does.*

"Sure, sweetheart. C'mere." Lex snuggled down on the bed and pulled her friend with her. "How's that?"

Amanda tangled her legs up with the longer ones of the rancher. "Perfect." She leaned up and kissed Lex on the jaw. "Sleep well, love."

"Mmm," Lex murmured, already well on her way to sleep.

****

Charlie opened the door to their hotel room and allowed Martha to enter before him. He followed behind her and closed the door. "That sure was a good lunch," he commented as he took off his boots and gunbelt, hanging the leather over a nearby chair.

"It certainly was." Martha sat down on the bed and removed her shoes. "Ohhh. That feels so good." She smiled at her fiancé when he dropped down beside her and pulled her legs onto his lap. He gently massaged her feet and calves, which caused her to moan in appreciation.

"You like that, huh?" Charlie teased, as the house-keeper fell back on the bed with a relaxed sigh.

Martha threw one arm over her eyes. "Mmmhmmm." She stretched out and exhaled heavily. "Have I told you lately what wonderful hands you have?"

He laughed, but continued his ministrations. "As a matter of fact," Charlie tickled the bottom of her foot, "I believe you mentioned something about that just last night."

"Oh, you." Martha kicked at him playfully. She sat up and pulled his cowboy hat off his head, putting it on with a sneaky grin. "Do you think that I'd make a good sheriff?"

"Sure. Want me to teach you the proper way to frisk someone?" Charlie crawled toward his intended victim.

She squealed and scooted backwards. "Charlie Bristol, you'd better not."

The ringing of the bedside phone interrupted the sheriff's retort. He changed direction and picked up the receiver. "Hello? This is Sheriff Bristol."

"Charlie. I've been looking all over for you." Robert Campbell sounded almost out of breath.

"What's wrong? Were you able to find Mark Garrett?" Charlie felt Martha crawl up behind him and wrap her arms around his waist. He patted her hands lovingly.

The young prosecutor took a calming breath. "You could say that. We tracked him to England. One of our guys is on the next plane out to make a positive identification."

Charlie turned his head to smile at Martha. "That's great. Do you think he'll give us much trouble?"

"Ah, no. I don't think he'll be any trouble at all, but no help, either. He's dead," Robert reported.

"Dead? What on earth happened?" The sheriff reached into his shirt pocket for his notepad and pen.

Robert shuffled through some papers for the information. "The investigators on the scene said he was standing on a street corner, when he somehow got in the way of a bus. They think that he may have been pushed, but no one saw anything. The bus driver complained that he was the third person this month who 'jumped' in front of her bus." He tried to keep from laughing. "It took three men to keep her from kicking the body in anger. Little brunette thing, they said. Wouldn't think she had the strength."

The sheriff snorted. "Good lord. Well, I guess there goes our best chance of proving who is behind this whole mess. What else could go wrong?"

* * * * * * * * * *

The agitated man rushed up to the nurses' station and looked around. He seemed out of place in the community hospital, although he appeared to have slept in his expensive clothes. His handsome face had a two-day growth of beard, and his reddish brown hair was in disarray. "Excuse me." He addressed the women that were bent over some papers on the back desk.

The two nurses turned around. The older one smiled and stepped closer to speak. "Yes sir? Is there something I can help you with?"

"I'm looking for my daughter. She was in Intensive Care, but the nurse in charge said that she had been moved to this floor." When Michael had first been told that Amanda was no longer in Intensive Care, he panicked. He had feared the worst until the woman had assured him that his daughter had improved and was resting comfortably in a private room.

"What's her name?" the nurse asked. "I'll see if I can find her for you."

Michael sighed in relief. "Amanda Lorraine Cauble." He watched as she scanned a clipboard carefully.

"Hmm, let's see...Solomon...Davies...ah. Here she is, Cauble." She looked up at him and smiled. "Room four-sixteen. Right down the hall and to your left." She pointed down the corridor. "But I'm afraid visiting hours aren't for another forty-five minutes. She's probably resting right now."

"Oh, okay." He smiled sincerely at the nurse. "Thank you for all your help. I'll just go grab some coffee and find a place to sit down for a bit."

The younger nurse looked at the rumpled man in sympathy. "There's a lounge just down the hall from her room. I think there's even a couch to lie down on if you want."

He returned her smile. "Great. I need to clean up a bit anyway. Wouldn't want to scare her." Michael winked and turned to leave. "Thank you again, ladies." He waved at them as he walked down the hallway.

Sometime later Michael stood outside the door. *Room four-sixteen.* He glanced down at his watch. *Only about fifteen minutes early. I don't see what it would hurt to just peek in and check on her.* He ran his hand over his clean-shaven face. *Cleaning up killed about half an hour. At least I look more presentable now.* The executive wiped his damp palms on his pant legs. *This is ridiculous. She's my daughter. Why am I so damned nervous?* He took a deep breath and opened the door slowly.

The late afternoon sun dropped rays of fading light across the two people snuggled together in one of the two hospital beds. Amanda had a tight grip on Lex, who was nestled face-first against the smaller woman's chest. Michael bit off the yell of disgust before it could leave his mouth. *Don't screw this up again, dumbass. It shouldn't matter who she's with, as long as she's happy.* He was about to step into the room when a strong hand grasped his shoulder and pulled him roughly back into the hallway.

"What are you doing here?" Jacob Cauble looked down on his son in anger. "Don't you dare disturb them." He grabbed the younger man's sleeve and shook him.

"Dad? Wait. I can explain." Michael covered his father's hand with his own and squeezed gently. "I've got a lot to tell you and to ask of you." He looked up into blue eyes that were filled with anger. "Please? Can we go somewhere and talk?"

Anna Leigh put her arm around her husband's waist and pulled him back. "Darling. Let's get out of the hallway and listen to what Michael has to say." She smiled at her son. "You look tired, honey." She offered her free hand to him and was surprised when he grasped it.

Michael almost broke down when he saw the look in his mother's eyes. *I've hurt them both so much. I hope that they can forgive me.* "I've never felt better in my life, actually." He smiled at Anna Leigh.

"Okay. Let's go into the waiting room. I think it's empty right now." Jacob loved his son, but was disappointed in how he had turned out. *I failed him, somehow. I should have never let my in-laws influence him so much when he was younger.* "C'mon, let's go someplace a little more private." He pulled the younger man to him and hugged him. "It's great to see you again, son."

"Thanks, Dad. I've really got a lot to tell you." Michael stepped in between his parents and allowed them to lead him down the corridor.

* * * * * * * * * *

Lex woke up when the sun began to shine in her face. *God. What time is it?* She blinked several times and slowly raised her head. Her partner was still sound asleep and had a tiny smile on her face. The rancher moaned when she tried to sit up. *Stupid, Lexington, sleeping in that position.* Her back still ached from the previous day's activities, and she had trouble stretching out.

"What's wrong?" Green eyes blinked open and peered upward. Amanda ran her hands down Lex's chest.

"Umm." Lex slowly pulled away and rolled over onto her back. "Nothing's wrong." When Amanda gave her a look, she turned her head and smiled. "I slept in the wrong position, and my back's a little stiff."

Amanda turned onto her side and propped her head up on one hand. She studied her friend carefully. "Since we're already here, why don't you have someone check it out? Nothing wrong with getting a second opinion."

The rancher shook her head. "I'm okay. Really." She reached over and caressed the younger woman's face tenderly. "Dr. A. told me that it would take several weeks for the bruising to heal completely. It's just something that I have to live with right now."

"I just hate seeing you hurting." Amanda leaned into the touch. "Do you think that we can just spend the next few days lounging around in bed? I'd really like to give you the chance to actually get over all of this."

Lex started to argue, but the sweet look on her lover's face silenced her objections. *She never asks me for anything. What would it hurt?* "Okay."

"I know that you have a lot to do at the ranch, and..." The blonde continued to babble.

"It's okay, sweetheart." Lex smiled at her friend's nervousness.

Amanda didn't seem to hear her. "You've got to make sure that the fence is finished, and check the cattle in the winter pasture, and..." A sudden finger over her lips stopped any more words from escaping.

"As you were so quick to point out to me recently, I pay the men at the ranch very well to handle those things." Lex sat up and leaned forward to look directly into the beautiful face across from her. "And to be stuck in bed with you for a couple of days? I think that I can handle the hardship." She replaced her finger with her lips and kissed Amanda tenderly.

"Mmm." Amanda tangled her fingers in the dark hair and pulled the older woman closer. She rolled slightly until she way lying partially on top of Lex, then reached under the rancher's shirt to explore.

"Ahem." A discreet throat clearing from the doorway caused the blonde to pause. "Don't you two ever get enough?" Jeannie teased, a large grin covering her face.

Amanda broke away from her ministrations regretfully. She turned around and slowly scooted back to her own bed. "No, we don't." She winked at Frank as he fought to control his laughter. "Are you jealous?"

Jeannie walked over to Lex's bed and sat down. "Of course not." She edged closer until she was almost sitting in the rancher's lap. "But," she leaned close to the dark-haired woman, "I certainly wouldn't turn Slim down if she ever got lonely."

"Give me a break." Amanda laughed. "She's got much better taste than that."

"Now wait a minute." Frank walked over and sat on Amanda's bed. "What does that say about me?" He looked over at Lex for help.

"Oh, no. Don't get me in the middle of this mess." Lex sat up and waved her hands around. "I'll get into trouble no matter what I say."

Frank laughed. "With these two, I *stay* in trouble." He reached over and gave the blonde's leg a light squeeze. "How are you feeling, Small Stuff?"

"I feel great. Do you think that you can sneak me out of here tonight?" Amanda covered his hand with hers. "I'd be eternally grateful."

The big man shook his head. "And I'd be eternally dead—your grandparents would kill me."

"We certainly would," Anna Leigh exclaimed from the doorway. She stood just inside the room with her hands on her hips. "You already promised me that you would stay the night, so I don't want to hear any arguments." She walked over until she was closer to her granddaughter's bed. "How are you feeling, dear?"

Amanda reached out with one hand to the older woman. When Anna Leigh grasped it, she pulled her grandmother closer. "I'm feeling much better, Gramma." She looked at the closed door. "Where's Grandpa?"

Anna Leigh smiled. "He's talking with someone, Mandy. Do you think that you're up to another guest?" She glanced at the others in the room. *I don't know if I should ask everyone to leave, or not.*

"Sure. Can I have a couple of minutes to make myself

a little more presentable?" Amanda ran her fingers through her hair. "I must look horrible."

Lex saw the look on the older woman's face and slowly climbed out of her bed. "You're always beautiful, Amanda." She kissed her lover on the top of the head and then slipped on her boots. "But I'll just run down to the gift shop and grab you a couple of things."

Frank could see the unspoken request on Anna Leigh's face. "I'll go with you." He patted Amanda's leg and jumped off the bed. "I need to stretch my legs anyway. See you in a few minutes, Lil' Bit." He hurried out after Lex.

Jeannie looked around. *Gramma's up to something.* "I think I'd better go supervise. No telling what kind of trouble those two will get into without me." She stood up and patted her sister's arm. "I'll be back in a minute, okay?" She left the room quickly, before Amanda could stop her.

The young woman on the bed watched them leave, then turned to give Anna Leigh a confused look. "What's up, Gramma? You practically chased them all out of here." When her grandmother sat down beside her, she began to panic. "Is Grandpa okay? What's going on?"

"I'm sorry, honey. It's just that our guest was a little afraid of the reception he might get. So I thought it would be best if it was just us here." Anna Leigh combed through Amanda's hair with her fingers. "You look fine, Mandy. Can I go ahead and bring him in?"

"Umm, okay." Amanda smiled nervously as the older woman crossed the room and opened the door. "Daddy?" She blinked as tears formed in her eyes.

Michael stepped into the room, unsure of himself. "Hello, Amanda." He almost cried when his youngest daughter opened her arms wide. "I'm so sorry, baby," he murmured, as he hurried across the room and pulled her into his arms. "Please forgive me," he whispered into her hair.

Amanda could feel her father's tears as they trailed across her cheek. "Oh, Daddy," she cried in relief, as part of her world righted after so many years. "I love you."

"I love you too, baby." Michael pulled back slightly and cupped her face in his hands. He gently wiped her tears away with his thumbs. "I'm so sorry for the way I've acted." He sniffled as Amanda used her hands to dry his face. "I've just had a long talk with Mom and Dad. I'd like to stay here in Texas for a while and get reacquainted, if you'll have me."

"Have you?" Amanda looked up into his eyes. "That's all I've ever wanted." She glanced over his shoulder when she heard a light knock.

The door opened slightly and a dark head popped in. "Oh." Lex saw Amanda wrapped in her father's arms. "I'm sorry. I'll come back later." She dropped a plastic bag just inside the room. "Here's some things for you, Amanda."

"Wait." Amanda looked at Michael. *Please, Daddy. Try.*

Michael turned around and looked at the young woman standing in the door. *I still think that my little girl could do better.* He thought about the scene in Los Angeles. *But then again, she's got more money than I do now. And I've learned the hard way that money isn't everything.* "Yes, please. Come in, Ms. Walters. I think I owe you an apology."

Lex walked toward the bed warily. "You do?" She stepped back a little when he rose to his feet.

"I don't know if I'll ever be able to like you, but I do want to apologize for my earlier behavior." Michael held out his hand. "It's apparent to me that you love my daughter, and that she loves you. So for her sake, I want to try and get along with you." He felt the strong grip as the rancher shook his hand.

"Sounds fair enough to me, Mr. Cauble." Lex glanced over his shoulder and saw Amanda smile. *I'd try to get along with Satan himself if it would keep that look on her face.*

He looked closely at the tall woman's face, and saw it soften as she met his daughter's eyes. *Mom and Dad think the world of this woman. Guess being a little nice can't hurt.* "Might as well call me Michael, since we're going to be seeing each other some."

She saw her lover's plaintive look, then looked down at him and grinned. "All right, Michael. Most folks call me Lex. At least that's what they call me to my face." She winked and smiled broadly.

Nice smile. Now I think I know what my daughter sees in her. Michael returned her smile. "Lex. It's going to be real interesting getting to know you, I think."

"Hey. Remember me?" Amanda waved her hands wildly. "Hello?"

Michael turned around and smiled at his daughter. *Thank God for my parents. They've done an excellent job with her and Jeannie. I couldn't ask for two more wonderful daughters.* "What's the matter, sweetheart? Feeling a little left out?" He sat back down on the bed and grasped her hand.

Amanda stuck out her bottom lip. "No. I'm fine. Just a little ignored." She saw the look on Lex's face and almost laughed out loud. "What?"

"You are a brat." Lex walked back to the other side of the room and picked up the plastic bag. "And after I bought you all of this...stuff." She brought the bag over and dropped it on the other side of the bed. "Now, if you two will excuse me, I'm going to go mug someone for a cup of coffee." The rancher ruffled Amanda's hair and started for the door.

"Thank you, honey." Amanda enjoyed the view as Lex walked away from her. *Definitely got to get her to rest and eat more. Those pants are a little baggy.*

Lex stopped in the doorway and turned. "Anytime, sweetheart. I'll be back in a few minutes. Give you two some time to talk."

"I really appreciate that, Lex." Michael nodded in her direction. "Thank you."

"No problem." Lex waved and closed the door behind her as she left the room. She had only taken a few steps when the two policemen from the night before caught her in the hallway. *Great. Just what I don't need. Backwater Vice.*

Sergeant Byers held out his hand to stop the tall woman. "Ms. Walters. Can we have a moment of your time?"

She glared at him. "Sergeant. I really don't think that this is a good time. I'm tired, sore, and there's a cup of coffee in the cafeteria with my name on it." She started to walk around him when the shorter detective grabbed her arm.

"You don't understand, Walters. That wasn't a request." He felt the muscles in her arm tighten before she shook his hand away. "You can either talk to us now, or I'll be more than happy to handcuff your sorry ass and drag you down to our office." *Oh, please. Give me an excuse to slam you face first onto the floor, you cocky bitch.*

"Let go of me, Officer," Lex purposely didn't use his title, "or I'll sue you for harassment and false arrest." She jerked her arm away from him and stepped closer, so that he had to strain his neck to look into her face.

Byers grabbed the detective's shoulder and pulled him back. "Dammit, Barry. Back off." He glared after his partner when the man threw up his hands and stormed down the hallway. The sergeant gave Lex an apologetic smile. "I'm sorry about that, Ms. Walters. He's been under a lot of stress lately."

Lex snorted. "Haven't we all? What the hell have I done to him, anyway?"

"It's not you, exactly. His wife just recently left him." The sergeant hoped that she'd understand, and not sign a complaint against the man he'd worked with for almost ten years.

"Yeah? Sounds like she got smart, if you ask me." The rancher was fed up with the stocky man's attitude. "Find herself a better guy?"

Byers ducked his head. "No. A better woman." He looked up into her widened eyes. "Just don't hold this against him, okay? He's normally a really good guy."

With a curt nod, she leaned back against the wall and crossed her arms over her chest. "What is it that you need from me, Sergeant? I really do need to get some coffee and maybe a little bite to eat." Lex refused to discuss the detective any further. *Serves him right. Hope she bagged a beauty.*

"I understand. How about if I buy you that cup of coffee, and we talk in the cafeteria? I really do need to get some information from you." He gestured for her to precede him to the lunchroom.

"Sure. But I need to get back soon to check on my friend, all right?" Lex accepted his offer and walked down the hallway. She stepped into the cafeteria and saw the detective brooding at a far table. She mentally shrugged her shoulders and went over to sit by the sullen officer. When he looked up with a sneer, Lex raised her hands in defense. "Don't look at me like that. You're the ones who want to talk." She pulled out a chair and sat across from Weingart.

"Thanks again, Ms. Walters." Sergeant Byers sat next to his partner and opened a manila folder. "We just finished going over some information that had been forwarded to us from your sheriff's department, and wanted to ask you a few questions."

"Okay, but I don't know how much help I will be." Lex leaned back in her chair and crossed her arms. "Should I call my lawyer?"

Detective Weingart stood up and leaned over the table. "Don't give us any attitude, Walters. You're in no position to be a smartass."

The sergeant grabbed the shorter man's shoulder and pulled him back to his seat. "Sit down, Barry." He gave Lex an apologetic smile. "I will try to make this as short as possible, Ms. Walters. I know you've been through quite a bit lately."

Lex nodded. "Thanks. I'll try to help you any way I can." She glared at the detective. *I don't care what Grumpy's problem is, but he's about to get an attitude adjustment, Walters-Style.*

Sergeant Byers consulted the papers in front of him. "All right. As I was saying, the sheriff's department has found some very relevant information. They sent it to us, in hopes that we can somehow tie it in to Miss Cauble's poisoning."

They did? Charlie hasn't notified me yet. Lex tried to appear unconcerned. "Really? What does that have to do with me? I haven't heard anything."

"I'm not surprised. Civilians aren't usually very high up on our need-to-know list," Weingart grumbled. A well-placed kick to his leg shut the detective up. He frowned at his partner. *I can't believe he's letting her get away with that attitude.*

"Ms. Walters, from what Sheriff Bristol told us last night, you've had some problems with Miss Cauble's family, correct?" the blonde man questioned carefully.

"What do you mean by problems? Her parents don't care much for me, but I get along just fine with everyone else." The rancher watched as Byers continued to take notes.

He looked up seriously. "Do you think that her father is capable of hiring someone to do you harm?"

Lex closed her eyes and thought for a moment about the man that she had first met in California.

Michael stood up and stepped around the desk, trying to distance himself from the imposing figure. "Because you're a woman? No." He went over and poured himself a drink, gulping the amber liquid down with a single swallow. He turned to face her and grimaced. "Unlike Elizabeth, I have resigned myself to the fact that my youngest daughter is unnatural. There's not much I can do about that. But," he pointed the empty glass in the rancher's direction, "I can try to make her see reason when it comes to dirt-poor farmers trying to sink their claws into her bank account." He filled the glass again, then drained it quickly.

Lex leaned back against the desk, arms crossed. "Dirt-poor farmer?" she laughed. "Number one, I'm a rancher. Second, I have no designs on Amanda's money." She stood up straight and walked over to stand only a step away from the shorter man. "Third, I have more than enough money of my own, that I certainly have no need for yours." She got right into his face. "Last, but not least, I love her with everything that I am. Nothing can change that." Hands grasped in her shirt took Lex by surprise, as she felt Michael pull her closer.

Amanda opened the door just in time to see her father grab Lex by the shirt and slam her into the bar. Before she could say anything, Michael had punched her lover in the face, causing her lower lip to bleed. "Stop it!" she shouted, scrambling across the room. She tried to pull her livid father off of Lex by tugging at his sleeve. "Daddy. Let her go, now."

Michael Cauble shook his head to clear it. He pushed the tall woman backwards again, happy to see that he was at least able to do some damage to her before his daughter interfered. "Get out of my house. You're not welcome here," he muttered, secretly hoping that the tall woman would try and retaliate.

"Gladly." Lex pushed by him and wiped her bloody mouth and chin with the back of her hand. She started for the door, trying to control her anger. Narrow-minded bastard. If he wasn't Amanda's father, I would... *Her thoughts ended there as she felt a small hand touch her arm.*

She opened her eyes and sighed. *Oh, yeah. He was more than capable.* Her mind then compared that scene with the man now sitting in Amanda's hospital room. "I'm not sure. I suppose that if he were mad or upset enough, maybe." She looked at the sergeant carefully. "What makes you ask that?"

"They found where Matt Sterling had been staying." the detective answered her. "He received several calls from a number in California, and the prosecutor's office traced them to a private office number in Los Angeles." He took the folder and passed a sheet of paper across the table. "The office was listed as Cau-King Enterprises, which is the name of the company for which Michael Cauble is the CEO."

"Cau-King?" Lex looked down at the paper on the desk and then reached into her pocket. *Of course. Cauble-Kingston. It's the combination of his last name and Elizabeth's. Damn.* She wadded up the scrap of paper from her pocket and tossed it on the table. *I wonder if he knew that I was one of the majority stockholders in his company.* "Great."

Sergeant Byers stopped writing when the paper hit the table. "What?" He looked at his partner in confusion.

"I just sold my stock in that company, recently," Lex mumbled. "But I had no idea that it was his."

"How much stock are we talking about?" Weingart asked.

Lex frowned. "Umm. Over forty percent. It had been my mother's." *And if the other stockholders bailed, that would just about ruin him.*

The detective snorted. "Guess he figured it would be safer to get you out of the way. According to our records, Michael Cauble lost everything." He gave the dark-haired woman an obnoxious smile. "Bet your little friend won't be too happy with you when she finds out you ruined her father." He leaned back in his chair and chuckled. "But then again, she'll probably dump you when she learns that her father nearly killed her while trying to get to you."

Dear God. I knew the man didn't like me, but I never thought he'd resort to attempted murder. If he did. He nearly killed his daughter trying to save his own rotten hide. Lex jumped up from the table in a rage. "That son of a bitch. He could have killed her." She knocked her chair down as she raced from the cafeteria.

Chapter
21

The enraged woman stormed down the corridor, oblivious to everything around her. *I should have never left him alone with Amanda. That son of a bitch nearly killed her.* She brushed by a group of people that had just stepped out of the elevator.

"Lex! Where are you...?" Frank was nearly knocked down by the distraught woman. He looked at his wife. "What's bitten her on the butt?"

Jeannie grabbed his arm and dragged him down the hallway. "I don't know but I think we'd better follow her."

Lex shoved open the door to Amanda's room causing it to slam back against the wall loudly. Michael was sitting on Amanda's bed with his arms around his daughter. Both appeared to be smiling. "Cauble! Get your slimy hands off of her." She rushed into the room and grabbed the man by his shirtfront. "You don't deserve to be anywhere near Amanda, you bastard." She picked him up and shook him roughly.

"Lex! What are you doing?" Amanda tried to break the rancher's hold on her father. "Have you lost your mind?" She frantically clawed at Lex's hands. "Put my father down."

"It's the money, isn't it? That's all you've ever cared about." Lex tightened her grasp on the flailing man's shirt. "I ought to toss your sorry ass through that window, but I'd probably be arrested for littering."

Michael fought the iron grip on his shirt in vain. "What the hell are you talking about? What's gotten into you?"

The rancher continued to shake him as she dragged the frantic man away from her lover. "The police traced the calls you made to Sterling and they'll probably connect you to the poisoning, too." Lex slammed him into the wall. "Amanda almost died, you greedy son of a bitch."

Jeannie and Frank burst into the room. "Daddy?" she yelled, as her husband rushed over to the older man's aid. "What's going on?"

"I don't know." Amanda was trying to pull the I.V. from her hand while she watched her lover manhandle her father. "Frank, do something, please."

"C'mon, Lex. Let him go." The ex-football player wrapped an arm around the tall woman's chest and pulled. "It's bad form to kill the in-laws, no matter how much they might deserve it." *And the way that he and Elizabeth have treated her, I don't much blame the woman.*

"I didn't have anything to do with this," Michael pleaded his case as Lex was forcibly pulled away. He rubbed his chest where her fists had dug into him. "Believe me, as much as I disliked you, I would never put my daughter in any danger."

"Let go of me, dammit." Lex strained to break away from the big man's grasp. "I'm gonna kill him." She kicked at the older man, trying to make some sort of contact. "Lying bastard."

Amanda had finally given up working the intravenous needle loose gently. She ripped it from her hand and rushed over to stand between Lex and Michael. "Honey, please." She reached up and touched the struggling woman's cheek. "What's going on?"

Lex looked into the blonde's eyes and stopped thrashing around. *Damn. I think I blew this one.* "Let me go, Frank," she requested quietly. *She's never gonna forgive me.*

He looked at Amanda, who nodded. With a heavy sigh, Frank released his hold on Lex. "You okay?" he whispered in the tall woman's ear.

"Yeah. Sorry about that." Lex glared at Michael. "You've got some nerve, showing your face around here." She calmed when she felt Amanda's hands on her stomach. Lex studied Amanda sadly. "The police traced calls from your father's private office to Matt Sterling." *Please understand what I'm trying to tell you. He almost killed you just to get to me.*

Amanda turned around and looked at her father. "Is that true, Daddy?"

"No. I swear that I had nothing to do with this entire mess. Someone else used my office while I was out of town." Michael looked back and forth between his two daughters. Jeannie stood skeptically off to one side, her arms crossed over her chest. Amanda was gently patting Lex on the stomach as she tried to calm the tall woman.

The rancher shook her head. "Yeah, right. Who else has access to your house? Are you trying to tell us that the butler did it?"

Jeannie began to laugh at the absurdity of Lex's statement, then paused. *The only other person who would be in his office is...*"Mother?"

"No way," Frank scoffed. "She's a lady, a..."

"Cold-hearted, two-faced, money hungry manipulator," Michael finished quietly. "She practically admitted everything to me before I left."

Amanda looked at her father with a shocked look on her face. "I don't believe it. Mother can be distant at times, but I don't think that she would ever purposely hurt anyone."

Michael watched as Lex put her arm around his daughter to comfort her. "I can prove it. All we have to do is find Mark Garrett and ask him. He's been working for her since

I fired him several weeks ago."

"Won't do you any good." Charlie stood in the doorway with Martha behind him. "What's going on here? We could hear you folks all the way down the hall."

Lex pointed at Michael. *I can't believe he's trying to shift the blame to his own wife.* "Ask him. He seems to have all the damned answers." She allowed Amanda to pull her back to the bed and sit her down.

"Calm down, love. Let's see if Charlie can make any sense out of this, okay?" Amanda sat down next to the rancher and held her hands. *I can't believe that my mother could have anything to do with this. Why would she want Lex hurt or killed?*

The sheriff moved further into the room. "I hate to ask you this, Mr. Cauble, but do you have proof that you've been out of town for the past couple of weeks?"

Michael nodded. "I do. Just not with me. But I can get my business expense receipts together in the next day or so." He paused momentarily. "Wait a minute. You said that Garrett couldn't help? Let me talk to him. I bet I can get him to cooperate."

"I don't think so. He's dead," Charlie informed the executive. "We've got a man flying to England to bring back his body."

Dear God. I wonder if Elizabeth had anything to do with that? Michael shuddered. "How did he die?"

Charlie released Martha's hand so that she could walk over to check on Lex and Amanda. The young blonde had tears in her eyes, and her companion was sitting with her head hanging down and her shoulders slumped. "He fell in front of a bus. Although witnesses said that he may have been pushed."

"How horrible," Amanda gasped. She tried to give Martha a smile when the housekeeper put a gentle hand on her shoulder.

Martha looked down at Amanda's hands and noticed that the top one was bleeding. "Oh, honey, let me call a nurse." She pulled out a linen handkerchief and covered the wound. The older woman was about to reach for the call button on the bed when Detective Weingart stormed into the room all out of breath.

"Walters. What's the big idea, running off like that?" He looked around the room at all the people now staring at him. *Shit. Now what's going on?*

Lex stood up and faced the heavily breathing man. "Get out of here, Detective. This is a family matter." She was still upset and was on the verge of losing complete control. *One wrong word out of you, and I'll gladly tear into your pathetic ass.*

"I don't think so." He stepped up until he was directly in her face. "Give me an excuse, lady..."

Sergeant Byers stood in the doorway. "Barry." He looked around the room. "I'm going to need everyone to leave, except the immediate family. We have a few questions to ask."

Michael shook his head. "No one will be talking to you without having our lawyers present, gentlemen." He glanced at Amanda, who was now standing behind Lex with one hand on the tall woman's back. "My daughter is still recovering from her ordeal, so I'd appreciate it if you would come back at a later time."

"Your daughter? So you're Michael Cauble?" Byers asked. At the older man's nod, he took a step forward. "I have some questions for you, sir. If you'll just come with me, we'll go somewhere that we won't disturb your daughter."

Charlie saw the worried look on Amanda's face. "Why don't you fellows step out into the hallway with me, and I'll update you on what's going on." *No sense in upsetting her any more than necessary. Poor girl.*

"Sheriff, you don't have any authority here." Detective Weingart turned around to face the lawman. *He's related to that...woman, somehow. She called him Uncle back in the office. Probably just as twisted as she is.* "We'd appreciate it if you'd just mind your own business." A firm hand on his shoulder caused him to jump slightly.

"I'd appreciate it if you'd show Sheriff Bristol the respect he deserves," Lex murmured menacingly as she tightened the grip she had on the detective's shoulder. *Cocky little bastard. No one talks to Charlie like that.*

Weingart spun back around and broke her hold. "That's it." He grabbed the tall woman's right wrist and twisted her around, bending her arm painfully behind her back. "I've had it with your attitude, Walters." He reached behind his back for his handcuffs.

Amanda stepped forward and reached for him when she saw the look of pain on Lex's face. "Stop it, please. You're hurting her."

Sergeant Byers sighed and grabbed his partner's arm. "Let her go, Barry. Let's see what Sheriff Bristol has to tell us."

Michael Cauble moved towards them. "I won't let you question me without my lawyer, but I can at least give you a little bit of information. I think I have a thing or two to add."

"She assaulted me, Kent. I have every right to book her," the detective objected, but pushed Lex away roughly.

Frank laughed. "Buddy, I've seen Lex in action. Believe me, if she *had* assaulted you, I can guarantee that you wouldn't be standing there."

When everyone in the room laughed, Byers tried to keep the grin off of his face. "Umm, right." He motioned for the other man to join him. "C'mon, Barry. Let's listen to what these gentlemen have to say." He looked over at Lex, who was cradling her right arm against her chest. "Ms. Walters, if you want to lodge a complaint against my partner, I'm obligated to give you my captain's phone number."

Lex felt Amanda's arm around her tighten. "No. I was out of line." She looked at the detective. "Sorry about that, Detective."

"Yeah." Weingart followed his partner out of the room. "Whatever."

"Are you all right?" Amanda stood in front of Lex and

looked up into her face. She raised her hand to touch the rancher's cheek.

"I'm okay." Lex covered Amanda's hand with her own. She frowned when she felt something wet and sticky. When she looked at her fingers, Lex saw that they were covered in with blood. "My God, Amanda, your hand."

The blonde woman tried to pull her hand away. "It's fine. I just had a fight with the I.V. and lost." She smiled at her friend.

Lex looked at her sadly. "My fault." She pulled Amanda back over to the bed.

Jeannie looked at Frank. They both realized that Amanda and Lex needed a little time alone. "I think we need to go see where Gramma and Grandpa are," she hinted.

"Right." Frank took his wife by the hand and quietly led her from the room.

The rancher sat down next to her friend and accepted Martha's handkerchief to staunch the bleeding. "I'm so sorry, sweetheart." She leaned down and kissed the make-shift bandage.

Martha patted Amanda's shoulder gently. "I called the nurse, honey." She bent down until she could look Lex in the eye. "And don't you start blaming yourself for any-thing, Lexie." She lightly grasped the dark-haired woman's chin to keep her from looking away. "Thank you for taking up for Charlie. You've always done me proud."

A middle-aged nurse wheeled a small cart into the room. She parked the vehicle next to the bed and shook her head at the three women. "Young lady," she addressed Amanda while checking out her hand, "we put those nee-dles in for a reason, you know." She turned to talk to Mar-tha. "Are you her mother?"

"No, she's mine." Lex offered with a grin. She enjoyed the happy smile on the older woman's face. "Is there a problem?"

"Oh, no. No problem at all." The nurse finished put-ting an adhesive bandage on Amanda's hand. "Dr. Barnes just called the nurses' station. He said that if Miss Cauble was feeling up to it, her family could take her home." She winked at Martha. "Personally, I think he's doing it in self-defense. We haven't had this much excitement around here in ages." She finished cleaning up her mess and rolled the cart away. "He'll be by in a bit to sign you out, honey."

Michael and Charlie stepped back into the room, parting to allow the nurse to leave. They wore matching grim looks on their faces. The sheriff put one hand on the younger man's shoulder and spoke quietly to him.

Amanda noticed the look on her father's face. "What's wrong, Daddy?"

"Your mother is gone." He sat down on the opposite bed. "She must have packed up right after I left."

The sheriff walked over to Martha and put his arm around her. "According to the household staff, all of her clothes and jewelry are gone, too. I don't think that she's planning on coming back."

Lex stood up. *Time to eat a little crow.* She walked around the bed to where Michael sat. "Mr. Cauble..." She stopped when he raised a hand and stood up.

"Lex, I don't appreciate being tossed around like a rag doll." He looked up into her eyes, which were filled with genuine regret. "Especially by someone that I'm trying to get along with."

"Daddy..." Amanda interrupted.

He waved his hand impatiently. "Just a minute, Amanda." Michael stepped closer to Lex and watched as she fought the urge to step back. "But I do appreciate your protectiveness of my daughter." Michael smiled at the tall woman. "Guess we're about even in the shoving department, huh?"

"What in the hell did you do to my daughter?" Michael Cauble yelled, when he spotted Lex and Amanda walking across the main foyer on their way to the stairs. He stormed towards the women, his fists clenched at his side. The younger woman had a large bruise on one side of

her face, which appeared to be in the shape of a hand.

"Daddy. Wait." Amanda stepped in front of Lex, hold-ing her hand out to block her father's path.

Michael pushed his daughter aside and shoved the tall woman up against the stairwell, his face red with rage. "You like hitting defenseless women, cow chaser?"

Amanda squeezed between the two of them. She reached forward and pushed her father back. "Stop it. Lex didn't do anything to me, Daddy. I was mugged at the beach."

"What? You were mugged?" Michael backed off a step and glared at the rancher. "Where the hell were you while my daughter was being assaulted?"

Lex wisely kept her mouth shut to give Amanda a chance to handle her father. She took a deep breath and released it, as she felt the younger woman's hand pat her gently on the arm.

"Lex was only a few steps away, and she caught the guy, then turned him over to the police." Amanda stated proudly. She stepped back and put a hand behind her to make contact with the silent woman. She could almost feel Lex's anger as the woman unconsciously put her hands on the small waist in front of her.

Michael prudently decided to let the matter drop. "Very well." He looked at their matching ragged shorts and frowned. "Is it too much to ask that you two change for dinner? We're not having a clambake."

Amanda felt Lex stiffen behind her, and the hands on her hips tightened slightly. "Is it too much for me to ask that you and Mother act civil tonight? If not, Lex and I can go out for dinner, then fly out first thing in the morning," she stated in a calm voice, halfway hoping his answer would be negative.

Damn. She's really grown up in the past year, hasn't she? Michael mused to himself, vaguely proud. All right. I'll play her little game. "Of course, dear. We just got off on the wrong foot, didn't we, Lex?" He reached forward and offered his hand to the dark-haired woman. "No hard feelings?"

"You still owe me a busted lip, too. I believe I man-
handled you on more than one occasion when you were in
California." Michael raised his chin in an exaggerated
manner. "Do you want to take it now?"

The rancher shook her head. "Nah. If it's okay with
you, I'll just take a raincheck." She offered him her hand.
"I'm really sorry about earlier, Mr. Cauble."

Michael accepted her hand and shook it. "Michael,
remember?"

Anna Leigh breezed into the room, carrying a small
bag. "Mandy. We just passed the doctor in the hallway. He
said that all of your tests came back negative, and we can
take you home now. We picked you up a few things so that
you wouldn't have to wear your nightgown home."

Jacob stood behind her, smiling. "That's right, Peanut.
Your grandmother made the ultimate sacrifice and went
shopping, just for you." He dodged his wife's playful swat.
"We saw Jeannie and Frank in the hallway. They told us
that we missed all the excitement." He glanced at Lex and
Michael. "Is everything okay in here?"

Lex nodded. "Other than me almost killing your son,
everything's just peachy." She grinned sheepishly. "I'm
afraid that I kinda lost my temper...again." She accepted
Amanda's outstretched hand and sat down next to her
friend.

"The police thought that Daddy had something to do
with what's been happening lately. They told Lex, and
she..." Amanda began to explain.

"Charged in here like a maniac," the rancher finished
helpfully.

Michael laughed. "Just remind me to try and stay on
your good side, Lex." He rubbed his chest with one hand.
"I'd hate to be on the receiving end of your temper again."

"I'm really sorry about that." Lex apologized again.
"Did I hurt you?"

"Only my pride." He looked at the other men in the

room. "Why don't we sneak out of here and let Amanda get dressed? I'll buy everyone a cup of coffee." He smiled. "If I could borrow a few dollars from someone, since I, umm, seem to be a little strapped for money at the moment."

Jacob chuckled and wrapped an arm around his son. "No problem there, son. C'mon." He led the younger man out of the room.

"Free coffee? Now that sounds like something I can handle." Frank kissed his wife's forehead and made a hasty exit.

* * * * * * * * *

"Are you sure you don't want to go upstairs and rest? It's after eleven o'clock," Lex asked the small woman, who was wrapped tightly around her. They were snuggled together on the sofa in Jacob and Anna Leigh's den, quietly watching the dying flames in the fireplace. Everyone else had made their excuses earlier, and the two women were the only ones left downstairs.

Amanda shook her head. "No. I'm so tired of lying in bed. This is very comfortable, believe me." She buried her face deeper into Lex's chest. "Do you think too many people would be upset if we just went home tomorrow? I want to sleep in our own bed, and get away from my helpful family." *If Gramma hadn't practically dragged Jeannie and Dad from here earlier, I think I would have gone off the deep end.* "Lord knows I love my sister, but she can be such a pain in the butt at times."

Lex laughed. "I thought your Gramma was gonna have to hog tie her to get her out of the room." *Although the thought had crossed my mind. Trouble is, she would have probably enjoyed it.* "And if you want to go home tomorrow, that's where we're going. I don't care what anyone else thinks." She paused for a moment in thought. "Umm. Do you want to invite your father out to the ranch? We have plenty of room."

"No. Not yet." Amanda looked up at her friend. *I know*

*how uncomfortable that would be for you, my love, and I
don't want to put you through any more than I already
have.* "But I really appreciate you asking, honey." She
reached up with one hand and brushed the dark hair out of
Lex's eyes. *She looks exhausted.* "Are you okay?"

"Yeah." Lex closed her eyes when Amanda caressed
her cheek gently. "Been a long couple of days, though."
She leaned into the touch and had to fight back a sudden
onslaught of memories. *I almost lost all of this. Her. Oh,
God.* Tears fell freely from her closed eyes as Lex remembered the events of the past couple of days.

The younger woman saw the wetness trail down her
lover's face. "Oh, Lex." Amanda crawled up the rancher's
body until she could look directly into her eyes, which
opened at her entreaty. "Honey, it's okay." She felt the
strong arms wrap around her tightly.

The dark head bent until it was buried in Amanda's
hair. Lex sobbed quietly, unable to stop. "God," she gasped
in between breaths, "I can't..."

"Shhh. I've got you. It's all right, baby." Amanda held
her lover close. *What do you do when the strongest person
you know falls apart? I'm at a complete loss here.* She
slowly rocked back and forth, running her hands up and
down Lex's back. "I'm here."

"I'm sorry," Lex whispered as she fought to control
her emotions. *Stop it, you damned fool. She's been through
enough without having to baby-sit you.* She pulled back
slightly and sniffled. The touch of Amanda's hands on her
face was nearly her undoing.

Amanda wiped at the tears with her fingertips. When
the blue eyes finally opened, they were red and puffy. "Hi
there." She smiled at Lex tenderly.

Lex smiled back, although hers wavered slightly. "Hi."
She blinked a couple of times and pulled in a deep breath.
"Sorry about that."

"Please don't apologize, honey." Amanda ran her
hands gently down the long arms in an effort to comfort.
"Do you realize how much it means to me when you let go

like that?" She fought back tears of her own. "I know how hard it is for you to open up, Lex. And when you let me hold you, it means more to me than you'll ever know." She leaned forward and lightly kissed Lex. "I love you and that means I love all of you, emotional or not. So don't ever feel that you have to hold back from me, all right?"

"Umm, okay." Lex smiled more sincerely this time. "It's just that I spent a lot of years trying to be more like my dad. I didn't think he'd respect me if I was any other way." She looked down for a moment. "Used to drive Martha absolutely crazy." Lex looked back up into the understanding eyes of her lover. "I love you, Amanda. Don't ever think otherwise, okay?"

The blonde ran her hand down Lex's cheek. "You've always told me that you love me. The way you look at me, the way you touch me, and with the little things you do for me. Every day you express what's in your heart with your words and your actions. I've never doubted your love for me." She hugged Lex. " Now, let's go upstairs and discuss this a little more." She kissed the rancher again, prolonging the contact. "In depth."

"Works for me." Lex stood up and brought the smaller woman with her. She made quick work of handling the fireplace by stirring the dying coals and then closing the glass doors. "You ready?"

"Yup." Amanda wrapped an arm around the tall woman and allowed Lex to lead her from the room.

Chapter
22

The following week passed uneventfully. Lex spent most of the time in the ranch house with Amanda, but would disappear for an hour or so every day. When her friend asked about where she had been, the rancher was very secretive.

"I'm just looking for something," Lex answered vaguely, as she knelt by Amanda's chair. She thought about her foray into the storage room. The rancher had spent over an hour each day searching for a small box that she had packed away years ago.

Eight years before, a severe thunderstorm had ravaged the ranch. Hubert had sworn it was a tornado, but twenty-year-old Lex was certain it was just high winds that had uprooted the old oak tree outside her bedroom window. She had been more than happy to stay in her own room after her father had left the ranch, and had purposely left the master bedroom just as he had left it. Just in case he decides to come back, *she thought to herself.*

The ancient shade tree by her room had crashed into the ranch house, destroying not only her bedroom, but her older brother Hubert's as well. The only room on that side

*of the house that was untouched was a small room used for
storage. Rawson had stacked several boxes in there before
he left, and they almost filled the tiny area.*

*Hubert had used the accident as an excuse to move out
of the ranch house. He had wanted to move into the house
that they owned in town, but could not get the family lawyer to release it to him without Lex's consent. After reluctantly agreeing to her brother's demands, Lex decided to
move into the master bedroom temporarily while she had
the other rooms rebuilt.*

*The day after the storm, Lex opened the door and
peered inside the master bedroom. She had not been in her
father's part of the house since before he left, and was surprised to see that it looked as if he was just out for the day.
The young woman glanced around the room as if it were a
museum, careful not to touch anything.*

*On the large dresser were several photographs, one
turned face down. Intrigued, she walked over for a closer
look. The center picture was of her father and mother on
their wedding day. The first one on the left was a rare
photo of Hubert smiling.* He looks like he was only five or
six, *Lex mused. Next to that one was another smaller
frame, with a happy ten-year-old Louis mugging for the
camera. The young woman fought her tears as she studied
the picture. She took a deep breath and focused on the
frame that was lying face down to the right of her parent's
picture. Lex lifted it and saw that it was of her when she
was fourteen. She was sitting atop a bale of hay with a
happy smile on her face. The picture was slightly off-cen-
ter, and it leaned off to one side.* I remember this one.
Louis took it. He was so damned proud of that silly camera. *She looked around the room sadly.* Guess I know what
Dad thought of me. *It never occurred to her at that time
that Rawson couldn't handle the resemblance between his
daughter and his deceased wife. Anger welled up from
deep inside her.* Nothing I did was ever good enough for
him. *She took the picture and threw it across the room.*

Within a few hours, Lex had packed up everything in

the master bedroom. Her father must have already packed up his wife's things, because the only thing that she had found belonging to Victoria was a small wooden jewelry box with her name on it. When she opened it, Lex found two gold rings nestled inside. Realizing that these were her parent's wedding rings, she quickly closed the box and packed it away with the rest of the stuff from the room. She had decided that since she ran the ranch, she would use the master bedroom herself. After all, I am in charge. Maybe Dad will come back, and then he'll realize that he was wrong about me. *She stacked the boxes at the end of the hallway where she had decided to remodel the house to enlarge the storage room and add a guestroom for her father, should he ever visit.*

She sighed happily as the younger woman ran her fingers through dark hair. "Where's Martha?" Lex asked as she looked around the empty kitchen. *Now if I could just find that damned box.*

"She ran back over to her house for something." Amanda wiped a smudge of dirt off an angular cheekbone. "Where have you been looking? Under the house?"

Lex grinned. "Nope. Been digging around in the storage room."

The blonde nodded. "Uh-huh. Would it make it easier if I joined you? I'd be glad to help."

"No," Lex exclaimed, then patted Amanda's leg. "What I mean is, there's no sense in you getting all dusty too." She bit her lip in thought. "I'm sure I'll find what I'm looking for soon. Don't worry about it."

"Are you trying to be sneaky? Because you know I'll figure it out." Amanda tapped the top of the dark head.

The rancher stood up and stretched. "Nah, not sneaky." She walked over to the refrigerator and pulled out a carton of juice. "I just didn't think you'd be interested in getting all dirty." She started to drink from the container when Amanda gave her a warning look. "Oh, all right." Lex reached into a nearby cabinet and grabbed a glass.

Amanda stood up and took the juice from her lover. "Don't let Martha catch you doing that. She'll take a spatula to you." She poured the glass of juice and put the carton back into the refrigerator.

"Doing what?" Martha stood in the doorway, glaring at the two women. "What are you up to, Lexie?"

"Up to? What makes you think that I'm up to anything?" Lex drained her juice and set the empty glass back on the counter. "You always complain that I don't drink enough juice. So I'm drinking juice." Her habits had changed quite a bit since Amanda moved to the ranch. Lex used to drink whatever was available; cans of soda or beer usually fell victim to her thirst, unless Martha actually handed her a glass of water or tea.

The housekeeper walked into the kitchen and shook her head. "You're not drinking directly from the carton again, are you?" She swatted Lex on the rear. "What have I told you about that?"

Lex wrapped her arms around the older woman and hugged her. "That you're glad that I'm drinking juice?" she ventured to guess.

"Brat." Martha pulled back far enough to tickle the tall woman's ribs. "I really should..." The phone rang. She swatted Lex on the arm. "Saved by the bell."

"I'll get it." Amanda laughed as she reached for the phone. "Rocking W Ranch, Amanda speaking." She saw the evil glint in Lex's eyes and stuck her tongue out at her friend. *She hates it when I answer the phone like that, because she thinks that I sound like a secretary.* "Just a moment, please." She handed the phone to Martha. "It's for you."

Martha frowned slightly and accepted the phone. "This is Martha." She listened for a few moments, then smiled. "Yes, that will be fine. Thank you." The housekeeper hung up the phone and looked Lex up and down.

"What?" Lex looked down at her favorite blue jeans and ragged denim shirt. "Is my fly open, or something?" *Looks okay to me. No buttons missing or anything.* She took an inconspicuous sniff. *Don't smell bad, either.*

"I want you to go upstairs and get cleaned up," Martha ordered. "I don't know how you do it, Lexie. You get filthy even when you don't leave the house." She threw her hands up in an exasperated manner. "Lord knows I've tried," she muttered as she walked out of the kitchen.

Lex watched her leave. "What's gotten into her?" She brushed her hands down the front of her ragged denim shirt. "I don't look that bad, do I?" she asked Amanda, who was leaning against the counter with her hand over her mouth.

"Don't get me in the middle of this." Amanda walked up to the tall woman and looked at her. "Hmm." She rubbed her chin with one hand and studied her friend. "You do look a little, umm, dusty." *And for some reason, the dirtier she is, the better she looks. Whew. Getting a little warm in here.*

"Dusty?" Lex reached out and grabbed Amanda and pulled her close. "I thought you liked it when I was a little dusty," she murmured in the smaller woman's ear.

Amanda wrapped her arms around Lex without any thought. "Umm." She tilted her head back as soft lips nibbled down her throat. "Oh, yeah." *Definitely getting warm.*

"Lexie!" Martha barked from the doorway. "Upstairs. Now." She spun around and walked to the laundry room.

The rancher jumped away from Amanda. "Damn. I swear that woman has eyes in the back of her head."

"I heard that." Martha's voice drifted down the hallway.

"Ooh, she's good," Amanda chuckled. She grabbed Lex's hand and pulled her to the doorway. "C'mon. I'll scrub your back for you."

"Cool." Lex followed dutifully. "You know, I think that's where I'm the dustiest." She took a long look at her companion's backside. "As a matter of fact, you look a little dusty yourself." She swatted Amanda on the rear end.

Amanda stopped in the hallway and spun around. "I'll tell you what." She released Lex's hand and took a couple of steps back. "If you catch me, you can dust me off personally." She poked the rancher in the chest and took off up the stairs.

Lex stood at the foot of the stairs stunned. "You little brat," she laughed, and raced up after the giggling blonde.

****

Later that afternoon, Lex and Amanda sat in the den watching an old movie. Martha had just left for the kitchen to get popcorn and sodas, after winning a good-natured argument with the younger women. Lex wanted Martha to relax and let them go for refreshments, but lost when the housekeeper stood up and tapped her on the nose.

"You two look too comfortable to disturb," she countered. "I want to check on the chili I have simmering on the stove, anyway."

Lex tightened her grip on Amanda. The blonde was sitting between her outstretched legs on the sofa. "Stubborn old woman," she muttered.

The younger woman turned her head so that she could look Lex in the eyes. "Must be where you get it," she teased.

A knock at the front door interrupted whatever Lex was going to say. She touched the tip of Amanda's nose with her fingertip. "I'll get you later."

"Promise?" Amanda grinned.

"Lexie? Could you get that? I'm busy in the kitchen!" Martha yelled from the back of the house.

"Jeez," Lex sighed. "I wish that she'd make up her mind. Stay put, get up." She waited until Amanda climbed off the sofa and extended a hand to her. "Thanks."

"Any time." Amanda pulled Lex up and looked at her. "Do you want me to get it?"

The tall woman shook her head. "Nah." She started towards the front door. "But you're more than welcome to come with me." Another knock caused her to frown. "Hold your horses, I'm coming." Lex opened the door and stood face to face with a handsome older man, although she had to look up to see his face. He seemed somewhat familiar but she couldn't place where she had seen him before. "Umm, can I help you?"

"Lexington?" Tears filled his blue eyes as he studied the young woman across from him. He ran a shaky hand through his thick silver hair in a familiar gesture.

Amanda stepped around her friend and looked at the flustered man. *Ooh. I bet I know who he is. The resemblance is uncanny. And he runs his hand through his hair just like Lex does when she's nervous or upset.* "Hi. My name's Amanda. Won't you come in?" She rubbed Lex on the back in a comforting manner.

He smiled at the cute blonde woman. "Nice to meet you, Amanda. I'm..."

"My grandfather?" Lex asked quietly, finally making the connection. *I thought he looked familiar.*

"That's right, honey." Travis Edwards nodded. He held out his hand cautiously. "It's really good to see you, Lexington." *God. She looks so much like Victoria, only taller and more sure of herself.*

Lex took his hand in hers and bit her lower lip in concentration. "Grandpa?" Sudden memories rushed back to her of this man from an earlier time in her life. Riding on his shoulders through a zoo laughing at his antics. Eating ice cream cones by a quiet river as an elegant woman looked on fondly. And of waving goodbye to them both on the day that her mommy "went away."

He hasn't changed much. Lex felt him pull her forward, and she gratefully lunged into his strong arms.

Travis wrapped his arms around his granddaughter in relief. "I've missed you so, little one," he murmured into her ear. "I'm sorry I've been away for so long, but I thought that you hated me."

She pulled back reluctantly from the embrace. "Hated you?" Lex took a deep breath and smiled. "Up until a few days ago, I thought you were dead. Then I just figured that you didn't want to have anything to do with me, like my father." She looked around sheepishly. "Why don't you come inside before we all freeze to death?" Lex wrapped an arm around her grandfather and led him into the house. She looked at the young blonde that stood just inside the doorway. "Amanda, this is my grandfather," she introduced with a silly smile on her face.

"Ah, yes. We've met." Amanda smiled at the older man. "Mr. Edwards come on in, and I'll get you some coffee." She was charmed by the childlike excitement exhibited by her partner. "Honey? Why don't you take your grandfather into the den while I go check on Martha?"

Honey? Travis looked at both young women carefully. The love between them was easy to see. *Ahh, so that's it. Hmm, Lester was right.*

Amanda cringed as Lex's grandfather studied them both. *Oh, rats. Guess I should have let him get to know her again, before announcing our relationship like that. Lex is probably gonna kill me.* "Umm."

When she saw the younger woman's discomfort, Lex put her free arm around Amanda's shoulder. "Why don't we all three go into the den? I think Martha is doing just fine." *Sneaky old woman. Gonna have to get her back for this one. I know she had something to do with this.*

"Okay." Amanda allowed Lex to lead them both into the room. She leaned close to her lover and whispered, "But if you want some time alone to talk, just give me a sign."

"Not gonna happen, baby," Lex whispered back. She looked up into her grandfather's face. "Are you okay with this? With us?" She thought that she'd better know now if he couldn't handle their relationship.

Travis inspected the two women carefully. "I won't lie to you, Lexington." He saw his granddaughter stiffen in reaction. "It's going to take some getting used to, because I still see you as an adorable four-year-old. Anyone that you're involved with is going to have to get used to me, as well." He held a hand out to Amanda. "I'd really like for you to consider me a part of your family too, Amanda."

Amanda took his hand and smiled warmly at Travis. "I'd like that, Mr. Edwards."

"You'd better call me either Grandpa, or Travis, young lady." He winked at Amanda.

"Okay, Grandpa," Amanda returned impishly. "I hope you don't have plans for Christmas, because Lex and I expect our families to join us." She stepped forward and wrapped her arms around his waist in a big hug.

Lex laughed. "Give it up, Grandpa. She never loses an argument." She shook her head and led them both into the den.

* * * * * * * * *

"He's so sweet," Amanda commented later to Lex as they got ready for bed. "Did you get him settled all right in the back guestroom?"

"Yup. Thanks for talking him into staying the night. I really didn't want him to drive back into town this late." Lex stood in the middle of the room as she took off her shirt. "I can't believe that I have a living relative that actually wants something to do with me."

Amanda rose from where she was perched on the end of the bed and crossed the room. "You're kidding, right?" She wrapped her arms around the tall woman and snuggled her face into the rancher's neck. "Any relative of yours would probably jump through hoops to be near you, honey. You're just too darned adorable."

Lex sighed. "Yeah, right." She moved Amanda's hair off her neck and nibbled the smooth flesh. "Mmm."

"Don't change the subject, Lex. You've just got to...ahhh..." The blonde squirmed in Lex's embrace when the rancher found a sensitive spot. "Oooh."

"You were saying?" Lex whispered in the younger woman's ear. She slipped her hands inside Amanda's nightshirt and up the smooth back. Small hands worked into the back of her jeans and slid the denim down her hips.

"You really smell good," Amanda informed her lover. She ran her hands over the older woman's chest and down her sides as she inhaled deeply.

"Uh-huh." Lex slipped the nightshirt over the blonde's head. "I've never quite figured out your fascination with how I smell." She reached down and grasped the smaller woman's rear and pulled her closer.

Amanda automatically raised her arms and locked her hands behind Lex's neck. She tilted her head upward and felt her lips covered immediately. "Mmm." She leaned into the kiss and almost squealed out loud when Lex tightened her grip and picked her up. "Lex. Put me down before you hurt yourself," she ordered.

Lex chuckled and trailed kisses down the younger woman's throat. "Nope. Can't let you get away." She walked slowly to the bed, never ceasing her exploration of Amanda's neck with her lips.

"As if I'd want to." Amanda tilted her head back to allow the rancher better access. "I'm not going any...AAAAH," she yelled when Lex tossed her onto the bed. "You scared me."

"Did I?" Lex stood beside the bed with a devilish grin.

"What are you thinking?" Amanda scooted back slightly. She almost screamed again as the tall form leapt at her, arms outstretched.

Lex laughed as she jumped onto the bed and covered Amanda's body with her own. "Gotcha."

Amanda swatted ineffectually at the warm body over hers. "You are such a brat." She thought for a moment and then blushed. "Oh, God. What if your grandfather heard us?" She covered her face with her hand.

"Let's give him something worth hearing," Lex murmured as she worked her way down Amanda's body with kisses.

"I can't believe that you'd..." Amanda paused when Lex found a sensitive spot and sucked lightly. "Ooh...umm..." She arched her back in response.

The rancher chuckled again and continued her exploration. "You were saying?" She bit down gently with her teeth.

Amanda tangled her fingers in the dark hair. "Uh...I...oooh..." She closed her eyes and fell back to the bed to enjoy the sensations coursing through her body. "Oh, yeah..."

* * * * * * * * * *

Early the next morning, Lex climbed out of bed and slipped on a pair of colorful boxers and a dark tee shirt. She looked down at the young woman who was still asleep, and smiled. *She looks so cute when she does that.* As soon as Lex had gotten out of bed, Amanda rolled over and wrapped her arms around the rancher's pillow. She shook her head and left the room quietly.

Maybe today will be the day that I find that damned box. Lex opened the storage room door and stepped inside. She flipped on the light switch, then frowned. "I really need to clear more of this junk out of here." She waded through several stacks of boxes until she was in the back corner of the room. Lex opened up a large box and sorted through it. Even with her height, she had to practically stand on her head to reach the bottom.

Travis appeared directly behind the jackknifed young woman. "Anything I can help you with, little one?"

"Aaaah!" Startled, Lex fell headfirst into the box, splitting it down one side as she landed face down.

Travis quickly bent over and grabbed the prone woman's hips. "Are you okay, sweetheart?" He helped Lex to her feet and tried to dust her off.

"I'm fine, Grandpa." Lex gently fought off his helping hands. "What are you doing up so early?" She realized how she must have looked to him and blushed.

"Early? It's after six. I actually slept in." He noticed her discomfort. "What are you doing here in your jammies?" Travis couldn't help but tease his granddaughter. *She looks just like she did when she was four. Always into something.*

She rolled her eyes and crossed her arms over her chest. "Umm. I'm looking for something."

He looked at the disarray around them. "I can see that, Lexington. What exactly are you looking for?"

"A small box that I packed away around eight years ago," Lex sighed. "But even if I find it, I'm afraid that it won't be what I'm expecting." She sat down on the dusty floor in disgust.

"Ooookay." Travis drew out the word and sat down next to his granddaughter. "What's so important about this box anyway?" He patted her on the leg. "If you describe it to me, I'll be more than happy to help you look for it."

Lex looked up at the older man's sincere face. "Well, it was a small wooden jewelry box that belonged to my mother." She saw a brief flash of pain cross Travis' features. "I'm sorry, Grandpa. I know this has got to be hard for you." She reached over and grasped his hand. "You don't have to help. I'll find it soon enough."

Travis shook his head. "No, I'd really like to help you, honey. Is there something special that's supposed to be in the box?"

"If I remember correctly, it had her wedding ring in it," Lex explained.

He thought for a moment. *Oh.* "Amanda means a lot to you, doesn't she?" He smiled to himself. *She's so cute when she blushes like that.*

Damn. He's a pretty sharp old guy. "She means everything to me, Grandpa. Although I took her for granted until I almost lost her last week." Lex looked down at their joined hands. "I want to give her something to let her know how special she is to me." She looked back up into his eyes. "Hell. I can buy her anything, Grandpa. But something that I've learned about Amanda is how sentimental she is; money means nothing to her. She'd probably treasure a rusted bottle cap if I gave it to her. That's why I was thinking about mother's ring."

"I don't think giving her your mother's ring is such a

good idea," Travis uttered quietly.

Lex sat up and tried to pull her hand away from his. "Why? I thought that you liked Amanda too."

Travis smiled gently and held her hand more tightly. "I do. Very much, as a matter of fact."

"Then why...?"

"She deserves better than a cheap stainless steel band," he muttered angrily.

Lex's jaw dropped. "What? Stainless steel? I thought that they wore gold?" *I knew Dad was cheap, but...*

He rubbed the back of her hand with his thumb. "Your father bought stainless steel bands and had them dipped in a gold-tone alloy. Turned Victoria's finger green after the first year when most of the gold color wore off. She finally took it off and put it away right before you were born, because she was afraid that it might hurt you when you were a baby."

"Damn." Lex fell back against the wall in defeat. "There goes that idea, then." She propped her chin on her bent knee. "Guess I'll just try to find something nice for her in town."

"Funny you should talk about rings, little one." He released her hand and reached into his pocket. Travis pulled out a small black velvet box and handed it to Lex. "Your grandmother's greatest wish was that I'd be able to reconcile with you." He wiped at a tear that escaped from his eye. "It was one of the last things she said to me before she passed away."

Travis sat gingerly on the edge of the large antique bed and picked up the small hand that was so pale, it was nearly translucent. "Hello there, beautiful."

The woman lying propped up on the bed opened her eyes slowly, then smiled. "My love," she whispered. With a concentrated effort, she lifted her other hand and gestured at her prone body. "I'm anything but beautiful, now." Her once long and luxurious dark hair had been cut very short, to make it easier to care for when she became bedridden.

Melanie Edwards had always been a small woman, but since she had been struck with a debilitating illness earlier in the year, the weight loss had left her frail and weak. She could barely hold her head up, and most days did not have the strength to open her eyes.

"That's not true, sweetheart." Travis leaned over until she could see the sincerity in his eyes. "You're as beautiful as the day I first saw you, over fifty years ago." He pulled her hand to his cheek and held it there. He had brought her home from the hospital the week before so that she would be more comfortable. The doctors had told him that there was nothing left to do for her, and it was only a matter of days before she passed away. "I got another letter from Lester today."

"Really?" Melanie's eyes brightened. "Read it to me, please?" A tinge of color returned to her cheeks from the anticipation.

Her husband chuckled. "I'm beginning to think you have a thing for my childhood friend, the way you perk up at the mention of his name." Travis searched his pockets with his free hand. "Now where did I put that darned thing?"

Melanie slapped at his arm. "Don't tease me like that, Tray." She used the pet name she had given him over half a century ago. Her hand dropped back to the bed, the effort tiring her.

"Just relax, Lanie. It's right here." Travis pulled an envelope from his inside coat pocket and tore it open. Quite a few pages here. I wonder what's going on? *He tried to scan the letter before he had to read it aloud.*

"Stop trying to edit it, honey. I'm a big girl," Melanie chastised. When she saw the frown on her husband's normally cheerful face, she reached up with her hand again. "What is it, love?"

Travis blinked, then successfully removed the worried look. "Nothing. You know how Lester likes to exaggerate." His hand shook slightly as he looked back down on the paper.

She tapped his elbow. "Don't give me that, Tray. Is our Lexie all right?"

"She's fine. Just had a bit of excitement at the ranch recently." He continued to scan the letter.

"Ahem. I can hear it much better when you read out loud, Travis Lee Edwards." Melanie pulled on his suit jacket sleeve. "My body's weak, not my hearing."

He looked properly chastised. "I'm sorry, sweet. I guess I got carried away reading it." Travis cleared his throat. "Travis, Hope this letter finds you and your beautiful wife well. Give her my best, and tell her that the next time I see her, I'll whip up a fresh bowl of my special chili. We've had a bit of excitement here at the ranch. The bridge that crosses the creek was washed out last week during a nasty thunderstorm. Young Lex dove right into the creek that day, after she saw a car get tossed in. She pulled out this sweet young thing, goes by the name of Amanda Cauble, and brought her to the house. Your granddaughter busted her ribs doing it, but didn't seem too bad off. It gets even better, though. Seems that there were these rustlers on the back side of the ranch, and Lex and her new friend saw them trying to haul off more stock. I don't know all the particulars, but part of them followed the girls back to the house and broke in. Lex was shot sometime during the mess, but it wasn't serious. They hauled the whole mess of 'em to jail, and I think things should be a little quieter now.

"I know this is more than I usually write, but I wanted to make sure you heard it from me, before some damned gossip called you. That Cauble girl is a sweet one, and I think your grand-daughter is quite taken with her. She's moved out to the ranch, and Martha has nothing but great things to say about her. As much as we fight, I gotta admit that the woman has good judgement when it comes to folks. But hopefully you'll meet her someday, and decide for yourself.

"Take care of yourself, Travis. Kiss your pretty wife for me, and tell her that if she ever gets tired of your ugly *face, to give me a call. Your friend, Lester."*

Melanie exchanged looks with her husband. *"It sounds
like she's had a rough time of it lately, doesn't it?"* She
leaned back against the pillows in exhaustion.

"She's a strong young woman. I just wish..." Travis
noticed his wife's increasingly pale features. *"Why don't
you get some rest, and we'll talk a bit later?"* He pulled
the comforter up around her chin to ward off the chill she
always seemed to have lately.

"No, not just yet." She looked up at her husband
sadly. *"You know I don't have much time left, Tray. Don't
let me waste it sleeping."* Melanie reached for her left
hand, and tugged at her ring. *"I want you to do something
for me. For us."*

Travis blinked the tears from his eyes. *"What is it, my
love?"* He watched as she pulled her wedding ring off her
finger, for the first time in over fifty years.

She opened his hand and placed the ring inside it,
closing Travis' strong fingers around the silver band and
jewels. *"I want Lexie to have this. Please try to reach her
again. She needs to know her family. I don't want you to be
alone when I'm gone."*

*"Please don't talk like that, Lanie. You're going to be
just fine."* Travis choked on his words, knowing them for
the untruths they were. I'm losing her. First Victoria, now
my Melanie. A man shouldn't have to outlive his entire
family. *"As soon as you're well enough, we'll both take a
trip to the ranch."*

"Tray." Melanie's voice faded into a near whisper.
*"We both know that I'm not going to get any better. Prom-
ise me that you'll try to talk to Lexie. She looks so much
like our Victoria, doesn't she?"* Her eyes closed for a
moment, then reopened. She looked up into the anguished
face of the man who had shared her life with her. *"Don't
cry, beloved."*

He pulled her hand up to his face and kissed the
paper-thin skin. *"I'm sorry, my love."* His tears continued
to drop onto her fingers. *"I swear to you that I will try*

again with our granddaughter. She deserves to know about her family."

Melanie closed her eyes again, relieved. *"Thank you, dearest. Now why don't you lie down with me, and hold me for a while? I need to talk to you,"* she finished in a near-whisper.

"Anything for you, my heart." Travis removed his suit coat and lay down next to his wife. He pulled her gently to him and felt her snuggle close.

The next morning, Travis woke up to find his wife gone. During the night, Melanie Edwards had passed away in her sleep, a small smile upon her lips. He buried his face in his hands and mourned the loss of his wife and best friend.

Lex accepted the small box reverently. "I wish that we hadn't wasted all those years apart," she whispered. "I would really have liked to have known you both when I was growing up. All I ever really wanted was to have a real family." She blinked as several tears dropped from her eyes while she studied the package in her hand. "What's in this?"

Travis put an arm around Lex and pulled her closer to him. "Open it, honey."

"All right." Lex lifted the lid and gasped in surprise. "Wow." Nestled atop dark blue satin sat a shimmering silver ring. It had a large square diamond in the center, with sparkling clear-cut sapphires on either side. "That's beautiful."

"It belonged to my great-great grandmother. Each generation it has been passed along as a wedding ring, except for Victoria. Your father refused to allow her to wear it. I gave it to my Melanie on our wedding day, and she had always wanted you to have it." Travis looked at the ring fondly. "Do you think that Amanda would like it? I know that your grandmother would be thrilled to keep it in the family."

She stared at the ring for a long moment. "She didn't

even really know me." Lex looked up into Travis' face. "Do you honestly think that she would have liked me? I'm not what you'd call normal."

The older man looked at her sadly. "Honey, she loved you. We've kept tabs on you all these years, you know." He winked at Lex. "Lester has kept us up to date on just about everything you've done. He and I grew up together."

"Really? You and Lester are friends?" Lex tried to reconcile this distinguished gentleman with the rough cowhand. "You've got to be kidding me. You two are nothing alike."

"He became cook on this ranch because I wanted someone close by to keep an eye on Victoria. I'm sorry to say this, honey, but I've never liked or trusted your father." Travis ran a hand across Lex's cheek. "I was afraid he was after your mother for her money. It wasn't until after she died that I realized that in his own way, he really did love her."

Lex wiped at her face with her hand. "Do you really think so?" She thought back to all the time she had spent with her father. *He never once told me he loved me. I didn't think he was even capable of such an emotion.* She shook her head mentally. *But I guess the same could have been said about me, until Amanda came along.*

Travis nodded. "I know he did, little one. He fell apart completely at the funeral." He reached over and wiped at the young woman's face with his fingertips. "Why don't you go get cleaned up? We can talk more later, sweetheart."

"That's probably a good idea, Grandpa. Amanda will be awake any time now." Lex leaned forward and kissed his cheek. "Thank you for not giving up on me."

"I couldn't give up on you any more than I could give up on myself, Lexie." Travis stood up and pulled her up with him. "I'll see you downstairs later for breakfast, all right?"

She wrapped her arms around Travis and hugged him tight. "You sure will. Thanks for everything, Grandpa."

Lex kissed his cheek again and practically ran from the room.

He watched her leave with a large smile on his face. "Well, Melanie," he addressed his deceased wife quietly, "looks like we've got a granddaughter again."

* * * * * * * * * *

Amanda wrinkled her nose when a light touch ran down her face. Another feather-like sensation caused one green eye to open slowly. "Lex?" She blinked both eyes open and studied the woman leaning over her. "What's going on?"

"Good morning." Lex leaned down and gave Amanda a long, sensual kiss. "Did you sleep well?"

"I always do, when I'm with you," Amanda answered. She reached up and fingered the dark hair, which was damp. "Did you just get out of the shower?"

Lex grinned. "Yup. I was kinda dirty, so I thought I'd better clean up." She ran a gentle fingertip down Amanda's cheek. "Talked with Grandpa for a few minutes this morning."

The younger woman squirmed to a more upright position on the bed. "Really? What did you talk about?"

"All sorts of things, actually." Lex rolled over to lie on her side, facing Amanda. She propped her head up with one hand. "I was in the storage room, and he came in and scared the daylights out of me. I landed face first in one of the big boxes in the corner."

Amanda giggled. "Bet that was a sight." She mirrored the older woman's posture and ran her free hand down Lex's arm. "You didn't hurt yourself, did you?"

"Nope. But I bet I looked funny with my butt sticking up out of that damned box. Grandpa pulled me out, and then we sat down and talked for a bit." Lex captured the small hand and brought it to her lips. "We even talked about you." *Don't chicken out, Lexington. That's a perfect opening, now use it.*

"Me? What did...?" Amanda asked, then blushed.
"He's okay with us, isn't he?" *He certainly seemed okay
last night. Unless he thought about it during the night and
changed his mind.*

Lex rolled over and crawled off the bed and stepped
into the bathroom. "Hold on a minute." She walked back
into the room carrying something in her hand and dropped
to one knee on Amanda's side of the bed. "I told Grandpa
how much you mean to me, Amanda. He asked me what I
was doing in the storage room, and I explained that I was
looking for something that I packed away years ago."

Amanda sat up and faced the kneeling rancher. "What
was that, honey?" She could feel Lex's nervousness as if it
were tangible. When the older woman held out her hand,
the blonde automatically accepted it.

"When I first took over the master bedroom, I packed
up all of my Dad's things and put them in storage. The one
thing I wanted to give to you, I haven't been able to find."
Lex kissed Amanda's hand. "I wanted to give you something to show you how much you mean to me."

"Oh, baby, you don't have to give me anything."
Amanda curled her hand around Lex's cheek. "You show
me all the time how you feel."

Lex nodded. "I try to. But I wanted to give you more
than just words, or actions. I want you to have a symbol of
my love for you. That's why I was looking for my mother's
wedding ring." She bent forward and placed her head on
the younger woman's lap. "I've already given you my
promise to love you forever, Amanda. I just wanted to give
you a token of that promise." She looked up with tears in
her eyes. "It took almost losing you for me to realize just
how precious you are to me. I can't allow one more day to
go by and not show you how I feel."

She looked down at Lex and at the remembered pain in
those blue eyes. When Lex took her left hand and kissed it
again, Amanda almost cried. "Oh, sweetheart."

"I couldn't find mother's ring. But Grandpa gave me
something that I think is more fitting." Lex opened the box

that she had hidden behind her back and pulled the ring out. "This ring belonged to my great-great-great grandmother. Grandpa said that it was passed down from generation to generation as a wedding present." She slipped the jewel-encrusted band on Amanda's finger and kissed the small hand again. "I would be truly honored if you would wear this ring and accept my promise to love you forever, Amanda Lorraine Cauble." Lex waited nervously to see what the younger woman's response would be.

"Lex." Amanda looked closely at the ring. "My God, it's incredible." She choked back a sob of happiness. "I'll cherish it as I do you." She reached out and pulled Lex to her in a strong embrace. "Always and forever, Lexington Marie Walters."

The dark-haired woman sealed the pledge with a tender kiss. She pulled back slightly to look into the green eyes, full of unshed tears. "Always and forever, my love."

Be sure to read the first book in this series by
Carrie Carr:

Destiny's Crossing

(Destiny's Crossing contains two stories)

Destiny's Bridge

Rancher Lexington (Lex) Walters pulls young Amanda
Cauble from a raging creek and the two women quickly
develop a strong bond of friendship. Overcoming
severe weather, cattle thieves, and their own fears, their
friendship deepens into a strong and lasting love.

Faith's Crossing

Lexington Walters and Amanda Cauble withstood raging floods, cattle rustlers and other obstacles to be
together...but can they handle Amanda's parents? When
Amanda decides to move to Texas for good, she goes
back to her parent's home in California to get the rest of
her things, taking the rancher with her.

Destiny's Crossing, 2nd Ed. may be ordered online at
www.rapbooks.com/orders.html or through booksellers.

Next book in this series by Carrie Carr:

Love's Journey

Lex and Amanda embark on a new journey as Lexington rediscovers the love her mother's family has for her, and Amanda begins to build her relationship with her father. Meanwhile, attacks on the two young women grow more violent and deadly as someone tries to tear apart the love they share.

Available Winter 2001 from
Yellow Rose Books

Available soon from
Yellow Rose Books

Take Time Out
By R. L. Johnson

Jessica Peters has just landed the job of her dreams—coaching Division I basketball at her alma mater. With an outstanding record, a positive coaching philosophy, and some excellent players, her career is headed for the fast track. What she doesn't count on is a spunky Economics Professor who is determined to turn her head. Coach Peters knows that relationships with women and Division I coaching careers do not mix. Besides that, she isn't interested in women. Is she? A year of practices, recruiting, competition, and playoffs, interspersed with fishing and hiking trips in spectacular Oregon locations, will take the two women through more ups and downs than they ever thought they could survive.

Lost Paradise
By Francine Quesnel

Kristina Von Deering is a young, wealthy Austrian stuntwoman working on an Austrian/Canadian film project in Montreal. On location, she meets and eventually falls in love with a young gopher and aspiring camerawoman named Nicole McGrail. Their friendship and love is threatened by Nicole's father who sees their relationship as deviant and unnatural. He does everything in his power to put an end to it.

Meridio's Daughter
By LJ Maas

Tessa (Nikki) Nikolaidis is cold and ruthless, the perfect person to be Karê, the right-hand, to Greek magnate Andreas Meridio. Cassandra (Casey) Meridio has come home after a six-year absence to find that her father's new Karê is a very desirable, but highly dangerous woman.

Set in modern day Greece on the beautiful island of Mýkonos, this novel weaves a tale of emotional intrigue as two women from different worlds struggle with forbidden desires. As the two come closer to the point of no return, Casey begins to wonder if she can really trust the beautiful Karê. Does Nikki's dark past, hide secrets that will eventually bring down the brutal Meridio Empire, or are her actions simply those of a vindictive woman? Will she stop at nothing for vengeance...even seduction?

Turning the Page
By Georgia Beers

Melanie Larson is an attractive, extremely successful business executive who shocks herself by resigning from her job when her company merges with another and relocating. While trying to decide what to do with her life next and at the urging of her uncle, Melanie heads to Rochester, New York, to stay temporarily with her cousin Samantha. She hopes to use her business savvy to help Sam sort out the financial woes of her small bookstore. During her stay, Melanie meets and becomes close to the family that owns the property on which Samantha lives, the charming Benjamin Rhodes, a distinguished, successful businessman, as well as his beautiful and intriguing daughter Taylor. Surprised by what and how she feels for each of them, Melanie is soon forced to face the facts and re-examine what's really important to her in life, career and love.

Other titles to look for in the coming months from *Yellow Rose Books*

Daredevil Hearts
By Francine Quesnel

Prairie Fire
By LJ Maas

Heartbroken Love
By Georgio Sicily

Many Roads To Travel
By Karen King and Nann Dunne

Ricochet In Time
By Lori L. Lake

Love's Journey
By Carrie Carr

About the author:

Carrie is a True Texan, having lived in the state her entire life. She now makes her home outside of Dallas, with her partner AJ. Her time is spent writing, traveling, and collecting television memorabilia. She can be reached by email at: carrie_carr@hotmail.com

Printed in the United Kingdom
by Lightning Source UK Ltd.
9572900001BA